FABLE FOR THE END OF THE WORLD

Also by Ava Reid

A Study in Drowning

FABLE
FOR THE END OF THE
WORLD

AVA REID

HARPER
An Imprint of HarperCollinsPublishers

To the young queer girls—your love
is going to save the world.

There's a lover in the story, but the story's still the same.

—"YOU WANT IT DARKER," LEONARD COHEN

ONE

INESA

Floris Dekker spreads his daughter's body out on the counter. "Please," he says.

Sanne is still wearing a limp white dress, stained at the hem with what might be rust, but I know better. The drab linen, gray-hued and rough from too many washes, indicates a Caerus online catalogue purchase. The seams are straining around her shoulders and elbows. Something from the back pages, cheap and mass-produced.

"No," I say firmly. "No way."

"*Please*," Floris says again. "This is all I have left."

Strictly speaking, he's wrong. Sure, his wife, Norah, has been dead since spring—from drinking contaminated water; if he lived in Lower Esopus with those of us who don't have indoor plumbing, she'd have known to boil her water before she drank it—but Floris still has plenty of her left. All her Caerus debts, floating around the empty house like ghosts, wrapping their cold hands around his wrists and ankles, spectral manacles.

And now, even with Sanne dead, he'll have company. She was twelve, old enough to accrue her own ghosts.

"I'm sorry," I say.

Sanne's hair is damp and tangled. If I didn't know better, I would say she died from drowning. But no one drowns here: as soon as we can walk and speak, everyone in the outlying Counties learns how to tell when the water table is rising and the ground under you can't be trusted. I didn't watch her die, unlike all the other inhabitants of Esopus Creek, their eyes trained on their tablet screens until they turned red and bloodshot—because how can you sleep, when you might risk missing the climax? The slaughter?

Her wet hair is all I can bear to look at. If I look at her face, or the utter stillness of her rib cage as it presses up against the fabric of the too-small dress—or, worst of all, the ring of bruises around her throat—I'll have to duck under the counter and retch.

You wouldn't imagine, in my line of work, that I'd have such a weak stomach.

Floris sets his jaw. "Is your brother here?"

My eyes narrow in response. I haven't been hard enough on him. "Luka would tell you the same. No human corpses."

I almost add another *sorry*, but if I do, he'll ask for Luka again.

"I can pay more," Floris says instead, voice pitching higher. "Sixty-five credits."

Our rate for white-tailed deer is sixty, and with the way they're dying off, soon we'll be able to charge twice as much. I'm not going to butcher a dead twelve-year-old for two extra packs of peach-flavored decon-tabs, even if it would make Mom happy.

Besides, Floris is lying. He can't pay more. If he had the credits, Sanne wouldn't be dead. This fact makes it difficult to pity him. If he runs up even more debts, he'll have nothing left to pay with but his own life. Sanne was a flimsy shield, thrown up between him and Caerus's collectors. Their cruel vengeance, disguised as justice.

Floris's lower lip quivers, and it makes the rest of his face look all the more gaunt and hollow. He's from Upper Esopus, which means he eats better than we do, but not by much. Though I know it wasn't food that racked up his debts. It never is.

I let my gaze slide down to Sanne again. Her eyes are half open, pale lashes like dandelions that could still be blown.

That's one little thing I've learned in this job: It's actually hard to get a dead person's eyes to close. Everyone thinks that when you die, you become limp and pliable, when really, it's the opposite. In death, the body seizes up. Rigor mortis. Eventually, of course, it rots away into nothing, but at first it stays stiff and still, as if trying to preserve itself as it was in the very last moment it was alive. In a way, it makes my work easier.

I always think of it like that—like the corpses are helping me as much as I'm helping them. We both want to stay alive, or however close we can get to it.

When that thought occurs to me, a stone lodges in my throat. Not for Floris, but for Sanne. Because maybe this is better than being buried in an unmarked grave and forgotten. And because maybe Floris deserves the constant reminder of what he did to her.

With a quiet, sharp inhale, I reach under the counter and pull open one of the drawers. Floris's brows leap hopefully.

I take one of the small glass bottles and hold it out to him, with no small amount of reticence.

"This is a mixture of alum and borax," I tell him. "They're both desiccants—they draw the moisture out of the flesh and help it last longer. I can't tell you exactly how—"

But Floris is already grabbing my hand and prying my fingers open. "Thank you, thank you."

"Wait!" I manage, as he's sliding the bottle into his pocket. "You have to get it under the skin and . . ."

I trail off, because in the end I still can't bring myself to give him step-by-step instructions about how to butcher and stuff his dead daughter.

Floris reaches for Sanne again. A little bead of water drips down her temple, and I have to fight the urge to wipe it away.

"Inesa," he says, "you're one of the good ones."

I'm not sure if he means one of the good residents of Lower Esopus, the ones who don't complain when the denizens of Upper Esopus flood our houses six times a year by keeping the reservoir too high; or one of the good taxidermists, the ones who don't charge for every stitch of thread or droplet of glycerin; or one of the good Soulises—maybe. With how much everyone in Esopus Creek hates Mom, that's not a hard title to win.

Or maybe he means I'm one of the people who doesn't judge him for what he's done. For paying off his debts with his daughter's life. But he would be wrong about that. I might hate him less for it than everyone else in our town, but it's not something I can forgive. Or forget.

I set my jaw and give him the coldest look I can manage, pretending that I'm eight inches taller, as tall as Luka. "I want seventy-five credits."

Floris doesn't say a word as he takes out his Caerus card and presses it against my cracked tablet, doesn't say a word as he sweeps his daughter's body off the counter and carries her toward the door. He forces it open with his foot, its rusted hinges creaking. When the door slams shut after him, the little wooden *SOULIS TAXIDERMY SHOP* sign clatters like a cheap wind chime.

I lean forward on my elbows and put my head in my hands. I have to breathe hard into the silence for several minutes and squeeze my eyes shut, until I stop seeing Sanne's face. When my heartbeat has steadied again, I sink down onto the floor behind the counter.

The desiccant I gave Floris was worth ninety credits, easy. Luka is going to kill me.

I find out quickly enough why Sanne was wet—it's raining. It hasn't rained in a couple of days (a small miracle, for Esopus Creek), so I have to dig my raft out of the clutter behind the counter. The sky is a dusky purple, striped with pink from the pollutants that are strong enough to slice through the heavy clouds. By the time I've finished closing up the shop, the water is knee-high and my jacket is soaked.

It's one of those rough, fast storms that sweeps in with little warning, the kind that's likely to raise the water table enough to lap at the legs of our couch. At home Luka is probably already laying down sandbags. I get on the raft and test the depth of the water with my pole—it's right up to the nine-inch notch—then push off into the rain.

The water is sluicing down Main Street, a murky, churning brown, rushing from Upper Esopus to Lower Esopus. It's after six now, so the evening commute has started, all the shop owners clambering onto their rafts and poling up toward their houses on higher ground. Across the flooded road, there's Mrs. Prinslew, down on her hands and knees on the porch of her shop, stuffing rags beneath the doorframe. All four of her sons moved south to the City, and now she runs the black market goods store all by herself. Wiping rainwater off her wrinkled brow, she sits back on her heels and swivels her head around, catching my eye.

The question rises instinctually in my throat: *Do you need some help?* But a second, stronger instinct pushes it down. Here in the outlying Counties, the offer is not a kindness. Because no assistance comes without gratitude, and no gratitude comes without debt.

That's what Caerus taught us—slowly, and then all at once—when the credits ran out and they came to collect.

The most I can give Mrs. Prinslew is a wave and a nod. She nods back, and I pole on.

At this hour, the punters are out in force, hawking fares from people who can't pole on their own. The punters have real boats, narrow and sleek, with a little platform to stand on and even a small carved seat for their passengers. It's fifteen credits for a ride to the residential district, ten if you live in the Shallows. On the rare occasions that Mom leaves the house, she always hires one. She says she doesn't trust my arm.

The streets of Esopus Creek run horizontally across the hill like striations on a cliffside, and the divide between Upper Esopus and Lower Esopus is stark. The houses in Lower Esopus have flat tin roofs and rotten wooden siding, paint stripped off after so many storms. They're held aloft over the hill by spindly cinder block columns, porches sagging precariously.

The houses in Upper Esopus are round and white like insect eggs, made of durable plastic that the rainwater rolls right off. They have sheet glass windows and covered porches that can fold and unfold, depending on the weather. They're Caerus pod houses, airlifted from the City and dropped right down on the hillside.

Mom says they're sterile and ugly. Luka says she's overcompensating.

Our house is at the very end of Little Schoharie Lane, the lowest street of the Shallows. Our neighbors have a bit of pride because there used to be a school here, ages ago, before learning was all virtual. Everyone likes to claim that *their* house is on the property of the old school, but Luka and I don't bother pretending our house has any sort of noble pedigree. I pole into the yard and hitch my raft to the foot of the stairs. Then I clamber up, boots sliding against the wet concrete, my hair drenched even under my hood.

There are sandbags on the floor and I can smell blood as soon as I step through the door. I shrug out of my soaked jacket and hang it on the hook beside Luka's. Mine is green, turned black by the rainwater. Luka's is black, turned blacker. Today's kill must have been messy.

He's sitting at the kitchen table, hair drying in stiff spikes. As soon as he sees me he says, "Did you board up the windows at the shop?"

"I never took them down from last storm," I say, and offer a huff of laughter, thinking he might laugh back. "Didn't see much of a point."

Luka offers only a grim smile in return. He's fiddling with his tablet, scrolling between a game app and a news app. We're both dancing around our twin questions.

How much did you make today?

How many did you kill today?

I blurt out my question first. "How many?"

"Two rabbits and a white-tailed deer." Luka's response is immediate, because he knows he did well. I could have guessed as much from all the blood on his jacket. "I was going to take them down to the shop, but then the rain started."

"I'll take them tomorrow." I swallow. "We should start up-charging for the deer. I had a City buyer in today who told me he wanted four mounted heads—*four*. I told him it could be a month."

"Bucks with antlers?"

I nod. "I had him make a nonrefundable deposit. Two hundred credits."

I was proud of my work today, until Floris Dekker. I never feel bad about being shameless with the City buyers. They come in wearing shining black boots and jewel-toned slickers, and when they take down their hoods, their faces and hair are dry. They're always jovial, remarking on the quaintness of the shop, politely ignoring the dripping ceiling and the buckets half filled with stale water. They don't blink or scowl when I list my exorbitant prices, and sometimes they even apologize to *me* when they have to press their Caerus card three or four times against my cracked tablet to get the transaction to go through.

They want stag heads for their "dining rooms" and "dens," places I've only seen on TV. The stuffed rabbits decorate their kids' bedrooms. The birds, which I mount to look as if they're midflight, wings fully spread, breasts puffed out proudly, are gifts for their wives.

It's the Outlier customers I feel sorry for, the ones who come from other towns in Catskill County or even as far as Adirondack County, the ones who can only afford the scrawniest, scruffiest rabbits or the tiny field mice we sell for twenty credits apiece. Taxidermies are a luxury, plain and simple. No one *needs* them. But there's a logic to buying them that City folk would never understand. Because when you're tabulating the entire worth of your life, a cheery decoration or an expensive bauble is more valuable than a bushel of half-rotted black-market apples.

At least, that's the logic that runs *Mom's* life. I can hear her shifting in her room now, her bedsprings creaking.

"Good," Luka says slowly. "So . . . how much did you make?"

He leans into the question carefully, like someone peering through the crack in a door to make sure the person on the other side is decent. I draw a breath. The down payment on the stags was nice, but losing the desiccant ate up almost half of that, and besides—the whole situation is humiliating to recount.

I tell Luka about Floris with as much dignity as I can manage, but my brother's face darkens and darkens. By the time I've finished, he's risen from the table and his jaw is clenched so tightly I can see the muscle feathering in his throat.

"Inesa," he says, "you can't keep pulling this shit."

Luka only curses when he's really angry, and when he's really angry, sometimes I forget he's my little brother. I was the one who made up stories to soothe him to sleep if the storms were too loud and the rainwater dripped relentlessly through the roof.

Now he easily clears six feet and is a deadly shot with a hunting rifle. I look up at him through my wet hair.

"I'll make it up," I say. "I can do the rabbits in two hours. And Floris was so happy he's going to be singing our praises to everyone in Upper Esopus—"

Luka scoffs. "You can't possibly be that naive."

"It's naive not to automatically assume the worst of people?"

"No," he says in a low voice. "It's naive to assume that anyone is ever going to look Floris in the eye again. Anyone but *you*, apparently."

I flinch, and my blood turns to ice. I saw Sanne, laid out on the counter, only two, three days dead. Dead to pay off her father's debts. What right did Floris even have to mourn her? And what business was it of mine, to help alleviate his guilt? Thinking back, what I considered inept kindness now feels like a cruel sort of apathy. Floris is a pariah now, marked forever by what we in the outlying Counties see as the most abhorrent and unforgivable crime. By doing so much as speaking to him, I've marked myself, too. I haven't helped our reputation—I've hurt it.

We really, really can't afford that.

"I'm sorry," I say. Useless, inane words.

Luka looks at me for a long moment. His eyes—the same brown-green color as mine—are hard and unrelenting.

"Maybe you should watch them," he says at last. "Maybe then you'd understand."

I kind of hate myself for it, but I can't help the angry bite of my next words. "Don't you think Mom watches them enough for the three of us?"

Mom is still in her bedroom, too far away to hear, or I never would've risked saying it. Luka inhales sharply. There's an unspoken rule between us not to bring up what Mom does, or doesn't do, and I've just broken it. And then, seeing the brief spasm of pain flit across Luka's face before he schools his expression into impassiveness again, I remember that the rule doesn't exist just for Mom's sake. The rule is like the house's shaky foundation—prod at it too much, and all three of us will fall through. Neither of us wants to be put in the position of defending Mom. And neither of us wants to hear the other defending her, either.

Luka is silent for so long, I wonder if he's going to pretend that I never spoke.

Finally, he says, "Whatever, Inesa. Everyone watches them. I don't know what point you're trying to make by tuning out."

I don't have an answer for him. It's almost a relief when the

11

curtain covering the doorway jerks open, and Mom steps over the threshold.

I hear her before I see her: she's doing her quiet, dainty coughs today, the kind that are meant to emphasize how unobtrusive they are. She's wrapped in the musty knitted blanket we've had since Luka and I were babies, but her hair is, as always, impeccable—sleek and black as the reservoir at night. Any fledgling strand of silver has been smothered by noxious (and expensive) dye.

"Can you two lower your voices, please?" she says. "I've had a pounding headache all day. A migraine. It's been terrible."

"Sorry," Luka says.

"Sorry," I echo.

Mom puts a hand to her temple and closes her eyes. "Inesa, you didn't patch the roof like I asked. The dripping water—I think that's what gave me the migraine. Or it could even be an ice pick headache."

It only just started raining, so I know the roof wasn't dripping all day, but there's no use pointing that out. There's also no use pointing out that I can't reach the hole in the roof to patch it, not without balancing precariously on one of our tottery kitchen chairs. Luka can. But she'd never ask him.

"I can do it tonight," I say. "Just rest on the couch for now."

Mom sighs thinly and makes her way to the couch. It's a staggering, arduous walk: she's still nursing a twisted ankle she claimed to have gotten from tripping up the front stairs. But I haven't seen her outside in more than two weeks.

"People die from ice pick headaches, you know." She collapses

12

onto the couch in a heap. "And it's not the headaches that kill them. It's the pain—so unbearable that they'd rather *die*. Dr. Kuiper had a patient with chronic ice pick headaches who *hanged* himself."

"Did you see Dr. Kuiper again today?" I'm glad it's Luka who asks, not me.

Technically Caerus is the only institution that grants medical licenses. They do virtual appointments, and airlift patients to City hospitals for more complex procedures or surgeries. You can get Dr. Wessels down on Main Street to set your bone or cure your cold for fifty credits (or a skillful barter), but Mom doesn't trust uncertified doctors. She shells out who knows how many credits a week to video chat with her Caerus doctor.

"Yes," she says. "I explained everything to him. He sent me another prescription. It needs to be taken with food."

And how much did he charge you for that? The words rise in my throat, but I snap my lips shut before they can spill out.

Beneath her silk housedress—which looks brand-new, probably delivered by Caerus drone while I was working at the shop—Mom's chest rises and falls slowly. She's curled in on herself like a mollusk, fists under her chin.

"I'll get you dinner," I say. I'm not hopeful about what's in the kitchen, but maybe I'll be pleasantly surprised.

"I don't want any of that instant garbage you eat. Dr. Kuiper says I need to be eating fresh fruits and vegetables. To keep my immune system up."

I want to tell her that she doesn't have to worry, because we can't afford to have the power turned on right now, so the microwave

13

isn't going to work anyway.

"We probably have some apples," Luka offers. "Let me check."

"No, let Inesa," Mom says. "You work hard all day. She just sits behind a counter. Come here and watch with me."

Her tablet is propped up on the arm of the couch. I glance over at the screen, and then wish I hadn't. It's open to the VOD of the live stream—paused, for now. Sanne is mid-leap, frozen in arrested motion, her white dress a blur against dark green trees. And behind her—

I look away, nausea pooling in the pit of my stomach. I know this isn't the first time Mom has watched it. She's one of the millions of citizens of New Amsterdam who caught the Gauntlet live, eyes trained unblinkingly on their tablets so they didn't miss a moment of it. I wonder if, in her rewatch, Mom is focusing on different things. Little things she might have missed, like the way Sanne's tears mingled with the rainwater until they were the same rivulets that ran down her face.

The thought jolts me, like an electric shock. While Luka settles down on the couch beside Mom, I go into the kitchen. My whole body feels strangely shaky, the way it does when I've gone a while without eating. But I'm definitely not hungry now.

The bruises around her throat—

I shake my head and blink, clearing the memory, and open the icebox. There are a few mealy-looking apples, but Mom won't want those. Instead, I light the stove and boil water for potatoes. We only have the powdered kind, but potatoes *are* a vegetable. I think.

Fixing Mom a meal she won't complain too much about is a

supreme feat. The potatoes are reconstituting, bubbling like a witch's brew. I take down two cups from the cabinet, fill them with water from the five-gallon bucket, and open a new packet of decon-tabs, peeling off the generic Caerus wrapping. Cherry-flavored, Mom's second favorite. We're out of peach.

The water in Esopus Creek, and in most of the outlying Counties, is far too polluted to risk drinking. Caerus's solution is decontamination tablets, chalky little pills that we drop into every glass. I watch the tablet sizzle and dissolve, dyeing the water a pale pink. The carbonation always makes my nose burn.

Caerus probably realized that they'd lose half the population of New Amsterdam in a matter of weeks if they didn't make the decon-tabs cheap, so we can almost always afford them, at least the unflavored ones. But Mom hates those, and since she's already in a bad mood, I use the cherry.

When I bring out the potatoes, Mom curls her lip.

"Sorry," I say. "We don't have much else. I'll go down to Mrs. Prinslew's tomorrow and see what she's got."

The VOD is paused again, thankfully. I don't risk so much as a glance toward the screen.

"Do you really think this is enough for your brother?" Mom protests. "He spends the whole day hunting in the wet and cold. I'm not asking for *me*. But for Luka—"

"It's fine, Mom," Luka cuts in, his voice muffled around a bite of potatoes. He's already wolfed down half the plate.

I don't take my own meals in front of Mom anymore. It's too much of an ordeal. She likes to pinch the bit of fat on my upper

15

arm, right above my elbow, holding on to it as proof that I could stand to eat a lot less than I do.

Mom eats in small, reluctant bites, letting the potatoes fall off her spoon and splatter on the blanket. In between mouthfuls, she gives dramatic, full-body shudders.

"It's so cold in here," she says. "Is the heat off?"

Her innocuous tone pricks at me. She knows the heat is off because we can't afford it at the moment, and it's gotten too embarrassing for Luka and me to keep begging coal off the Mulders next door. Maybe if I weren't so tired, so rattled by my experience with Floris, I would keep my mouth shut and let Luka handle this one. But he's still shoving potatoes into his mouth, and his finger is hovering over the play button on the tablet, threatening to turn the video back on.

So I bite out, "Yes. It's too expensive right now."

I can't bring myself to add a *sorry*. But as soon as the words are spoken, I regret them. I've summoned up an even uglier side of Mom. Maybe the ugliest.

"Inesa," she says, her voice pitching up, high and reedy, "I cannot deal with your selfishness right now."

I suppose it *is* selfish, if you look at it the way Caerus wants you to. Because that's the whole point of their credit system. Everything is affordable—if you're willing to go into the red. I doubt there's one person in Esopus Creek who isn't at least a thousand credits in debt to Caerus. You can keep buying and buying, watching your account sink further into the scarlet ledger, until the collection alerts start popping up. And if you sink far enough, they'll send one of their

16

employees—Masks—to come and collect you. Then you can labor away in one of their packaging plants, for however long it takes to pay off what you owe.

But sometimes, there's too much debt for work to wipe it clean. Five hundred thousand credits. That's what Floris owed.

Unlike our neighbors, we refuse to let ourselves go into the red. For Luka, I know it has a lot to do with Dad. For me, there's nothing quite so principled behind it. I'm just afraid. I'm afraid all the time. And maybe that's the real reason I refuse to watch the Gauntlets. I don't want it to feel real. I want to pretend it's just a show.

It's hard to pretend, when I've seen Sanne's body stretched out across the counter.

So I let Mom have her little fit, scowling at my laziness, criticizing my lack of compassion. She goes on for so long that eventually Luka gets up and retreats to his bedroom in silence. He might think he's the protector of the family, now that Dad is gone—and that's probably how it looks to everyone in Esopus Creek. But behind closed doors, I'm still the one protecting him. I take Mom's bullets every single time.

Eventually I manage to escape to my bedroom. It's just a cot shoved up against the east wall of the house, with a bedsheet strung as a curtain between Luka's section and mine. We can see each other's shadows passing behind the curtain and hear the low murmur of each other's voices, though we both keep our headphones on most of the time. I don't know what he does on his tablet. And I'm glad he doesn't know what I do on mine.

17

I force myself to choke down some leftover pasta—out of Mom's sight—and set the empty plate on the floor, then prop my tablet up on my pillow. From the other side of the curtain, I hear Luka roll over in his cot.

I put on my headphones and open the $ponsor app, checking to see if any of my subscribers are online. After dinner is usually a good time. Everyone is home from work and there are a few hours to kill before bed. The little counter in the top right corner shows 172. Good enough. I turn on my front camera and click the red button that says STREAM.

"Hi, everyone," I say, keeping my voice to a whisper. "Sorry I have to be quiet—my mom and brother are both trying to sleep."

My subscribers know more about my life than anyone, because they pay me just to talk. They'll pay to watch me eat pasta in bed and recount my day. I wondered, at first, what they could possibly get out of it—and sure, there are a fair number of men with shudder-inducing intentions. But if they say anything too creepy in the chat, I can click a single button and block them. They're all anonymous, a string of random numbers—Caerus account numbers—with no picture attached. Still, I've come to recognize their different typing styles, if they watch my streams often enough.

A lot of them tell me about themselves, too. There's the same thread that runs through every story, whether it be a negligent spouse, grown-up children moved far away, a luckless love life, a failed marriage. Their loneliness pulses through the screen.

Sometimes I wonder why they choose to watch me, when there are thousands of other streamers out there, and a lot of them much more, well, *forthcoming* than I am. As I stream, I watch my face, warped slightly by the cracks in my tablet. My skin is olive-toned, and I suspect it would be almost as dark as Dad's if I didn't live in Esopus Creek, where the sun only peeks out from the clouds one out of every three days. My hair is the same shade of ash brown as his, my eyes a wavering hazel, my brows arched and dense, my lips full. It's hard to look at myself without thinking of what Mom would say: that I look too much like my father.

"Luka takes after me," she always says proudly, one of her more egregious delusions. Luka and I are mirror images of each other. Some people in Esopus Creek still mistake us for twins.

It's funny, how the same features can look so different on different people.

The streams are something I keep secret from Mom, and even from Luka. We don't judge each other for the things we do to survive, whether that's swiping coal from the shed in the Mulders' yard or sucking the marrow out of rabbit bones while Mom turns her head away in disgust. On that front, we're a team, just like we are when it comes to running the shop—him hunting, me mounting. But streaming feels like a different kind of desperation, one that embarrasses me too much to share.

"It's raining so hard today," I tell my chat. "And I had this one client come into my shop—you won't believe what he wanted me to do . . ."

I just talk and talk and talk, into the fuzzy tablet screen. I answer questions from the chat and sometimes they tell me about their days in return. With my longtime subscribers, I know what kinds of questions they're going to ask, and how they expect me to reply. It's five credits for every question; five more if they want the app to read their questions aloud in a staticky, robotic voice. Some nights I can make more in an hour than I do my entire week at the shop.

It's easy to lose track of time when I'm streaming. At first it was awkward, but now I can talk almost nonstop for hours. The things I find impossible to say to Luka are somehow simple to say to strangers. My subscribers know about Mom and all her dramatically feigned ailments, about how long it took me to realize that when Dad disappeared, he was never coming back. Topics that Luka and I have a silent agreement to never touch.

Seven turns into ten turns into midnight so quickly. When I finally switch off my camera, I'm so tired I can hardly keep my eyes open. Some of the subscribers linger a little while after I'm gone, their questions hanging limply in the chat, unanswered. I think they watch me because they can feel my loneliness echoing back, identical to their own. While my voice and face fill up their empty houses, their questions build like a seawall. A barrier against the bleak, oblivious silence that would crush me, if I let it.

I scroll through the remaining messages in the chat. One comment sticks out to me, from a user that I don't recognize. A new subscriber.

have u seen it??

Then they post a link.

Usually the only commenters who post links are bots, trying to send me to spam websites, and I block them immediately. But I know this one isn't a bot because they've actually subscribed to my stream—though only as of ten minutes ago. Not long enough to be aware of my personal convictions. All my other subscribers know better than to ask.

I recognize the link. It's the same one at the top of Mom's browser screen. **Caerus.gov/Gauntlet.**

Luka's words drift through my mind. *Maybe you should watch them. Maybe then you'd understand.* And then I think of my humiliating encounter with Floris, how I've damaged our reputation, all because I'm too much of a coward to so much as peek at what everyone in New Amsterdam watches greedily, eagerly, or with a repulsed sense of obligation.

I click the link.

The page takes a few agonizing seconds to load, and I steel myself to see Sanne—blue eyes flung wide in silent horror, skinny legs pumping desperately as she runs, stained dress streaking against the trees. If I can imagine it first, maybe seeing it won't be so bad. But it's stupid of me to think I can conjure anything more nightmarish than the truth.

When the page finally loads, I don't see Sanne at all. Instead, I see the dark belly of a helicopter lowering itself over a familiar patch of forest. I hear the deafening whir of its blades. It hovers a few feet above the ground, stirring up dead leaves, mud flecking its sleek black hull.

Then the camera cuts to a close-up. I see a sheet of blond hair, so pale it's almost white, pin-straight and shimmering. An oval face, equally pale, as pristine as the snow that hasn't fallen over

New Amsterdam in decades. Angular cheekbones and lips set in a thin, impassive line. A girl, no older than me.

I almost catch myself thinking she's beautiful. But then I remember that she's not a girl—not really. She's a cold creature that was crafted in the Caerus labs, starting with a human body and then adding or subtracting whatever they need to turn her into their perfect weapon. She wears a girl's face, and maybe it is an exceptionally lovely one. But inside, she's wires and hardware, alloys and electrical circuits threaded around flesh and bone.

Caerus calls them Angels, the name fitting in its cruel irony. Yet I find that I'm captivated, sickeningly, just like everyone else in New Amsterdam, by the coldly beautiful face of Sanne's killer.

TWO

MELINOË

⟢

When the lights go off, my real eye shuts and my prosthetic blinks to life. My artificial eye sees everything in a different way: streaks of heat, blue and red and yellow, motion and stillness. The little girl's movement pattern is erratic. She's stumbling in the dark; I can hear her clumsy footfalls and labored breathing. Against my temple, the feed from her tracker throbs like a second pulse.

In the darkness I lift my gun, tracing her heat signature. Sometimes my targets stop, freeze, try to make as little movement as possible, try to not even breathe. That's how prey animals survive. But people aren't rabbits or mice, and as much as I sometimes wish it, I'm no snake or raptor.

The little girl whimpers as my prosthetic eye blinks, adjusts, and trains on her like the scope of a rifle. Then I line up my shot, finger brushing the trigger.

At the exact moment my bullet meets its mark, the feed from her tracker goes dead silent. I can only hear my own heartbeat, so loud in the empty room, almost angry in its determined bragging.

The lights flicker back on, and fifty yards down the shooting range, the girl's body is slumped against the cold metal floor. There's no blood, and I don't see the bullet wound until I get closer.

With every step toward her, my heartbeat grows louder. I feel it throbbing in my throat, making my gorge rise. By the time I reach her, the vision in my real eye has blurred, and I have to lift my hand to close the lid over my prosthetic, because it's programmed to stay open always, even when I sleep.

I turn the girl over. Dead bodies are heavier than you think they'd be. Her stained white dress is limp and her hair looks damp—why is it damp? The stains are dark, but they aren't blood. Where did they come from? My vision doubles and then fractures, like the whole room is a broken mirror. I can't even feel the ground as I kneel beside her. My gloved hand spreads over the bullet wound.

Both of her eyes are still open, glassy and staring at nothing. There's a choking sound that I know comes from me, but it feels so distant, like something I'm hearing from underwater. I rub at my real eye over and over again until it stings, until the pain driving tiny needles into my skull brings me back.

I let the eyelid over my prosthetic slide open. And then I can see the perfect falsity of her limbs, the tough silicone flesh that doesn't give way when I touch it. Her eyes are spheres of plastic. The wound is just a hole with mesh and wires and circuit boards inside. There's no sinew, no muscle, no blood.

The girl isn't real. But all the others have been. I get to my feet again, breathing in short, hot gasps. There's no mud seizing at my boots, sticking me down. I'm inside—standing in a stark, familiar metal gallery.

When I look up to the observation chamber, Azrael is frowning at me from behind the glass. His arms are folded over his chest. He used to think that killing was harder in the dark, when I had to rely on my prosthetic and heat signatures and the auditory implants that make my hearing as sharp as any hunting dog's. But he must know now that he's wrong. It's so much harder to kill in the light, when I have to see everything, with all the human parts of me that are still left.

"Melinoë," he says, his voice low and grainy through the speaker, "let's talk."

It's not a long walk from the shooting range to the lab, but it feels like it. My knees are weak and trembling. As I approach, Azrael scans me up and down, eyes zeroing in on all the little chinks in my armor: the way my hands are shaking inside my gloves, the way my breath is coming too fast, the way I can't stop blinking, trying to make the memory of the dead girl stop playing on the insides of my eyelids.

"It's been three Wipes now," he says. His voice is still low, though it's not quite gentle.

"I know."

"We need to find a solution. You need to move on from this, Melinoë."

There's nothing in the world I want more. To move on from

this. To forget. I could start sleeping at night again. I could take a shower without ending up curled on the bathroom floor, breathing hard and clasping my hand over my mouth as the water pours down and down around me.

I could do another Gauntlet.

Azrael starts to lead me to the lab, but then stops, right there in the middle of the hallway. I stare up at him, gaze running over his familiar features. The dark hair that betrays no trace of silvering, the eyes that seem almost pupilless, the white skin pulled taut over his bones. He's all sharp edges, from his cheeks to his chin to the crisp lines of his black suit. I know that he's getting transfusions, like all the high-level Caerus employees, and that's why he looks so young. Why he hasn't changed at all since I first met him, when I was eight years old and still asking after my real father.

I take a deep breath, because I don't want my voice to betray any hesitation.

"Wipe me again," I say.

Azrael's mouth twitches. "You know it isn't that simple. Every time we Wipe, we risk losing something we didn't intend to lose."

Memories, as he's explained to me, are tricky things. Even Caerus's top scientists can't figure out why certain ones hang on while others slip away, eroded by time. Why certain ones get buried in us like shrapnel so we can't move without feeling the pain of the thing that's killing us slowly.

"I don't care." I'd rather die than see the girl again.

Azrael inhales, and then he lays a hand on my shoulder.

"I know you're desperate to get back into the field," he says.

"But you're too valuable to risk. What happened with Daena—it can never happen again."

We've heard the story a hundred times by now, all of us Angels. Daena was Caerus's best killer, equal parts ruthless and beautiful. Her record was impeccable; the streams of her Gauntlets were replayed millions of times, to the point where anyone you met could recount them, almost beat for beat. The time she chased down her mark in the middle of a crowded street and still managed to get off the perfect shot, clean and almost bloodless, a bullet right through the heart. Or the time she found her mark cowering in a hollow tree and, holding the woman's hand, slit her throat so tenderly it seemed almost a kindness.

Daena's icy smile was projected onto the sides of buildings, and she was rented out almost every night for parties with the City's elite. Even now you'll hear some of them talk about her, in low and wistful tones, eyes darkening over their glasses of Scotch. The City folk loved her, and the people in the outlying Counties feared her, which was the best you could hope for as an Angel.

It shouldn't have happened the way it did. Now Caerus has a system in place to prevent us from ever getting assigned marks we know. A more extensive program of memory wiping, so after our parents hand us over to Azrael, we're blank slates. If we don't remember who we were before becoming Angels, there's no chance of us encountering someone we recognize on a Gauntlet.

Daena's mark was an old woman, more than eighty, which is an astonishing age for an Outlier—even more astonishing for a Lamb. It's usually the opposite way, parents putting up their children, but in this case, the woman's son had racked up a huge debt with Caerus, buying bottles of sapphire-blue liquor and collectible action figures, of all things. So Daena was dropped into some tiny mountain village in Adirondack County, where she found her mark sitting on the porch of her house, a serene smile on the woman's face.

But the house had once been Daena's house. And the mark was Daena's grandmother. If she had laid down her rifle then, she'd still be an Angel. She'd still be hired out for parties and put up on every holoscreen in the City. But instead, Daena had killed her, and only afterward did she realize that it was her grandmother's blood pooling on the porch.

Caerus tried an initial Wipe, of course. It didn't take. Then Azrael tried an Echoing—the opposite of a Wipe, where the memory is replayed over and over again so that we become inured to it. But that only made it worse. It brought Daena to a precipice he was afraid she couldn't return from. So he tried another Wipe, and that time it *did* work—except it took everything else with it. Everything that made Daena who she was—all the people she'd known, places she'd been—all of it, gone. She was a mute, empty husk. The City folk were repulsed by her, and the Outliers no longer feared her, and that's about the worst you can imagine, as an Angel.

Azrael thinks the moral of the story is that you shouldn't get too arrogant or trigger-happy when trying to erase someone's memories. But I think the moral is that there's always one memory that will ruin you, no matter how perfect your record, no matter how many times you've killed and felt nothing at all.

I'm afraid this is that memory for me.

With the utmost tenderness, Azrael brushes back a bit of hair from my face. Usually I don't let a single strand escape from my tight white-blond ponytail.

"All right," he says, softly now. "Let's try. Just one more time."

My stomach contracts with relief and fear, both at once.

And then he takes me into the sterile, metallic room, everything gleaming silver. I lie down on the cold table. I don't need the straps anymore; I've trained my limbs not to protest when he presses the nodes to my temples and drives the needle into my throat. All the clear liquid from the syringe drains into my bloodstream.

"Please," I whisper, but I don't know if I'm saying it aloud or speaking it into the silence of my own brain. "Please work."

After that, there's only darkness.

I wake back in my room. I only know it's been hours because the sky outside my window is a deep, jewel-toned blue, gashed through with white streaks of ever-present smog. There's a steady hum of yellow radiating from the skyline as lights all across the City are turned on for the night.

With a deep breath, I sit up in bed. I'm still wearing my black hunting suit, but my hair has been let down. I imagine Azrael combing it himself, equal parts dutiful and tender. He must have remembered that I'm due at the CTO's party later. The diamond-encrusted dress I took out this morning is still folded over the back of my chair, glittering like broken glass.

There's only one way to tell if the Wipe worked. I can remember our walk down the hallway, Azrael's hand on my shoulder. His fingers gently brushing the hair from my face. I can remember the syringe draining and the cold metal against my back. Before that is a rheumy gray space, vague and ill-defined. The lights dimming over the shooting range—

I walk to the bathroom, my gait swift and purposeful. I peel off my hunting suit. Even though I usually try to avoid it, I catch a glimpse of myself in the narrow mirror. My hair, long and bone-straight, falling to the small of my back. In this light, it looks more white than blond. My cheeks are utterly drained of color. When I do blush, which isn't often, my face turns a bruised shade of purple—thanks to Caerus's physiological alterations. They slow our heart rates to make us better snipers; the side effect is that our blood is blue, not red.

I don't let my eyes linger on the scars that ring my wrists and ankles, my elbows and knees, my hips, even my throat. The only other people who have ever seen them are Azrael and the surgeon who worked on my anesthetized body. They're otherwise hidden under our hunting suits, and Caerus provides us with civilian clothes that are fitted to cover them completely. The scars are just for us to look at in private, to remind us we're not quite human. Not anymore. That there's no life for us, other than this.

Turning my back to the mirror, I scroll through the tablet screen outside the shower door, selecting the coldest possible setting.

I can feel the memory start to creep into the corners of my mind—*the girl's wet hair, the girl's wet dress, the mud-stained hem*—but as soon as the water hits my skin, the world behind my eyelids explodes in a riot of color. I'm there again, in the woods, in the pouring rain, the green smell of rotten leaves and damp wood flooding my nose. I can hear the girl crying, pleading, and I can see my arm rising alongside the rifle, like the rudder of a boat and the black wave that follows it.

I'm hardly aware of collapsing onto the shower floor, knees hitting the tile with a flinching but hollow sound. With one hand, I feel for the interior control panel, fingers scrabbling against the waterproof screen, and manage to switch the setting to *HOT*. Steam clouds around me.

We've all gone through rigorous neural reconditioning, which blunts the edges of our emotions, but the closest thing I know to anger is flooding my chest. What's the point of keeping us just human enough to feel? They've grafted titanium onto our bones and pumped hormones into our blood, but they've left something essential at the core of us unchanged.

I know what Azrael would reply.

"Think of it as a means of communication, Melinoë. Otherwise, Caerus might as well send the Dogs."

The Dogs are quadruped robots programmed to do one thing only: kill. Their AI is simple and brutally efficient, and their armored hulls, heat-seeking vision, and clutch of titanium bullets ensure they get the job done. They never falter.

But there's no tension to watching a Dog take down its target. It's like watching the wheels of a car turn a skittering creature into roadkill. Ugly and inevitable. Being struck down by an Angel is meant to be a beautiful thing: riveting, theatrical, perfectly paced, like your favorite TV show. That part is for the City dwellers, the ones who will never have to worry about seeing their loved one as the Lamb in the Gauntlet.

Most important, though, it's meant to impart a message, a warning to the Outliers: *We will take your son or daughter from you. And we will bite our nails and murmur anxiously and, in the end, breathe a sigh of relief as they're slaughtered.*

Duty trumps my pathetic sentimentality. Two hours later I'm smiling over cocktails with the Caerus CTO, Hendrik Visser.

The blood infusions from young donors make him look no older than forty, but there's an undeniable falsity to his smooth face. When he smiles, the corners of his eyes don't crease and his cheeks don't wrinkle. He's sipping a sickly purple cocktail that makes my eyes water when I get near enough to smell it.

"Debts are piling up in the Valley," he says to the HR director, whose name I haven't bothered to learn. "Every time a big storm comes in—and the thing is, these people don't even want canned goods or Mylar blankets or whatever the fuck. They want candy bars and sixty-inch tablets. I kid you not. And they blame *us* when they're five hundred thousand credits in the red."

He's drunk already, slurring his words. He's slipped from Damish, the language of the City, the language of newscasts and board meetings and political speeches, into English, the informal tongue of the Outliers. It's what we're all raised to speak until the Damish consonants and vowel sounds are drilled into us for the sake of job interviews and corporate shop talk. Mostly, we speak

32

in Damish to separate ourselves from the Outliers. When I'm on my Gauntlets, sometimes I have to remind myself to moderate my City accent.

"Cheers to that," the HR director says, his artificially white teeth gleaming. "And cheers to second-quarter profits up ten percent."

They clink glasses. I stay quiet, cradling my glass of water. Angels aren't supposed to drink. We aren't supposed to have any vices, anything that might compromise our missions. The neural reconditioning means I'm not even tempted. Not by alcohol, not by cigarettes, not by anything the other people at this party are enjoying—or craving.

As I stare into the middle distance with practiced blankness, Visser's arm slides against my back.

"I hear we might have another Gauntlet soon," he says.

If he weren't already slipping back and forth between English and Damish, this is how I would know for certain that he's drunk. Even the HR director flinches. I seize up, my fingers curling into my palm.

Everyone knows about my last humiliating, disastrous Gauntlet, and everyone knows I haven't been on one since. The guests around us go quiet, their gazes darting anxiously toward me. As if I'm a mine, rigged to explode. As if I'm going to collapse onto the floor at any moment. Just like I did during the live stream, for every pair of eyes in New Amsterdam to see.

The clip of it went viral, of course. Last I checked, it had been viewed over twenty million times. I'm sure it fills the Outliers with a vengeful satisfaction to see an Angel on her knees for once. And the City folk must watch it out of morbid curiosity—the same thing that keeps them glued to TV shows where garishly horrible fates befall the characters. I'm no more real to them than I am to the Outliers. No more human.

In a flat, measured voice, I say, "Who's the Lamb?"

More silence. There are a few titters from the other guests, dressed in their suits of gunmetal gray and adorned with glittering silver jewelry. The head of HR gives a quiet cough, clearing his throat.

"I've only heard rumors," Visser says—too loud, oblivious to the discomfiting silence. "A girl in the Valley, her mother with some kind of addiction. It's always the same, isn't it? Same old tragic story."

Yes, I want to say, *it's always the same.* Because that's Caerus's design, and nothing exists outside of their design.

I take a sip of water, but it burns my throat like acid. The guests return to their conversations, but it seems that Visser's hand has found a permanent place against the small of my back.

My next sip of water chokes me, and I cough, trying to use that as an excuse to dislodge Visser's hand. But I can still feel it, hot and clammy through the fabric of my dress. It's a thin silver nylon, encrusted in diamonds to hide all the places no one is supposed to see. Not just my breasts or my privates, but the scars ringing my wrists and elbows, my neck. A diamond choker covers that old wound easily.

As if on cue, Azrael sweeps over to us. As if he means to rescue me. Just like he did the day of my last Gauntlet, the black Caerus helicopter whirring overhead. I remember him reaching out his hand, gathering me into his arms, and not much after that. They left the girl's body on the ground, rain drenching her, sinking slowly into the mud.

My heart leaps a little bit, seeing him. I wish it didn't. I wish the voice inside my head didn't cry out to him, *Save me, please, get me out of here.* But it does. It always has.

"Mel," Azrael says, "having a good night?"

"Yes," I answer. It's as quick as a reflex.

"Good," says Azrael. "And you, Hendrik?"

Visser nods gruffly, his nose in his cocktail glass.

The holoscreen in the corner is playing back the live stream of another Gauntlet, volume muted. Another Angel is running along the edge of a cliff, blue-brown water foaming and churning below. The video drones buzz around her like flies. Her helpless Lamb must be close.

The stream cuts to the live feed from her prosthetic and I see a young man stumbling down the cliffside, his shirt and pants torn. Even though there's no volume, I can still hear the thrum of his tracker in my ear, the hitch of his panicked breathing.

I turn my eyes away as the Angel lifts her gun. But then she's here in front of me, not a hologram, not a playback. She slinks through the crowd toward me, her frosty auburn hair looking radioactively bright.

"Azrael," she says with a demure smile when she reaches us. "Mr. Visser." When she turns to me, the smile vanishes and her nostrils flare. "Mel."

"Lethe," I greet her. "I see we're celebrating your Gauntlet."

Lethe's smile returns, a cold beam of pride. "Last week. Nineteen-year-old boy put up by his grandfather. It took him eighty years, but eventually he reached the threshold."

Five hundred thousand credits. That's how deep you can go into the red before Caerus comes to collect. How long you can go on buying until one of the Masks shows up at your door, demanding payment. Demanding a name.

There's not a Mask in sight tonight. No sleek, featureless silicone with a voice modulator—required dress for all Caerus employees when they're on the clock. Caerus is meant to be a total meritocracy, and the masks ensure that no one is treated any differently because of their looks, their gender . . . anything.

Supposedly. Once you get to upper management, though, the masks are cast aside. I recognize everyone in the room, a sea of pale, artificially unwrinkled male faces.

"Good job," I say to Lethe. "It looks like he didn't put up much of a fight."

Lethe's eyes narrow—the real one, and the prosthetic, which is black from end to end.

"More of a fight than a twelve-year-old girl," she says.

I draw in a sharp breath. I feel like a knife has been jabbed between my ribs.

"Enough, Lethe," Azrael says stonily. "You're not each other's competition."

Not officially. But it's kind of inevitable, when you have viewers in the chat commenting on who their favorite Angel is, when you have people in upper management asking for one of us specifically, when you have Caerus's ad department deciding whose face they should put on their holoboards. Lethe hates me because she thinks I'm Azrael's favorite and, by extension, Caerus's.

Lethe sniffs. "I wish I had weeks to mope around in my room instead of working, that's all."

It isn't often that Azrael looks truly angry, but the way his eyes flash now—it scares me, even though I'm not the target of his cold fury.

When he speaks, his voice is deathly quiet. "I said *enough.*"

Lethe's mouth snaps shut, but she still glares at me. At least Visser is too drunk to have noticed a thing.

Relief shudders through me. Relief and gratitude. I'm not naive enough to think that Azrael is silencing Lethe just to protect me. He doesn't want to draw attention to his own mistakes. It was him who put me through a week of Echoing, thinking he was fixing me. He was wrong; we both were. All it did was force the memory further into my head, like a hammer driving in a nail. Forcing me to relive that moment over and over again in the hopes that it would eventually settle within me, as harmless and innocuous as a layer of dust. But the Echoing had the opposite effect. Now the memory is planted so deeply, I'm afraid I'll never dig it out.

There's some murmuring among the guests, and suddenly the crowd parts, forming a path wide enough for two people to walk through. One of them is Caerus upper management—head of accounts, maybe. I've seen him a couple of times before. But my eyes glide over him to the woman on his arm. Her black hair is loose around her shoulders and she wears a deep-blue gown with sleeves down to her wrists, its collar buttoned up to her chin.

"Keres," I whisper.

She can't hear me, of course, and she doesn't see me. As she gets closer, I notice the patch over one of her eyes. They took her prosthetic out, and the wound hasn't healed enough to set the new one in. One that doesn't have night vision or heat tracing or anything else we use to hunt.

But Keres was one of us. She was the one who trained with me at the shooting range, our rifles aimed at identical targets, our trigger fingers perfectly in sync. We ducked Azrael's rules to sneak into each other's rooms at night, speaking in hushed tones until the sun rose over the City and turned all the glass faces of the buildings to liquid gold. She used the shower in my room once, and I watched her, guiltily, through the crack in the door, marking the places where our bodies were identical. Wrists, ankles, elbows, knees, throat. My eyes had lingered, more guiltily, on other parts of her, until I was so flushed I turned away and bit down hard on my lip.

Thinking of that now, with Visser's hand against my back, makes me want to retch.

It's wrong of me, but I leave him. I almost can't help it—my body floats through the crowd, as if buoyed on invisible strings. I ignore the protests of the other guests, the livid look of disapproval on Azrael's face. When I reach her, my chest is heaving.

"Keres," I say again. "It's you."

She blinks her real eye, lifting one hand to her mouth. It's a gesture I've seen a million times, but it looks different now. It looks like I'm watching a disembodied hand, a disembodied mouth. The man next to her gives a disgruntled huff.

"Melinoë," he says. "I didn't think I'd see you here tonight."

I scarcely hear him. My pulse is pounding in my ears. I stare at Keres, watching her blink, waiting for her to smile back at me.

She doesn't. Her hand drops from her mouth and falls limply to her side. It doesn't reach out for mine. She looks back at me as if I'm a stranger.

And then Azrael grabs me by the elbow, dragging me away as Keres continues on, fixed to the man's side. Karl van Something, I think. Like all the others, his face is pale, stiff, and artificially young. Azrael's grip on my arm feels like fire, searing through my flesh.

When I've been pulled off to the side, Lethe gives a wide-toothed smile.

"Oh, you didn't hear?" she asks, all too innocently. "Keres was decommissioned. Van Wyck wanted her."

Azrael lets my arm drop. I look up at him, bewildered, full of both stupid hope and plunging despair. He doesn't speak.

I've spent the last few weeks in isolation, shuffled from the shooting range to the lab to my bedroom, my life made simple and monotonous, a dull and grinding rhythm. Rifle in my hands, back against the cold metal table, knees digging into the shower tiles, water running over me, real and not real. So many half-failed Wipes that I'm not even sure it's been *only* a few weeks. It could've been a year.

Long enough for Keres to get pulled from the Angel program. Long enough for her to get *married*.

"I didn't want to put any extra strain on you," Azrael says at last, his voice soft. "I know you were such close friends."

Water, unreal water, is rushing all around me, pulling my head under.

Keres is older than me, twenty. That's a short life span, even for an Angel. And Keres was good—better than Lethe. Her record was almost as perfect as mine.

"Why?" I whisper.

"Keres asked, Melinoë," Azrael says. His voice has gained a sharper edge. "When I told her you were out of commission, she said she didn't want to be an Angel anymore, not without you."

You're lying. It's the first thought that leaps into my mind, and it shames me. Azrael has no reason to lie. But . . . my gaze travels to Keres in the crowd, her sleek black hair shining under the lights, empty expression on her face. She wouldn't choose this. Not if there was a chance I might come back. We had talked about it, before. Promised each other we would retire *together*.

Lethe's voice plays over again in my mind. *Van Wyck wanted her.* I blink and blink and blink. Caerus dulls the nerves around our tear ducts so we can't cry, but I feel it rising in me, the urge to sob. I want Azrael to fold his arms around me, press my face into his chest, so I can hide my shameful, distraught expression.

I know if I asked, he would.

Did Keres think of me, when Azrael strapped her to the table for the last time? Does it even matter now? All the nights we spent huddled under the covers together, laughing and whispering, all the times she helped me take down my hair, peel off my sodden hunting suit, her fingers dancing gently along the notches of my spine—gone. I'm left holding on to them alone, and the memories are so, so heavy for one pair of hands.

Visser sidles up to me again, seemingly oblivious to the disruption. And then I can't—I can't take it anymore; the water is rising up and drowning me. I lift my gaze to Azrael's. I don't speak, but he knows me well enough to recognize the desperate pleading in my eyes.

Save me, please, get me out of here.

And he does. With a few polite words, he shakes off Visser. Then it's Azrael's arm sliding around my waist and down to the small of my back, leading me out of the room. In the hallway, I take off my heels, leaning heavily against Azrael to steady myself. Neither of us says a word.

He walks me to my room in utter silence. When we're standing outside the door, an almost-memory rises in me. Somehow, I can gaze through his crisp black suit to his bare chest—I know what it looks like; I've seen it before. And then the not-memory dissipates, as quickly as it appeared.

"Get some rest, Melinoë," Azrael says. "We'll try again tomorrow."

Tomorrow, and tomorrow, and tomorrow.

Inside, I strip off my dress, my jewelry. My scars look cartoonishly ugly in the bathroom's fluorescent light. I choose the shower's coldest setting, and step into the unforgiving stream.

In the morning, I'm at the shooting range again, rifle in my hands. I see the girl at the end of the long gallery, blond hair flashing, the pulse of her tracker pounding in my left temple. It matches my steady heartbeat. My breathing is measured, even.

I kill her twelve times. Thirteen. I let the memories run over me like rainwater. This time, they slide off my back, painless, disembodied. I was in the wet tangle of those trees once, but I'm not now. I killed the girl as she sobbed and begged for her life, but it's what I was made to do. She was doomed long before I cornered her in the forest. I'm Azrael's instrument, a mere extension of the rifle in my hands. Her death had already been determined by a tally of red marks, by a Caerus algorithm, by a Mask tapping numbers into a tablet.

When the girl's tracker has gone silent and I let my rifle fall, Azrael walks down from the observation room to join me. He holds my face in his hands delicately, turning my head slightly from side to side. As if to examine me, very intimately and with pride. I am, after all, his greatest creation. There's more of his machinations within me, titanium and circuit boards, than my own parents' DNA.

"Melinoë," he says, voice soft and thin with relief, "I'm so proud of you."

I want to say that it was easy once I realized I wasn't just doing it to put on a show for the anonymous live stream audience. Once I realized it was a fight for survival. Every Lamb I kill is more distance between Visser and me, more distance between a final Wipe that will turn me into an empty, mindless doll, opening my legs numbly for a husband three times my age who I barely know and could never love.

It was easy once I understood that it was the girl's life or mine. Survival is the most natural thing in the world, as natural as breathing. Stripped down to its essence, any creature will choose to save itself. Even if it means stealing the breath from another.

The next girl, whoever she is, will be no different.

THREE

INESA

The next weeks pass in a rush of storms, relentless and torrential.
If I didn't know better, if I hadn't lived in Esopus Creek all my life,
I'd worry they would never end. But they always do. Eventually,
nature permits us a bit of sun.

I pole down to the shop before dawn, the sky humming a
tender, pretty blue-pink that belies its ugly origins: air pollution
wafting from the City that traps all sorts of noxious gases beneath
the smoggy stratosphere. Mom and some of the older folk in Esopus say the air used to smell different, fresher. They always talk
about some mythical "before" time, when seasons were drier and
milder, when white-tailed deer were abundant, when the trees were
filled with birdsong.

It bothers me to hear them talk about it, not because I'm envi-
ous, but because this is the only world I've ever known. They treat
it like the dismal end of some story, but for me, it's the beginning,
whether I like it or not. I'm seventeen, and I'll never see a dull sunrise.

Main Street is already busy with punters and rafters, people from Lower Esopus shaking out their wet hair. I'm relieved to see Mrs. Prinslew hunched on one of the punts. The deck of her shop is soggy and rotted, the sandbags split open, but the cinder blocks beneath have held firm.

Dr. Wessels is stepping through the door of his shop; his son lingers behind on the porch. I remember when Jacob Wessels was five inches shorter and following Luka, ever popular, around like a puppy. Now his limbs have lengthened, wiry but strong, and his dark curls are cut close to his scalp. His skin is a deep bronze even in this sunless place. He gives me a wave, and my heart flutters.

"Hey, Inesa," he calls.

I pole over to him and step off my raft onto his porch, stamping my boots dry. "Hi," I say. "You're here early."

"Shadowing my dad," he says. "He finally decided he was sick of me turning green at the sight of blood, so we're doing a bit of exposure therapy. Someone is bound to come in needing stitches."

Hardly a day goes by in Esopus Creek without someone slipping down their steps and gashing their head, wobbling on their raft and falling face-first against the wood, or, when the water is treacherously low, crumpling their raft against one of the sharp rocks that jut upward like shark fins. When Luka was twelve, he crashed into a rock, stripping all the skin from his left forearm and chipping one of his front teeth. I've heard girls whispering about how cute his slightly imperfect smile is.

"I was probably just as squeamish when I first started," I say, which is an understatement. I used to keep a bucket under the counter so I could periodically lean over and retch. "And I only deal with dead things."

Jacob laughs. "Will it sound creepy if I say sometimes I hope you get hurt—just a little—so I can see you?"

That *is* creepy, but also kind of sweet, in a weird way. My cheeks are warm. "Best of luck overcoming your phobia of blood. We're going to need another doctor someday. Already we could do with more than just one."

Jacob's smile falters. "Well . . . he's training me so I can apply for medical school. In the City. Get an actual Caerus license, get out of here."

The flush leaves my cheeks, and my veins grow cold. People my age are always talking about leaving Esopus. They wistfully recount their plans to move to the City, or at least to take off to a different town, one on higher ground. Esopus Creek sits in a valley right between the Catskill and Adirondack Mountains, so all the rainwater that gathers on top of those peaks slides down and puddles into our town.

But I've never thought about leaving and, as far as I know, neither has Luka. Where would we go? What would we do? The City feels too distant to even imagine. I've never even seen one of those sleek high-speed trains that connects the outlying Counties to the metropolitan region downstate. Our dad was born in Esopus, and so was his father, and his father. We're four generations deep in this water.

Not that this legacy seemed to have any sentimental effect on Dad. He made leaving look so easy. But Luka and I couldn't abandon Mom. She'd die without us.

I'm about to reply to Jacob when there's a sudden, powerful gust of wind and a warbling, uneven call that sounds like wood groaning under my feet. Everyone on Main Street looks up, gripped by identical terror.

A winged shadow passes over us, blotting out the shy light of sunrise. We all recognize the creature right away, with its enormous scaly wings and cruelly curved beak, its jagged proportions. It dips and reels overhead, awkward with the novel bloat of its body.

Once upon a time it was a gull, obnoxiously loud and bolder than it had any right to be, but now it's something else, something treacherous and terrifying. A mutation, transfigured by the polluted air and radiation but most of all by evolutionary necessity.

Everyone ducks and scrambles for cover, and fear rolls over me. I've seen gull mutations carry off cats and dogs, and there are rumors that one of them even snatched up a small child.

Larger wings make it easier to stay in flight for longer periods of time. Given the near endless stretches of flooded land in New Amsterdam, you could go for miles without so much as an outcropping for a bird to rest. Water glints off its scales, turning them iridescent as it circles and circles, looking for prey. Scales are better than feathers for sloughing off thick, fetid water. It's survival of the fittest taken to its most extreme and appalling end.

There's the crack of a gunshot, and the gull mutation plummets out of the sky. Its body falls into the flooded street, where it floats with its wings outstretched, easily the size of my raft. Blood, almost the same color as the muddy water, trickles from its breast.

Jacob glances at me questioningly, but I'm a taxidermist, not a trash collector. Like everyone else, I'm going to leave the ugly gull mutation where it is, until another rainstorm comes and flushes it away or its body decomposes and joins the water itself.

"Shit," Jacob said. "I haven't seen one get this close in a while. Disgusting."

It's hard to defend the mutations, especially the ones fabled to carry off small children, but they're also the only reason I have a job. The faunae of New Amsterdam have been mutating for generations. We have squirrels and deer with scaled bellies, rabbits with webbed paws and canine teeth, and birds grown to monstrous proportions. Changed by the hostile world around us, driven by the bone-deep need all organisms share: to survive.

Everyone thinks they're hideous, a grotesque reminder of the planet's inexorable decay. That's why the work Luka and I do, killing and preserving the last of the unchanged deer, rabbits, squirrels, and birds, is valuable. If it weren't for us, they'd disappear completely. Stuffed and dead, they'll exist forever. Mounted in the studies and dining rooms of City folk, they're immortal.

But seeing a mutation turns my stomach all the same. It's a reminder that our work has a planned obsolescence, an expiration date. One day we'll wake up and all the ordinary animals will be gone. Only the mutations will be left, and the lab-grown meat that Caerus drones carry to our doorsteps.

Our livelihood will die with them. To Luka, I know it's just a paycheck, a shallow cushion between us and a steep pit of debt. Maybe I'm the only one who assigns a deeper meaning to it. Even

Jacob talked about leaving like it's the simplest thing in the world. I can't help feeling like I'm holding on to something that is slipping further and further out of my grasp with every passing day. I say goodbye to Jacob and step back onto my raft, poling toward the shop.

The stubborn leak in the ceiling has filled the bucket beneath to its brim, but the shop is dry—a relief. I empty it and then unload Luka's latest haul. Two rabbits, already stiff, and the deer, which is so heavy in death that I'm panting by the time I've dragged it onto my worktable. Since we have a down payment on the deer, I start with him first. He's young—still a few fading white spots on his flank—but his antlers have come in nicely, a broad and curling coronet of bone.

With my buck knife, I cut a seam down his belly, careful to puncture just the skin and not any of the muscles or organs underneath. It took me a long time to be able to make such precise cuts—it pains me to think how many potential mounts I ruined back then, all those credits down the drain. At least we could eat those deer. We had venison stew and venison jerky for weeks afterward.

I like to think of it as taking off the animal's shirt and pants. That makes it easier to stomach. Like the heart of the animal isn't its skin, or its meat, or even its actual heart. There's something enduring but invisible that constitutes the very core of the creature. I'd call it a *soul*, but even I wouldn't take myself seriously if I spoke the word aloud. And Luka would laugh at me.

Unlike with Luka's hunting, there was no one to teach me

taxidermy. I figured it out by myself, over the course of several bloody, woozy months. My early mounts were overstuffed and lopsided, and they looked half like mutations themselves. People bought them anyway; people from the outlying Counties, at least. We didn't start getting our City customers until my work started getting decent, only a year and a half ago. It was convenient timing, because that's when Dad disappeared for good.

I slip the young buck out of his skin, taking care not to rip the hide. He's so freshly dead that there are still some oils in his coat, and it's soft under my hands as I lay it out on the drying table.

Dad approved of the business. He approved of doing anything outside Caerus's control. *A system of exploitation*, he called it. The more dependent we are on Caerus, the more power we give them. Dad's whole life was about outsmarting, evading. When he was around, we never went without power because he figured out sly—and very illegal—ways to wire us to the grid. As far as I know, he never had a single credit on his account. When he needed something, he bartered for it, offering his skills as a self-taught electrician, handyman, or hunter. He patched roofs and fixed plumbing. He rebuilt Mrs. Prinslew's crumbling porch, with Luka hanging around to hand him wrenches or hammers. I could tell from Luka's furrowed brow that he was trying to commit everything Dad did to memory, so that one day he could do it, too. I know he imagined they'd be a team, father and son evading that *system of exploitation* together.

My chest tightens suddenly, surprising me. I thought I'd gotten numb to memories of Dad, but now they wash over me like floodwater. I can feel his strong arms around my shoulders, and see his warm brown eyes crinkling when he smiled. The knife wobbles in my hand and I have to put it down and draw in a breath so I don't make the wrong cut.

Dad was born in Esopus Creek, but he spoke differently and thought differently than everyone else. His mother was a schoolteacher. She had a lot of pre-Caerus books around, histories that were otherwise obliterated. People and places we were never supposed to know, or at least were supposed to forget. I wish I had paid more attention to the things he told us, but that's the way it always is: You never really understand what's important until you lose it.

Dad was the one who told me about evolution and natural selection. Only the strongest creatures survive, so their traits are passed down to their descendants. Gulls with larger wingspans were more likely to survive, so with each successive generation, their wings grew larger and larger. The new replaces the old. The powerful replace the powerless.

"Don't let Caerus think there's anything *natural* about what they're doing, Nesa," Dad had said. "They've created conditions that allow some organisms to thrive and others to die—all by their design. It's *intentional*. We aren't less-evolved creatures. We're just land animals in a sinking world, and they're the sea animals. If the lakes and rivers were drying up and the sea level was falling instead of rising, they'd die like beached fish. Do you see what I mean?"

To tell the truth, Dad drank more than he should have, so when he talked, his eyes turned glassy and far away, and his stories meandered and zigzagged until he was slurring words and dropping syllables. And I didn't usually understand him, not really.

Most of the time, it was hard to imagine how he and Mom had ever ended up together. But in those moments, I could see it. In their own ways, they both thought they deserved more from the world than it had given them.

Dad coped with it by slipping further and further off Caerus's grid, and ours, until one day we woke up and he was gone. Mom copes with it the way she does. And Luka and I just try to keep our heads above water.

But Dad leaving ripped a wound in Luka that I don't think will ever heal. As much as he thinks I'm the softhearted idealist between us, he's the one who believed the things Dad said about escaping Caerus's system, about being free. I'm not sure I can believe it the way Luka does.

And anyway, right now I'm up to my elbows in dead deer.

I should've started with the rabbits. I didn't eat anything before I left the house and I feel lightheaded. I salt the deer's skin and then take a step back, drawing in a shaky breath. I'm suddenly overcome with the desperate desire to do anything but this ugly, bloody, *small* work. I march up to the counter instead and turn on my tablet.

I scroll through my receipts and accounts, my virtual ledger. There's the City buyer who wanted four mounted stag heads, Arend Meester. I could barely understand his thick Damish accent. Next to him is Floris Dekker, and I flinch at the sales column: seventy-five credits. It should have been ninety at least. And that's not even accounting for what I risked by helping him.

But Floris hasn't left his house since the day he spread his daughter's dead body across my counter. I wonder if he'll ever leave again. Someone—I really wonder who—splashed black paint across the door of his Caerus pod home. *Coward.*

I shake my head, as if to clear it of the memory, and keep scrolling through the accounts. It's almost impossible to tell a City resident from an Outlier by name alone, because New Amsterdam's provincial government offered an incentive program a while back for Outliers to change their names to Damish. Ten thousand credits of debt, erased—we really could have used that, but Mom had refused. She said people had been trying to make us change our family name for centuries, including the officials at the City immigration port where our great-great-great-whatever ancestors first landed. They came from a small village in some old country thousands of miles away, where they ate mostly cabbage and didn't work on Saturdays, which doesn't sound too bad.

In the Dominion of New England, just north of us, they offered a similar financial incentive for people to change their names to things like Prudence and Bartholomew. I don't think I'd ever do that, not even for fifty thousand credits.

I'm so zoned out staring at my tablet that I hardly notice when the door of the shop swings open. I only startle when I hear how heavy the footsteps are on the floor. Thick, weather-resistant boots made of durable rubber. No one in Esopus has boots like that.

Slowly, my gaze rolls upward, from the boots to the pale gray suit, inexplicably dry and entirely featureless, save for the Caerus insignia on the breast.

I can't make eye contact with the Mask, of course, but I fix my stare about where I think its eyes should be. I can't see anything in the smooth metal visor except my own reflection, warped and tiny, like a fish trapped in a bowl.

"Hello," I say. "Welcome to Soulis Taxidermy Shop. How can I help you?"

We've had Masks in here before, sent by Caerus to appraise the shop. Sometimes they offer to buy it, but Luka and I always refuse. Even though I didn't understand everything Dad said, I know when someone is trying to stiff me.

I assume this Mask is here for the same reason. Usually they send us a notification, my tablet screen momentarily blinking red. Not this time, though it doesn't matter. I'm not selling the shop.

I'm preparing my most polite refusal when the Mask shocks me by saying my full name aloud.

"Inesa Yael Soulis."

It's not a question. I cringe at hearing it in the Mask's staticky, monotone voice. "Yes?"

"Account number 6415506781."

With its flat, robotic tone, it's hard to tell if *this* is a question. "Yes?" I try again hesitantly.

"You have been nominated for the Lamb's Gauntlet beginning March eighth. More information will be forwarded to your tablet."

"What?" The word comes out strangled. I stare at the smooth metal visor, my mind racing, and I don't understand.

"The Lamb's Gauntlet," the Mask repeats. If there's a tinge of annoyance to its voice, I can't suss it out. It just sounds like the buzz of black flies as they hover around a corpse. The memory of

54

Sanne flashes through my mind, the muddied hem of her white dress, her still-open eyes. And, then, worse: the flash of the Angel's white hair. Her gloved hands, sliding up the barrel of her rifle. The utterly inhuman coldness of her stare.

This all happens to other people, not to me. To people who carelessly let themselves slip so far into the red that they can't dig themselves out. My thoughts skip around, scattered. We've never gone a single credit into debt. Luka and I work so hard to keep our family out of the red. It *can't* be me.

"Your Gauntlet will begin in twelve hours. Please refer to your tablet for the countdown."

There's a roaring in my ears, my blood pounding like rainwater down a mountainside. It can't be me. Unless—

"Who?" I manage.

"What?" I imagine some impatience in the Mask's voice.

"My sponsor," I say, my voice a weak croak. "Who is it?"

But I already know.

"Account number 8148775617, Janina Soulis."

The words should hit me like a blow to the head. Instead I just stand there behind the counter, staring blankly at the Mask. My brain is sparking like a cut wire. My throat is dry.

And then the Mask steps forward. All it takes is one swift movement and their fingers close around my upper arm. I don't have the time, or the reflexes, to react. The Mask jerks me forward until I'm bent over the counter, knocking the breath out of me.

"Please," I gasp. "Don't—"

In the Mask's other hand is something that looks like a syringe, only appallingly large, as wide around as my two fingers. Three needles protrude from its end, each one shiny and solid-looking and terrifying. The syringe is made of sleek metal, opaque, so I can't even tell what's inside.

"Your tracker will be inserted now," the Mask says. "Hold still."

All I can do is choke out a wordless protest, tears blurring my vision.

The Mask plunges the syringe into my throat and immediately the counter flies up at me. I hear the crack of my head against the wood, and then everything goes black.

FOUR

MELINOË

"Full name: Inesa Yael Soulis. Account number: 6415506781.
Age: seventeen. Legal residence: Eighteen Little Schoharie Lane,
Esopus Creek, Catskill County. Is there anything else?"

I stare at the girl's picture on the holoscreen. It's an older photo,
probably self-taken, since the camera is angled slightly downward
and the poor lighting makes everything look grainy. Still, I can
make out a ripple of dark brown hair, wavy and casually messy. Full
lips and thick brows. A mole under her left eye. The eyes are peculiar, requiring an extra moment's attention. They're a deep, murky
color, and I can't quite decide if they're brown or green.

But it's not worth mentioning. She looks nothing like my last
target, and that's what's most important.

"Occupation?" I ask.

"She runs a taxidermy shop in Esopus Creek with her younger
brother. Luka Elian Soulis, account number 43678812131." Azrael
puts another picture up on the holoscreen. Side by side, the siblings
look like twins, with the same brown-green eyes and olive skin. But

Luka has a defiant slant to his gaze. Inesa looks cheerful, innocent.

I can't stop the next thought that flashes through my mind: *Just like a Lamb should.*

"The brother," I say. "He hunts?"

Azrael taps something else onto the screen. Photo after photo of Luka beside dead deer, dead rabbits, their bodies hung from tree branches in lifeless suspension, letting the blood from his kills drain out. But he doesn't wear the kind of gloating smile that most hunters do when they pose with their prey—the ones who hunt for sport. I've seen enough already to know that for the Soulises, every dead deer is another day of food, hot water, electricity.

"By all accounts, the Soulis children are hardworking and well-respected in their community," Azrael says. His tone is careful. He's worried that if he humanizes the Lamb too much, I'll get weak again. That I'll balk at killing her. He taps to the next screen almost hesitantly.

There are pictures of Inesa standing at a worktable in a too-long apron, medical-grade gloves, and plastic goggles. Even under the goggles I can see the furrow of concentration in her brow. Clearly she's not the indolent, surrendering type who usually ends up five hundred thousand credits in debt. The ones who are addicted to television or alcohol or sour green soda or greasy delivery food. There's another story here, lurking under these photos and statistics. She must have a sponsor.

"The mother," I say. "What does she do?"

Azrael doesn't reply. Instead he taps through to another screen, which shows Janina Soulis's account history. Her charges fly past me: two hundred thirteen credits for an appointment with a neurologist. Another three hundred for a surgery consult. A monthlong prescription for pain pills that cost forty credits apiece. The doctor's note reads that the pills are prescribed for patients who live with *severe and life-inhibiting levels of pain.*

If Azrael wants me to be strong and heartless, I don't know why he's showing me this. "She's sick?"

Peppered among the medical debts are the small, idiosyncratic indulgences I've come to expect. Eighty credits for top-of-the-line hair dye, jet-black. Peach-flavored detox tea. Boxes of chocolate-covered macadamia nuts. Chenille slippers.

"Sick in the head," Azrael says, tapping his own temple. "Convinced she has every disease and ailment under the sun."

I wonder why none of the many doctors she's seen have told her that. Maybe she's gotten adept at tricking them. Or maybe they have no incentive to tell her the truth. It's more profitable to treat someone for a disease they think they have than to cure them of an illness that never existed.

But there's really no cure for her kind of sickness, anyway. The brain isn't like other organs. You can't suture its wounds and wait for new skin to grow. Even the scientists at Caerus don't fully understand it. If they did, I wouldn't feel my fingers start to shake when I look at the Lamb's picture on the holoscreen. Inesa Yael Soulis.

She's nothing to me. Nothing except a heat flash in the scope of my rifle. The hum of a tracker in my ear. The promise that I'll go another cycle without being decommissioned.

"So," I say, my voice cracking a little, "is there a father?"

Azrael gives me a grim look. He taps around on his tablet until the screen shows a man's face. He has echoes of Inesa's features, only harsher, leaner. Black hair. Scornful, angry eyes. A sneer pulling back his lips. It looks more like a mug shot than an ID photo. When his vital info appears on the screen, the text is red.

"Dead?" I ask.

"Unclear," says Azrael. "Our last records of him are from two years ago, but no one in the family ever registered his passing. They would have good incentive to, because a death certificate qualifies them for welfare benefits. But there's nothing in the system." When I don't reply, Azrael goes on. "I suspect ugly business, probably with the mother."

Domestic abuse is more common in the families of our Lambs than not, and it's easy to imagine that's the *ugly business* Azrael means. I try to bridge the distance between the waifish, sickly looking mother and the angry-eyed father. But the connection fizzles out. The more I look at the photo, the father's gaze seems turbulent, not hostile. It's the mother's eyes that have a sheen of malice in them, glossy and cold as water under moonlight.

But none of this matters. Not really. As much as people like the Soulises want it to be, anger isn't strength. Hate isn't power.

"The parents won't be a concern, then," I say.

"No." Azrael taps away from the father's photo. Inesa's face reappears, and Luka's beside it. "And there's nothing to suggest the Lamb herself will be capable of putting up a fight. The brother, though . . ."

I stare at Luka's face on the screen. He's a hunter—like me, I suppose. I measure myself beside his vitals. He has six inches on me, and more than fifty pounds. But he doesn't have state-of-the-art Caerus rifles, a prosthetic eye that sees in the dark and can follow heat signatures like a hawk, and other enhancements that are under the surface, invisible. Still, brute strength shouldn't be underestimated. And in terms of sheer numbers, I'm sure he's killed more than I have. *His* survival means making new corpses every day.

Animals, though. Deer and rabbits. Not people. In that, I'll always have the upper hand.

"He'll help her," I find myself saying. "He'll do everything he can to save her."

"I expect so," Azrael says. "Be prepared."

There are no rules against having help during a Gauntlet—for the Lambs, at least. They're allowed to do whatever it takes to survive. Still, help usually isn't enough to level the playing field. It just gives the illusion of hope. Of choice, of freedom. Although having another player in the Gauntlet can make aiming trickier—Angels aren't allowed to harm civilians. That will be Inesa's advantage.

Azrael selects his Lambs carefully. Every day, dozens of people reach the limit of their credits, but if we gave them all a Gauntlet, it would become too mundane. More a snuff film than a riveting spectacle. It's important not to let the banal barbarity of it all settle in. So every two months, Azrael chooses Lambs that he can build a narrative around, something that keeps eyes glued to tablet screens and fingers typing furiously in the live chat. At the CEO's instruction, he coordinates the timing carefully to coincide with product releases and key marketing moments.

It's easy to see the narrative he's building around Inesa. Her relationship with her brother, her embittered mother and absent father, her traumatic past—huge entertainment value. It doesn't hurt that she's pretty. My skin prickles at the thought; I'm annoyed at myself for noticing. But it's just a fact, like her height, or the color of her eyes. That elusory brown-green.

It has all the contours of a good story, and I have my own role to play in it. This is the sort of Gauntlet I was made for. The kind where my legendary coldness contrasts with the warmth and spirit and unaccountable hope of the Lamb. Inesa Soulis's vitality seems to pulse through the screen. It will be something to watch, when I drain that life from her.

This is my territory; my act. I wasn't created to kill the hopeless, the helpless, the utterly innocent. That was always Keres's purview, and she was skilled enough that she could make murder seem like mercy. I kill the ones who seem like they might have a fighting chance.

After my last Gauntlet, someone hacked one of the holoboards in the City. It showed me in a clip from the live stream, the camera roving around for a 360-degree view. Beside it were words in a harsh red font: *The most hated face in New Amsterdam.*

Caerus had the image taken down instantly. I don't know what they did to the hacker—probably something too hideous to imagine. But enough people had seen it, and I couldn't exactly argue the fact. I read all the chat logs from the live stream. I searched my own name and found message board upon message board, pages and pages and pages of vitriol and rage. There was even talk of boycotting the Gauntlets, which provoked an irate threat, directly from Caerus's CEO, to cut off power to the Valley if they went through with their plan.

If it were any other Angel, they would have been decommissioned immediately. They would be more trouble than they were worth. But I'm not just any Angel. Not to Azrael.

"The CEO will be watching," Azrael tells me, and the words break my reverie. "Give him a good show."

The remark is a veiled threat. I know the CEO wanted me gone after my last Gauntlet. I know Azrael fought for me to have another chance, a chance at redemption. And I know what fate awaits me if I fail this time. The memory of Visser's hand on the small of my back makes me shiver. And Keres's blank, empty eyes—

"I will," I say, lifting my chin. "I promise."

"Good girl." Azrael rests his hands on my shoulders, and they feel inexplicably heavy, as heavy as steel. Then he moves them up to cup my cheeks. His flesh is warm where mine is cold. "You'll do well, Melinoë. You'll do perfectly."

I return to my room and find Lethe standing outside the door. I stiffen, my shoulders going up around my ears and my black-gloved hands curling into fists.

"*You're* on the next Gauntlet," she says, before I can utter a word. "Azrael picked *you*."

Her voice drips with poison. It's almost enough to make me flinch. "Yes."

"It's not fair. It should be me."

Lethe's eyes gleam like knifepoints. She can't disguise the anger in them, or the hate. Our natural tears have been replaced with a synthetic saline solution that our eyes only release when we need to flush out foreign matter, never when our emotions reach a pitch—but Lethe looks about as close to crying as an Angel can.

"It wasn't my decision," I say. It's true, and she knows it. Azrael plots out every aspect of the Gauntlets, maneuvering us like game pieces. Even if I wanted to, I couldn't refuse him.

But Lethe just says again, "It's not *fair*. All you've done is fail, over and over again. You should've been decommissioned. Like Keres. Everyone knows it."

Keres's name is a blade twisted between my ribs. "Take it up with Azrael."

"Azrael plays favorites. I don't know what you're doing to make him give you so many extra chances, but it's disgusting."

Something shimmers up in my mind, a whaleback breaching the water's placid surface. Another half memory, flickering across the inside of my eyelids. I remember cold metal against the bottom of my belly. A flash of silver. My stomach turns over on itself, but then the not-memory dissipates, curling into the air like smoke.

My tone is flat and chilly. "I'm not doing anything. And you'll get your chance soon enough. There's never any shortage of Lambs."

Lethe sucks in a breath. "I hope you fail. I can't stand to see your face on another holoboard."

"If I fail, you'll never *stop* seeing it."

Our failures as Angels—those rare occasions when the Lambs

actually triumph—are as famous as our successes. Maybe more. Most of the time it's because they find somewhere to hide, somewhere deep or distant enough that it muffles the frequency of their trackers. They can wait out the timer. But sometimes, very rarely, it's because they fight back. That's what the audiences ache to see the most. A dead Angel, blood pooling around her head like a halo.

Lethe's nostrils flare. "I don't know why you think you're so superior. You're just going to end up on Visser's arm."

That's what Lethe is really jealous of, I think. The more successful and famous an Angel is, the better her position when she's decommissioned. When they do the final Wipe and we become what people call, in whispers, *corporate concubines*. A bauble flaunted on the arm of a Caerus executive.

Lethe stands there seething at me, but I'm cloaked in coldness. I don't know anything about her. With precision and efficiency, Azrael turns us all into blank slates the moment we come to him. Her past is a black hole, like mine. She's beautiful, I suppose, like all Angels are meant to be. No more or less than I am, really.

But this is why I'm better than Lethe, even with the unwashable stain of my last Gauntlet: because I can just push past her, as her lips tremble and her eyes blaze, and feel almost nothing at all.

I close the door to my room, leaving Lethe to rage outside. The lights come on when I enter, overly bright at first, before calibrating themselves to a dimmer, warmer glow. One of the maids has been in here, and she's tucked in my sheets and fluffed my pillows.

The entire west wall of my bedroom is a window, facing the

City skyline below. Against the darkness, the buildings glow like a tangle of circuitry. Holo-ads beam into the starless dark. Tonight they're advertising my upcoming Gauntlet. My face, flickering with static, and beside it, the Lamb's. Inesa's. Animated by Caerus's media department, her eyes widen and her mouth opens ever so slightly, as if she's shocked to see herself there in the sky above the City.

I press the pad next to the window and the City view vanishes. I scroll through the list of possible holograms to replace it: a field of flowers, the ocean at night, mountain peaks wreathed in mist. But in the end I choose nothing at all, and just let my window turn black. I can't afford to be distracted.

I take out my tablet and pull up the map of Esopus Creek. I don't need to memorize it. Tomorrow, all this information, along with the pulse of the Lamb's tracker, will be fed into my brain via my prosthetic eye and the comms chip in my temple. To see it, all I'll have to do is blink.

I type in Inesa's address and the map zooms in. Her house is tiny, made of wood and perched precariously on cinder block pillars that hold it above the flooded street. Once, winter turned the outlying valleys crackling dry, brown leaves and brittle branches crusted with snow. It hasn't snowed for as long as I've been alive. Now every season is the rainy season and every day the water rises farther than before. I wonder how long it will be before Inesa's house goes under.

There's something oddly familiar about it, something that jabs at me like a needle to the throat. The words themselves, *Esopus*

Creek, blink across my vision. They're familiar, too. But I can't quite knit the sensations together into thoughts, into revelations. Maybe it's a false familiarity. My mind is pitted with black holes. There's no use puzzling over it.

My childhood is almost entirely gone, but a few memories have survived the countless Wipes. I remember that during my first days with Caerus, I would come to the window and press my palms flat against the glass, staring down at the City below. Sometimes I would imagine that the glass would shatter and I would plummet through it. But sometimes I imagined that instead of falling, I would fly. I was an Angel, after all. I spread my wings, and I was free.

FIVE

INESA

I wake with blood in my mouth and someone jostling my shoul-der. There's a white-hot pain in the middle of my forehead and it hurts to open my eyes to the light. The vague, blurry outline of a face is hovering over mine, but I have to blink a few times before its features sharpen and clarify. Jacob.

"Inesa," he says, voice high and tight with panic, "are you all right?"

Even in my semiconscious state, it strikes me as an absurd question.

There are more voices, and more blurry faces. I think I hear Mrs. Prinslew sniffling. Someone else lets out a choked sob.

I try to get up. Instantly, Jacob reaches around to cradle my back, easing me into a sitting position. My vision ripples. I lift a hand to my forehead, and wince when I touch that sore, throbbing spot in the center. I remember now: I hit my head on the counter.

The room returns to me in increments: the bucket of filthy water in the corner; the damp, creaky floorboards; the sharp, acrid

68

smell of preserving chemicals. And the crowd of people around me, their heads bobbing like buoys in the water. Their eyes are bleary but bright, tearful with concern.

"We saw the Mask come in." Mrs. Prinslew's voice is so hushed I can barely hear her. "We thought—and then we got the notification on our tablets. But it didn't seem real until . . ."

"Until?" I prompt. My tongue is swollen in my mouth and it hurts to talk.

Silence. Mrs. Prinslew's gaze drops to the floor. When I shake Jacob off and push myself onto my knees, the crowd shifts away from me, as if tragedy is radiating from me like an illness they're afraid they might catch.

In the silence I can hear something like a second heartbeat, staticky and incessant—the tracker that the Mask implanted in my throat. Like water dripping from the ceiling, the beat is so measured, it could drive me mad. But I'll be dead long before I have the chance to lose my mind.

"Inesa, wait," Jacob says as I lurch unsteadily to my feet. "Your head . . . you need to take it easy."

"Let her go," someone says gruffly. Mr. Hallick, I think. Luka and I used to sneak into his yard and play on his tire swing when we were kids. "She doesn't have time to rest."

The Mask's voice echoes in my ears. *Twelve hours.* Twelve hours for the Lambs to prepare, to say our goodbyes, to scrounge together a plan that might give us the slimmest chance of survival. Twelve hours for Caerus to run their ads, to promote their Gauntlet-themed and -adjacent products, like VR headsets for better viewing and energy drinks to keep you awake so you don't miss a moment of the slaughter.

How many of those hours did I lose while I was unconscious? I stagger toward the door, but my vision is still swimming. I catch myself on the windowsill. Through the gaps in the wooden slats I can see that evening has fallen, the sky a smoky, mottled gray.

There are murmurs of protest as I jerk open the door and stumble onto the porch. Then, instantly, the crowd hushes. At first, I don't understand. Then I look up. My face is projected into the sky, a pale hologram against the storm-swollen clouds. The weather in Esopus is usually too bad for us to see holo-ads. But this one is as clear as a bolt of lightning. My face, my name—and next to it, seconds ticking away, the countdown until my Gauntlet starts.

"Inesa." Jacob grasps me by the wrist, turning me toward him. "Listen—we'll help you. My dad and me . . ."

He keeps talking, but white noise builds like a wall between us. The hum of the tracker and the more distant sounds of rumbling thunder make Jacob's voice fade to an unintelligible murmur. It's like I'm underwater, everything muffled and dim, and I'm sinking and sinking and sinking.

I almost drowned once, when I was nine. I slipped off the porch at the house during a storm, and the water almost swept me downstream. It happens to pretty much everyone in Esopus Creek at one point or another. I managed to grab hold of a rock and hang on until a passing punter fished me out. I don't remember the almost-drowning itself, except that it was loud. So loud. And I remember, afterward, the punter delivering me home, and Dad wrapping me in a Mylar blanket while my clothes dried on a line in the kitchen.

And I remember, maybe a couple of weeks later, watching a TV show set in the City. The characters lived in a massive apartment building, hundreds of stories tall, all glass and sleek metal. The building had a huge room with a giant pit in the ground, which was filled with impossibly clear, teal-green water. I had never seen a swimming pool before. They dove in and splashed around, doing handstands and somersaults. Every so often they would swim to the edge of the pool to catch their breath, laughing, just kicking lazily to keep themselves afloat.

I didn't think it was real at first. A lake in the clouds. But Dad told me that almost every apartment building in the City had a pool, that they laced the water with chemicals to keep it that clean, and that the City folk swam all the time, just for fun. I watched that episode over and over, fascinated by the way the water clung to their skin like drops of dew, crystalline, almost otherworldly. I remember their wide, white-toothed smiles.

I blink, and the pain brings me back to the present, searing through my forehead again. The tracker fizzes and hums. Jacob is still talking, eyes huge and frantic with worry.

"I need to get home," I blurt out. "Please. I just need to get home."

"Did you hear me? I said we can help. My father has—"

"*Please.*" I raise my fingers and press two of them over his mouth. "Let me go home."

Jacob stares back at me, mollified and silenced. My hand against his lips is trembling. He just nods.

Dr. Wessels offers to pay for a punter to take me back to the house, and I'm too exhausted to protest. I don't think I could make my knees steady enough to stand or my hands firm enough to grip an oar. The punter poles me silently upstream, both of us pretending we don't see my face in the sky, flickering like the most ominous constellation.

I can hear Mom and Luka before I even open the door.

"What else could I have done?"

"You know what."

Luka's voice is as cold as ice. I've heard him talk this way before, but not to Mom. Ever. I push open the door.

Their heads shoot up as I enter. The door creaks shut behind me, and with the force of the wind it slams too loudly, making the whole house shudder. Such a fragile, pitiful little house. Its walls feel thinner and its floor more unsound than ever.

For a long time, no one speaks.

"Inesa," Luka says at last. His gaze meets mine.

It's always like looking in a mirror, but now, our expressions are perfectly twinned: watery, haunted stares, lips pressed together, cheeks bloodless.

Mom crosses her arms over her chest. She's wearing the same nightgown I left her in this morning, with a blanket draped over her shoulders. Her mouth twists into a defiant scowl.

"Don't start with me," she bites out. "I'm not going to apologize."

I didn't expect her to.

"You can't be so naive. You know how these things work. This just made the most sense. Luka hunts. He takes care of the family. We couldn't get by without him. Putting him up wasn't an option."

Of course she'll never state the obvious aloud: that she could have offered *herself* up. For *her* debts. Not Luka's. Not mine. The air crackles around us.

"It doesn't matter how many deer I kill if Inesa isn't there to mount them," Luka says icily.

"Don't you try to make me feel guilty." Mom's pitch rises, and color comes into her cheeks. "It's my right, as your mother. Neither of you would be here without me."

She'll always have this as her trump card. The debt that every child owes their parent, a levee that never breaks, no matter how hard the water rushes against it.

"I sacrificed everything for you," she chokes out, forcing tears into her eyes. I've heard this a thousand times before, too. "I came to this miserable place for your father, and look what happened. I could have lived in the City. And I never would have gotten so sick. I'm doing what I have to do for our family, and look how you're treating me. Trying to make me feel *guilty*—"

"There won't be a family anymore, after this," Luka says. "It'll just be you and me."

I fix my eyes on Mom. I've gone so long without speaking that my voice is hoarse when I say, "I know that's what you've always wanted."

Her shoulders rise to her ears.

"You're ridiculous, Inesa," she says. "I can't reason with you. You blame me for everything wrong in your life—you never take responsibility for yourself."

My chest tightens and the tip of my nose grows hot, like it does when I'm about to cry. And I hate myself as much as I hate Mom in this moment, because I can't stop my eyes from welling, can't stop myself from being the weepy, weak, pathetic daughter she thinks I am. Because I can't stop myself from crying over something I should've seen coming. Because I'm mourning a corpse that's long dead. It feels like all I've ever done is cared for things that everyone else has left to rot.

"You've always wanted me to be the worst mother ever," Mom goes on. "Are you happy now that I've proved you right?"

"Am I happy? Am I *happy*?" My voice rises, and I'm shouting now, playing the daughter who's too unstable, too emotional. When the cameras come on, this is what everyone in New Amsterdam will see. Tears blur my vision, and I try to blink them away.

"Why don't you ever blame your father for anything?" Mom snarls back. "At least I'm *here*. I'm the one who stayed."

She surges toward me, all her false fragility forgotten. I put my arms up over my head—it's been a long time since she's laid a hand on either of us, but I remember the sting of her palm against my cheek. The way she gripped my face so tightly that her nails left half-moon gouges in my skin.

This time, Luka steps between us before she can reach me. He's as impenetrable as a wall of steel, and Mom collapses against him. She inhales sharply and then lets out a great, heaving sob, eyes squeezed shut, hands balled into fists. Ordinarily Luka would let her lean on him, help her to the couch, lay her down and cover her with a quilt. Now he lets her slide to the ground, onto her knees, the blanket pooling around her.

She wails and blubbers, wordlessly now. It's hard to feel sorry for her, but it's also hard not to. Her sicknesses are feigned, but the pain behind them is real. The feeling that gathers in my chest is mostly pity. It thickens over my own hurt like a scab.

My bedroom isn't private enough. I can still see Mom's silhouette from behind the curtain and I can still hear her bawling. The sound is punctuated by the incessant dinging from my tablet, notifications from the $ponsor app from all the people who searched my name the moment the Gauntlet was announced and found my account. Messages piling up by the dozens. New subscribers that are worthless to me now. I'll be dead before I can stream again.

I march out onto the porch. Luka follows me. The storm clouds have gathered, fat and gray-bellied, blotting out my face and name from the sky. The air is heavy, almost unbearably so.

I lean against the side of the house, head tilted back, and close my eyes. I can't hear anything except the eerie, unrelenting buzz of the tracker, counting down the seconds until I die.

"Nesa."

I open my eyes. Luka is standing in front of me, slightly hunched so that our faces are level. I see the faint, pale scar that cleaves his left eyebrow. I gave it to him when he was seven and I was eight, sword fighting with sticks on the hillside. He gave me an almost identical one on my left pointer finger, a small crescent above my knuckle. Sometimes I think that's what love is, really— giving each other matching scars.

"I'm going to die, Luka," I say.

There's a strange relief in speaking it out loud. A dragonfly flits through the air above us. They were smaller when I was little. Now some of them are the size of sparrows, the hum of their wings as loud as helicopter blades.

"No," Luka says, voice low. "You're not."

"You saw what happened to Sanne." The image of her laid across the counter flashes in my mind.

"You're not Sanne."

"No," I say, "but I'm not strong, or brave, or smart. You've watched the Gauntlets. Everyone knows how this story ends."

Before Sanne, the Lamb was a man in his mid-forties, thick and muscled, who had carried a machete in his belt. If there was no mercy for a twelve-year-old girl and no bloody, hard-won victory for him, there's no chance for me.

"We aren't like everyone else," says Luka.

"Yes, we are!" The anger that spikes in my chest surprises me. "We're exactly like everyone else—that's the problem. Land animals in a drowning world, like Dad said."

"I didn't think you listened to anything Dad said."

"Well, I did."

Luka pretends he's the only one who really knew Dad, the only one who misses him. Sometimes I pretend, too. But deep down, both of us know the truth. Deep down, where we have another set of invisible, identical scars.

"People have survived their Gauntlets before," says Luka.

He takes out his tablet. There's a notification on the lock screen that shows my face, my name. He swipes on it and opens up the countdown clock. Ten and a half hours until the Gauntlet starts. I feel nausea overtake me when I look at the numbers, so stark, so cold and unforgiving. I wonder how many people will tune in to watch the live stream of my death. Thousands. Millions. The tracker whirs in my throat.

"Not people like me," I say.

"Maybe not alone." Luka looks up from the tablet and meets my eyes. "You're not helpless, Nes. You never have been. You're not just going to trot off to your death like a lamb to the slaughter—" He stops abruptly. I know he didn't mean to call me a lamb, but the metaphor is too apt. That's why Caerus picked it, after all. He clears his throat and then goes on. "I'm not going to let you."

His gaze is fierce, steady. I don't feel quite *hopeful*, but some of the nausea begins to recede.

"I'm not exactly what you'd call competent with a rifle," I mumble.

Luka lets out a breath. "I won't argue with you there. But I am. We just need . . . a plan."

"An escape plan." Running is better than fighting. No Outlier is any match for an Angel. Just a few minutes of watching Sanne's Gauntlet was enough to convince me of that. The Angels are more machine than human. The Angel that killed Sanne certainly looked more than human. Or less.

"Yeah," Luka says. He runs a hand through his hair. Then he turns away from me for a moment, staring out over the railing of the porch at the black water below. It's too dark to see much beyond that. But the forest is out there, the damp knot of trees and bushes, disguising dangers that are only kept at bay by Esopus Creek's electrified barbed wire fence.

Luka's eyes are narrowed, a little too bright. I haven't seen him cry since we were kids. Even now, the tears gather, but they don't fall. He's always been so much better at staying composed than I am.

His gaze follows the line of the fence, a slash of silver in the dark. "I think I have an idea, though."

I push myself off from the side of the house and square my shoulders. I will my voice not to tremble when I reply, "What is it?"

Finally, Luka looks back at me. There's a defiant glint to his stare, one I recognize but rarely see in myself.

"I'll show you," he says.

When Dad first left, we all thought he would come back. It wasn't unusual for him to disappear for a couple of days—once he was even gone for nearly two weeks. But he always returned, full of booze and whimsical excuses that were half true at best. He'd pass out on the couch for hours, in a deep and impenetrable slumber, while we all tiptoed around him and tried to convince ourselves that this would be the last time, that nothing would pull him away from us again.

I wish I had known, before he left for good, that it would be our final day. I don't even remember it well. I didn't say anything special to him. I poled down to the shop as he smoked on the porch. He and Luka talked; I don't know about what. There was nothing, not even a subtle sign, to suggest that he was saying goodbye. Or maybe I just wasn't paying close enough attention.

Clearly Luka knows something I don't, because he marches back inside, wordless, not even sparing a glance at Mom, who's huddled on the couch. She looks over at him hopefully, as if she thinks she'll be forgiven. She doesn't even try to meet my eyes.

Mom's bedroom is a proper room, with a door and everything, unlike the curtained-off space that Luka and I share. Ordinarily, neither of us dare to step past the threshold of Mom's room. But now I follow Luka inside, with only a split second of hesitation.

It's an unholy mess of open boxes, packing supplies strewn across the floor, and a pile of blankets so thick that I can hardly see the bed underneath. Luka clicks on the battery-powered lamp, and I step over crushed cans of diet soda to join him as he pauses in front of the closet door.

He opens it and pushes aside an overstuffed rack of musty-smelling clothes. There are sequined dresses, woolen slacks, even shiny patent-leather heels, though I haven't seen Mom out of a nightgown in years. Bitterly I picture her scrolling through Caerus's clothing catalogue, adding items that she'll never wear to her cart, oblivious to her account plunging further and further into the red.

Luka flings away a fur-lined coat and a silky button-down shirt. Underneath, layered in dust so thick that my nose instantly begins to itch, is a gray metal box. I watch in shock as he removes a key from his pocket, fits it into the lock, turns it, and flips the lid open.

I don't say anything, but I can't stop my sharp inhale of breath. I'm not offended that he and Dad had secrets just between the two of them. I'm just hurt that even after Dad left, Luka kept them from me.

Almost as if he can read my thoughts, Luka says quietly, "This is why I thought he might come back."

I understand now. Luka's secret wasn't the box itself. The secret was that he had kept hoping, kept believing, even when I had long since given up.

With deliberate, practiced motions, Luka begins to remove the items from the box. It seems almost depthless as he piles its contents on the floor. I can tell he's done this before.

There's a vinyl backpack. Binoculars. Weatherproof ponchos and a drinking straw. Bandages and gauze and antiseptic wipes. Steel pliers, screwdriver heads, and even a hand chainsaw. Waterproof matches, work gloves, two sleeping bags. A flashlight and fishing line. Iodine tablets. There's even a gas mask.

And, last of all, Luka removes a small object of tarnished gold. Unlike the other items, it looks old, as if it's passed through many pairs of hands. When Luka holds it out, his fingers shake a little bit, but he manages to flip open the tiny clasp. It's an analogue compass, probably a hand-me-down, maybe the closest thing we have to a family heirloom. They don't sell anything like this in the Caerus catalogue.

All together it's a treasure trove of survival gear, clearly accumulated over the course of years, packed and prepped and ready. I can't believe Dad left all this behind. But then again, he left us behind, too.

I sit back on my knees and let out a breath. The tracker hums and pulses in my throat. It's not quite hope I feel—not yet, maybe not ever again. But Luka is beside me, his body radiating a steady warmth, and I know that when the cameras turn on and the Gauntlet begins, at least I won't be alone. And with this, with Luka, there's the slimmest, farthest-flung hope that I might survive.

SIX

MELINOË

The live stream is hosted on the Gauntlet portal's landing page, with a moderated chat room for users so that anyone who watches can leave their comments and reactions in real time. Caerus automatically saves the transcript of the live chat after the stream is over, so I can go back and read the chats from my past Gauntlets.

Azrael uses the transcripts to teach us lessons, because with millions of people tuned in, nothing will escape some eagle-eyed viewer's attention. The transcripts are the reason for some of the Gauntlet's unofficial rules.

<user1033485234: is it just me or does mel look like sh*t here hahaha>

<user4435668902: no lmao was thinking the same thing. legit so off-putting looks like she hasn't slept in days>

Most of the uglier comments are censored by the moderators, but occasionally some slip through.

<user893045860: idc her body is insane. so f*ckable>

It's three hours before my Gauntlet, and I'm in the holding room in front of a huge, lighted vanity. A Mask leans over me, dabbing concealer onto my face. Their touch isn't gentle, and I flinch when they start covering up the circles under my eyes. They're deep and purple, and there isn't enough makeup in the world to hide them completely.

I steal glances at myself in the mirror while the Mask works. They've layered on the palest shade of foundation and have moved on to contouring my cheekbones. I got my new lash extensions last night and lip injections four days ago, long enough for the swelling and tenderness to subside. My eyeliner is tattooed on and permanent.

"I've recommended a brow lift," the Mask says in their hollow, robotic voice. "Azrael says for next time."

That the Angels have to be beautiful is one of the Gauntlet's unofficial rules. And if we're not beautiful when we enter the program, Azrael fixes that right away. Lethe was twelve when she got her nose job.

I used to try to keep track of the changes made to my face and body, as if there were some clean delineation between real and fake, natural and unnatural. But there have been too many now, and I've lost count. My cheekbones, high and prominent, are real—at least, I think they are. My nose is my own—or is it? The memory of a rhinoplasty could've been Wiped away and I'd never know it. My breasts are my own, but for how much longer? I stayed at Keres's bedside after her implants were put in. Helped change her bandages, trying not to see the bruises patterned all up and down her chest and rib cage. I held back her hair when she vomited, nauseous from the anesthesia.

We Angels were made to fulfill Azrael's archetypes: Keres was the maternal one—beautiful, of course, but with softer edges. Kinder eyes. They sent her on all the Gauntlets with young children. Lethe is the fiery one, with her red hair and quick temper. I'm supposed to be the deadliest one, unflinching and emotionless, armored in coldness. The audience likes us better if we fit into boxes.

"There," the Mask says, after dusting highlighter onto the tip of my nose. "Look."

I turn toward the mirror. Melinoë stares back at me. Long, white-blond hair pulled back into a high ponytail, no strands escaping. I asked Azrael if I could cut it once, but he said the viewers would hate it. He's probably right. My real eye is so dark, it's almost black, which makes the prosthetic seem not quite so aberrant in comparison. Wide-set, slightly overlarge; a few years ago, there was a running joke in the chat that I looked like a praying mantis. The comments made me avoid mirrors for weeks.

"It's perfect," I say, averting my gaze.

The Mask gives the slightest nod in return. Then they leave without a word, the door to the holding room sealing shut after them.

I only have a few minutes alone before the door slides open again. I expect it to be Azrael; he's one of the only people who has clearance to come into the holding room.

But it's not Azrael. It's Keres.

I lurch up from my seat, sending it toppling to the ground. I can't understand what emotion overtakes me in that moment, but it's so strong that my hands start shaking and my stomach goes slick.

"Keres?" I whisper.

The eyepatch has been removed, and a new, more natural-looking prosthetic has replaced the old one. It doesn't quite match her real eye, though. The shade of blue is wrong, icier and too pale. But the blank, wondering gaze is gone. Keres stares back, and this time, she knows me. She remembers.

"Mel?"

Her voice is so quiet, hesitant, like she's not quite sure how to use it. A lump invades my throat. "How did you get in here?"

"I don't know."

The only thing I can think is that Azrael didn't erase her biometrics from the fingerprint reader outside the door. It doesn't seem like the kind of careless mistake he would make, but it's hard to focus on anything else right now except for Keres. I take a careful step toward her.

She just stands there, mouth hanging open slightly. Her black hair is loose around her shoulders, shorter and more untidy than when she was an Angel.

"Keres," I say again. "What happened—why—"

My stammering is cut off as Keres steps toward me, close enough that she's within arm's reach. Her blouse is sleeveless, exposing the scars that ring her wrists and elbows. The ones that look so ugly on me but never seemed anything less than beautiful on her. Very slowly she reaches her hands up, until she's holding my face.

"I'm sorry," she says, and she almost sounds like herself again, with just the faintest tremor in her voice. "I didn't want to. I didn't—"

The door slides open, and we both flinch. Keres drops her hands. Azrael is standing in the threshold.

He takes in the scene, and his eyes narrow. It's rare for him to look truly angry; he's the one who's supposed to teach us apathy, after all. So the emotion fades quickly, replaced by his usual cool, unflappable expression.

"Keres," he says, "what are you doing here?"

Her gaze clouds again. Her brow furrows, and she replies, in that distant, childlike voice, "I don't know."

I try to capture her stare, but she won't look at me. She doesn't recognize me anymore.

The pit in my stomach widens and deepens. Azrael puts his arm around Keres's shoulders and leads her gently toward the door. Her steps are clumsy, staggering, like a patient still half anesthetized. She doesn't turn back. Not even for a second.

When Azrael returns, I'm sitting on the stool with my elbows balanced on my knees, hunched over. I feel sick, but there's nothing in me to vomit. In preparation for the Gauntlet, I've had nothing but intravenous fluids.

"Melinoë."

I don't look up.

He steps toward me. "That was a mistake. Keres should never have been able to get in here. I've removed all her biometrics now. It won't happen again."

I still don't move or speak.

"She shouldn't have been able to get to the basement in the first place. I've asked Karl to keep her on a tighter leash." He must mean her husband. More gently, Azrael goes on, "You know how it is sometimes, with the Wipes. They don't take completely. The old memories are stubborn. She seemed to be slipping in and out of awareness. I'm sorry if it alarmed you, but there's nothing to worry about. There will be another Wipe, and then another, if need be."

I look up. "No."

Azrael frowns. "What was that?"

"You lied." I can only manage a whisper. "You said she chose to be decommissioned, but she didn't. She *wouldn't*. She wouldn't leave me."

Azrael's gaze doesn't shift. His gray eyes look frozen solid, like chips of ice. And that unflinching silence is my answer.

I'll never know how many times he's lied to me. How many memories of mine he's stolen. Maybe I watched him haul Keres from her room, latch her to the table, jam the syringe into her throat. Maybe I saw it all, heard her screams echoing through the empty halls. And maybe then he slammed *me* down onto the table, shoved the needle through my skin, and took *that* memory, too.

We stare at each other without speaking. Moments tick by, like droplets from a tincture.

And then, at last, he says, "It was for her own good. Keres was compromised."

I think my body is collapsing in on itself. I feel pressure on my throat, as if someone is crushing my windpipe. Is *this* a memory? The slow squeezing of my throat by strange hands? Has it happened to me before? It seems familiar, somehow, just like the desperate, gasping breaths I have to take so I can stammer out, "W-why?"

Azrael regards me without emotion, but when he speaks, his voice is gentle.

"She could no longer cope with the rigors of the job," he says, and this is corporate talk, boardroom talk. He even switches to Damish. "It was better for everyone that she was able to retire gracefully and discreetly."

"Better for *you*." I shock myself with the venom of my words.

The Angel program is Azrael's invention, his brainchild. I don't know much about his past except that he was once a midlevel Caerus employee, and it was this idea—the Lamb's Gauntlet—that propelled him upward through the company's ranks. The CEO has always been a big fan of the Gauntlet, considering how much ad revenue the live streams bring in, but even more for the message they send. They keep New Amsterdam both riveted and cowed. Entertained and subjugated.

But Azrael's position is dependent on the Gauntlet's success. On *our* success. The CEO hears dozens of pitches every day. He's equal parts capricious and unsentimental. He could choose, at any point, to pull all his funding and support. And after my last performance, I'm sure it's more than crossed his mind.

Then, astonishingly, Azrael lowers himself to the ground. He kneels, so we're at eye level—I think it must be for the first time in my life.

"Keres was good," he says softly, "but she was imperfect. Over the years, I've refined my technique and made each successive Angel better than the last. It has been the work of my life. And all of it, leading up to this. To you, Melinoë. You are my perfect creation."

I open my mouth to protest, but he goes on. "I was the one to fail you, not the other way around. You never should have been on that Gauntlet. But I've learned from my mistake. This is my chance for redemption. You won't fail again."

He slips from the first person to the second person so fluidly I almost don't notice. My throat feels too thick to speak. I can't move a muscle as he raises his hand, cups my face, and tenderly strokes my cheek. The hand that has whittled me, carved me, shaped me, *made* me, in every sense of the word. When I was little, I always wanted to call him *Father*.

The same childish impulse rises again, along with an equally childish question. *Why are you doing this to me?*

But I keep the words tucked down deep. And when Azrael stands, I stand, too.

"Get in the helicopter, Melinoë," he says quietly.

And I do.

From ten thousand feet, the land is scraggly, half drowned. The outlying Counties of New Amsterdam are green with veins of brown, muddy rivers flooding down thousands of tributaries, overflowing their banks, creating lakes and ponds where there were once valleys and gorges.

The white specks, like lichen on a mossy log, are Caerus pod houses. I can't see any other buildings until the helicopter dips closer. Then tumbledown wooden structures come into view, partially camouflaged by the damp woods around them. We pass a hundred identical towns that are barely more than a scattering of these houses, clustered together like bodies around a fire.

The North River lies against the land, a length of filthy rope, weaving through the Catskill and Adirondack Mountains. I tap my temple to activate the comms chip, and information scrolls across my vision. A map of Esopus Creek. The photos of the Lamb and her brother. And her tracker, a pulsing red dot on the map. It has an electric hum to it, like a live wire.

As the helicopter starts its descent, Azrael reaches out and grasps my arm. The wind and the whirring blades make it impossible for me to hear him, but I can read the shape of the words on his lips.

The Lamb has to die.

His grip on my arm is tight enough to hurt. I mouth back: *She will.*

Then he lets go.

The helicopter doesn't land; it hovers about ten feet off the ground, a rope ladder is unfurled so I can climb down. The propulsed air from its blades blows back the trees, sending dead leaves fluttering off limp branches. And the noise draws the inhabitants of Esopus Creek out of their houses, onto their porches, squinting through the wind to watch me drop.

I'm required to start my Gauntlet at the Lamb's legal residence, which means she's had a head start of several hours. My hair blows around my face, partially obscuring the sights around me: the anxious faces of the Outliers, their precariously perched houses, the muggy smell of the churning water below. All these outlying towns are the same, more or less; I've seen half a hundred of them.

But as I look around, a powerful sensation shoots through me. An image flashes through my mind, just a brief burst of light. My limbs quiver and my cold blood runs hot.

There's no proof of it, no proof except that full-body shuddering, that burst of light, but somehow I *know*, down to the very marrow in my bones—Esopus Creek is not new to me. The memory isn't false familiarity.

I've been here before.

SEVEN

INESA

The Wesselses are the only people in Esopus Creek who own a car. I've never been inside one until now. It's boxy, with two rows of seats and no doors, so you can fall right out on a sharp turn if you aren't buckled in. There's mud caked over the hubcaps and so much dirt splattered up the sides that I can't tell what color the paint beneath is supposed to be. It looks nothing like the cars I've seen on TV. Dr. Wessels says that's because it runs on gas, not electricity. Luka is loading red gasoline canisters into the trunk.

"Practically a fossil," Jacob says, slapping the hood. "But it still runs fine."

He urges me to get in and try driving. I turn the key in the ignition and the engine growls to life so furiously that it shakes the entire car. My stomach lurches.

"I don't know if I'm cut out for this," I say, feeling nauseous for too many reasons to count.

"You'll be okay," says Jacob, buckling himself into the passenger seat. "Just take it slowly at first."

At his direction, I drive three jerky circles around their house. The whole time, my knuckles are white around the steering wheel. Dr. Wessels is standing on the porch, his arms crossed over his chest, clearly not impressed with my driving. He probably thinks I'm going to crash his car and die in a fiery explosion before the Angel even gets her hands on me. There's at least a 30 percent chance.

"Good job," Jacob says, overgenerously. "Now try going a little faster."

The speedometer ticks from fifteen to twenty.

After a few more circles, my stomach is too upset to continue. Bile clogs my throat—just bile, because I haven't eaten anything, even though Luka tried to force bread and soup into my mouth earlier. "Don't be stupid," he said, "you need the energy." But whenever I think about eating, I just hear the hum of the tracker and my gorge rises again.

I get out of the car and walk over to Luka. "I think this might be hopeless."

"You're doing fine," he says, but his teeth are gritted. "Let's just get out of here."

It's not just that he wants to get as big a head start as possible. He's uncomfortable with the whole situation. He doesn't trust the Wesselses' generosity; help never comes without strings attached. And we all know the danger of being in debt.

There's also the fact that we're being very blatantly watched. A small crowd has gathered around the Wesselses' yard, craning their necks over the fence. Lucky for them it's not electrified. I can pick out a few faces—including, to my shock, Floris Dekker's. This must be the first time he's left his house in weeks. In any other circumstance, he'd probably be harassed and heckled back inside. But no one is thinking about Sanne anymore. The voyeuristic anticipation of a new Gauntlet eclipses everything else.

Floris's eyes betray no empathy, even after what I did for him. In fact, there's a subtle shimmer of glee in his stare. He's just here for the show. And in just a few hours, the show will be live streamed to an audience of millions.

I don't want to look at the crowd, and I figure it's best to try to get in at least one more test ride before we go, anyway. I walk back over to Jacob, my boots sinking slightly into the mud with each step. It's a warm morning for the season and his T-shirt sticks to his skin, slightly translucent with sweat, so I can see the muscles in his back. The sight of those muscles takes me a little by surprise. I mostly think of him as the kid I played video games with in his living room—the kid who didn't mope when he lost and never gloated when he won—but he's grown up. So have I.

"Hey," I say. Jacob turns. "I don't really know how to say thank you. For all of this."

Jacob smiles, showing the dimples in his cheeks. "It's nothing, really. Just don't total my dad's car."

"I'll do my best."

Luka is giving me an impatient glare, so maybe it's better to just get out of here as soon as possible. But before I can turn away, Jacob grabs my wrist.

"Listen, Inesa," he says softly. "When you come back, I want things to be . . . different."

"Different how?" He's looking at me so intently that my skin prickles.

Abruptly, he leans forward and kisses me. I'm so shocked I can't react—I don't even know *how* to react. It's quick, over before I have enough time to be embarrassed that I'm not sure what to do with my lips. Jacob pulls away, cheeks flushed.

Neither of us says a word. My mouth feels completely dry. Luckily, he speaks first.

"I'm moving to the City," he says. "I want you to come, too."

And then I really don't know what to say. Luka approaches us and Jacob steps away, rubbing the back of his neck. My cheeks are blazing. Now I'm mostly just embarrassed that Luka saw what happened. The whole situation seems more transactional than it did before.

"We'll pay you back for everything," Luka says tersely, as if reading my mind.

"Don't worry about it," says Jacob. His face is still faintly pink. "Just focus on making it out the other side. It's just thirteen days."

Thirteen days. An unlucky number. I can't help but feel Caerus did that on purpose. Although I'm sure they beta tested and focus grouped the time limit to make sure it was long enough to keep people engaged but not so long that they lost interest. Everything about the Gauntlet is precisely, shrewdly arranged. I feel nauseous again, for a whole host of new reasons.

"I'll try," I say uneasily.

It's time. I climb into the car and buckle my seat belt. Luka gets into the passenger side and rests his hunting rifle between his knees. Neither of us speak as I carefully put the car into drive and inch out of the Wesselses' yard. From the porch, Dr. Wessels waves, but it's a stiff, self-conscious motion. His lips are pressed into a thin line.

The crowd backs up as we drive through the gate, parting to let us onto the road. Faces blur past. Neighbors and clients and people I've watched grow from toddlers to lanky preteens, adults to old-timers. With each face I pass, I wonder if it's the last time I'll ever see them. I know they're all wondering the same thing.

"Wait!"

I slam down on the brake pedal and the car shudders to a halt.

It's Mrs. Prinslew, pushing her way through the crowd. The sea of bodies parts for her, but by the time she reaches us, there's a dew of sweat on her brow. Or maybe it's rain. The sky has started sprinkling and I barely even noticed.

She stops at the driver's-side door and looks up at me, her eyes glazed with unshed tears. Wordlessly, she holds out a satchel. Her arms tremble as she lifts it, and when I take it from her, I'm shocked by its heaviness. Peering inside, I see dozens of cans. They're unlabeled, like all black-market goods, but she's written their contents on the side in black marker: peaches, carrots, cream of mushroom soup. Spaghetti, spinach, Spam.

Abruptly my throat clogs. It's the equivalent of a hundred credits, at least. I look down at Mrs. Prinslew's face, open and waiting, but I'm too stunned to speak.

"For you," she says quietly.

No one has ever given me a gift before. Offered me something without the expectation of repayment. She must read my befuddled expression, because she goes on. "It's a shame we've started believing that credits are worth more than a life."

Regret and grief pile down on me. I remember how I poled past her as she piled sandbags on her porch. I could have—*should* have—stopped to help. I thought I'd been doing her a kindness, by moving along without a word. Who would want to be in more debt?

All I can manage is a nod. My feelings are so tangled up inside me. The words *thank you* feel as foreign to me as Damish. I wonder what the Damish word for *thank you* is. They must have one. They're not afraid of owing.

Mrs. Prinslew steps back, and slowly I press down on the gas, letting the car roll forward, through the gate. Luka takes the bag of cans off my lap in silence and chucks it into the back seat. His mouth twitches, and I can tell he's thinking that this is another debt we can't afford. He's probably wishing he could castigate me for not refusing the gift. But he does me the courtesy of keeping quiet.

Esopus Creek vanishes in the rearview mirror. Mrs. Prinslew's words echo. *For you. For you.* And then Jacob's words return to me. *I want you to come, too.* The seeds of an imagined future bloom up, layering over my vision. A future where I survive this, where I leave Esopus and move to the City with Jacob. It's what most people in the outlying Counties dream of. Getting out of here. Except when I try to pull the images together, they keep slipping away. I don't know if it's because I can't focus on anything except surviving the Gauntlet, or because that future, Jacob's future, isn't really what I want.

The tracker pulses, reminding me that not even my next breath is guaranteed. But this part of the Gauntlet I'm prepared for. It's how I've lived my entire life: as if at any moment, the ground under my feet could crumble.

I steal a glance at Luka. Now he's staring straight ahead, eyes narrowed. I wonder if he's thinking about Jacob kissing me. I still feel embarrassed by it, like I've unknowingly exchanged something I didn't want to exchange in return for a car and some canisters of gasoline. But Luka and I have never judged each other for what we do in order to survive. I don't want to believe he'd start now.

We drive on for a while in silence. Then Luka reaches over and covers my hand on the steering wheel, just for a moment, and gives it the faintest squeeze.

Five minutes until the Gauntlet. My tablet won't stop vibrating. Dusk is settling in an uneven, hazy way, shadows long and sunlight still beaming through gaps between the tree branches. After a few moments of ceaseless rumbling from my tablet, Luka picks it up and shoves it into the glove compartment.

The first part of our plan is just to get as far away from Esopus Creek as possible. According to the Gauntlet's rules, the Angel has to start at my legal residence. So at least we have a head start.

But just running away is easier imagined than done. To say that the roads in the outlying Counties are treacherous is an understatement. The ones that were once paved are now pocked with low, deep potholes. The dirt roads are so uneven that sometimes I have to slow to a ten-mile-per-hour crawl just to make it through in one piece. Some of the lanes we try to turn down are completely flooded, or lead to dead ends, which means I have to make creaky, perilous U-turns to get out. My driving is still liable to get us killed before the Gauntlet even starts.

We're not completely directionless, though. Luka's tablet is propped up on the dash, giving me, at the very least, the vague sense that we're heading north. North and north and north.

One thing Dad believed—one thing he never stopped talking about—was that there was a place completely off Caerus's grid. A place where even the feed from my tracker would go dead. I could never really make myself believe it, since Dad mostly brought it up when he was a few beers deep, but we don't have a solid plan otherwise, and it's worth exploring.

I know Luka believes it. And I know he believes Dad made it there.

"It would have to be somewhere around the contested territory," Luka murmurs. He scrolls up on the map, zooming in and then out again.

The contested territory he's talking about is in the far northwest of New Amsterdam, where it shares a border with the Dominion of New England. Historically, the border was the lake that we call Lake Renssaeler and New England calls Lake Burlington—a lake that, a long time ago, everyone called Lake Champlain. But then there were the storms, and the lake overflowed its banks, drowning nearly the entire county on New Amsterdam's side.

New England seized the moment and invaded. The marshy remains were occupied by the Dominion, its residents placed under martial law. New Amsterdam fought back. New England fought back harder. Then came the Era of Atomics, and once both sides got their hands on nuclear weapons, every border skirmish instantly exploded—for one terrifying moment—and then turned cold. Mutual assured destruction granted the contested territory a reprieve, but I wouldn't quite call it peace.

Because both sides are afraid of igniting that powder keg again, Drowned County, as it's been nicknamed, exists in a sort of limbo. New Amsterdam's government won't officially confirm anything, of course, but there are rumors that it's a blackout zone. The residents aren't even wired to a power grid, so electricity is scant, and of course there are no Caerus helicopters airlifting rations to its residents, which might be construed as taking sides. It does seem like the sort of place Dad would go.

Unfortunately, even if you do believe Drowned County is some kind of rebel's paradise, there's still about two hundred miles between it and Catskill County. Miles occupied by half-sunken roads, impassable mountains, and dark, swampy forests, where things even worse than Angels lurk.

In the back seat, my tablet suddenly stops vibrating. There's a single, almost musical *ding*, and then it goes totally silent. We're driving through an impenetrable canopy of trees, so I can't see any projections in the sky, but with cold-blooded certainty, I know that my Gauntlet has begun.

Luka looks over at me, like he's expecting me to break down, to start hyperventilating or sobbing. Strangely, I feel almost nothing at all. It's just my body that reacts, not my mind, bile churning in my empty stomach and adrenaline spiking through my veins. But it's fair enough for him to wonder. Mom always mocks me, saying that I cry over every little thing.

I didn't speak to her again after last night. I know I should try to erase her from my mind. Yet even now I feel a petulant hint of pride that I'm not being weak the way she thinks I am.

But then of course there's the sneaking doubt that follows. The small voice that tells me Mom was right to do what she did. That between the two of us, Luka is always the one worth saving.

I bite down on my lip, hard. Because I feel like I have to break the horrible silence, I ask, "How long have we been driving?"

"About three hours now." Luka's voice is tense.

That doesn't mean much—I've only reached a peak speed of forty miles per hour, and every thirty minutes or so we've come upon a flooded road and had to backtrack. I steal a glance at Luka's tablet. We've only managed to put about twenty miles between us and Esopus Creek.

I wonder if the cameras have flickered on to start the live stream. They're microscopic, flitting through the air like the ever-present mosquitoes, and I can't hear them over the growling engine and the clatter of the wheels on the uneven terrain. I try to tell myself it doesn't matter, that the only thing I should focus on is surviving. But it's hard when I know there are millions of people tuned in, watching and analyzing my every move.

"Do you really think this will work?" I whisper—because I'm self-conscious about the cameras, and afraid of speaking my fears aloud, as if that will make them more real. "Do you really think Dad is . . . alive?"

Luka is silent for a long moment.

"I do," he says at last. "Dad is a survivor."

"Yeah. Like a cockroach."

Luka lets out a breath that's almost a laugh. "A cockroach that couldn't stay off the booze."

"A cockroach that thought it was stronger than the shoe about to squish it."

Luka's laugh is genuine and unmistakable this time. "Yeah."

This is probably the most we've talked about Dad since he left, and probably the closest we've come to discussing our feelings. Mom, on the other hand, is a topic that feels impossible to broach at the moment. Somewhere in the lowest, darkest parts of my mind, I wonder if Luka agrees with her. If he thinks I'm the weak, expendable one between the two of us. He criticizes me all the time for being overly charitable with our clients, for still getting woozy at the sight of blood. For not believing the worst in people after they've proven, over and over, that they're as much our enemies as the water lapping at our door.

Night falls, and the world becomes eerie.

It's not just the darkness. It's dark enough at night in Esopus, where only about half the town can regularly afford electricity. But here, miles away from anything that could reasonably be called *civilization*, it's the silence that's terrifying. There are the perfunctory noises of the mosquitoes, of the animals moving through the brush that lines the road, but there are no human sounds. No generators being pulled, no parents shouting for their children to come in for dinner, no punters poling furiously against the churning water. I start to wonder about those animals in the brush. Some of the noises are too loud to just be scurrying rabbits and squirrels.

My suspicions are proven right when something darts out into the road, a brown-and-white streak in my headlights. I yelp and slam on the brakes. The creature freezes.

The deer stares me down with two sets of eyes. There are webbed feet where its hooves should be. Its fur is matted with a wetness that makes it look sleek, and dangerous. Even from the safety of the car, a shudder of fear goes through me.

Luka bangs his hand against the dashboard, hard, and the sudden sound spooks the creature. It flicks its antlered head and then vanishes into the woods again.

"Those things are hideous," Luka mutters.

I press slowly on the gas again, skin still prickling. Despite my line of work, I don't find the mutations as repulsive as most people do.

"They're just surviving," I say. "Four eyes are better than two at spotting predators. Webbed feet are better for swimming."

"They're not just surviving—they're overpopulating. They're driving the real deer to extinction. I'd shoot them all, but it would be a waste of bullets." Luka's rifle is still wedged carefully between his knees.

I can't really refute that, so we just lapse back into silence. The car rattles on down the dirt road. My driving slows to little more than a crawl, because the headlight beams only illuminate about ten feet in front of us, barely able to penetrate the muggy darkness.

"I don't want to hit a deer," I say, and then, before Luka can roll his eyes at my sentimentality, I add, "It might damage the car."

"Yeah," Luka says tensely. "Be careful."

And then—something. It bolts out of the tarry blackness. There's a thud, and the whole car shakes. My instinct is to slam on the brakes immediately, but I don't even have time to lift my foot. There are several more thuds—louder, closer—and then she drops onto the hood of the car.

I try to scream. The sound just lodges in my throat.

The Angel's hair is practically white, streaming out behind her. In the shuddery gleam of the headlights, her skin is almost translucent, purple veins showing like a leaf held up to the sun. Her eyes lock on mine and pin me into place. They're so dark I can see my reflection in them, warped and tiny, terrified.

The empty quality of her stare was something the cameras didn't pick up, that I didn't notice, during the few minutes I watched of her last Gauntlet. There's nothing behind her eyes at all, not even cruelty. They're as cold and bleak as the river on a winter night.

"Inesa, *go!*" Luka shouts.

I slam the gas pedal all the way to the floor.

Somehow, even as the car crashes down the dirt road, juddery enough to make my teeth rattle in my skull, it doesn't dislodge her. The Angel crouches on all fours, lithe and agile as a spider in her skintight black suit. The metal of the hood crumples under her hands. Sharp, glinting claws emerge from the fabric of her gloves, extending her fingers to a gruesome-looking length.

With one hand braced on the hood, she reaches for the rifle strapped to her back.

Instinctively, I raise an arm to shield myself, squeezing my eyes shut—but the blow I'm expecting doesn't come. Instead, the glass of the windshield cracks. The Angel thrusts the butt of her rifle against it, over and over, tiny fissures spiderwebbing outward from the point of impact.

I think I catch some expression of anger flit across her impassive face as the windshield holds—maybe just the flaring of her nostrils—but in another half a heartbeat, it's gone. And then she is, too.

I still have the gas pedal pressed to the floor, so I think maybe I've jostled her loose at last. But the relief doesn't even have a chance to settle. Quick as a strike of lightning, the Angel appears on my left, clinging to the roof of the car, limbs splayed to wedge herself in the empty doorway. Her face is ghostly white, a bright, spectral shock in the darkness. And now she *does* look angry, teeth flashing, predator-sharp.

This time, I scream.

I raise my arm again, the other still braced on the steering wheel. I don't know if it's some sort of Caerus technology, but when she locks eyes with me, I find that I can't look away. I can't even blink. Hypnotized into total stillness, all I can do is stare into her empty gaze, her black prosthetic whirring and clicking.

She reaches for her rifle. I can see that, even as I'm frozen. Another scream gets caught in my throat, and only a pitiful, choking sound comes out. My tracker throbs in time with my racing heart. *I'm going to die*, I think, and the realization is like a kick between the shoulder blades, the tinny taste of blood in my mouth—

Bang.

The Angel's face crumples, brow furrowing in shock, mouth twitching with bewildered, bridled rage. There's blood in the air. But it's not mine.

Behind me, Luka is drawn up almost to his full height, rifle held aloft and aimed over my head, through the empty door. Smoke curls from the barrel into the air. A slow, dark stain spreads across the Angel's shoulder, turning the fabric of her suit somehow blacker. Her body spasms, her long, thin arms shuddering, knees buckling. Those unnatural claws retract into her gloves and her fingers slip from the roof of the car.

And then she's gone.

I can't tell if she leapt away or just fell, inertia dragging her to the ground. I can't hear anything over my panicked, sputtering pulse.

"Inesa," Luka snarls, "*drive!*"

Without noticing, I've let up on the gas. I slam the pedal back to the floor. Luka spins frantically in all directions, rifle cocked, as if he's expecting her to drop onto the car again. My vision warps and blurs with what I think are tears. I can't connect them to any emotion. My heart is just beating so fast, I think it's going to crack through my chest.

EIGHT

MELINOË

The bullet only grazed me, skimming off the curve of my shoulder. It's happened before. The car's taillights disappear down the road, leaving me in near total darkness. The moon shines weakly through a cobweb of cloud. Blood is sluicing from the wound in my shoulder all the way down my arm, dripping past my fingertips.

It would be easy to panic. Not because of the blood, or the solid, pitiless darkness, but because I failed. It was never supposed to be this way. Her death should have been quick, merciless, a testament to my skill and cruelty, redeeming my grievous mistake. And it would have been. If not for the brother. I underestimated him.

The night vision in my prosthetic eye flickers on. At least for now, I'm alone. I venture just slightly into the woods that line the road and slump down against the trunk of a tree. The movement makes pain shoot through my arm. I bite my lip before I can cry out. I don't want the things that lurk in the forest to hear me, and I especially don't want my weakness live streamed to millions. I'm already humiliated enough.

I dig through the hidden pockets of my hunting suit until I find the roll of bandages. I tear off a strip and then slowly begin to unzip the suit. I'm careful not to reveal any more skin than necessary, since I know the cameras are zeroing in on me right now, greedily trying to capture as much as possible. There are entire archives of photos online showing me in suggestive poses, grainy screenshots taken from the live streams. I already know pictures of this moment will end up there, too.

The wound isn't deep and there's no bullet to dislodge, so I just grit my teeth and apply the bandage. It stings for a few moments and then it dissolves into my skin, forming new flesh where mine was torn open and absorbing the spilled blood. There are powerful painkillers inside the liquid bandage, and after a few moments, when they've soaked into my skin, the throbbing in my shoulder fades to a dull and distant ache.

This comes with the downside of making me groggy, a little removed from my immediate reality. Sloppy. So I just huddle there against the tree, waiting until the tiredness fades.

My comms chip beeps. I tap my temple twice to activate it.

Slightly corrupted by static, Azrael's voice is in my ear.

"Melinoë," he says, "what are you doing?"

I flinch.

Tucking my head into my knees so the cameras won't pick up on my words, I whisper, "I'm sorry. It was a mistake. I wasn't expecting the brother—"

"I briefed you on him. It shouldn't have come as a surprise."

"I know." I try to close my eyes, but my prosthetic stays stubbornly open. My vision is grainy black and green. "I won't fail again. I promise."

A beat of silence. Azrael exhales, and when he speaks again, his voice is gentle. "It's not the worst thing that could've happened. The viewers are definitely engrossed now. We're gaining thousands by the minute. But they'll be expecting a dramatic finale. And their attention won't hold for long."

"I know," I repeat.

"Then get it done."

With another fizzle of static, my comms chip goes dead. I draw in another tremulous breath, my head still cradled in my knees, and tap my temple again. A three-dimensional map unfolds across my vision, a second, false world overlaid upon the first. Roads spread out around me like a complex network of tree roots. And there in the distance is the Lamb's tracker, a pulsing red light. It moves in halting, sluggish increments, pressing farther north.

Her face suddenly invades my mind. Fear-stricken, eyes wide, just like all the rest. But even when I blink, it doesn't vanish. I keep seeing her stare, fixed so unflinchingly on mine. In the watery, inconstant light, her eyes wavered between brown and green. A dynamic color, something as alive as the earth, both essential and changeable. Her brother's stare was cold and sharp enough to cut. But her gaze had no scorn in it.

No matter how I try to banish the memory, I keep seeing her eyes.

NINE

INESA

I drive for an incalculable amount of time until my heartbeat returns to something approaching normal. Luka slumps in his seat, but keeps his rifle across his lap for easy access. Outside, the dark is seething and silent again, the air as thick as water.

I've taken a series of random turns down obscure roads, too panicked to pay attention to the map at all, so now I have no idea where we are. Also, the cracks in the windshield—rippling outward from the point of impact—make it nearly impossible to see what's ahead. I keep having to stick my head out the window to my left.

Eventually, my body just seizes up on me. I no longer have the strength to press down on the gas pedal, and my fingers go slack around the steering wheel.

The car slows to a jagged halt.

"Sorry," I mumble, staring vaguely out the cracked windshield. "I just . . ."

And then, almost unconsciously, I slump over, resting my forehead on the wheel. I squeeze my eyes shut until my vision pricks with stars.

Luka is silent. I can't even hear him breathing.

"I just want it to stop," I finish in a whisper.

"I know."

I lift my head, slowly. My voice is hoarse. "Do you think she's dead?"

"I don't know." Luka glances down at his rifle. "It wasn't a very clean shot. I couldn't see well."

"Yeah. It's dark."

My words sound like they're coming from the mouth of a stranger. Even my tongue feels numb. It reminds me of when Luka and I were little and we found huge bushels of pokeweed in the woods. The delicate white flowers and shiny black berries are poisonous, but the shoots and leaves are edible. We hadn't eaten all day, so we'd tried to boil the leaves like Dad had taught us. But it tasted so sour that our tongues itched and stung for days.

The memory brings me back to myself, like a ghost possessing a body. I'm in the driver's seat of the Wesselses' car, who knows how many miles from home. Luka is sitting across from me. I'm three hours into my Gauntlet. An Angel almost killed me.

The Angel. Her face returns to me, so appallingly, unnaturally white. I've seen corpses that aren't as pale.

Nothing I can envision is so white. Her hair, too blanched to be called blond. And her eyes. Black and unfathomably deep. As hypnotic as a snake's. The memory of them makes my heart leap and lodge in my throat.

"Let's just hope she's dead," Luka says at last. "Good fucking riddance."

The venom in his voice makes me shiver. It's not hard to be afraid—whenever I close my eyes, I see her face and my stomach hollows and my blood turns to ice. But it's harder to hate. I fish for anger, for the righteousness that Luka seems to feel. I can't find it. I just feel a horrible, dragging heaviness, as if there's water sucking at my feet.

Maybe this is why I'm weak. If I could hate her, maybe I would have done something—*anything*—instead of sitting there gaping, frozen with terror. If not for Luka, I would be dead. Everything is tangled up inside me, all of it so muddled and bleary, and when I get this way, there's only one thought that cleaves through the murky depths. It's a phrase that's almost soothing in its brusque simplicity.

Mom was right.

"Still," I say thickly, "we should get going again."

"Yeah," Luka says.

For the first time, I notice how tightly his fingers are clenched around the barrel of his gun. His knuckles are white, bone straining against skin. *He's sixteen*, I think. A year younger than me. Sometimes it's too easy to forget.

The cracks in the windshield are so bad that it's impossible to keep driving. We come up with an inelegant solution, which involves

Luka standing on the hood and bashing the butt of his rifle against the glass until it shatters, while I watch from the road and wince.

"It's not Dr. Wessels's day," I say, as Luka jumps down from the hood.

"Yeah, well, he should've known the risks. We'll pay him back when this is over."

I'm not sure how we'll manage that when we barely make enough to feed ourselves most weeks. But then, I'm not sure if I'll even be alive when this is over. *One thing at a time.* I walk over to help Luka brush the shards of glass off the seats.

We work in dutiful silence for a few moments, until I say quietly, "Thank you."

We never say it to each other, not even for small things, like, *Thanks for putting up the sandbags,* or *Thanks for fixing the hole in the roof.* And we certainly never say things like, *Thanks for risking your life in the woods every day to hunt for our dinner,* or *Thank you for being up to your elbows in deer guts so neither of us have to go into the red.* Expressing gratitude so openly feels strange. Because *thank you* implies debt, and you never want to owe anybody anything, not even your own family.

Especially not your own family.

But part of it, too, is that I've always seen the things we do for each other as separate from the tangle of favors and dues, tallies and tabs. If we started keeping track of our respective balances, it would never end. Should Luka say, *Thanks for letting me crawl into your bed when I was five and Mom and Dad wouldn't stop fighting?* Should I say, *Thanks for punching Adrian Pietersen after he pinned me down and tried to stick his hand up my shirt behind Mrs. Prinslew's shop?*

The silence is long, and it seems to stretch out between us, a physical thing—between our hands, nicked with tiny scratches from the glass, toiling at the same task. His hands are bigger, rough with calluses, and mine are smaller and softer, but the olive tone of our skin is the same.

At last, Luka says, "If only it'd been a better shot. Then we'd know for sure that she's dead."

The Angel's face flashes through my mind. Those black, black eyes. "I thought it was a pretty good shot."

"That's why Dad never trusted you with a gun."

There's just a fleck of humor in his voice, and it defuses the seriousness of the moment. I huff out a laugh. "At least we know he's right about one thing, then. That's a good omen, right?"

"I'll take it." Luka brushes the last bit of glass off his seat. "Come on."

We climb back into the car. Even the air feels colder now, sharper. Hostile. Whenever I blink, I see the Angel, her pale hair rippling. Sometimes she even appears in the path of the headlights—but that, at least, I know is a mirage, a trick of my exhausted and panic-stricken mind.

Sometimes it's Mom who darts across the road, blanket trailing behind her, feet bare. I resist the urge to slam on the brakes. I press down steadily on the gas and keep driving, as the vision dissipates like smoke.

———

It's less than an hour before the car starts making troubling noises. I pull over and Luka opens the hood. There's blue-white smoke wafting from the engine. Not that either of us has a single clue what that means. We both stare down, brows furrowed, eyes narrowed in bewilderment. Luka dares to reach down and touch the bizarre metal tubing, but he jerks his hand back almost instantly, fingertips singed bright red.

"Fuck," he says.

I squint at the engine, then poke one of the tubes gingerly. Nothing happens, except that the smoke grows thicker and more acrid. Luka pulls down his sleeves to cover his palms and fiddles with some of the knobs. They make a sinister grinding sound.

My brain has literally never felt smaller. It doesn't help that I've gone almost twenty hours without sleep. Luka takes out his tablet and tries to give himself a crash course on repairing an engine, but it's hard when all we can search is "what does that nozzle thing do" or "why is there black stuff dripping from the undercarriage."

"Even if we figure out what's wrong," I say, "we probably don't have the tools or the parts to fix it."

Luka scrolls through a page of dense, incomprehensible automobile repair tips. "And I doubt there's anyone nearby who knows how to fix a gas-powered car."

"Probably not."

Silence covers us, unpunctuated by bird trills or cricket warbles. I shiver at the eerie quiet.

"As long as we're just waiting here, we're sitting ducks." Luka turns off his tablet with a furious exhale. "Damn it."

I didn't expect to hear the pitch of frustration in Luka's voice. Usually he's the epitome of the strong, silent type. Strangely, though, his anxiety makes me calmer. "It's all right. We'll just—we'll have to continue on foot."

Luka gives me a scornful look. "You saw how quickly she caught up to us when we were driving. We don't stand a chance on foot. Even if we run. And no offense, but I don't think you have the stamina for that."

The back of my neck prickles. "I'm sorry I'm such a liability."

"That's not what I said."

"That's what it feels like."

A part of me knows I'm not being fair. But Mom has poisoned my brain, and that poison is spreading, seeping into everything. *Weak. Stupid.*

Luka stares at me, unflinching.

"Just leave me, then," I say. I draw in a breath that puffs up my chest, feigning strength where I don't feel it. "Go back to Esopus. You and Mom will manage fine without me."

"Fucking stop it, Inesa. Don't do this right now."

"Do what?" The tip of my nose is growing hot. "This was never going to work. I'm not . . . Mom was right. I can't do this, I can't—"

A short, rough sob wrenches itself from my throat, and my eyes water. A thousand emotions flit across Luka's face, because this is part of our silent agreement: not to make each other cry, not to burden the other person with your fears, to pretend you don't *have* any fears. I reach up to brush away the tears before they can fall.

As Luka opens his mouth to reply, there's a strange, guttural noise from the bushes beside us.

I watch the color drain from Luka's face. Every drop of blood in my body turns to ice.

Another sound, like twigs snapping under a boot. The bushes rustle.

Very, very quietly, Luka says, "Let's go, Inesa."

Go where? I want to ask. But my mouth is too dry to speak.

We've been so terrified of the Angel that it was too easy to forget the reasons no one leaves Esopus Creek unless they have to. Reasons why the town is surrounded by an electrified barbed wire fence. Reasons why if you do leave Esopus Creek—especially alone, at night—there's a chance you're never coming back.

Luka and I take a few cautious steps away from the trees, but there's not much room between us and the now useless car. Eventually I'm standing flush against the side of it, hands clenched into fists, while the rustling sound grows louder and closer.

We're pressed shoulder to shoulder, and I can feel Luka trembling. His rifle is still lying across the passenger seat. Without turning, he reaches his arm around his back, through the window, and grabs it. The car's headlights blink off, and there's only the scant light of the moon, which casts everything in an icy, alien silver. Briefly they blink on and then off again, plunging us into total blackness.

Something launches itself out of the brush and the shadows, but I only catch a glimpse of it. Luka catches my wrist and hauls me around the other side of the car.

"Inesa, *run!*"

I stumble across the empty road, blood roaring in my ears.

Without hesitation, Luka plunges ahead into the woods, dragging me after him, the growling, snarling creature just steps behind.

In the pitch dark, we scramble over tree roots and rocks, branches scraping my cheeks, thorns tearing at my clothes. Luka pulls me along with such relentlessness that I'm afraid he's going to yank my arm out of its socket. I'm more afraid he's going to let go. But he doesn't, and we stumble on through the darkness.

My lungs are burning. I want to say, *stop, please, I can't do this*, but my throat is too parched to speak and my tongue feels dry and heavy in my mouth. I don't know how long it takes, how many steps we've put between us and the road, but eventually, the rustling and snarling behind us ceases.

We've lost the thing. For now.

Luka's chest is heaving. He lets go of me and rests his hand against a nearby tree, doubled over. He's still clutching the rifle in his other hand, but his arm looks limp, trembling like a leaf in the wind.

I'm woozy with the ebbing of adrenaline, and I feel like I'm going to be sick. My vision blurs and sharpens and blurs again. I lean back against the tree trunk, eyes swimming. When I wipe at my budding tears and runny nose, my palm comes away bloody.

It doesn't seem real. Nothing seems real anymore.

Luka coughs, then straightens up abruptly. He was one of those kids who always seemed to get sick: from the rocking of a raft in the water, from eating food that didn't quite settle right in his stomach. He's mostly grown out of it. You'd have to, living in Esopus Creek.

But seeing him like this, face pale and slightly green, eyes damp and cracked through with red, he looks like a little boy again.

We stand there in utter silence, while time seems to warp and bend. The sun comes up again, finally. Just the faint glimmer of it over the horizon, dewy and barely yellow. It casts the trees and the grass with a light like honey. It illuminates the sheen of cold sweat on Luka's brow. It shows me my shaking hands, blood dried into the creases of my palm.

"Where are we?" I ask, at the same time Luka says, "What was that thing?"

The answer to both is *I don't know*, so we lapse back into silence.

"Your face," Luka says quietly, after a moment. "It's all scratched."

"Yeah." I wipe it again. "I must have run into some brush."

The burgeoning light mottles the forest floor, squeezing between the gaps in the tree canopy. The ground is remarkably dry, mostly dirt instead of moss and the long, bright green grass that I'm used to. The trees are all pines, the lower level of their branches brown and dead because not enough sun or rain can reach them. It gives the forest a sense of bleak strangeness. I feel impossibly far from home.

If the ground were wet, we would've left tracks, a path to follow back to the car. But the forest floor is carpeted with dried pine needles. We had to flee so quickly we couldn't carry anything with us, except Luka's rifle. No food, no water, not even my tablet. Even though I can't tell how much time has passed, how much time is left in my Gauntlet, the tracker still pulses like a second heartbeat.

I swallow around the lump in my throat. "We have to get back to the road."

Luka's face is hard. I can't bear to speak aloud the hopelessness of our situation, and neither can he. But then, to my surprise, he reaches into the front pocket of his coat. He takes out Dad's compass and holds it out on the flat of his palm.

"We have to go north," he says.

"Is that the way to the car?" I wonder if somehow, he's managed to keep track.

"I don't know," he admits. "But it's our best chance of getting to safety. Of finding . . ."

He trails off before he can say it. Invoking Dad's name is kind of like proclaiming you still believe in Santa Claus. I know some imagined version of Dad still lives in Luka's head. A version of Dad who's a hero, who outsmarts the system, who maneuvers out of the restraints that keep the rest of us held down.

But there's nothing else to believe in, here in the forest, miles away from any semblance of home, with the Angel trailing us and worse things lurking among the dense and shadowy trees. So when Luka points the way, I follow him. Following some dream of our father that might as well be a ghost.

The scenery changes as we walk. The ground becomes hilly, uneven. The trees are at least more familiar, spiky conifers bleeding into deep-green deciduous brush. Lichen ladders up their trunks and bulbous moss grows on their branches. There's the ever-present sound of rainwater trickling from the leaves.

All of this could let me believe we're in the woods around Esopus Creek, with our house and the shop close enough to see between the gaps in the trees. But as we stomp through the leaf pulp, my spine is stiff with fear.

Luka and I don't talk. I can't even think, really. My mind feels fuzzy, like static. And always, *always*, when I allow my thoughts to wander, they return to the Angel's face, that shock of white in the murky darkness. I get so lost in the memory—*those impossibly dark, empty eyes*—that I stumble over an upturned rock. Luka turns around.

"I'm okay," I say.

He just nods.

In the absence of adrenaline, I start to feel the weight of the hours. Hours without sleep, food, or water. My throat is dry and my empty stomach is in knots. And the exhaustion makes my vision blur as I try to tread carefully along the edge of what has become an increasingly steep ravine.

Luka stops so suddenly that I slam into his back. I stammer out an apology, but he gives me a fierce look, finger pressed to his lips. That's when I see it: strips of fabric draped among the tree branches.

My blood turns to ice.

It's not just tattered cloth. There are crude stick sculptures, twigs held together with dried mud. There are wooden signs driven into the tree trunks, the writing too weather-blanched to read.

Luka takes a hesitant step forward. I follow, heart lodged in my throat. The stick sculptures grow more elaborate as we make our way through the arbor. They hold stones with strange markings etched into them, clumps of moss the size of my head.

I stop to examine the nearest one. Inside is a bundle of small, dried-out bones, wrapped in twine and smeared with still-drying blood.

"Animal bones?" I whisper to Luka.

He doesn't reply. He just raises a trembling finger to point.

Just ahead of us, nailed to the trunk of a large, spreading oak, is an arrangement of sticks and bones. In the very center is a human skull. It's crowned with a set of enormous antlers, and where its eyes should be are two smooth, white stones.

There are people who choose to unplug from Caerus's grid entirely—either because their debt is so staggering, it would take seven lifetimes to repay, or simply, like Dad, out of high-minded dogma. But unlike Dad, who vanished like a ghost, a lot of those people hang around.

Once, in the woods outside Esopus Creek, I came across one of these off-gridders in his campsite. It was just a tarp pulled between tree trunks, hanging limply over a wooden raft. I wondered how he didn't drown when the water table rose.

"You can never win with Caerus," the man said.

Luka would have told me to run, but he looked too thin and too worn-out to be dangerous. At least, not yet.

"It's not a game," I replied warily.

"Not to us."

I was lucky the man I encountered was still sentient and mostly human. His mind untainted and his appetites contained. By now, though, I'm sure he's far gone.

The off-gridders have to hunt for their food—no Caerus drones airlifting them freeze-dried chicken thighs—and what they hunt, of course, are mutations. Sometimes in the outskirts of Lower Esopus you can find the picked-over corpse of a deer mutation, its antlers still dripping with moss, flesh hanging in strips from its rib cage, all four eye sockets empty. I saw one once, and the swarm of blackflies was so loud, I couldn't even hear my own breath. I fled before I could catch a glimpse of the thing that killed it.

There's a reason no one hunts the mutations for food unless they have no other choice. The animals are corrupted, irradiated, their gene pools so tainted that eating their flesh is like swallowing poison. If you consume enough of their meat, you become something corrupted, too: feral, violent, not quite human.

Wends, we call them. I've never seen one up close. Sometimes there are flashes in the brush, a quick snatch of grayish skin. The smell of decay, heavier than swamp air, thick enough to make you retch.

Now a breeze picks up, ruffling my hair and carrying a scent toward us. The scent of rotting flesh, of meat gone bad. The bones in the trees rattle like wind chimes. And then, in the distance, there's an ear-splitting, unearthly howl.

TEN

MELINOË

One of the advantages of being an Angel is that I don't need much sleep, though that's mostly for the audience's benefit, not mine. It would be horribly boring to watch a live stream of me napping. If I really can't fight the exhaustion, I can usually climb into a tree, strap myself to a sturdy branch, and get in an hour or two.

But I can't afford it now. Not on this Gauntlet. I've already spent far too long hunched on the side of the road, waiting for the bullet wound in my shoulder to knit shut and for the blood to stop running. The viewers are probably starting to get restless and fed up. So I use one of the other tools Azrael has granted me: stimulants.

The sleek, silver capsules turn my veins into live wires and fling my eyelids open. My limbs feel lighter, my muscles stronger. They come with the slight drawback of increasing my heart rate—and thus making me a slightly worse shot. And when the effects of the pill wear off, my body feels unbearably heavy, heavier than it did before, and dark thoughts crowd my head like storm clouds.

I know the risks of taking a stimulant right now. But I tell myself that I'll be dealing with the withdrawal symptoms from the safety of a Caerus helicopter, away from the cameras, the Lamb's body growing cold hundreds of feet below. Azrael will tuck me under an electric blanket for the chills and smooth back my hair, letting me sleep until the drugs pass through my system. Or at least until the post-Gauntlet parties and photo shoots start.

So I take one of the pills and swallow it. The capsule slides coldly down my throat. The effect is almost instantaneous: My muscles seize, my heart starts to pound, and my real eye fills with a rush of blood. A little bit of moisture pools along my lash line, and I raise my hand to dab it away.

There. Now I can run for hours.

The sun is up, and even though the dark is better, because I can see in it and my prey can't, the light makes me feel hopeful. Or maybe it's just the stimulants. Either way, I streak through the forest. I leap over rocks and roots, dodge tree trunks and bushes.

The red dot of the Lamb's tracker is pulsing in front of me. She's moving—but not fast enough. I'm gaining too much ground on her. The trees, the bushes, the rocks all blur as I run past them, just smudges of green-brown. There's a faint crackle of thirst in my throat. I swallow hard to shove it down. I have to redeem myself with a swift kill, calculated and brutal. If I stop now, I'll lose. I'll lose the Gauntlet. And then I'll lose myself—or whatever part of me I have left. She'll vanish with the plunging of a syringe.

I keep running.

The forest opens onto a scraggly clearing, tree branches arching overhead like a dome. The beat of the tracker is close now, so close. Yards, not miles. Just another few minutes. My mouth tastes like metal, the way it always does when I'm on the stimulants. The way it always does before a kill.

The tracker blares an alarm, and my vision burns red. I throw out my arm and grasp a nearby tree trunk to stop myself. I've built up so much momentum that my elbow joint nearly tears out of its socket.

I bend at the waist, gasping for air. Pain shudders from the wound in my shoulder and down my arm, but the stimulants keep it dull, at a distance. With this exertion, there's a risk of the skin tearing open again. It's a risk I'll have to take, though. I need the Lamb dead. I'll deal with the fallout later.

Still panting hard, I whip my head around the clearing. No movement.

My comms chip must be glitching. I exhale with annoyance. I tap my temple to reset the tracker, but then catch something out of the corner of my eye: a length of red fabric knotted around a tree trunk.

It's a strange sight, here in the middle of the woods, miles away from civilization, and my curiosity is piqued enough to examine it. My comms chip buzzes, like a fly trapped in my ear. I tap my temple again and the nasally sound fades to a low whine. I'll have to call Azrael; he can fix it.

I reach the tree and tug at the red fabric. It's ratty and a little damp. When I touch it, my thumb comes away dirty. With something the color of rust.

I stagger backward, brushing my palms to try to get the blood off. It's not that I have a weak stomach—but the breeze is carrying an even stranger scent toward me, one of rotting meat, and the stimulants are coursing through my body, making me feel sick with unspent adrenaline. My vision rocks. My hands are trembling.

Overhead, the sky darkens. I only notice because it happens so suddenly, the scattered light fading from gold to gray. My palms feel sticky. And the smell is getting stronger, thicker on the wind that blows my pale hair around my face.

I raise a shaking hand and tap my temple again. Once. Twice. There's only the fuzzy sound of static. Panic surges up my throat, squeezing out my breath in short, quick gasps. I wish I hadn't taken the stimulant, because now I can't tell if the rocketing of my heart is because of the drugs, or because I'm really in danger. Caerus has ripped everything out of my brain and installed new wiring. But there are tangles and faulty connections, short circuits and cables with fizzing, frayed ends. My body and mind don't quite work in sync anymore.

But the screaming I hear is real. So are the footsteps. I snap my head up, and my vision explodes with red.

The Lamb breaks through the trees, her brother right behind her. She skids to a halt when she sees me, letting out a choked sound.

The brother reaches for his rifle. But my muscles are coiled and taut with the effects of the stimulant, and my instincts are quicker. I unsheathe the knife from my boot and hurl it at him.

It spins through the air, catching the sleeve of his jacket just as

I intended. I can't kill him, but I can stop him. The blade sinks into a nearby tree trunk with a *thwack*, pinning him there. The brother lets out a furious snarl of protest, straining and fumbling to free himself.

I'm across the clearing in seconds. I grab the rifle from his hand and toss it into the bushes, out of reach. The brother's face is red with the flush of anger and his eyes are full of hate. He reaches for me with his free hand, but I take a quick step back, and his fingers just claw at the air.

"Fuck you," he bites out.

I suppress the instinct to strike him. The rule is that I'm not allowed to kill anyone on my Gauntlets except the Lamb, but the guidelines are a bit fuzzy when it comes to how much "nonfatal" damage I can cause. But rage and temper don't fit with my Angel persona, and torture isn't part of my repertoire of skills. I'll leave that to Lethe. My kills are cold, swift, precise. Bloodless, mostly.

"Bitch," he hisses.

I hope the cameras don't catch the slight clench of my jaw.

With the brother still stuck fast to the tree, I turn around to take my kill. But before I can, my rifle is snatched off my back. It's so sudden and so forceful that I topple backward, onto the ground.

When I scramble to my feet, the Lamb is holding my rifle aloft. Her whole body is shaking. There are scratch marks across her nose and though her earth-colored eyes are bright, her gaze is unsteady.

"Don't move," she says, voice thick.

I still myself.

I'm not afraid of her. From the way she's holding the gun, I can tell she doesn't know how to use it. Moreover, I don't think she really would. It took years of training before I could pull the trigger without flinching, knowing there was a person at the end of the barrel. Years to annihilate my conscience, my pity, my weak human heart. To become the frigid killing creature I am now.

By contrast, the Lamb's humanity suddenly overwhelms me. It's the dried blood on her face. The warm color in her cheeks. The way her chest heaves with every breath. The way her finger trembles against the trigger and her throat pulses as she swallows. In the mingling of terror and blustery courage, she looks so *alive*.

Overhead, the sky darkens further. There's a rumble of thunder, and lightning cracks through the coal-colored clouds.

The Lamb's gaze flickers upward, and I seize the moment. I launch myself at her, knocking her over and pinning her to the ground. My rifle slips from her grasp.

She chokes out a wordless protest as I straddle her hips, one hand pressing down on her throat.

Thunder crashes. Tears squeeze from her eyes.

I press down harder.

It takes five minutes to strangle someone. So it won't be my quickest kill, but it will be bloodless. The Lamb reaches up and claws weakly at my face.

"Please," she croaks.

I can hear the low hum of the cameras flitting around our heads, capturing every twitch, every breath. The Lamb's eyes are shining, the color of damp leaves, of moss soaked with morning dew, deep green with flecks of brown. I feel her start to go limp.

And then I feel a droplet on my back. The coldness seeps through my hunting suit. At first I think it's sweat, or moisture from the trees. The wind comes howling into the clearing, whipping my hair around my face, nearly tearing it loose from its sleek ponytail.

The downpour comes with another strike of lightning.

I flinch as the rain gushes over me. It's only a matter of seconds before I'm soaked to the skin. The Lamb's hair is plastered to her face, her eyelids fluttering. Her lips move vaguely, but I can't hear her desperate, feeble pleas over the deafening rush of rainwater.

My vision ripples. Steadies, then ripples again. There's a fizzing, staticky sound—water leaking into my prosthetic?

When I blink through the rainwater, the Lamb is gone.

There's a body beneath me, but it's not hers. It's a small body, delicate, frail-limbed. Blond hair spreads out around the girl's head. Her face is bloodless, blue eyes wide and fixed on nothing. Blood stains the front of her dress, spouting from a bullet hole in her chest.

From *my* bullet. The water washing over me, weighing my limbs down. Every other sound fades into the periphery. There's only the pounding rain, my heart skipping beats as I stare at the girl who is not the girl, at the blood that trickles from the corner of her mouth.

No.

No.

It's not real. I'm not here again. I raise a hand to wipe the water from my face, but I can't even feel it. My fingers are numb and so are my cheeks. The scene in front of me flickers, like a tablet screen trying to load, and then I see the Lamb again. She's moving groggily but determinedly, trying to wriggle out from underneath me. In lifting my hand from her throat, I've given her just enough slack to get loose.

"Don't," I pant, but the word is swallowed by the roar of the rain.

Her throat is red, red, red where my hands have pressed down on it. I reach for her again.

And then I feel a sudden, breathtaking pain as something is thrust hard against my temple. Static crackles agonizingly in my ear, driving needles into my brain. I sway for a moment, my body going limp.

I fall. Blackness swallows my vision and pulls me under before I even hit the ground.

ELEVEN

INESA

The Angel topples over and I shove her limp body off of me, gasp-ing for air. My throat is burning, and my breaths come in uneven, choking spurts. I push myself to my knees, palms sinking into the newly wet earth. Mud seeps from between my splayed fingers and water falls in freezing rivulets down my face.

I feel pressure on my back. Luka. He grabs me by the elbow and hauls me to my feet. My arms and legs are pricking with a thousand pins and needles and they feel as heavy as lead.

"Inesa," he pants.

I blink droplets from my lashes and look around the clearing. It's hard to see anything through the torrent of rainwater: tree branches sagging and swaying in the storm, the grass pressed flat to the muddy ground. And there's the Angel's body. She's on her stomach, limbs starfished out around her. Her head is turned to the side, so I can only see her profile, so impossibly pale against the dark, damp earth.

I see the beginnings of a bruise on her temple, pale purple, where the butt of Luka's rifle landed. A single brusque, brutal blow.

"Is she—" I try hoarsely, then clear my throat and try again. "Is she dead?"

"Who fucking cares?"

I shouldn't. But my stomach clenches as I look down at her unmoving body. With her limbs spread out like that, her eyes closed in a peaceful way that belies the circumstances, she really does look like an angel. Obviously. And she's beautiful. Obviously. All the Angels are supposed to be beautiful. Raindrops track down her face, clinging to her full, heart-shaped lips.

"Come on," Luka urges.

I tear my gaze away.

He could have put a bullet through her brain, ending all this for good. He must have considered it. I look over at Luka. He's breathing unevenly, and shivering, not just from the rain and the cold.

We've always done what we could to survive, and made no apologies for it. But the gulf between survival and murder isn't an easy one to cross. Killing someone—even an Angel—is something that, deep down, his instincts protested. Just like mine would.

Maybe the viewers are typing their grievances furiously into the chat, castigating him for his hesitation, for his weakness. But I can't call reluctance to murder someone *weakness*. And I don't think I would be able to live with myself if I made my brother a murderer at just sixteen.

Luka drapes my arm around his neck and helps me stagger forward a few steps. I cough again, covering my mouth, and blood splatters my palm. *That can't be good.*

The rain is still gushing down in heavy, translucent sheets. I bend over, with a bolt of excruciating pain, and pick up the Angel's rifle. It's sleek and black, so different from Luka's, with its rusted barrel and wooden stock. I've never used a gun before. But I guess if I'm going to learn how, it's now or never.

As I straighten up again, Luka says, "Come on, Inesa. The Wends won't be far behind."

I cast one look back at the Angel. She's not moving, eyes closed, mouth open slightly. Rainwater slicks her white-blond hair to her cheek and the cold brings a blue marbling to her skin. I think I see her chest rising and falling faintly, but I'm not sure. I might have just imagined it.

If she's not dead already, the Wends will tear her to pieces anyway, when they come across her unconscious body. Maybe, in some way, that still makes Luka and me murderers. But the slight uncertainty, that crucial *maybe*, transforms it into something I might be able to live with. If I survive, that is.

I let Luka help me stagger out of the clearing, as the rain pelts down, and the Angel lies still and silent in the dirt.

As it usually is with these sudden, soaking downpours, the rain stops almost as quickly as it started. In the aftermath of the storm, the forest is uncannily peaceful. The animals are still hidden in their dens and tree holes; the birds are too timid to sing. The only sound is that of water dripping from the leaves and onto the dirt. And, of course, of Luka and me stumbling through the dead, muddy leaves.

We try to be as quiet as possible, but it's difficult when my limbs feel so unwieldy. My throat burns agonizingly with every breath. There must be bruises pulsing there already, in the shape of the Angel's fingers.

Luka has Dad's compass out and is staring down at it determinedly. But it just keeps spinning and spinning, the needle never resting at true north.

"Maybe it got damaged in the rainstorm?" I suggest meekly. My voice is so hoarse, it's almost comical. Almost.

"Maybe," Luka mutters. There's a crease in his brow. No, not a crease. A crack. He's close to breaking.

I stand up straight and gently remove my arm from his shoulders. "I can walk on my own now, I think."

Luka doesn't respond. He watches the needle spin and spin.

Looking at him, a memory floats up. It was not long after Dad left, in those first hazy weeks when we were all quietly convincing ourselves that he'd just disappeared temporarily like he always did, that he'd be throwing back beers on the porch again soon enough.

Luka kept clenching his jaw and grinding his teeth. I assumed it was just stress—he had plenty of reasons to be stressed. But then one morning he coughed, and a tooth came out in a rush of blood.

We took him to Dr. Wessels, who pried open his mouth and peered into it with a tiny flashlight.

"There's an abscess," he said. "I'll give you some medication to clear the infection. If you'd come in earlier, I might've been able to save the molar."

"It's fine," Luka said, voice tight.

Dr. Wessels gave him some pills and a handful of gauze pads to stanch the bleeding. While Luka busied himself transferring credits for the visit, Dr. Wessels pulled me aside and said, "Why didn't you come in here sooner? A tooth abscess is one of the most painful conditions I can think of. Didn't he mention the pain?"

I lifted my head to glance at Luka. He was clenching his jaw again, moving his tongue around the inside of his mouth.

"No," I said.

That was when I realized I couldn't remember the last time I'd seen him cry.

I blink, returning to the present. Luka puts a fist to his forehead, brow still furrowed as if he's concentrating, but there's an empty sheen in his eyes that tells me he's not really seeing what's in front of him. Very cautiously, I put a hand on his shoulder.

"Let's stop for now," I say. "Rest up a little."

His head snaps up. "We don't have time to rest. The Wends—"

"We have a better shot at outrunning them if we're not absolutely exhausted. How long has it been since either of us slept?"

Luka's mouth twitches, like it's forming a protest, but instead of speaking, he looks down at the compass again. A moment passes in silence. Water drips down from the leaves and onto our shoulders, dampening our already soaked jackets.

"I should've known," he says quietly. "I should've known all he'd leave us with is a worthless piece of junk."

And then he hurls the compass across the clearing, hard. It hits a nearby tree trunk and drops to the ground.

Luka draws in shallow, shuddering breaths. His eyes are red

with exhaustion and there's just the faintest hint of tears in them, a bright, shining wetness.

It would be easy if I could hug him. If I felt like he would find any comfort in it. My arms seem locked at my sides.

I realize, though, in this moment of silence, that I don't hear the cameras anymore. The soft, insistent buzzing is totally silent; there's only the hum of my tracker. And while I'm not normally disposed to conspiracy theories, it occurs to me that Caerus wouldn't want the audience to hear us talking about Dad, about the Drowned County. They must have cut the cameras, or sent them flitting away from us and back to Melinoë.

A sensation of hope rises in me—or maybe it's just the subtle, sudden absence of total despair. Stiffly and awkwardly, I walk over to where the compass landed and pick it up.

The impact and the fall have broken the hinge. Now it's in two pieces: the tarnished and scuffed golden case, and the compass itself, glass cracked. The needle has stopped spinning entirely. I dig around through the leaf pulp to see if I've overlooked any crucial pieces.

And that's when my fingers find a tiny, rolled-up scrap of paper. I would've missed it completely in the mud if it weren't so white against the forest floor, curiously unstained. It's tied with a thin, gossamer string that looks almost like dental floss (Dad was nothing if not resourceful).

I tear off the string and unroll the paper. In Dad's familiar, barely decipherable scrawl is a series of numbers. I stare at them for a moment, squinting, trying to make sense of them. Luka strides over to peer over my shoulder, and of course he recognizes what we're looking at immediately.

"They're coordinates," he says. There's a breathy awed quality to his voice. "Dad *did* leave us a map."

I wouldn't exactly call it a *map*, but it's something. Something we can use. And maybe more than that, it's proof that he didn't abandon us in the devastatingly complete manner I thought he had. A warm sensation brims in my chest, making my heart beat quickly. And I'm certain this time—it's just the barest glimmer of hope.

"This must be where he is," Luka says, in a heated rush. "We just need to get back to the car—get our tablets—and then we'll know exactly where to go."

I'm almost as relieved to see the spark back in Luka as I am at finding the note. Dad's trail. I roll up the scrap of paper again and hold it in my fist, clenched tight enough that my fingernails bite into my palm. I wish that I could feel something radiating from it, some kind of love, but to my surprise I feel a spark of anger instead.

You left us with a scrap of paper, and we're supposed to be grateful?

When I look at Luka, his eyes blazing, I can't bring myself to say it. Instead, I hold out the pieces of the broken compass to him.

"Here," I say. "These are still yours."

Luka looks down at my open palm for a long moment. Then he shakes his head.

"You keep half," he says. He points to the golden case, the part without the compass inside. "This part. Maybe you can trap rainwater inside it."

"No, you take it. You're better with this survival stuff than I am."

"*You* take it. You need all the help you can get."

A smile tugs at the corner of my lips, and I slip the case into my pocket. Luka takes the compass itself. Standing there in the muggy aftermath of the storm, the air both cold and dense at once, and so familiar, because we've lived in this drowning world all our lives, I realize that we have to make our own hope. And I think maybe we can.

Without our tablets, I don't know what time it is, or how much time has elapsed since the start of my Gauntlet. All I can hear is the incessant humming of the tracker, reminding me that every single breath is a stolen one. Oddly enough, I still can't pick up the buzzing of the cameras.

Luka and I are actually pretty good at finding our way. We spent enough time in the woods with Dad when we were kids, back when his mood swings were more fun than scary and we still believed everything he said, even after four or five beers. He taught us which plants were safe to eat and to boil our water before drinking it—and, most important, how to tell when something was too irradiated to do either. We both know the difference between real deer tracks and the webbed prints of the deer mutations. We can mostly figure out which direction is north by looking at which way the moss grows on trees and rocks, though Dad warned us that this method wasn't always reliable.

Still, it's the best we have to go on at the moment. We trek through the forest, mostly in silence, the mud sucking at our boots. And in the silence, my mind keeps drifting back to the Angel—her face hovering over mine, flashing white like a strike of lightning. And her eyes. One dark brown, the other black from end to end, throwing my terrified reflection back at me.

The Angels have a number of unnatural features, cyborg traits that Caerus has imbued them with to craft the deadliest killers. Even though I've never watched any of the Gauntlets all the way through, it's impossible to escape the viral clips, usually only a few seconds long. The moment of the kill—a bullet through the heart, a knife to the throat. I remember a red-haired Angel driving her knife right between a teenage boy's legs. The comments from the live chat were divisive.

<user193848697: so f*cking badass>

<user04955866850: it's not really. I hate these types of gauntlets tbh. like it's not even a fair fight>

<user559506032: lol why don't you volunteer then>

Another memory keeps rising in my mind, just as persistent as the first. The Angel lying face down in the dirt, as still as a corpse, mouth open in arrested protest. The echo of Luka's voice: *Who fucking cares?*

I shouldn't. I should be cheering for what he did. I'm sure everyone watching the Gauntlet cheered. If the Angel really is dead, Luka will be famous. I can imagine the chat's comments so easily.

<user099485437: inesa is so pathetic. like really b*tch you can't even get up to help? brother doing all the heavy lifting lol>

I lose myself in these self-pitying and fairly embarrassing thoughts until Luka says suddenly, "Wait. Stop."

I skid to a halt. "What?"

Lowering his voice, Luka asks, "Can you smell that?"

I draw in a breath. The rain has brought out all the scents of the forest, the earthiness of the moss and the bark. But under it, just barely detectable, is the bitter, curling smell of rot.

Luka and I press close together, our gazes snapping wildly around the clearing. There are no bones—animal or human—strung up in the trees, no strips of cloth, but the scent of decay is familiar and unmistakable. We got away quickly enough last time that we didn't even get a good look at the Wends. This time—

"We have to run," I whisper.

A throaty, inhuman growling sound seems to come from everywhere at once.

Luka lifts his rifle. I fumble with mine—the one I stole from the Angel—but it's heavier than I expect it to be, and difficult to heft up to my shoulder. My eyes blur as I try to look into the scope, and my hands are shaking so hard, I'm not sure I'll have the strength to pull the trigger.

They burst from the bushes, three at once. Their skin is the mottled gray of meat gone bad and their clothes hang off them in filthy rags. Their flesh has peeled away in places to reveal the bloody sinew and muscle beneath. Their lipless mouths are open, exposing yellow teeth sharpened to jagged points.

Worst of all are their eyes. The pupils are dilated, whites cracked through with red, but there's no emotion in them. No hatred, no anger, no wrath. There's only hunger. A desperate need that animates their spindly limbs and slouching bodies, so when they launch themselves at us, I'm too shocked to shoot.

Wham. My back is against the earth, stars blinking across my darkening vision. The Wend is on top of me, panting, slobbering, arms flailing. Spittle drips down toward my face. The smell of decay is so strong that my stomach heaves. With all the strength I can muster, I let the rifle slip and then shove my hands against the Wend's bony chest.

It falls over, yowling like a cat. I scramble to my feet, clumsily grabbing the rifle again. Across the clearing, Luka is fending off the other two Wends at once. He swings his rifle and knocks one of them in the head. There's a garbled wail of pain as its frail skin folds inward, and I can hear the crushing of bone as its skull splinters.

I try to swing my own rifle, but I'm clumsier than Luka, and the barrel whistles through empty air. The Wend lunges at me again. This time, it manages to grab my jacket in its gnarled hands. There's soft, webbed skin growing between its fingers.

The Wend's grip tightens and its razor-sharp nails slice through the fabric, into the skin of my arm. I suck in a breath at the sharp, sudden bolt of pain. I find myself locked in a terrible and furious game of tug-of-war, where the Wend tries to reel me in closer and I desperately try to yank my jacket out of its grasp.

"Inesa!" Luka shouts. "Look out—there's more!"

They break through the bushes and lurch across the clearing. Three, four—too many to count, their grayish bodies all blurring together into one snarling, lumbering mass.

I manage to pull free of the Wend, but the momentum sends me stumbling backward, and I collide with another. This Wend has a third eye, still milky as an infant's, budding on its forehead.

They howl like wolves and hiss like snakes. One of them tangles its claws in my hair. Another digs its teeth into my shoulder—not quite hard enough to break the skin, but with enough force to make me cry out. I jerk away, and end up falling to the ground.

On my hands and knees, I crawl through the crush of limbs and claws and teeth. I can't even see Luka anymore; I can just hear him breathing hard with exertion. A shot rings out. There are more yowls, and one of the Wends crumples.

Its blood is black, like tar. I know it's not really human, not anymore, but I still feel a lump in my throat as I watch its eyes lose their gleam and its chest rise and fall unevenly with its very last breaths. I try to tell myself it's more like an animal, and Luka has killed hundreds of those before.

Still. Once upon a time, this was someone's brother or sister, son or daughter, neighbor or friend.

My vision blurs. I don't have time for this strange, mangled sort of grief. The Wends scramble backward, making too-human whimpering sounds. Luka struggles through the mass of them, but he can't reach me. There's blood running from his nose.

Luka manages to break through the crowd of clawing, snarling Wends. "Inesa, *run!*"

It takes me a moment to force my legs to move. Luka and I skid through the mud and leaf pulp, the Wends loping after us. Tree roots make each step perilous and rocks jut up menacingly from the ground. We come along the edge of a ravine; a sheer, steep drop on the other side.

Luka stops suddenly and turns, readying his rifle. I try to lift mine, too, but I'm shaking all over with adrenaline and terror. I don't know why I think this will stop them. They aren't human enough to remember how to be afraid. They just hurtle forward, and even Luka isn't fast enough to fell them all.

They're almost on us. I stagger back, and my ankle curls inward with a jolt of pain. I skid along the very edge of the ravine. One of my legs slips out from under me, and I claw at the leaves and the dirt to try to pull myself up again.

"Luka!" I cry.

He turns, but it's too late. In that moment of hesitation, the Wends are on him. Their gray limbs pull and grasp.

"Inesa!" he yells back. The blanched look of horror on his face is more terrifying than anything else. I've never seen him so afraid.

My fingers scrabble against the earth, but they can't find purchase. My heart drops into my stomach.

Please—

And then I fall.

TWELVE

MELINOË

I should have slit her throat.

That's my first thought upon waking. Blood in my mouth and mud caked to my face, I push myself up on trembling limbs. Rainwater is beading along my lash line; I wipe it away. Then I scrub at the mud. But I don't make much progress before a searing, fiery pain splits through my head.

I double over, gripping my temples and squeezing my eyes shut, as if I can will the pain away. Instead, I vomit.

Bile splatters the mud and burns my throat. I sit back on my heels and draw in a shaky breath.

I'm not dead. At least there's that. But every nerve ending in my body is burning like a live wire and a quick glance around the clearing tells me that my rifle is gone.

A heaviness settles in my stomach. It's more grief than fear. The rifle is my signature weapon. It feels as much a part of me as my own limbs. Without it—

I stand, with another tremor of nausea. I manage to cross the clearing to the tree where my knife had pinned down the Lamb's brother. There's nothing except a nick in the bark. They must've taken my knife with them, too.

My body feels unbearably heavy. The adrenaline from the stimulants has obviously long faded, and although I was unconscious through most of the withdrawal, the wash of the drugs through my system leaves me exhausted, barely able to walk. I put my hand against the tree and lean over, bile rising again in my throat.

I try to stay rational. I try to consider my options. But I just end up berating myself.

I was too reckless. I thought this would be easy. The Lamb looked so defenseless in her file. I underestimated the brother—not just his strength, but his tenacity. I didn't really believe he would fight so hard for his sister. Azrael tells us to think of the other Angels as our sisters, but I can't imagine putting myself in the line of fire for any of them. Except Keres. And if anything, Keres was just a lesson in the futility of fighting for anyone who isn't yourself.

Maybe I wasn't reckless. I was just desperate. Keres's face flashes through my mind—her blank stare, her eyes wide and dull, nothing behind them. No memory of me, of anything. I feel sick again and clap a hand over my mouth. I don't want to keep vomiting on camera.

The cameras. I listen for them—if I'm very still, I can usually hear them buzzing faintly around my head, like tiny winged insects. But as I stand and wait in the silence, I hear nothing. Just the breeze through the wiry branches and the wet leaves. And of course the pulse of the tracker, dimmer now, as the Lamb moves hopelessly far away.

My veins turn to ice. I try to remind myself that this isn't the first time I've failed to hear the cameras; sometimes they just take a little while to catch up with me. Sometimes there are glitches in the system. Gaps. Even with Caerus technology, there's always a margin for error.

I'm really just trying to put off the inevitable: calling Azrael. I don't want to hear the disappointment or the barely cloaked anger in his voice. I don't want him to tell me how the chat is flooded with comments celebrating my failure. Maybe they're even disappointed to see me getting up now. After all, there's no bigger plot twist than an Angel dying.

I examine my face in the small piece of reflective metal affixed to my wrist. It's supposed to help my peripheral vision when I'm fighting, but I always end up using it more for vanity purposes. My eyes are bloodshot and my face is a waxy yellowish color. My hair has come loose from its neat ponytail and falls in damp tendrils over my shoulders, down to the middle of my back.

Every cruel comment comes ringing to life: the people who called me too skinny, too fat, too ugly to be an Angel, too pretty to be kept under lock and key in Caerus's clutches, too sexy for seventeen, not sexy enough.

My fingers tremble as I brush the rest of the mud from my face.

I can't put it off any longer. I'm shivering even inside my insulated hunting suit. I tap my temple and wait for the fizzle of static that tells me I'm connected to the Caerus mainframe.

Silence.

I blink my prosthetic eye, expecting the map to layer across my vision.

Nothing.

Panic rises in me, with astonishing coldness. I tap again, blink and blink and blink, but everything is still quiet.

My heart hammers in my throat. *There must be a delay in the transmission, that's all, some wires getting crossed.* I wait and wait. The chill seeps further, into my bones, and the wind blows my damp hair around my face. My teeth chatter.

Silence is the most terrifying sound. The utter absence of life. I remember pressing two fingers to the girl's throat and feeling no pulse under her cold skin. I remember leaning over with my ear to her chest, waiting to hear the hum of her heart. The silence yawned below me, like a dark, bottomless pit. I tumbled into it. The next thing I remember is waking up in the helicopter, trembling beneath a Mylar blanket.

I can't fail again. I tap my temple one more time, hard enough to hurt, to shock my body into action and start the synapses firing in my brain. Nothing.

My comms system is totally down, crumpled like a house on a fault line. I can't even access my own vitals. The only thing that works is the night vision in my prosthetic, which I test by burying my head in my arms and blocking out the watery sunlight.

The throbbing pain moves from my temple to the center of my forehead. There's a staticky itch under my skin, and I want to claw into my flesh to dig it out. I curl my fingernails into my palm again.

The brother hit me right where my comms chip is implanted. He must have damaged it. Crushed it into pieces, maybe, and sent them scattering through my brain. The realization floods my veins with ice again. I try to swallow the bile in my throat, but then I think—*why?* If I'm disconnected from the Caerus mainframe, then the cameras have lost track of me, too.

I vomit again.

All that comes out is sticky, clear saliva. The acid churning in my empty stomach. With nausea still shuddering through me, I look up at the sky, half obscured through the dense canopy, just jagged strips of blue-gray between gnarled branches.

"Please," I whisper, as if anyone can hear. "Save me, please, get me out of here."

There's no answer, of course. I might as well be in another universe, and Azrael some other, far-flung planet's god.

I switch my brain into survival mode. No thinking, just acting. I unzip the small compartment in my suit that holds meal-replacement packets. I tear one open and squeeze the nutrient paste into my mouth. It tastes like cereal milk left to sit in the bowl. But it's better than nothing. I have decon-tabs in my suit, too, which I can use as soon as I find water.

The rote, simple procedure of nourishing my body makes me calmer. Warmer. There's still that splintering ache in my head and I want nothing more than to swallow a painkiller and crawl into a nearby bush to sleep until the pain passes through me. But I can't afford to rest now.

My best chance is to get out of the woods. Find somewhere with a signal and contact Azrael. He'll be looking for me, too. Maybe he's as panicked as I am. I try to imagine it—fear passing across his cold, stoic face. Strangely enough, this makes me feel better, picturing his terror at the thought of losing me. Maybe enough fear can add up to love.

I have no idea how close I am to even a speck of civilization. Until now, my hunts have been brutally efficient and short. I've never spent any more time than necessary in this ugly, half-drowned world. Who would, if they had any other choice?

My gait is more limping than walking, really. My legs still feel so heavy. With enough time I know my muscles will strengthen again, but for now, every step seems more tremulous than the last. It has to be the withdrawal. I'm shaking and drenched in cold sweat.

I go in the direction I think is south, hoping that I'll stumble upon some semblance of civilization, somewhere Caerus can find me again. But after what feels like hours, I've found nothing. And the woods are growing denser, deeper. The bark on the trees is black with rainwater and the leaves are a rich, water-fed green. Scummy white moss is growing on every rock, and bizarre mushrooms unfold from the ground like frilly fish gills. I don't recognize anything in this alien place. I might as well be walking on the bottom of the ocean.

The thickly interwoven tree branches blot out most of the sun. What does leak through is thin, bleary light, more gray than gold. The air is so heavy with humidity that every breath is like drowning—in slow, painful increments. I wonder again how anyone manages to live out here. I suppose they just adapt to it, just like they adapt to everything else.

Or maybe they don't. In the several hours I've been walking, I haven't seen a trace of another human being. Not that I would necessarily know what to look for. Azrael never prepared me for this situation, for the possibility that I'd be disconnected from the Caerus mainframe entirely. Because nothing is supposed to exist outside Caerus.

I have to stop for a minute to catch my breath. There's a stitch in my side and the headache is returning, a dull throb behind my temples. I limp over to the nearest tree and steady myself against the trunk, panting. I want to collapse, to slide down into the dirt and leaf pulp of the forest floor. But if I do, I'm not sure I'll be able to get up again.

There's a rustling sound, like a shiver of wind, only nothing shifts in the air. My head snaps up.

She steps out of the trees, nimbly parting the branches. I didn't think I was at the stage of withdrawal where I'd still be having hallucinations, but my brain refuses to accept that this is real. That the Lamb is walking toward me in slow, deliberate paces, my own rifle held aloft on her shoulder.

Our eyes meet, and neither of us speaks. Her finger hovers over the trigger. The bruises of my failed strangulation are blooming on her throat, garish red marks in the shape of my hands. Drawn up to her full height, with me still doubled over, she seems suddenly tall, strong, though I felt how weak she was beneath me. How weak she was *supposed* to be.

But strange metamorphoses are happening all the time. Who says prey can't become predator?

Her gaze is unflinching. I look up into the barrel of my own rifle, and my stomach lurches. My skin is prickling with heat. I wonder if this is how my Lambs die—in a knot of terror and righteous fury, fearing me and hating me in equal measure.

Except. The Lamb hasn't blinked in so long that her eyes turn glazed and wet. And her finger is still dancing over the trigger, trembling like a leaf in the wind.

All of a sudden, my vision flashes white. *I'm dead*, I think—but then the light dissipates just as quickly as it came. My connection to the Caerus grid, maybe, flaring up and then fading again. Her tracker is a pulse in my ear, a second heartbeat. Her life, just as fragile as mine.

My voice is hoarse when I finally manage to speak.

"If you're going to kill me," I say, "you should probably cock the rifle first."

Immediately her face flushes. Her left hand fumbles around the barrel, trying to pull it back like it's a manual, like her brother's gun. I knew she wouldn't understand the difference. I just need a second of hesitation, the briefest slipping, and I can have her on the ground again, my rifle jammed against her throat.

Only when I try to launch myself forward, my tired body won't move. Not even the fear shooting up my spine can give me enough adrenaline to tackle her the way I want to. Exhaustion lies over me like a sodden blanket.

Her fingers are still scrabbling at the gun, panic in her rich green-brown eyes. "We have to get out of here."

I just blink, puzzled by her use of the plural.

"The Wends," she says. "They're coming."

I'm so baffled all I can do is echo, "The Wends?"

"*Yes.*" Her pitch rises. "They'll kill us. Kill us and eat us."

I have no idea what she's talking about. But the fear in her voice is obvious, and my heart skips its beats.

"Go, then," I say. I almost ask: *Why are you bothering with me?*

The sound of her tracker flutters in my ear. For a brief moment I entertain the hope that the tracker is still online, that the cameras will find me now. But when I listen, I still hear nothing. Just the link between whatever's left of my comms system and the pulsing chip in her throat. The Lamb swallows.

"I can't do it," she whispers.

"Just pull the trigger. I was lying before. You don't have to cock it."

I don't know what a Wend is, but I'd rather die cleanly with a bullet to the brain than be torn to pieces and eaten.

"No, I mean . . ." She draws in a shaking breath. "I can't run anymore. They're too fast. There are too many of them."

My sluggish brain finally catches on to the fact that she's by herself. I stay silent for a moment, waiting for her brother to burst through the trees, but he doesn't. The Lamb is just as alone as I am. And judging from the tears in her eyes, her ripped jacket and blood-streaked face, I can guess that their parting wasn't peaceful.

"They're coming," she goes on hoarsely. "Can you—can you smell them?"

My sense of smell is tainted by the iron tinge of blood on my tongue and the leftover bile in my throat. With one hand still braced on the tree trunk, I push myself up to a standing position. I reach out my other arm, even as it shakes.

"Give me the rifle," I say.

At once, her eyes harden. She clutches the gun to her chest.

"Listen." I can't exactly blame her for not trusting me, so I soften my voice. "You don't know how to use it. But I do. I'll kill the . . . the Wends. If you help me get somewhere safe."

Every atom in my body resists using the word *help*. The Lamb doesn't move. Her gaze is reproachful.

"I'm not going to kill you," I say.

And I'm not. The realization comes to me at the same time I say it aloud. I can't kill her, not now, not yet. I *do* need her help. I can barely walk on my own. But more important, the cameras are gone. If I kill her off-screen, it won't count. Azrael will mark it as a failure. After all, what's the point of a Gauntlet without the spectacle?

I have to keep her alive until I can make sure the cameras are on and the world is watching. Then I'll slit her throat or bury a bullet in her brain. I'll give her the most lurid death I can imagine. It'll play over and over again, on every holoscreen in New Amsterdam. They'll forget her name, maybe even mine, too, but they'll remember the arc of my blade and the spray of her blood.

The Lamb's eyes waver. Her body is tensed, shoulders raised, but I can sense the exhaustion beneath her stiff posture.

"I won't kill you," I say again. I stretch out my hand even farther, fingers reaching. "I promise."

Moments pass, like drops of rain from damp leaves. The wind picks up, making her dark hair ripple around her face.

Then, without a word, she reaches toward me. She joins our hands and laces our fingers. And then she slides the rifle into my arms.

THIRTEEN

INESA

The Angel's hand is as cold as naked bone. There's no warmth at all radiating through her black gloves. As soon as she has the rifle, she lets go of me and slings the gun over her shoulder. But her movements are jerky, sluggish. Nothing like the fluid way she threw her knife, pinning Luka to the tree, or the way she landed on the car like a mountain cat dropping onto its prey.

She could be pretending. Playing at weakness so that when I turn my back, she can put a bullet through my heart. The possibility doesn't escape me. But I've weighed the risks. Run through it all in my mind. Without Luka, I don't stand a chance against the Wends. I can't allow myself to imagine him dead. If I do, I'll crumble.

The Angel staggers forward, legs trembling under her own weight. Her steps are uneven. If she is pretending, she's very committed to the performance. I notice the bruising on her temple where Luka hit her. It's a slow-spreading purple, almost black.

If Luka's blow had landed with just a little more force, it

might have killed her. All of this would have been over. But if Luka couldn't bring himself to do it, I don't know if I'll ever find the strength.

Helplessness turns my stomach hollow. Because now, with Luka gone, I know this is what it will take. The Gauntlet will only end with a death—hers or mine. And I'll have to be the one to strike the blow.

"Where are they coming from?" the Angel asks, voice low. "The . . . Wends?"

I gesture behind me, to the unmoving brush. "They were chasing me. I only lost them because I fell down a ravine."

She looks at me with her lips pursed. When I say it out loud, I'm embarrassed. But why bother trying to pretend I'm strong or competent? She knows I'm weak, ill-equipped for any of this, helpless and hopeless without Luka. After all, she's almost killed me. Twice.

Almost. I remember the odd way her expression shifted when she leaned over me, pressing down hard on my throat. There was fear on her face, surfacing like a silver-backed fish from the water. She had let go. I know I didn't imagine it. The sudden relief of pressure on my throat. The widening of her eye—her real eye—in horror.

Even so, I wouldn't be alive without Luka. Thinking of him makes a flash of tears well up.

You might never see him again. The Wends might have already ripped him limb from limb.

I try to push the thought out of my mind. If I'm going to make it through the Gauntlet, I have to believe that Luka is okay. He's stronger than me. He can survive.

"Then let's get as far away as we can," the Angel says. "Quickly."

But she doesn't move. She just stands there, trembling slightly. I notice again how pale her face is, impossibly pale. A reminder that no matter how fragile she seems, the stories are true: The Angels are more machine than human, designed only to kill.

I start off in the opposite direction I ran from—my best guess at north. The Angel follows, her footsteps dragging in the dirt. Hearing them, I grind to a halt.

"I'm not going to walk in front of you," I say. "I'm not that stupid."

Her eyes flash. Well, one of them. The left one, the one that's black from end to end, just throws my reflection back at me.

"Fine," she says. "Then tell me where to go."

I try to imbue my voice with confidence. "This way."

She walks forward with agonizing sluggishness. I keep my gaze fixed on the rifle slung over her back. Her narrow shoulders are pinched together, and under her skintight black suit, I can see the outline of every bone. Her painful-looking thinness didn't occur to me when I was pressed to the ground beneath her, her cold hands around my throat.

"What happened to you?" I ask. The question just spills out before I can stop it.

The Angel turns, her eyes narrowed. "You tried to kill me."

"That wasn't me," I protest. "That was Luka. And you tried to kill me first."

She just stares back balefully. I feel five inches tall.

"Well, you're still alive," I say.

"So are you."

We lapse back into silence, but the air between us crackles. I shouldn't waste time with conversation. I should be focused on not getting eaten alive.

Just make it through. Get back to Luka. Then you can—

I squeeze my eyes shut briefly, as if to banish the thought. I don't want to imagine it. Killing her. It makes my stomach turn. I just have to hope that when the time comes, I'll find the strength to plunge the knife in.

Vaguely nauseated, I follow the Angel out of the clearing. It feels like we're wading through swamp water. If I had any doubt she was faking her frailty, it's gone now. She's practically dragging herself forward, one aching step at a time. I can hear her labored breathing, even the gritting of her teeth.

This has to be something worse than a head injury. Not that I'm an expert, and not that I think she would tell me the truth, if I did ask. So I just follow, with the same brutal slowness.

We're barely more than a hundred yards from the clearing when she falls. It happens so suddenly that I nearly trip over her as she crumples to her knees in the dirt.

The Angel gives a small, pained exhale. Her hair, loose from its high, neat ponytail, falls over her shoulders in tangled strands. I don't know what comes over me—*instinct*, I tell myself, *nothing more*—but I drop to my knees beside her.

"Here," I say. I drape one of her thin arms over my shoulders. "Come on."

Even now, her real eye flickers with suspicion. I half expect her to shove me off. But instead she just hangs on to me limply as I haul us both back to our feet.

As her grip on my neck tightens, I'm aware of how easy it would be for her to start squeezing. My throat is still an unending pulse of pain, garishly purple. But I only feel a faint fluttering of fear. It's not that I trust her, not really. If she were strong enough, she'd probably try.

Her body feels as limp as a cut sapling. I realize, very abruptly, that if it came to blows, I could win.

She knows it, too. That's why she tenses around me, jaw clenched, muscles tightening in her throat.

After we've hobbled a few steps, I blurt out, "This isn't just because of Luka, is it?"

Her gaze clips to me, cold as quicksilver. "No."

"Then what happened?"

She lets out a breath. "Withdrawal. From stimulants." When I stare back at her blankly, she adds, "Drugs."

"I know that." My mother has taken every medication in Caerus's arsenal, including the little white mood-elevating pills we call lifters. They didn't make her happy, though. Just paranoid. She kept scratching at her skin, accusing me of stealing food from her, accusing Luka of planning to leave her.

There's also a fairly active black market trade for drugs in the outlying Counties. It's not so bad in Esopus, but in Schuyler, the town across the reservoir, the pills move like flotsam down the flooded streets. I've seen the twitchy, glassy-eyed, cold-sweat withdrawals. I just never imagined people in the City abused them, too, much less the Angels.

It makes sense, though. The lifters give powerful but temporary bursts of energy. Enough energy for the Angels to execute their quick and ruthless kills.

"I guess I just assumed you were powered by batteries, not pills."

She blinks at me. "Is that really what you Outliers think?"

Oddly, there's no judgment in her voice, just curiosity. Still, my face flushes. "To us you seem like machines."

"You haven't seen real Caerus machines."

Again, her tone isn't harsh. It's flat. Observational. She has a heavy City accent, suggesting that she grew up speaking Damish as a first language. Only the most elite City dwellers do. She's probably thinking that I have a thick Outlier accent, coarse and provincial.

"What do they look like?" I ask.

Her real eye fixes somewhere in the distance, over my left shoulder. "Nothing like people."

It feels surreal that I'm having a conversation with an Angel and she's not actively trying to slit my throat. We stumble on a bit farther. I can tell, sort of, from the moss and the position of the sun, that we are heading vaguely north. I don't exactly have a plan except to put as much distance between us and the Wends as possible.

But I'm very aware of the fact that the farther I get from the Wends, the farther I am from where I last saw Luka. A lump invades my throat. It's hard not to feel like I've made a stupid and traitorous choice: the Angel over my own brother.

Just survive. Then you can find him.

I repeat the words in a steady rhythm in my mind as I shuffle through the mud and the dead leaves, the Angel's arm braced over my shoulders. But we don't even make it another ten yards before the wind picks up, feathering the Angel's pale hair across my face and carrying the smell of rot, thick and pungent as smoke.

FOURTEEN

MELINOË

I smell it now: the scent of decaying flesh. In my current state, it's enough to make my gorge rise, and I have to swallow down the bile that fills my throat.

The Lamb stops dead. For a moment, neither of us even dares to breathe. I tighten my grip on her shoulder—an instinct that makes me even more nauseous, repulsed by my own weakness.

The moment the cameras are back on, I tell myself, *I'm putting a bullet between her eyes.*

But right now there are more pressing matters to worry about.

There's the low sound of leaves rustling, something moving among the trees just beyond the clearing. The Lamb's hold on me loosens, as if she's thinking of dropping me to the ground and just running. I wouldn't blame her. But then it tightens again. I'm amazed by how warm she is, still—the heat of her body bleeding through my damp hunting suit.

"They're coming," she whispers hoarsely.

With all the strength I can muster, I jerk the rifle up, bracing it on my shoulder. I need my other arm to steady it. So I slide myself free of the Lamb and hold the gun aloft. My knees tremble. My vision darkens at the corners.

But then the Lamb's arms are braced around my waist. She holds me upright, hunching down so my upper body has free range of motion. We both tense. I can't help but resist it, her touch. I can feel her pulse against my thigh, beating in time with her tracker and with my own heart.

I don't want to feel it—any of it. I don't want any reminders that she's human or that I'm going to be the one to make her heart-beat stop.

The Lamb's fingers curl, nails digging into my hunting suit. I know I disgust her, the frigid, half-human creature that I am.

To us you seem like machines.

The rot smell grows stronger until it has a weight, the air growing thick and close. I shudder, and the rifle shudders with me, my eye briefly losing the scope. I pretend that I'm back at the shooting range, nothing but silicone torsos staring emptily back at me, Azrael watching from behind the two-way glass.

But the thing that bursts into the clearing is anything but lifeless. It's a snarling mass of mottled gray skin and flailing limbs. It snarls, guttural and rasping, a sound no human could make.

It's a good thing my first instinct is always to shoot. I pull the trigger and within an instant, the creature crumples. There's only a high-pitched whine as it dies, scrabbling pitifully at the mud and the leaf pulp.

The Lamb lets out a breath. I feel her shoulders slump, but her grip on my waist is still tight.

In the silence, I peer at the creature. In death, it's easier to see how it resembles a human: the same-shaped limbs, covered in a waxy gray skin, bones pushing tautly through. The face, still mostly recognizable, though transfigured by a grimace of pain.

But when I look closer, I see the little things that are off. Wrong. It has too many fingers on its left hand. There's a pale webbing of flesh between them, delicate and translucent. Along the side of its neck is a faint patterning of scales, shimmering even in the weak light.

"What is it?" I ask, repulsed.

"A Wend." The Lamb inches slightly closer to me. Her cheek is a breath away from my rib cage. "Some people try to live off the grid—the Caerus grid. So they go into the woods and they start eating the mutations. It changes them. Their appearance. Their . . . appetites."

I stare down at the slumped pile of bones and rotted skin. "Mutations?"

"Yeah." She blinks up at me. "You know, the deer with webbed feet or third eyes. The birds with scaled wings. They're everywhere. They outcompete the ordinary animals. That's what Luka and I do in our shop. We hunt the ordinary animals and stuff them, so they'll be preserved, even when they go extinct in the wild."

"I've never seen them before."

"Really?" Her mouth hangs open, just slightly.

"They're not roaming the streets of the City, if that's what you mean."

"No." A flush tints her cheeks, illuminating a subtle scattering of freckles. "I just figured—on your . . . hunts."

I press my lips shut. I'm not going to confess that I've never been on a Gauntlet that lasted so long or took me so far into the unmarked wilds of the outlying Counties. I never expected an Outlier to make me feel naive, unworldly. But I feel an odd and unaccountable pull of curiosity.

I want her to keep talking.

But neither of us gets the chance to say more. All of a sudden, the clearing is flooded. Wends are lurching through the brush, grasping and growling. Some of them crawl on all fours, their spines arched like cats. Revulsion climbs from my stomach to my throat, more powerful than even fear. It's the revulsion that moves my rifle, sends bullets sliding cleanly through the barrel and burying themselves in the Wends' mangled bodies.

One in the throat. Another in the temple. These are killing places, sites of instant death. A feeling of calm overtakes me as I shoot, banishing the nausea and the cold sweat of withdrawal. This is what I was made for.

Blood, more black than red, splatters the earth. A numbing silence clouds my senses, like cotton crowding my ears, insulating me from the smell of decay and the sounds of choking and howling.

Something pierces through the silence. A very human cry.

One of the Wends has survived. It's grasping at the hem of the Lamb's jacket, yanking her down and dragging her across the forest floor. She thrashes and kicks as it sinks its sharpened nails into her thigh. Clambering up her body like a vine on a tree.

Her eyes are flung open in horror as its foaming mouth hovers above her throat.

My gunshot cracks the air.

The Wend collapses, arms and legs folding in on themselves. Gagging, the Lamb shoves its limp corpse off her. Her chest rises and falls in short, panicked breaths. Tears shine in the corners of her eyes.

Then her gaze lifts to mine. I can see the deep-earth shade of her irises perfectly—not quite green, not quite brown. A color I don't have a name for.

"Thank you," she says softly.

The wooziness is returning, and I don't trust my voice not to shake. I just nod.

The Lamb gets to her feet, panting, hair strewn wildly about her face. It's dark brown, somehow both soft and deep. She brushes it back with shaking hands.

I don't tell her the truth. I can barely even admit it to myself. Instead it hardens inside me like a pearl, this shameful secret. It would have been easy to let her die like this. Azrael wouldn't have blamed me—neither of us had prepared for the Wends. But I never once considered letting them kill her.

FIFTEEN

INESA

The clearing is littered with the bodies of the Wends, some of them still twitching. Hideous, gray, rotting things that had looked half dead even when they were alive. The smell that clouds the air is thick and oily enough to taste.

A few of them, including the one that nearly killed me, still have their eyes open. On its back, gaze flung skyward, the last thing it saw were the gauzy gray-blue clouds, speared through with thin beams of sunlight. I wonder if its mind was too far gone, or if it could still recognize this as something beautiful.

Luka thinks I'm crazy for believing that anything about this world is beautiful, from the vivid, irradiated sunsets to the reflection of the moon on the murky reservoir. If he were here, he would tell me I'm insane for feeling a knot of pity in my stomach for the Wends. Why should I feel anything but hate and revulsion for these barely human creatures, creatures that almost tore out my throat with their teeth?

Beside me, the Angel sways on her feet. The rifle has slipped from her grasp, the exertion of the past few minutes overpowering her at last. Instinctively, I move to catch her, and manage to grab her arm before she collapses.

"I'm fine," she bites out.

I struggle to sling her arm around my shoulders. "You need to rest."

Her eyes shift blearily around the clearing. "Will there be more?"

"I'm not sure." I bite my lip. "I think . . . I think we're safe for now."

The Angel gives a small, tight nod. The bruise that Luka left on her temple looks more black than purple now, darkened with deep, tar-like blood.

"I'm sorry," I blurt out.

As soon as I speak, I realize how absurd I sound. How absurd it is that I'm helping her limp across the clearing instead of running without looking back—or, better yet, sinking my knife into her chest. Well, *her* knife, the one Luka jerked from the tree in the clearing. It would be a tragically ironic, cinematic ending—if only the cameras were here to capture it.

The Angel just stares at me, gaze remarkably steady. Even her left eye, the prosthetic, seems somehow focused. There's a depth to it that I hadn't noticed before. I can see more than just my own reflection.

At last, she says, "I don't blame you." A pause. "Or your brother."

"We all do what we have to do in order to survive."

The response is automatic, conditioned. Dad repeated it so many times that it's engraved in my mind. The law that governs all nature. The law that can be used to justify anything, if you can twist and warp the words to fit. Dad was especially clever about it. I'm sure, in the end, he convinced himself that he left us behind in the name of *survival*.

The Angel blinks slowly. Her white-blond hair falls like a sheet over her shoulder, shimmery as silk, seemingly unaffected by the dense, humid air.

"Yes," she says. "We do."

We stagger through the woods like a single awkward, lurching creature. I'm not even trying to orient myself anymore. I'm too exhausted to pay attention to the placement of the moss or the weakening, watery shafts of sunlight.

Inevitably, the rain picks up again. It's just a light patter at first, gentle, almost soothing. I can imagine myself back in Esopus, tucked into my cot while the rain beats against our tin roof. I can see Luka's shadow through the curtain that divides our beds, silent but steady. Neither of us needed to speak. The air was heavy, and I could feel the pulse of the words that rose in both our chests. *I'm here. I'm here.*

The Angel tenses suddenly, jolting me from the memory. Her head snaps up, panic in her eye.

"We have to get out of here," she says hoarsely. "To shelter."

Her teeth are chattering, and her skin is mottled blue. The abrupt switch in her demeanor unnerves me. I shift my position so

I can get a better grip on her, wrapping my arm more tightly around her waist and dovetailing our fingers together.

I expect her to flinch, but she doesn't. We're both still for what feels like a very long time.

The rain grows almost hopelessly heavier, and the Angel clenches her jaw. I hesitate for just a few more seconds, and then I haul us forward again.

By the grace of some nameless—and otherwise mostly indifferent—god, I spot a cave up ahead, through the unforgiving sheets of rain. As we approach, I realize that *cave* is probably a little generous. It's just an outcropping of rock, offering only a sliver of shelter. But I'll take even the most pathetic miracle.

The sight seems to give the Angel a sudden surge of energy. I've been more or less dragging her, but now she takes deliberate, if shaky, footsteps. When we reach the cave, I give it only the most cursory check for things that might be hiding themselves in the dark, and then we both collapse onto the ground.

The Angel doesn't even bother pushing herself into a sitting position. Instead she just curls up, arms under her head in a makeshift pillow, her long, lithe body going limp. When we were standing it was easy to see she was taller than me by a few inches, but folded like this, she looks tiny. Fragile.

Her lashes flutter. The rain is falling in relentless gouts, and she shivers. I pull my knees to my chest, unsure what to do, my vision blurring with exhaustion.

And then I hear it. Her voice, so faint that the words barely register over the sound of the rushing rain.

"Thank you," she whispers.

She must be delirious with lack of sleep. I must be, too, because I find myself whispering back, "What's your name?"

"Melinoë."

"Melinoë," I repeat. The four syllables dance lightly on my tongue. "I'm Inesa."

"I know," she says.

And then she's gone.

SIXTEEN

MELINOË

My dreams are languid and strange, darkness slurring around me like soiled water. I dream that I'm sinking into a sandpit, slowly, inch by agonizing inch, while a crowd gathers around me and watches. Some of them take photos with their tablets. They jostle and whisper to one another, eyes alight with perverse glee. Azrael is among them.

Please, I try to say, but the words won't come out. *Save me, please, get me out of here.*

The crowd just titters and murmurs. And Azrael looks on, gaze cool. My limbs are glued in place. I know it's a dream because I'm crying, and I haven't been able to do that since I was a child. They're silent, salt-laced tears that taste like blood when they reach my lips.

The Lamb is in my dreams, too. A different dream, this time. We're on the ground in the woods, kneeling face-to-face. I can feel the heavy humidity of the air and the cold, damp leaf pulp beneath us, the water seeping through the fabric of my hunting suit. It all feels real.

She leans forward, until our foreheads are nearly touching, her nose a breath away from mine. The Lamb. Inesa. Her earth-colored eyes gleam, almost giddily, and the corner of her mouth lifts in a smile.

I try to speak, but the words curdle in my throat again.

In a flash, she's on her feet, bounding into the trees. But it's not a fearful flight. And she doesn't go far. She hangs along the edge of the clearing, peeking her head out from behind one of the trees. Her smile widens, as if beckoning me to join her playful chase.

And I want to. My chest burns with how much I want to. But when I rise to stagger toward her, the forest floor falls out from under me. The whole dream shatters like glass.

SEVENTEEN

INESA

In sleep, it's hard to think of her as dangerous. Hard to recall how painfully her hands circled my throat. Hard to remind myself to be afraid.

Even with the bruise darkening her temple and the bloodless pall of her face, she's beautiful. I know that the Angels are supposed to be, but it's still impossible not to notice. The perfect bow of her mouth, the high, taut cheekbones, the brows and lashes surprisingly dark for someone with such pale hair. It falls nearly to her waist, a blond more silver than gold.

My fingers inch across the ground. I want to touch just the ends of it, to see if it's as soft as it looks, but I stop myself. Exhaustion is clearly doing strange things to my brain.

I rub my face with my cold hands, trying to enliven my muscles. My thoughts are racing. I should look for dry wood to start a fire. Who knows if there are more Wends out there. I should take her rifle while she's sleeping and run. Find Luka. I should look for the car with all our gear. I should at least look for clean water, because my throat is as dry as sandpaper and my tongue feels huge and heavy in my mouth.

I should kill her.

The thought slips into my mind so easily, like a key into its lock. The rifle lies beside Melinoë's sleeping body, mere inches from my fingertips. Now that I've watched her use it, I know how easy it is. Brace. Aim. Fire. I could do it.

There's also the knife. Her knife, which Luka passed to me and I slipped inside my boot. I withdraw it now, turning it over in trembling hands. It's lighter than the knives I use in the shop and narrower than Dad's buck knife, the one that Luka carries with him when he hunts. The blade is sharpened to a fine and deadly point. Knives I know intimately, and this one looks both sleek and brutal. Like her.

I grip the handle and shift my body slightly so I'm crouching over her. The blade hovers above her throat. I imagine the cut, the gush of blood. If people bleed as much as animals do, the ground would be soaked with it, my hands covered, her black suit turned blacker. I imagine her eyelids flying open in shock. Her body writhing in the dirt. Her stare glassy as the blood drains into the earth.

The thought turns my stomach into an icy pit. I hurl the knife away from me. It skids across the ground and lands at the very edge of the cave mouth, blade glinting cruelly.

I'm not a murderer. I'm certainly not an executioner. Because that's what it would be—an execution, cold and detached. They say the Angels aren't human, but she looks perfectly human to me now. And I can't force myself to believe that slitting someone's throat in their sleep is an act of survival. I'd like to think even Dad would balk at that. Luka did. He could have shot her or stabbed her, guaranteeing her death. But he's not a murderer, either.

I curl my fingers into fists. I wonder whether the Angel would hesitate, if I was the one sleeping defenselessly beside her. When she was fighting the Wends, she had a thousand chances to turn her gun on me. Or she could have let them kill me. It would have been easier than saving my life.

My head is throbbing. My exhaustion is like black water closing over my head. In the end, the choice is really no choice at all, because my body overrides my brain. I slump over onto the ground, my vision filmy and gray.

The one thing I make sure to do before sleep overcomes me is to lie down facing Melinoë. I place my hand gently against her arm, so that if she wakes up, her movement will jostle me awake, too. That's all I can manage before my eyelids slide shut and I drown.

EIGHTEEN

MELINOË

I wake slowly. Excruciatingly. My eyelids are weighted with lead and every muscle in my body is aching. If I really was a machine, like the Outliers apparently believe, I would be some long-defunct model, dusted off and powered on for the first time in years.

I blink away the film of sleep and look around. It's bright— brighter than I've ever seen it in these woods. Sunlight falls gently through the patchwork of leaves and branches, a deep, pure gold, as if the sky above is cloudless. A cloudless sky in New Amsterdam? Maybe I am still dreaming.

My memory returns to me in increments: the Wends with their rotting gray skin and slavering mouths. The Lamb bracing her arm around my waist, holding me upright. Carrying me. Helping me into the cave. The last thing I remember is my face dive into the dirt.

The Lamb. My eyes open fully and I see her sleeping body next to mine. Her knees are pulled up to her chest and one arm is pillowed beneath her head. Her other arm is stretched out, and her fingertips are—just barely—brushing my arm.

My heart jumps into my throat. I'm sure she didn't mean to touch me. She was probably tossing and turning in her sleep. But the way she's reaching out feels intentional, fingers splayed so they're almost grasping me. Almost.

I want to pull away, but I don't. Instead, I keep my body still and slow my breathing. Rainwater drips from the cave overhang, bright and delicate as beads of dew. A band of sunlight stripes across her face, illuminating the scattered freckles on the bridge of her nose, her long, thick, dark lashes. Her brows are full, with a canny sort of arch that makes her look playful, even in sleep.

It recalls my hazy dream: her peeking out at me from behind the tree, teasing smile on her face. Blood rushes to my cheeks. I jerk my arm against my chest and push myself into a sitting position.

Her eyes fly open instantly. She scrambles backward, away from me, to the opposite side of the cave. Then she stops and draws a breath. We stare at each other, unblinking.

A swallow ticks in her throat. The bruises I left are even more vicious-looking in the light, purple and lurid.

"Just give me a head start," she says at last. Her voice is hoarse.

"What?"

"Before you start hunting me again."

Oh. I push myself up onto my knees. "I'm not going to chase you."

She stiffens. Her hand searches the leaves, and her knuckles whiten as she takes hold of something. The handle of a knife. *My* knife.

"No," I say quickly. "I mean, I'm not going to kill you."

Her brow creases with confusion. "But you have to."

My rifle is right between us, just out of my reach. I could lunge forward and grab it, but she already has the knife, and she would be faster. My body still feels sluggish, my instincts dulled. I don't think I could chase her even if I wanted to.

Slowly, she draws the knife upward, until the hilt is pressed against her chest, blade pointed out. She lets out a trembling breath.

"So kill me, then," I say. "Why don't you?"

"I don't want to." She swallows again, hard. "I don't want to be a murderer."

"You said it yourself—I'm barely human."

"I didn't mean that. I was wrong." Her gaze flicks up and down my body, and red tinges her cheeks. "I'm sorry."

The absurdity of her apologizing to me when my bruises are pulsing on her throat almost makes me laugh.

"I'd rather die quickly than starve to death out here. I'll even show you where to cut."

I'm bluffing, of course. Sort of. With no connection to the Caerus mainframe, only a few days' worth of meal replacement packets in my suit, and no way of navigating out of the woods, the odds of survival aren't exactly in my favor. The only thing I can hope is that Azrael is looking for me. That he'll find me.

Please, that pitiful voice in my mind cries out. *Save me, please, get me out of here.*

"I know where to cut," Inesa says. For the first time, her voice is sharp.

Right. "You're not a murderer, but you have plenty of experience with dead things."

"*Animals.* Not people." She glares at me. "Are you really trying to convince me to kill you?"

"Are you really going to refuse the quickest and easiest way to win your Gauntlet?"

She falls silent. We stare at each other as the seconds pass, punctuated by the trickle of rainwater from the cave overhang. Her eyes shift from green to brown to green again, changing, like nature does all the time.

"Has it ever happened before?" she asks finally. Softly.

Even without elaboration, I know what she means.

"Of course it has. Not often. But there's always a chance. That's what makes the Gauntlet entertaining. The possibility that the roles could reverse. That one of you could kill one of us."

Inesa just watches me, frowning.

"Haven't you ever heard of Mara?"

She shakes her head.

"Mara was an Angel before me. Twelve years ago." I was too young to remember it when it happened, or maybe my original memory has been mangled, cut into pieces, like so many others. But Azrael has forced us to watch the recording of her Gauntlet over and over and over again. "She was . . . a child. Well, not really. She was seventeen, like me. But she was small. She looked younger. So Azrael always sent her on Gauntlets against these enormous, burly men, because the contrast was fascinating. It seemed like it might be an even match."

182

Inesa purses her lips. "I didn't realize so much thought went into it. The . . . the pairings."

"It's never supposed to look like cold brutality." I glance down at my fingers, then back up at Inesa. I can't risk taking my eyes off her for too long. "Azrael works very hard, deciding who to send on which Gauntlet. The optics of it."

"So we're always supposed to believe we have a chance." Inesa's voice is low. "Even when we don't."

I nod.

Silence again. Inesa stares at me intently, but I can't read the emotion in her gaze.

"What happened to Mara?" she asks.

"Exactly what you'd expect to happen, eventually." I press my nails into my palm. "Azrael sent her out on a Gauntlet against some bigger, stronger-looking man. It turns out he actually *was* stronger. He bashed her head in with a rock. So hard you could see the white of her skull. The cameras caught a very good angle of it. Of her brain seeping out between the splinters of bone."

Inesa's face goes pale, then slightly green.

"I'm surprised you haven't seen it before," I say. "The footage is famous."

"I don't like watching them. The Gauntlets." Inesa's gaze drops, but just for a moment. "It's easier to pretend they don't happen. Even when they do."

For some reason, I feel my chest tighten with some emotion— relief? *She hasn't seen my last Gauntlet.* The dead girl, my pitiful breakdown. And maybe that means she never saw the hacked holoboard, projecting my image into the skies with the headline *The Most Hated Face in New Amsterdam*. Maybe, somehow, I'm less of a monster to her than I am to the rest of her kind.

I shouldn't care what she thinks of me. Not when I still have to kill her. I draw in a breath and reply, "Fair enough."

More silence. Inesa's eyes are damp as she looks at me from beneath her lashes.

"Who's Azrael?"

I'm taken aback by the question. It's something I assumed the Outliers knew. Isn't he as famous among them as we Angels are?

"He's our handler," I say. There's a catch in my throat. "He invented the Angel program. He trains us, decides who to send on which Gauntlet. He decides how we're supposed to look and act. And he fixes thing when they go wrong."

The pitifully hopeful part of me is still waiting to hear the faint buzz of the cameras. To hear his voice in my ear. I would even take his anger, his disappointment, if it meant he would save me.

"When things go wrong," Inesa repeats. "You mean, like when an Angel fails to kill her mark?"

My teeth come together with an audible *click*. Inesa watches me intently.

"I've never failed before," I say. My tone is flat and cold—the way it should have been this whole time.

Inesa's fingers tense around the handle of the knife.

Maybe I should just kill her and be done with it. But I know it wouldn't be over, not really. A Gauntlet that isn't live streamed is just a murder. Quotidian and forgettable. I'm a performer just as much as I am a killer. And I can't perform without an audience.

It's not exactly a novel realization, but in this moment, it hurts. It hurts to know that I'm nothing without Caerus. I'm the creature they made me and nothing more. Just a cold body in a hunting suit.

Another realization, equally painful: I need Caerus, but right now—I need the Lamb, too. Inesa. This is her world. She knows about the Wends and the mutations, how to survive in this drowning, irradiated wasteland. I won't make it without her.

And she needs me, too. She's useless with a gun, and until she finds her way back to her brother, she's easy prey for anything in these woods. I can see the exhaustion that's gouged black circles under her eyes and the thirst that has turned her lips white, cracked and dry.

We need each other, as much as the thought turns my stomach. And I think she knows it, too.

I reach over, slowly, and unzip the compartment of my suit that contains the meal replacement packets. There are four left. I remove one and hold it out to her. My hand trembles as it breaches the space between us.

"Here," I say. "You must be starving."

NINETEEN

INESA

I never thought any food that came in a vacuum-sealed plastic package could look so appetizing. But the Angel is right, of course. My stomach is so empty that it's gnawing on itself, like a dog chewing on the same old bone.

Still, I hesitate. I would be stupid not to consider that she's offering me poison. But that would make for an anticlimactic ending to what has surely been one of the most exciting Gauntlets in years. I remember what she said about her handler—Azrael—making sure the Gauntlets are gripping, dramatic. If she were planning to kill me, she would try harder to make a spectacle of it.

Besides, I haven't heard the cameras in hours. A sense of wrongness pricks at me. I don't think any of this is going according to Caerus's plan.

Slowly, I reach forward and take the packet. It crinkles in my fingers. Melinoë looks relieved. She almost smiles, but catches herself and thins her lips into a line.

I tear open the packet with my teeth while keeping one hand

braced on the knife. It's nutrient paste, the same kind Luka and I sometimes eat when things are really dire. It has a queasy, jellylike consistency that normally makes my stomach turn. Not this time, though. I suck it all down in a matter of seconds, not caring how feral I look to her.

I crumple the empty packet and squeeze it in my fist. Glancing back at Melinoë, I say, "Thank you."

She nods.

A moment passes. Then she says, "I only have three left."

My stomach drops. Even if we ration ourselves as strictly as possible, it's not enough to last us more than a few days. But maybe that's all I need to find my way back to Luka.

And maybe that's all she needs to kill me.

"What about Azrael?" I ask. "He'll pull you out, if he thinks you're in real danger. Won't he?"

Instantly, her gaze shutters. This whole time, she's barely taken her eyes off me—because she doesn't want to give me a chance with the knife, I'm sure—but now she glances away, to the darkened half of the cave, and says, "Not exactly."

"What do you mean? You said he fixes things when they go wrong."

"When things go wrong that are out of my control." Her voice is cold. "This kind of failure is my fault. *I'm* supposed to fix it."

I stiffen, drawing my shoulders around my ears. Rising up farther onto my knees, knife still gripped in my fist, I consider whether I should make a lunge for the rifle lying between us. Then I decide it's better just to run.

But before I can move, Melinoë says, "Besides, the connection is dead."

This throws me off. "What connection?"

"Between me and the Caerus grid. Ever since your brother hit me here." She delicately touches a finger to her bruised temple. "My comms chip shattered. Even if Azrael wanted to find me—"

She cuts herself off abruptly, glancing over to the dark half of the cave again. With only her black prosthetic eye turned toward me, I can't read the expression on her face.

Is she lying? Trying to lull me into a false sense of security? It would be a pretty elaborate game. And this explains a lot: why she was wandering aimlessly in the woods when I found her. Why she accepted my help instead of killing me. Out here, severed from the Caerus grid, she's as alone as I am.

My voice trembles as I ask, "Do you know how much time is left?"

I wish Dad had left us a watch instead of a broken compass. If, somehow, I manage to survive for the rest of the thirteen days—however long is left—this will all be over, Mom's debt erased. Everything since the beginning of the Gauntlet has felt hazy and unreal; I can't account for the hours. I think at least two cycles of day and night have passed, but really, there's no way to be sure. I should have taken my tablet from the car before running away.

I should have done a lot of things differently.

Melinoë looks down at her arm. She tugs back the sleeve of her hunting suit to reveal a small black-and-white screen affixed to her wrist. It shows four sets of numbers: hours, minutes, seconds, and milliseconds. A countdown. Ticking away the time of my Gauntlet.

She angles her wrist toward me, so I can see: 264 hours.

Too many. My heart plummets with despair.

"What about my tracker?" I ask. I can still hear the hum of it when I stay quiet and listen, but I've grown so accustomed to the sound that it fades into the background if I'm not paying attention. There's something blood-chilling about that realization. That the tracker has become such an innate part of me, as quietly essential as my own heart. "That must still be connected to the grid, right?"

Melinoë shakes her head. "Something must have gone wrong with that, too. You haven't heard the cameras in hours, have you?"

I fall silent, straining my ears. But I still can't pick up their low, whirring hum anywhere. Ever since Luka and I ran from the car, it's been oddly and eerily quiet.

"No," I say. "I haven't heard them in hours, either."

We fall silent again, just for good measure. But there's nothing except the gentle rustling of damp leaves.

"The only thing I can hear now is your tracker." Melinoë's voice is low, as if her words are a confession. For some reason, heat rises to my face.

"I can hear it, too," I say. "When I listen for it."

Her gaze darts away briefly, then lifts to meet mine. "So at least I'll always be able to find you."

The longer this quiet, awkward stalemate lasts, the better it is for me. Melinoë has tugged her sleeve back down to conceal the timer, but as we stare at each other from opposite sides of the cave, I know the seconds of my Gauntlet are ticking away. At any moment she could breach the space between us and close her hands around my throat.

Now I understand what's really stopping her, other than the shaky vestiges of withdrawal. Is a Gauntlet even a Gauntlet if it's not live streamed? Killing me off camera probably violates the terms and conditions.

If no one watched me die, the audience would feel outraged, and Caerus would be humiliated. They're probably scrambling behind the scenes right now, because here's proof that their system isn't perfect. There are gaps in their control, large enough for someone like me to slip through.

"They have to be able to fix the connection soon," I murmur.

"I don't know." Melinoë rubs her temple, as if she's feeling for the pieces of her shattered comms chip. "Nothing like this has ever happened before."

"Is there a protocol? Did Azrael ever tell you what to do?"

She shakes her head, just once. She's not much for words, this Angel. It's probably for the best, though. Unaccountably, Mom's voice echoes through my mind: *Inesa, you talk enough for two. You'd go on for hours if no one stopped you.*

Mom must be at least a little right, because I feel a strong compulsion to fill the silence now. "You said you only had three meal packets left. He must expect you to be finished soon."

"Gauntlets aren't supposed to last longer than a few days. The audience would lose interest."

"Well, it's very generous of you and Azrael to think about the interests of the audience."

The coldness of my voice surprises me, as does the angry knot that forms in my belly. With her saving my life, limping around so pitifully, talking to me like a human being—it's been easy to forget that we're not the same. She grew up in glass skyscrapers and climate-controlled domes, eating as much or as little as she pleased, never worrying about what will happen when the water table rises too high or the last deer is finally dead.

Melinoë's shoulders rise and her gaze grows hard. "Caerus makes the rules. Not me."

"Well, you and your kind benefit from those rules a hell of a lot more than we do."

I don't know how Dad's words, in his exact tone, have snuck into my mouth.

Melinoë doesn't reply. The utter blackness of her stare reminds me of that first night, when she landed on the hood of the car. There was nothing behind her eyes then, not even hate, just the icy, inhuman determination to complete her mission.

But because I never seem to know when to just shut up, I rush on: "You're lucky you were born inside the City instead of out. That's it. Luck. Or else you'd be the one staring down the barrel of a gun."

She blinks. I realize for the first time how rarely she does. Maybe it's a quirk of the prosthetic, or one of her other technologically augmented features. Flat-voiced, she says, "You're the one holding the knife."

I'd almost forgotten. Instinctively, I tighten my grip on the handle.

For the first time, I consider another reason to kill her. One driven by the righteous anger that always burned so brightly and fiercely within Dad, the anger I could never quite bring myself to feel. I think I'm finally starting to.

If I did kill her, I'd be a hero among the Outliers, that's for certain. Dad, wherever he is—if he managed to see it—would be proud. But no matter how easy it is to imagine—*the slash of the blade, the bright red spout of blood*—I can't make myself lunge for her.

Weak. This is why Mom will always choose Luka over me. I'll never have the guts to just drive the knife home. I've had plenty of experience with dead things, but only to mend them. To make them look and feel alive again.

Once I've had the thought, the words just leap out of my mouth.

"How old were you? The first time?"

She doesn't ask me to clarify. Her gaze doesn't even shift as she replies, "Fifteen."

The same age Luka was when he started hunting on his own. I remember the first kill he ever brought to me. A fawn, spindly legged, too green to recognize the scent of a predator and too slow to get away. I looked up taxidermy instructions on the internet. Bought the supplies I'd need. But when it came to the point where the deer was lying across the table and I was standing over it with my carving knife in hand, my gorge rose and I vomited.

"Who was it?" I ask.

"A boy," Melinoë replies.

I just blink at her, feeling that knot of righteous fury tighten in my belly again. "That's it? That's all you can say?"

"We're not supposed to remember."

"What does that mean?"

Finally, a flicker of *something* in her gaze. Not anger. Not grief. Not even a bit of reproach. It's a strange look of longing, and it seems so out of place, I'm certain I imagined it. And then, as quickly as it appeared, it's gone again.

"It makes it easier," she says. "If people had a choice, everyone would choose not to feel."

Revulsion. That's the most powerful emotion that rises in me. I think I can see Luka's side now, understand what he feels when he looks at the mutated animals, the disgust that makes his lip curl. Ugly things that outcompete their weaker counterparts. Even the deer are growing sharp teeth.

"Well," I say at last, "you're lucky that I don't get to choose not to feel. Or else you'd be dead already."

A beat of silence. I think I see her mouth quiver.

"I suppose so."

So here we are, hating each other, repulsed by each other, both standing to gain from the other's demise. And yet—I owe her my life. And she owes me hers.

Debt. Every Outlier knows how dangerous it is. But in Esopus Creek, it's also our only hope. The thing that's keeping us alive but also killing us slowly.

And that's how I find myself saying, "Let's make a deal."

She arches a brow. "A deal?"

"Yes." I draw a breath. "We find our way out of here . . . together. You keep us from getting torn to pieces by the Wends, and I make sure you don't turn into one by eating the wrong meat. And then, once the cameras are back on . . ."

"The Gauntlet begins again?"

Melinoë watches me like a cat, wary. Cats are peculiar animals. Predators to mice, but prey to hawks. And they don't do especially well with water.

"Yes." My voice is scratchy and low. I clear my throat. Then, without wavering, I repeat, "Yes."

And then, so she knows that I mean it, I lower the knife. I place it on the ground between us, equidistant from her reach and mine. I flex my fingers. It hurts to unclench them after being kept in a white-knuckled grip for so long.

Her eyes dart from the knife to me, then back again. I tense. She could grab it in an instant and have me pinned to the ground even faster, blade to my throat—

But she doesn't. Instead, she raises her empty hand, fingers outstretched.

Slowly, I reach back. Our hands are almost the exact same size, and our fingers lace together easily.

"Deal," she says quietly.

"Deal." I squeeze her hand, and she squeezes back.

Strangely, it makes me think of Jacob's kiss. I was acutely

aware of how long it lasted, my stomach clenching as I waited for it to be over. Melinoë's hand is warm and her grip is soft, but certain. Maybe it's just hunger and exhaustion doing odd things to my brain, but I'm surprised by how much I don't want her to let go.

TWENTY

MELINOË

It's done. I let go of Inesa's hand, flexing my fingers. The agreement has been made. Like signing a Caerus contract. Now we sit in silence, staring at each other guardedly. The knife and the gun still lie between us. My gaze skims over them, muscles itching to reach out.

"You should take it," Inesa blurts. "The rifle, I mean. I don't know how to use it."

I nod, still wary. But if she really were planning to spring at me, she's had plenty of better chances to do it. As I reach forward, I feel a prickling in my hand, my skin still humming with the memory of Inesa's touch. The strange heat spreads, and I hope it doesn't reach my face. I don't need her to see me flush.

When I have the rifle in my grip, I'm overcome with relief. Just the smoothness of its barrel, the familiar weight, makes me feel like myself again. Well, like an Angel, at least.

Inesa isn't stupid. As I was reaching for the rifle, she grabbed the knife, slipping it into the shaft of her boot. Mutual assured destruction. It ended—tenuously—decades of war between New England and New Amsterdam, so maybe it will work for us, too.

I meet Inesa's eyes, as if to ask, *Now what?*

She inhales. Then she pushes herself to her feet, brushing the dirt from her knees. "We should get walking, I guess. If you're feeling up to it."

"I'm fine." I don't mean for the words to sound cold, bitten-off, but it's just instinct. I stand up, faltering a bit, which definitely undercuts my point.

Inesa's gaze is concerned. It seems genuine, but I have to remember that it's not concern for my well-being, not really. I'm a sentient weapon to her, just something to keep the Wends and the other dangers of the forest at bay. I should be used to it. I'm just a sentient weapon to Caerus, too.

"Are you sure you're all right?" Inesa asks, brow furrowing.

"Yes," I say curtly.

She doesn't look convinced. "It'll help both of us if we can find a source of water. Unless you somehow have that in your suit, too."

"No. But I have decon-tabs." I feel a surge of unexpected bitterness toward Azrael. Why wouldn't he at least supply me with clean water? And why was I too stupid to think of bringing it myself?

Because it was supposed to be easy. Because it was supposed to be over in a matter of hours. My gaze zeroes in on the bruises around Inesa's throat. If I had only pressed down a little harder—

"That's good," Inesa says. "I think I know where to find something to drink."

She starts out of the cave, beckoning me after her. I follow slowly, still unsteady on my feet. As she steps into the sun, the light casts a dappled pattern on her face, drawing out the flecks of green in her eyes. I freeze for a moment, just watching her.

Inesa pauses, too. "Come on. I'm not going to try to poison you."

"I wasn't worried about that," I bite back, too quickly.

The corner of her mouth twitches. "Then let's go."

That's not what I'm worried about, her killing me. Not anymore. If I unfold my fingers, I can still feel the warmth her hand left behind. And if I close my eyes, I can see her face from my dream, the playful quirk of her lips, the dancing, mischievous gaze. I sling my rifle over my shoulder and blink repeatedly, trying to dispel the images. They're more alarming to me than a knife to the throat.

I stand still and let the coldness seep back into my bones, ice forming a wall around my heart. When the time comes, I know I can still find the strength to kill her.

Inesa is not quite the unflappable navigator I hoped she would be. Once we're out of the cave and into a small clearing, she pauses. Her eyes dart around uncertainly. Then she walks over to a tree and examines its lichen-crusted trunk.

After a few moments, she says, "This way."

"Which way?"

She indicates with her chin. "South."

"Why south?"

"The farther north you get into the outlying Counties, the

wilder the woods are," she says. "We're looking for civilization, right? That means our best bet is south."

It's logical enough. "How do you know which way is south?"

"The way the moss grows on the rocks and the trees," she says. "It's usually on the north side, where it's darker and damper."

The word *usually* doesn't fill me with unreserved faith, but Inesa's tone is assured. "Where did you learn that?"

"My dad." She doesn't look up when she says it, and there's a faint tremor in her voice. "He wasn't good for much, but survival was kind of his specialty."

Her father, the one who fell off Caerus's grid. Or maybe jumped off. I don't want to let Inesa know I've been briefed on her background; I feel creepy, suddenly, carrying around secrets I shouldn't have. Secrets that should be hers to keep. But Caerus sees everything, and through them, so do I.

We walk without speaking for a while, under the deep-green canopy, through the clutter of fallen leaves and the damp soil. Now that the withdrawal has mostly passed and my exhaustion has ebbed, the moist air doesn't feel quite so oppressive. There's a strange clarity to it, a coolness that isn't artificial, like what we breathe inside the City buildings. No air conditioners rattling away in the background—just the trees, quietly and gently stretching their branches over our heads.

Inesa stops so suddenly that I have to skid to a halt to avoid crashing into her. She crouches down and says, "Look."

I squint over her shoulder, but I don't see anything except mud and mashed leaves. "What?"

"Deer tracks," she says triumphantly. "That means they're close. And if they're close, water is nearby, too. Every creature needs to drink, so animals tend to stick near a source of water."

I would never have noticed the small indentation in the earth, and I certainly wouldn't have identified it as evidence of animal life. Studying it carefully, I can make out the vague outline of a hoof. Maybe. But then it stretches outward, in five odd, uneven points.

"It doesn't look like a deer print," I say at last.

"Most of the deer don't have hooves anymore," Inesa says. "They're mutations. They have webbed feet. Even scales, some of them."

The idea of a deer with scales and webbed feet makes my skin chill. "I'm not eating one of those."

And, then, unexpectedly, Inesa laughs. It's a clear, bright sound, like water from a spout. "No, that would be a bad idea."

"You said that's how the Wends become Wends." I can hazily recall the conversation we had before I passed out, when the withdrawal was still clouding my senses. "By eating the mutations."

She nods.

"And you said the mutations are outcompeting the unchanged animals," I say. "So the Wends must be outcompeting people."

Inesa doesn't reply. She glances away from me, casting her gaze around the clearing. Her eyes are shining and slightly damp, but they're elsewhere. Watching something that's invisible to me. Replaying a memory I wasn't briefed on. A secret she's managed to keep.

After a few moments, she turns back and says, "We'll see."

———

We don't talk for another long bout. Inesa dutifully follows the deer tracks, and I dutifully follow her. My tongue is thick and fuzzy in my mouth, and my throat is hollow with horrible, scraping thirst. I'm almost tempted to start licking rainwater off the leaves, but I have a feeling that that, like everything else, is contaminated. It seems perverse and cruel that anyone could die of thirst here in the outlying Counties, in the drowning world.

Inesa pauses, less abruptly this time. She falls silent, her gaze traveling slowly over the nearby trees and rocks. Before I can ask what's wrong, she puts a finger meaningfully to her lips.

And then, in the silence, I hear it: trickling water. It's faint, but unmistakable. My knees go weak with relief.

We walk on for a few moments more, and then, mercifully, we reach a small stream. It's a tiny furrow carved into the earth, and again, I'm not sure I would have noticed it on my own. It burbles softly as it runs over tree roots and its bed of gray stones. I'm surprised by how clear the water looks—but maybe that's just my own wishful thinking.

Then I make a gutting realization. "I don't have anything to drink it from."

As tempting as it is, scooping the water up with my hands is not an option. It *looks* clear, but I don't trust that the water is potable. It'll need a few fizzling decon-tabs before we can drink it without worrying about bacteria, or worse.

Inesa frowns. She casts her gaze around the area again. Then she says, "Wait here."

I do, staring longingly down at the stream at first, and then letting my eyes creep over toward her. She's on her knees, rooting around in the fallen leaves. Her dark hair is tumbling over her shoulders in loose, unruly waves. I suddenly become self-conscious about my own hair and take the opportunity to pull it back into its usual sleek ponytail, leaving no strands to flutter around my face. It should make me feel better, more like myself, but instead I just feel stranger. More out of place.

Inesa gets to her feet, holding something up with a pleased expression. It's just a piece of wood. Part of a fallen tree, by the looks of it, spongy and slightly porous with termite erosion. She doesn't wait for me to question her; she just removes my knife from the shaft of her boot and starts sawing at the wood.

It bothers me a little bit to see my knife, with its artfully honed black steel blade, used for such ignoble purposes. But I'm not in any position to be sentimental. Carefully, Inesa whittles away at the piece of wood, curly slivers falling to the ground. Her brow is furrowed with concentration, and when she clenches her jaw, a small dimple appears in her left cheek.

I'm annoyed at myself for noticing that.

Finally, she manages to carve a distinct depression in the wood, a smooth indentation deep enough for water to settle. It would be a bit too generous to call it a bowl, but it will get the job done.

I can't bite back my curiosity. "How did you learn to do that?" If she can handle a knife this well, maybe I have more to fear than I thought.

"Dad again," she says.

I picture her father's face on the holoscreen, the defiance

burning in his gaze. I shouldn't say anything, but this time, the words seem to just spill out before I can stop them.

"I heard he was gone," I say, trying to keep my tone light.

Surprise briefly flickers across Inesa's face. "I suppose you know everything about me, don't you."

"Just what Caerus was able to compile." Unaccountably, heat begins to creep up my cheeks. "Just what Azrael needed to create a narrative."

Inesa arches a brow. "So what was his narrative about me?"

Shame forms a knot in my stomach. When I speak, I fumble over my words.

"Well, the audience likes an element of tragedy. So with your missing father, and your sick mother . . ." I pause. "And then your relationship with your brother; that was a key selling point, too. The audience is also, well . . . shallow. The fact that you look like— that you're so pretty . . ."

My voice drops off. My face is burning.

The corner of Inesa's mouth twitches. There's a faint flush painting her cheeks, deepening her freckles. After a moment, she says, "That's very shrewd of him."

I just nod, wishing Caerus had taken away my ability to blush entirely.

We fall silent for a few moments. There's something charged in the air, like the static around a circuit board. Inesa's fingers tighten around the bowl.

"So you really don't know where he is, either?" she asks quietly.

It takes me a second to realize she's talking about her father.

I'm not sure why, but the question makes me feel bereft. Like I've lost something I'm not sure I even had in the first place.

"No," I reply. "There's been no activity on his account. If he were dead, Azrael figured you would have applied for a death certificate. To be eligible for benefits."

Inesa's mouth tightens. "You can't apply for a death certificate without a body. We just woke up one morning and he was gone."

The tremor in her voice seems to ripple the air itself. I don't probe any further.

Inesa crouches down beside the creek and tries to scoop up some water, but the bowl is shallow and hard to fill. After a few increasingly frustrated tries, she sets the bowl aside and takes something out of her pocket. It's a piece of metal, small and scuffed, and it glints in the sunlight.

"What is that?"

"A compass. Well, part of one." Inesa's gaze is fixed on it. "One of the more useless things we inherited from Dad. Luka has the other half."

She uses the broken piece to scoop up water from the stream and fill the bowl. Though its construction was slapdash, the bowl works well: No water leaks out from the wood as she lifts it from the ground.

I remove the decon-tabs from a pocket of my suit. It's not much water, and I can't afford to be wasteful with them, so I only put one in. It fizzes for a few seconds before it dissolves, leaving the water slightly carbonated.

Inesa holds out the bowl with two hands. "You first."

Considering she's the one who found the stream and made the bowl, it seems unfair. "No, you."

Her eyes gleam. "Afraid I'm poisoning you?"

"No." My skin prickles with heat. "Okay. Fine."

I take the bowl from her and tilt it to my mouth. Cool water trickles down my parched throat, and almost immediately I feel woozy with relief. My instincts tell me to gulp it all down, remorselessly, but Inesa is waiting, so I ration my sips.

Somewhat reluctantly, I offer the half-filled bowl back to her.

She puts the compass case away, so both of her hands are free, then takes the bowl. While she drinks, I watch her. I find myself oddly fascinated by the way her throat pulses when she swallows, distorting the garish bruises that are turning from red to violet. When I remember how I touched her there, I feel a jolt of heat.

My temple throbs, reminding me of the thrust of the rifle against it. Finally, I bring myself to ask the question that's been on my tongue since we first ran into each other in the woods.

"What happened to your brother?"

Slowly, Inesa lowers the bowl. There are a few beads of moisture clinging to her lips, and she wipes them away. My heart does an odd little stutter in my chest.

"I told you," she says at last, "we got separated when the Wends were chasing us."

The bowl has been completely drained. Inesa takes out the compass piece again to refill it. Wind comes shuddering through the trees, lifting my hair and making goose bumps rise on the back of my neck.

Inesa looks up at me from under her lashes.

"I'm going to find him," she says. "I don't care how long it takes. I know he's looking for me, too."

I don't reply. There's a sheen of pain in her eyes, but underneath it there's determination, fierce and bright. I wonder if there's anyone in the world I love enough to never give up on. To follow to the end of the world. Maybe Keres, but she doesn't see me anymore. I'd be chasing a ghost. Azrael? He's looking for me. He must be. But I don't know if he's looking for Melinoë, because he can't bear to lose her, or for his perfect Angel, his most adept creation—and is there any difference between the two?

Inesa might be chasing a ghost herself. Luka could very well be dead, and we're both aware of it, though it doesn't bear speaking aloud. I should hope for my own sake that he is. But when I look into Inesa's burning gaze, there's a tiny flare in my own chest to match it.

I try to stamp it out as quickly as it sparks to life. We drink our fill of water in silence, though I never quite manage to return my heart to a steady rhythm. And, as always, there's the hum of her tracker, pulsing faithfully alongside it.

TWENTY-ONE

INESA

The crackling ache in my throat is gone, my muscles are strong instead of shaky, and my eyes are fully open for what feels like the first time in days. Even the sunlight seems brighter as it breaches the canopy of leaves, warm and pale yellow. I stand still for a moment, tilting my face toward the slashes of unobstructed sky.

I don't let myself bask too long, though. Melinoë is watching me.

If the sunlight is coaxing me back to life like a wilted flower, it's having quite a different effect on her. Her shoulders are raised up around her ears, her body tensed and gaze narrowed. It gives her the appearance of a wary cat, not even trusting the impartial brightness of the sun. I remember thinking of her as spidery, when she first dropped onto the hood of the car, her long, thin limbs clad in black, her eyes wide-set and night-dark. Now I can't shake the feline aura she exudes.

"Are you feeling better?" I ask. It still feels like an absurd thing to say, considering we were quite literally at each other's throats no more than a day ago.

She gives a stiff, tight nod.

"Okay, then." I draw a breath. "We should probably go."

Another silent nod. The compass case has gone back into my pocket, and I decide to bring the bowl with me as well. It will save me the trouble of having to whittle another one later. Her knife is made of more expensive materials than our entire house on Little Schoharie Lane, but it's very much a killing tool, not a crafting one. Made for carving flesh, not wood.

I put that in my pocket, too. Melinoë's gaze follows my hand as I do.

You're not getting it back, I almost tell her. *I may not be much of a fighter, but I'm no fool.*

Her eyes flicker to my face again. "Which way?"

"Following the stream." I indicate it with my chin. "Eventually it will take us to a lake or a river. And where there's water, there's civilization."

I'd stick close to the stream anyway. Just in case I'm wrong, I don't want to be too far away from our only source of water. The animals will stay by the stream, too, which will make hunting easier when we exhaust our meager supply of nutrition paste.

Plus, Luka is also smart enough to seek out a source of water. If he's nearby, he'll find the same stream. Melinoë doesn't have to know what I'm thinking.

I try to let the idea of seeing him again lift my spirits, but my stomach is hollow with hopelessness. Over and over again I see his face in my mind, stricken with horror, screaming my name.

He's alive, I tell myself firmly. *He has to be.* If I'm still here, as weak and inept as I am, Luka has survived, too. He's always been better, stronger than me.

Melinoë and I end up walking side by side, neither of us willing to turn our back to the other. The silence that stretches between us isn't quite companionable, but it isn't hostile, either. Melinoë keeps her head down, though occasionally her eyes dart over to me, both the real one and the fake one. I realize that I've started to not even notice her prosthetic. It just seems like such a natural part of her.

"Did Azrael put that in?" I blurt out, and almost clap my hand over my mouth. What a presumptuous question to ask someone who knows three dozen different ways to kill me.

But Melinoë doesn't look offended. She lifts a finger to her cheekbone, right below the false eye. "We have them implanted when we're children."

Her voice, as usual, betrays nothing, but the way she touches her face seems self-conscious.

"Sorry," I say. "I didn't mean to pry."

"It's okay," she says, and then lapses back into silence.

I'm left with the image of a child strapped down on an operating table, sharp medical tools hovering over their face. I'm sure the process was brisk, anesthetized, and clean. But I can't dispel the barbarity of it. The idea of going to sleep and waking up with such an essential piece of you ripped away and replaced.

"Did it hurt?" I ask softly.

Another too-probing question. Melinoë stops walking. The wind lifts the long strands of her ponytail and makes her white hair shiver around her face. I stop, too, and just watch her. Beautiful and pale, she's too bright in this world of muted browns and greens.

She's silent for so long that I give up on her answering, and start to turn around again, but then—her voice.

Quietly, without looking over at me, she says, "Yes."

The forest changes around us. It's subtle, but not below my attention. The trees are thinning. White birches begin to emerge among the thick deciduous brush, like slashes of light. More of the sky shows through the canopy, larger swaths of gray-tinged blue. I hope this means we're getting close to the edge of the woods. Close to civilization.

At the same time, I hope we're not. Because the minute the cameras click on again, Melinoë will have her rifle drawn and I'll be staring down the barrel with nothing but a flimsy knife in my hand. Maybe I can convince her to at least give me a head start.

Or maybe we'll find Luka first.

Just as I feel a flicker of hope kindle in my chest, a branch cracks nearby. I stop instantly, boots skidding in the dirt.

Melinoë heard it, too. She pauses, fists clenched at her sides, so still she looks almost lifeless.

I inhale, searching for the scent of rotting meat, but I don't find it. Not a Wend, then. I'm not quite optimistic enough to imagine that it's another person, appearing to lead us triumphantly to civilization.

Another twig snap. For some reason, I have to restrain myself from reaching out to Melinoë. I don't even know what it would achieve, to touch her. I just want to.

The leaves rustle, and then a flash of brown and white darts out from the brush. Before I can react, before I can even register that it's a deer, Melinoë's rifle is lifted. The bullet cracks the air. The deer gives a plaintive honk and then collapses in the dirt, limbs spasming for a moment before going still.

I let out a breath, half shock and half relief. Warily, Melinoë lowers her gun.

"It's just a deer," I say.

Very slowly, I walk over and examine it. Melinoë follows. It's definitely dead, but there's almost no blood—her bullet went right through its eye. Its tawny fur is matted and damp-looking, with a shimmery pattern of scales emerging on its chest. Its antlers are draped with moss. And where its hooves should be are webbed feet instead, only lumpy and misshapen, the transformation not quite complete.

"A mutation?" Melinoë asks.

I nod.

I've seen a hundred of them before. Luka doesn't kill them, because there's no point in wasting the bullets, but every so often a group of men in Esopus will round themselves up and go hunting for mutations. Obviously there's no eating the meat, and the pelts are usually too disfigured to do anything with, either, the antlers too yellowed and ugly to display. But it's an exercise in camaraderie, one of the rare times that people from Upper Esopus and Lower Esopus voluntarily mingle, bound by a shared purpose.

More than that, it's a release. A necessary one. All the small, daily humiliations people face eventually build up and harden into rage, and it's better to take that anger out on mutated deer than on each other. The more powerless you are, the better any shred of power tastes. It's like taking a lifter.

"Oh," I say suddenly. "Oh, no."

Melinoë's head snaps up. "What?"

"The scent of the kill will draw the Wends here." The thought sets my hands shaking. "I've heard they can smell fresh meat from miles away."

Melinoë draws a breath. "I shouldn't have killed it. It was just instinct."

"It's okay. You didn't know." I stand up straight, drawing in a breath of my own. "It just means we should get out of here—fast."

After the hunts, the men pile up all the deer and set their bodies alight, precisely so the smell doesn't attract the Wends. I can build a decent fire of my own, given enough time, but we don't have that time. The Wends could be on us in minutes.

I zip my jacket up to my throat, because the rare sunlight is already waning, and set off at a quicker pace, almost a jog. But I don't get far before I realize Melinoë isn't following me.

I turn around. "What is it?"

She's staring down at the deer's body, eyes oddly unfocused. A small furrow emerges in her forehead, marring a face that is otherwise as smooth and flawless as marble.

"I'm sorry," she says. Her voice is low and distant, like an echo of itself. "It was just instinct."

TWENTY-TWO

MELINOË

On the move again. My muscles are still twinging. Even now that the worst of the withdrawal has passed, running isn't exactly easy, and my ribs feel like they're going to crack. After a few moments of breathless scampering through the brush, I realize this is the first time in my life that I've been the one being chased. Hunted. I've only ever been on the other side. I've only ever been the thing people are running *from*.

I still manage to keep pace with Inesa. I would be embarrassed if I couldn't. She surprises me by having decent stamina, if not being particularly fast. The earth seems to roll steadily under her feet, as if it's carrying her. Meanwhile, the ground seems to sense that I'm an intruder in this world and is throwing up all its defenses against me, thrusting rocks and roots into my path.

Inesa doesn't say anything else about it, but I do regret shooting the deer. Not just because it's forced us to flee again, but because it was pointless. It makes me feel like I don't have control over myself. Like I really am just a mindless killing machine.

And it makes me think of the girl. Even after so many Wipes, I can't erase her face from my mind. And I can't think about death without remembering her limp body in the rain.

Stop. I squeeze my eyes shut, just for a moment, to make it vanish.

When I open my eyes, all I see is Inesa, her long, dark hair streaming over her shoulders. Somehow, this is no less distracting. I find myself watching her so intently that I nearly trip over another tree root.

Over the sound of my labored breathing, I strain to hear the cameras. But there's still no humming in the air. And, unaccountably, the knot in my stomach loosens with relief.

It appears out of the woods like a desert mirage. Slapdash and tiny, made of rain-dampened wood, it blends in perfectly with the trees and brush around it. The roof is a sheet of corrugated tin, striped with flaky orange rust. Inesa skids to a halt and darts behind a nearby tree trunk. Then she beckons me over.

It's not a broad tree, and in order to fit myself behind it, I have to press close to her. Our bodies are almost touching. I can see the faint sheen of sweat on her face, the way her tongue darts out to lick away the salt on her lips. My heartbeat stutters. I dig my fingernails into my palm.

"Do you think anyone is in there?" I ask in a whisper.

It seems like too advanced a structure to be the work of the Wends, but it's not exactly what I'd call civilization, either. I listen again for the cameras. Nothing.

"I don't know," Inesa admits. "There are some people who live out in the wilderness . . . to get off the grid. But I assumed they'd live together, in some sort of community. I don't know how you'd survive alone."

"I can't imagine that anyone who chooses to live out here alone would be very welcoming to unexpected company." I reach over my shoulder for my rifle.

"Probably not."

I can't hear anything from the vicinity of the cabin. It would be wisest to give it a wide berth and continue along, but my mind and body are buzzing with the possibility of food, sleep, and shelter. It's a difficult siren song to resist.

Inesa must be thinking the same, because she says, "Maybe it wouldn't hurt to just check it out."

There's a flicker of emotion in her eyes that I can't quire read—hope? Fear? Maybe both. I nod.

We creep forward, slowly. I'm aware of how heavy Inesa's foot-steps are—she's no hunter, after all. I open my mouth to tell her to stop and let me go first, but she shoots out an arm to hold me back.

"Wait," she says.

"What is it?"

She points at her feet, where something gleams like a thin rib-bon of silver.

"A trip wire," I say in surprise. "It must wrap around the perim-eter of the house."

I'm rather impressed by this Outlier's precautious ingenuity, and more impressed that Inesa thought to look for it. She points above my head. I look up and see rusted metal half camouflaged among the tree branches. Dented old cans, connected to the trip wire, no doubt, and rigged to alert the cabin's owner if anyone comes too close.

"Well, there goes the theory that they're friendly." Inesa gets to her feet. "There could even be mines, bear traps . . ."

"I doubt someone who uses a trip wire rigged to tin cans has that kind of sophisticated technology."

Inesa bites her lip. "I suppose."

"Let me go first."

"Wait." Inesa reaches out and grasps my wrist.

The warm, soft pressure of her fingers stops me instantly. She kneels down and combs through the leaves until she comes up with a fist-size rock. Before I can say a word, she chucks it in the direction of the cabin.

My eyes go wide. We wait in silence. Inesa is still holding on to my arm.

After a few moments, she shrugs and says, "Just testing for land mines."

"You've ruined my stealthy approach."

The corner of her mouth quivers upward. "Sorry. But better than being blown to pieces, right?"

The fact that no one has come bursting out of the cabin door, guns cocked and knives drawn, is encouraging. I take hesitant, prowling paces toward the house, balancing my rifle against my shoulder. When it's within reach—and when I'm satisfied I won't step on any bear traps—I press myself against the outer wall and test the door handle.

Locked, though that's not enough to deter me. I can tell by the way the handle rattles that it's a latch lock, flimsy. I jam the end of my rifle beneath the handle in one brisk, powerful thrust.

There's a clattering sound, and the door creaks open.

Inside is a yawning darkness, heavy and silent. I step over the threshold, rifle aloft, finger hovering over the trigger. The night vision in my prosthetic clicks on, and the interior of the cabin glows in its eerie green light.

Inesa has joined me at the door, but I raise an arm to hold her back.

Casting my gaze around, I see mostly ordinary things: A small bed with a tattered cover. A cast-iron, wood-burning stove. A table and two very wobbly looking chairs. My vision flickers briefly with bands of static—I wonder if Luka's blow damaged my prosthetic after all.

When the static fades, I notice something draped over one of the chairs. At first I think it's just a heap of clothes. But as I zoom in with the prosthetic, I make out the limp, slumped body of a man.

The shock is fleeting. There's no heat signature, so I know instantly that he's dead. Still holding Inesa back, I take another step into the cabin. Except for the corpse in the chair and a few other battered pieces of homemade furniture, it's empty.

I press a finger to the man's neck and check for a pulse—just in case. His skin is cold and there's no give to his flesh. Rigor mortis, the stiffening of the flesh before rot. That explains why the Wends haven't found him yet. No blood, no smell of decay.

After a few moments of fumbling, I find a half-melted candle and a box of matches. I light the candle and hold it out, washing the cabin in a pale, waxy yellow glow.

From the doorway, Inesa lets out a squeak and claps a hand over her mouth. "Is that—"

"He's dead," I say.

She steps cautiously into the cabin. The wooden floor groans under her feet. By the time she joins me at the table, her face is white, almost sickly.

"Are you sure?" she asks in a whisper.

I wave the candle over his body, illuminating the grayish cast to his skin. His empty, glassy eyes. I nod.

A swallow ticks in her throat. She leans over—close enough to feel the man's breath on her cheek, if he were breathing. Then she recoils, looking equal parts repulsed and relieved.

"Who was he, do you think?"

"Some Outlier."

It sounds too callous. Inesa's face falls.

I try to soften my voice. "Someone who lived and died off the grid, I suppose."

Inesa examines the man again, this time from a distance. Her eyes are damp and gleaming. Then she looks up at me and says, "We have to bury him."

"Why?"

"Because he's a human being," she replies. "Someone's father or brother or son."

I open my mouth to argue. Why should I spend hours digging a grave for some nameless Outlier just because we happened to stumble across his cabin? But Inesa's jaw is set. I can tell that no matter what I say, she'll do it herself.

"Fine," I say, letting out a breath. "He'll be less likely to attract the Wends that way."

We find several small oil lamps around the cabin and light them. We also find a treasure trove of supplies: canned food, carving knives, a small rusted axe, a bristly coil of rope, wire saws and carabiners and half a dozen flashlights with dead batteries. There's gauze and tweezers, alcohol pads and tourniquets. There's a half-crumpled paper map, yellowed with age. I set it all aside to look through later. There's an ancient bolt-action rifle, like the one Luka uses. I'm dying to reach for it, but Inesa's warning gaze stops me.

Among the supplies, we also find a shovel.

"With all of this stuff," she murmurs, "I wonder how he died."

"Heart attack. Brain aneurysm. Maybe starvation, if he couldn't find any edible meat or potable water." So far we haven't turned up any decon-tabs.

Inesa presses her lips together. "I guess it doesn't matter, in the end."

We drag his body outside. He's not a large man, but corpses are heavy. We're both panting. Rather unceremoniously, we drop his body a few yards from the back of the house. I want to suggest that we bury him farther away, but it's already growing dark, which makes us easy prey for whatever else is lurking in the woods.

With only one shovel, it's slow going. Inesa does all the digging and doesn't complain, doesn't ask for help; even when I offer, she just shakes her head. Determination has furrowed her brow. When she's dug up to her shoulders, she tries to climb out. I kneel down and offer a hand to haul her up, and when she takes it, I feel the raw, angry blisters forming on her palm.

"Stop," I say. "Let me do the rest. Go inside."

She frowns. "No. I'm fine."

"It's going to be full dark soon. You won't be able to see. I'll finish."

Inesa's gaze drops. I can tell by the way she clenches her fingers around her palms that the blisters hurt, badly. After a moment's hesitation, she nods, then heads back into the cabin.

There's not much digging left to do. I shovel out a few more inches of dirt and then start to push the Outlier's body into the open grave. I don't have the strength or the proper equipment to lower him down delicately and somberly, so he just flops over the edge of the hole and lands face down. I wonder if this counts as desecration of a corpse. That's against the rules of the Gauntlet. We're supposed to let the Lambs' families recover their bodies in as intact a state as possible.

But this man wasn't a Lamb. I don't know who he was, and I never will. If he does have family, they won't find him now. If they're even looking.

I cover the body as best I can. The sun sets behind the trees, and the night vision in my prosthetic clicks on, casting the world in that ghoulish green. When I'm finished, I tamp the soil flat, disguising any trace of the body buried beneath it.

I brush the dirt from my hands and turn to go inside. But before I reach the cabin, I stop. There's a strange, hollow feeling in my chest, one that seems to have the centripetal force of a black hole. Possessed by some odd and unnameable sensation, I search through the leaves until I find a rock. It's a perfectly ordinary rock, flat and about as long as my arm from elbow to wrist.

I drive it into the ground so that it juts up from the earth. A makeshift gravestone. I wonder what Azrael would say about it, if he were watching. What messages would be pinging through the chat. I'm not even sure what I feel. I just turn away and head back into the cabin, my palms prickling.

Inesa is standing by the table, utterly still. She's found and lit several more oil lamps, and it's light enough that I don't need the night vision in my prosthetic anymore. My gloves are filthy from digging, so I slip them off and set them down on the table.

"It's done," I say. "He's buried."

"Thank you."

Her voice is low. She steps closer to the table and puts her hands on the back of the chair, then lifts them up abruptly, as if she's just remembered a dead man had been sitting there. I'm gripped by the sudden worry that he died of an illness and we're infecting ourselves by being here, but if that's true, it's probably too late already. I'm exhausted, and the fear just falls through me like water through a sieve.

Water. "I should fill up something from the stream."

"Later," Inesa says. "It's dark now."

"I can see in the dark, you know. It's fine. I'll go." I turn and head for the door again.

"No!" The urgency in her voice stops me dead. "Wait. I don't—"

I turn back, frowning. "What?"

Her eyes skim the floor. "I don't want to be alone."

Silence washes over the cabin. I'm not sure where to look. A lump forms in my throat. Then I hear the sound of something dripping, very faintly. It takes me a few moments to locate the source. It's Inesa's blood, falling from her clenched fists and splattering the floor.

"You're bleeding," I say, in a voice that seems too distant to be my own.

She blinks, as if roused from sleep, then uncurls her fingers and looks down at her palms. "Oh."

I feel frozen, stuck fast to the floor. And then, like before, I'm possessed by some strange force that carries my body across the room. Makes me dig through the supplies until I find the alcohol pads and gauze bandages. Makes me bring them over to Inesa, my heartbeat pounding in my ears.

"Let me see," I say.

"No." She folds up her fingers. "It was stupid of me, to dig a whole grave."

I just watch her, clutching the gauze, feeling like I'm standing at the edge of a cliff. Height pulses in the soles of my feet.

At last, slowly, she holds her hands out to me.

The sight is more gruesome than I expected. There are twin gashes across her palms, blood welling up bright and ruby-red. The pads of her fingers are swollen and pink, giving the skin a taut, painful look. My own hands sting in sympathy.

I've bandaged my own wounds before, but it's different, dressing someone else's. I dab gently at the cuts with the alcohol pad, and Inesa sucks in a sharp breath.

"Sorry," I say. It comes out in a whisper.

"It's okay."

The alcohol pads turn rosy with Inesa's blood. When I'm satisfied that I've done enough to prevent infection, I try to wrap the gauze. This involves taking one of Inesa's hands in both of mine. Cradling it. It feels almost impossibly fragile, like a creature just hatched and entirely new to the world.

My fingers are trembling as I wind the gauze around her palm once, twice. I try to tear the strip off the roll once I finish, but it holds tight. My nails aren't sharp enough to pierce it, so I have to lift our joined hands to my mouth and bite through the bandage.

When I do, my lips brush her finger. My teeth graze her knuckle. We both freeze.

Heat rises to my cheeks. I snap the bandage free from the roll and step back. A flush is painting Inesa's face, too.

A few moments pass, light flickering in the long chimneys of the oil lamps. At first, I think Inesa is going to pull away from me. But instead, hesitantly, she holds out her other hand.

I bandage it in silence, my fingers trembling slightly. Inesa's throat bobs. She doesn't say a word until I've finished, until I let go of her hand. Then—

"Thank you," she says quietly.

I just nod. I swallow and try to ignore the fact that my lips are burning, like I've kissed an open flame.

We decide that I'll take first watch. Since I'm the one who can see in the dark, it seems only fair. Plus, Inesa has completely exhausted herself from digging. She climbs into the bed and pulls the tattered blanket up to her chin.

I go around the cabin and extinguish the lamps. I don't need them to see, and they'll only draw more attention to us. We might as well conserve the oil, too. I make a clumsy effort to bar the door by jamming one of the chairs against the handle, which won't hold against much, but will at least give us some warning. Luckily the trip wire and the tin cans are still in place.

Inesa faces outward, her hair spilling across the pillow. I sit on the floor, my back against the wall, a few paces from the bed. The coldness of the wood seeps through my suit. I consider trying to light the cast-iron stove, but I'm not convinced I won't burn down the cabin in the process. I'm sure Inesa knows how. Maybe in the morning.

My night vision clicks on. Inesa is the only warm, bright thing I can see. I'm aware of every aching moment that passes, the twin hums of her tracker and my heart, her eyes remaining open all the while.

"Can I tell you something?" she asks softly.

I nod. Then I remember she can't see my face, so I reply, "Yes."

"When we first found this cabin, I thought it might be my dad's. The trip wire and all the survival stuff . . . it seemed exactly like him. It's what he always wanted to do, living off the grid." She pauses. In the eerie green light, I see her run her fingers along the edge of the blanket. "And when we saw the body inside . . . I was almost sure it was him."

I open my mouth to reply, but there's a lump in my throat.

"It wasn't," she says. "I mean, it's not him. The thing is . . . I'm not sure if I wanted it to be. If it were him, at least I would know for sure. I wouldn't have to wonder anymore. Because I do wonder, every time I see one of the Wends. I wonder if it's him. Maybe he's one that I killed."

"I killed them," I say. "Not you."

"But you killed them for me." Her voice is almost inaudible now. "I brought you the gun."

"They would have killed us both, otherwise."

"Yeah." She unfolds her hands, straining to see the bandages in the dark. "But that's the same reason pretty much anyone kills anything. So they can survive. If it's all survival, who am I to judge what someone does? We're all the same, deep down."

I stare ahead, eyes unfocused.

She lets out a huff of air. "I don't know if that makes me feel better or worse. I suppose it's easier, like you said, to not feel anything at all."

"Yes" is all I can manage to reply.

Another moment passes in silence. There's only my breathing, and Inesa's, shifting through the cold and empty air.

"And now," she says, her voice barely louder than a whisper, "I have to wonder if Luka is out there, too. If he's become one of them. If I'll have to kill him someday. If I've killed him already."

"That seems unlikely."

Inesa doesn't answer. She just shifts under the covers, closing her fingers over her bandaged palms. In the dark, dense quiet, her tracker pulses in my ear like blood behind a bruise.

"How do you do it?" she whispers finally.

I don't need to ask her to elaborate. I glance over at my rifle, propped up beside me. It's a killing tool that feels utterly mundane to me, as uncomplicated to use as a fork or a knife. I try to think back to a time when it terrified me, to hold the power of death so casually in my hands. I'm sure I was scared, once. But all those memories have been stolen from me, scattered like leaves in the wind.

"I was eight when I was brought to Azrael," I say. "That's when he starts training you. Not just physically. They inject us with serums, hormones and chemicals to blunt our emotions. We don't feel things with the intensity that other people do. And things like guilt, regret . . . we're not supposed to feel them at all. Then, after a certain amount of time, living this way is all you know."

Inesa nods slightly. Her fists are clenched under her chin.

"And," I go on, the words rising from me almost unbidden, "it helps that I never have to worry that I'll encounter someone I recognized on my hunts. Someone I . . . love."

"I suppose that is an advantage," Inesa says. Her voice is hollow with black humor.

"But it is like the Wends, in a way." Some unaccountable force has pried my lips open and made me keep speaking, even though I know I shouldn't. "The way they're not quite human . . . it's how we're trained to see you. Outliers, I mean. And not just the Angels. Everyone in the City. So it's not—it's not like killing people. It's more like . . ."

I trail off. I was supposed to be defending myself, but hearing my own words, a hard knot forms in my stomach. It's something akin to nausea. Revulsion. And it's powerful enough that a thin bile rises up my throat.

"Animals?" Inesa supplies.

Her tone is so flat as to be unreadable. Now I can't summon up any words at all. I just nod, even though she can't see, and let the air fill with that one unspoken syllable, the one that is running through both of our minds, as ceaseless as a beating heart.

Yes.

The silence is thick, like spoiled water.

"How unfortunate, then," Inesa says at last, "that you have to share a cabin with one of us. That you had to *touch* one of us." Her voice is veined with ice.

"No," I say, and I'm surprised at the readiness of the word as it leaps from my tongue. "I don't believe that. Not anymore."

Despite how much more difficult it makes everything, some metamorphosis has happened inside me, invisible at a mere glance.

I can hardly even explain it to myself. All I know is that I've seen the way the light reflects in her hazel eyes and illuminates the freckles on her cheeks, and I've felt the warmth of her touch, the way her flesh gives way under my hands.

"No," I repeat, with more certainty this time, as Inesa just stares into the darkness. "I'm convinced that you're human now."

TWENTY-THREE

INESA

Morning comes. Softly, slowly, like the sun has surprised itself by rising. Somehow, I have survived another night of my Gauntlet.

Somehow, too, it seems like Melinoë has managed to stay awake all night. She's exactly where I left her when I fell asleep, sitting on the floor, knees pulled up to her chest. Her head is bowed over, nestled in the crook of her knees. But the moment I shift in the bed, her head snaps up in response.

"Good morning," I say. "You should rest now."

With the effects of the withdrawal now gone, she looks a little less pale, but not by much. There are also bright violet circles beneath her eyes, and her lips are closer to blue than pink. She squares her shoulders and says, "I'm fine."

I slide out of the bed and pull on my boots. "Just sleep. You're no use if you're too exhausted to hold a gun."

"I'm not too exhausted."

I tilt my head. "You're not a very good liar, you know."

Maybe that's why she doesn't talk much. When she's not

speaking, she's excellent at keeping her expression neutral, cold. But speaking, she gives herself away.

Like she did last night. In the quiet darkness, she was more honest with me than I had any right to expect. Without being able to see her, I could only hear the faint tremor in her voice; it made her seem so vulnerable. Not like the mindless, unfeeling killer I once imagined her to be.

I'm convinced that you're human now.

In the revealing light of day, maybe she's changed her mind. Caked in days of dirt and sweat and blood, I probably look plenty like an animal. And now that I can see her clearly, too, with that impossibly pale and perfect skin, stretched taut over titanium-reinforced bones, my brain should switch back into survival mode, and I should think of her as more machine than girl.

I blink and blink, but I can't manage to shift my vision. After last night's conversation, she seems vulnerable in a way I never imagined an Angel could. And everything is even more tangled and dangerous than it should be, because now I'm convinced that she's human, too.

Melinoë's jaw sets. There's a spark of defiance in her eyes that somehow seems to even animate the prosthetic. My heart thumps unevenly.

"Fine." I sigh. "I'm going to get us some water."

Slowly, Melinoë starts to push herself up from the floor. On instinct, I hold out a hand. Melinoë hesitates for a moment, then slips her fingers through mine and lets me pull her to her feet.

My bandages stayed in place overnight, and all the blood has dried and scabbed, but my hands are still throbbing a little. The pressure of her palm is slightly painful, and I bite my lip. She notices that, of course, and drops my hand like it's a burning coal.

"It's okay," I say. "Thank you—again. You didn't have to."

She just nods. Still not much for words, my Angel.

I wonder when I started thinking of her as *mine*.

Maybe it was even before we spoke last night in the dark. Maybe it started when she wrapped the gauze gently around my wounds. When she lifted my hand to her mouth. I can still feel it, if I focus on the memory—her lips grazing my skin. I have to clench my fists to stop thinking about it, stop feeling it, drag myself out of the past.

Melinoë is watching me. I wonder if she can tell, somehow, that I'm remembering it, and the thought makes heat rise to my cheeks.

She's probably just watching me because she's still afraid I'm going to try to kill her. When I realize that, I feel enormously stupid and even more flushed in the face.

I could. When her guard is down, when her back is turned. The knife is still wedged in the shaft of my boot.

But we're no closer to civilization than before, and four rickety wooden walls and a trip wire with some rusted cans are not going to stop the Wends. I'll have to wait a little longer for salvation. Or rather, a little longer until I'm safe from the Wends and Melinoë is my only enemy.

I'm convinced that you're human now.

Such simple words, spoken in the safety of darkness, but they unbalance me. They make everything inside me muddle and spin.

I have to turn away from her, because I find that when I'm looking into her eyes, there's nothing I can do to make my heart keep a steady rhythm.

The dead man's cabin comes equipped with a wooden bucket, which I clear of cobwebs and dust and then carry down to the stream. I take deliberate, inching steps, careful not to disturb the trip wire. On my way out, I notice something sticking up from the ground, something that wasn't there when I went inside last night.

Warily, I bend over to examine it. It's a piece of shale, driven into the earth like a stake—or maybe like a gravestone. I'm standing precisely where I dug the man's grave. But I didn't put the stone there.

Melinoë must have done it.

Why? *Some Outlier,* she had called him, her tone contemptuous and remote. And that's all he was, really. Not my brother, not my father. He has no one to mourn him. I stand up, my skin prickling.

Melinoë marked his grave.

I can't stop thinking about it, as I walk to the stream. She told me last night that City folk think of us Outliers as no better than animals. So why go to the trouble? Burying a total stranger and marking their grave is more than a lot of Outliers would do for each other, in truth.

Beneath the bandages, my skin pulses with the memory of Melinoë's touch. Her hands were warmer than I thought they would be. Gentler. She only looks cold from a distance. But up close—

I stop that train of thought in its tracks. I'm being sentimental, reckless. Because even a wolf can be gentle if it wants, but you should never forget its teeth.

It takes the better part of an hour to fill the bucket. I'm grateful for the distraction. I fix my mind on the task at hand and try not to think about my Angel or her hands or how Luka would roll his eyes at me in disgust. He would tell me to run and leave her for dead. Or maybe he's overcome his inhibitions. Maybe he'd tell me to stick a knife in her back and be done with it.

My clean, bandaged hands make it apparent how filthy the rest of my body is. There's a stark white line on my wrist where clean skin gives way to the dirt that's ground into my arm, the accumulated grime of these past miserable days. It's on all my limbs, my face, even my hair. Normally I can go a day or two without bathing, especially when we don't have electricity to heat the water, but it's been far longer than that, and I feel absolutely gamy. My clothes are so textured with dirt that they've all turned a drab shade of gray.

When I return to the cabin, lugging the heavy bucket and splashing a not insignificant amount of water on the floor, Melinoë is curled up on the bed. I'm relieved to see her resting—even with the rifle propped against the wall within arm's reach.

There's something shudder-inducing about wearing a dead man's clothes, but my urgent need to be clean overpowers those qualms. I find a thick pair of cargo pants and a long flannel shirt unfolded in a trunk.

Melinoë stays asleep as I undress, quickly. I scrub at my skin

233

until it turns pink. Beads of dirt roll off the crevices of my elbows and knees. I even manage to dip my hair into the bucket and comb through the knots with my fingers.

Goose bumps are rising along my limbs by the time I finish. The cabin doesn't offer much heat on its own, and I haven't gotten around to fiddling with the stove. But the pants and shirt are made of durable, moisture-wicking material, even if both are comically large on me. The shirt reaches almost to my knees, and when I stand up, I have to hold the waistband of the pants to keep them from falling down.

I'm holding up the pants with one hand and trying to wring out my hair with the other when Melinoë stirs.

"*What* are you doing?" she demands.

"Bathing," I reply.

She looks at me as if I've grown a third eye and fins.

"I'm going to wash my clothes," I say. "I'll wash yours, too."

"No." Her cheeks fill with color. It's a strange color, more purple than red, and maybe I didn't recognize it before—but now she's definitely blushing.

I have to bite my lip to keep from smiling. "Okay. Suit yourself."

Melinoë sits up in bed. Very tensely, she watches me, fists clenched at her sides. I try to focus on scrubbing the clothes, but now I'm all too aware of her unblinking gaze. Water sloshes over the edge of the bucket and soaks the floor.

"Are you accustomed to doing this?" she asks.

"I'm a lot better at it . . . usually."

"I didn't think anyone washed clothes by hand anymore." Her eyes flick from my face to my arms as I twist and swirl the fabric of my shirt.

"Most people can't afford washing machines in Esopus Creek." Or, in our case, can't even afford the electricity to turn them on. The Wesselses have a washing machine. Sometimes, when it's so cold that a layer of ice coats all our drinking water and I'm afraid I could lose a finger to frostbite, I'll pole down to their house and Jacob will let me use it. For days afterward, I'll find myself sniffing the sleeves of my shirts, relishing in the floral, faintly artificial scent of their detergent.

"It's a useful skill to have," Melinoë says.

I snort. "Yeah. Laundry. Cleaning animal carcasses. My illustrious claims to fame. Hard to believe my mother chose me for the Gauntlet over Luka."

Unfortunately, I fail to keep my voice even, and the attempt at humor drifts to the ground between us. The wound is still too fresh.

Silence falls over the cabin, and Melinoë's gaze fixes firmly on mine. Her lips are pressed into a thin, white line, and for the first time I see their faint twitching, betraying the effort that it takes to maintain such a stoic face.

"You know, don't you?" My throat tightens over the words. "Why she put me up for the Gauntlet?"

Slowly, Melinoë nods. "Her file said she's sick."

There must be hundreds of stories like that. Thousands. It's an age-old narrative: the child sacrificed for their ailing parent.

Giving back the life their mother or father gave to them. It's tragic on all sides, and I can't imagine it's ever failed to evoke an emotional response from the audience. I wish it were so simple.

Or maybe it never is. Melinoë said that Azrael crafts his narratives carefully. Maybe he's adept at eliding the nuances, the ugly little truths behind all the stories of valiant sacrifice and long-suffering martyrdom. If I were smart, I'd stick to that straightforward, reliable fiction.

But the cameras are off. There's no one to hear the truth except Melinoë.

"Kind of," I say at last. "It's complicated."

"I'm smart," she says—in a bald, unassuming way that makes me bite my tongue on a smile. A fact, not a boast.

"I know." My mouth quivers. "It's just difficult to understand, if you haven't lived the way we have."

"Try."

There's an earnestness in her voice, a faint gleam of curiosity in her eyes. I'm not sure if she's even aware of them herself, these tiny, almost imperceptible cracks in her facade. But I know I'm not imagining them. In the light of day, with my senses sharpened by a night of sleep, it's so clear to me.

"Well," I begin, "my mother isn't from the outlying Counties originally. Her family is from the City. She fell in love with my dad and moved to Esopus to be with him. I don't think she was much older than I am. But by the time they had Luka and me, my parents couldn't stand each other. They were just too different. I guess they weren't ever in love."

"They could have been." Melinoë's tone is light, but her gaze is intent. "Sometimes love isn't enough."

"I think it is. I think it has to be. Otherwise, it's not really love. If the world can break it . . ." I trail off, cowed by the unexpected intensity of Melinoë's stare. And the fact that I'm not even sure where I stand on the subject. I've never been in love before.

Has she?

"The world can break anything," she says.

"Then maybe no one has ever really been in love," I suggest dryly.

"Maybe you have too much faith in people."

"Luka is always telling me the same thing."

Bringing up Luka shifts something in the air. Melinoë's eyes lose that earnest gleam, and her face seems to shrink into itself, becoming icy and remote again. I stare down at my hands, at the now damp bandages that have been dyed pale pink with my blood. Even her cold stare can't erase the memory of her touch. The brush of her lips against my palm.

"Anyway," I say, lifting my gaze, "staying in Esopus made my mother miserable."

"Why didn't she leave?"

It's an unexpectedly hard question to answer. "She didn't have any family left in the City by then. And we didn't have any money, because Dad refused to take on Caerus debt and Luka wasn't old enough to hunt. People just get stuck. Sometimes you don't even realize that you're drowning until the water closes over your head."

Melinoë's expression doesn't shift. "So then what?"

"Mom started to . . . deteriorate, I guess." I pick at the bandages, just for something to do, somewhere to look. "It started with this one cold. Just a cold. It passed in a few days, but she still refused to leave her bed. She started snapping at me, and Dad, and even Luka. Ordering us to bring her things. I mean, I understood, at first. We all thought there might be something deeper going on. We even had Dr. Wessels come up to examine her, but he said there was nothing wrong with her. Physically, at least. And then . . . and then there was the year of silence, where we couldn't even be in the house unless we whispered, and if we did so much as close the door too loudly, she'd fly into a rage . . ."

Once the words start coming, I can't stop them. I've never spoken about this before, to anyone. Luka and I don't talk about it, because we've lived it, and what is there to say? But there's an odd relief in being able to piece it all together into a story. A weight lifts from my chest. It's like the first breath after surfacing from the water.

"Luka was always her favorite," I go on. "She never yelled at him the way she yelled at me. He always seemed to know how to do the right thing. And if she was angry, he could shake it off. He never complained. Never cried. Not even when Dad left, even though I know how much it hurt. I suppose . . ."

I trail off, a lump hardening in my throat. Melinoë is still watching me steadily.

"I suppose," I say, voice thick, "that if I were my mother, I'd have chosen to keep Luka, too. He's the strong one. He's the one worth saving."

A little bit of fresh blood seeps through the bandages. I fold my fingers shut over my palms.

"I've never heard you complain," Melinoë says quietly. "And I've never seen you cry."

I can't help but give a short laugh, because my eyes are almost watering as we speak. "Maybe you haven't been paying attention."

Moments drip by, like water through a crack in the wall. Then, in the same low tone, she says, "I've been paying attention."

TWENTY-FOUR

MELINOË

My hour or so of sleep has just left me more disoriented. At least, that's the only reason I can imagine why my heart hums as I listen to Inesa speak. It's not a droning, choppy sound like helicopter blades, but a soft, insistent murmur that warms me from my cheeks to the tips of my gloved fingers.

Inesa stands up, hiking the borrowed pants up around her waist. "Well, come on," she says. "I'll show you how to light the stove."

"You look ridiculous," I tell her, gesturing at the oversize clothes.

The corner of her mouth lifts in a deadpan smile. "Maybe Caerus should outfit the Lambs with fancy suits, then. It's only fair that we should get to look so graceful and pretty, too."

She says it in an offhand way and then immediately turns her back to me, so I'm sure that I've misheard. I stay glued to the floor, heat rushing to my face. *She thinks I'm pretty?*

She's been paying attention to me, too. I still can't believe those words slipped from my tongue. We must both be decompensating from hunger.

Inesa kneels in front of the stove and opens the firebox. There's nothing but soot and ashes inside, the remnants of a fire that burned out a long, long time ago. There's also no wood or coal to be found in the cabin. It makes me wonder again if the owner died of sickness, because something must have prevented him from chopping down the trees just outside.

As it turns out, it's even simpler than that—we don't need the axe at all. There are enough fallen logs on the ground, and branches that we can break off with just our hands. Carefully avoiding the trip wire, we gather as much wood as we can. Then we bring our piles inside and heap them next to the stove.

The main problem is that all the wood is damp. Inesa strikes match after match, trying to get the wood to catch, but the flame keeps sizzling out against the wet bark. Her eyes search the room. Then she stands up, suddenly, and seizes a white bottle tucked in the corner behind the door.

"Kerosene," she says. "It's what's inside the oil lamps. We can use it to start the fire, too."

She starts to douse the wood, then stops. Giving a humorless laugh, she says, "My dad would be so ashamed of me, if he could see this. No *real* survivalist would have to resort to kerosene to make a fire."

"You've survived longer than ninety-six percent of Lambs." Azrael's statistics are stamped inside the most rigid part of my brain. "That must count for something."

"I think it's possible there are other explanations for that."

My cheeks prickle with warmth.

When she's finished dousing the wood, she places the kerosene bottle at a safe distance, then goes over to rinse her hands in the bucket. The bandages on her palms have become almost completely saturated in blood, both old and new. I'll have to replace them. For some reason, my skin prickles at the thought of this, of touching her again.

"Just to be safe," says Inesa when she returns. "It's not as flammable as gasoline, but—well, you'll see."

She strikes a match and tosses it inside, then quickly slams the door to the stove shut. The explosion follows a fraction of a second later. I find myself jolting slightly forward, as if to pull her back, but I manage to quash the instinct. Behind the door, flames burst to life, roaring red and orange, licking ferociously at the soot-stained glass. Heat swells outward.

Something pulls my gaze to the fire behind the glass. I can't blink, and I can't look away. It happens so suddenly that I'm stunned to silence, just watching the flames flicker and rise, yellow tongues licking within the wisps of smoke, and I think, *I've seen it before.*

A memory, surfacing from somewhere deep within me. Layered across my vision, another fire blooms. A sensation unfurls from the pit of my stomach—the shaky juddering of adrenaline. And for some reason, my brain forms a word, a name.

Keres.

And then, just as abruptly as it appears, it's gone. The glass fragment of a memory and the sensation that accompanied it.

Keres's name sinks back down into the murk and depths of my black-pitted mind.

When I come to, Inesa is watching me intently.

"You aren't afraid of fire, are you?" she asks, brow furrowed.

"No."

At least, I don't think I am. Surely Azrael would have wiped that phobia out of me, like I'm certain he did for many others. But I don't mention that. And I don't mention that what I felt when looking at the fire wasn't fear. It was closer to anger. Closer to defiance.

Those are definitely not emotions an Angel is supposed to feel. I'm grateful that they've vanished so quickly. I shake my head, as if to clear the last of the fuzzy memory from my brain.

I hold my hands out toward the rising heat, relieved at how it chases away the chill from the tips of my fingers. Inesa holds hers out, too, and I'm equally relieved to see her visibly relax, her shoulders slumping. At least for the moment, we're both safe and warm. All thanks to her.

"Maybe survivalists would be better at surviving if they took some tips from you," I say.

Inesa laughs. It's a clear sound, bright and somehow shining, almost visible in the air.

"It's just a shame," she says, "that we don't have anything to cook over it."

"I think I can fix that."

If I've been feeling slightly useless to our survival efforts so far, this is the perfect remedy. Hunting is something I know I can do. It's as instinctual as breathing. Granted, I've never tracked animals before, but it can't be any more difficult than tracking people.

Unless it isn't. Animals might technically be less intelligent, though in a way they're more adept. Their brains are optimized, dedicated solely to survival. They aren't clouded with things like empathy, or tripped up by tangled human questions of morality. Their memories are short, and full of holes, but they preserve the essential things: how to escape and how to stay alive.

Azrael's voice echoes through my mind, quick as a fizzing bar of static. *You are my perfect creation.*

If only he could see me now. Digging graves for Outliers. Bandaging the hands of my Lamb. I wonder how many Wipes it will take to mend these cracks in my facade. To obliterate all memories of this weakness.

Fire erupts across my vision, that same outward, blooming heat. And this time, it's his face I see within it, his name that catches on my tongue. My stomach clenches with revulsion.

Stop, I tell myself sternly. *Snap out of it.* These are false memories, I decide, something going wrong with the circuitry in my brain. The blow Luka struck me with his rifle must have done more damage than I thought. A tiny fissure in the glass. That's all. Azrael will seal it up and make me new again.

But my fingernails are digging so hard into my palm that I've broken the skin beneath my gloves.

I start pacing through the forest, silent and swift on my feet. The biggest challenge will be finding a deer that isn't too irradiated to eat. Inesa told me the best places to look: upstream, where the water is fresher, and where the woods are damper and denser. I make sure to stick close to the creek, though, so I don't get hopelessly turned around.

But even if I do lose the creek, Inesa's tracker is still pulsing in me like a second heartbeat. All my other systems have collapsed, except for this one. I'll always be able to find my way back to her.

The sun slowly works its way across the sky as I walk, draining toward the line of the horizon. Evening settles thick and heavy across the forest, shadows stretching and air bristling with cold. I'll have more luck now. Inesa told me that deer come out to graze at dawn and dusk, when the light is muddled and they're safest from predators. Or so they think.

The stream diverts into a small pool, with deer droppings ground into the dirt around it. It's not something I would've picked up on before, but being out here has reframed my vision. Made me notice things that I would never even have bothered to look for. For as long as I can remember, the air has just felt like dead space around me. Now it seems like I can sense every atom, seething and blooming with life.

This new awareness is equal parts blessing and curse. I narrow my eyes, trying to focus on nothing more than the hunt. I clamber up into a nearby tree and cache myself among its low-hanging branches. Then, with my rifle propped against my shoulder, I wait.

I don't have to wait long. The deer come trotting out of the trees in a group of three: a mother and two fawns. They're still young enough that their pelts are dappled with white. It's not dark enough yet for the night vision in my prosthetic to click on, so I have to strain with my real eye to see if I can spot a third eye or a webbed hoof. They all look like ordinary deer to me. Anxious, trembling, gentle things.

Using the scope, I train my rifle on the mother. My artificially slowed heart gives an inexplicable stutter, and I wonder which is crueler: to kill one of the shaky-legged fawns before it's even had a chance to outgrow its white spots, or to kill the mother and leave her children to fend for themselves? Crueler to make a child live without its mother, or a mother live without its child?

It's nothing I've ever had to consider before. These are the types of inane human concerns that make a person weak. Concerns that should be below me. I shoot the mother because she's bigger, which means more to eat. But when I see the fawns scatter at the gunshot, still unsteady on their legs, their large, black eyes damp with uncomprehending terror, I feel another tremor in my heart. Another crack in my system, spiraling outward from the first.

The temperature drops violently while I'm hauling the deer back to the cabin. All of a sudden, my breath is clouding in front of my face and the air is taut with cold. Under my hunting suit, gooseflesh rises on my arms and legs.

Careful to avoid the trip wire, I drag my kill into the cabin. As soon as I open the door, I'm met with a flushing wave of heat. Relief makes my bones quiver. The stove in the corner is steadily crackling, chuffing gray-white smoke. All the oil lamps have been lit, casting the room in a sheen of gold.

Inesa has spread out a series of tools on the table, most

prominent among them a knife and a handsaw. She's still wearing those ridiculous clothes. When she sees me, her head tips up and a smile stretches across her face, one that shows the dimple in her cheek.

"You did it," she says.

I drop the carcass on the floor with a heavy *thud*. "You didn't think I would?"

She gives a coy shrug. "I've never seen one of your Gauntlets before."

"You're one of the few."

She's mentioned it before, but it still surprises me to hear it; I almost can't believe it. The Gauntlets get millions and millions of views. They're the height of entertainment, better than any soap opera or sitcom Caerus could dream up. There are streamers who build their entire careers off live-reacting to the Gauntlets. Online retailers who sell merchandise bearing the images of Angels and Lambs. Websites that use AI technology to transpose my face onto naked bodies, so men don't even have to use their imaginations.

"Yeah," Inesa says. She picks up one of the tools, turns it over in her hands. "I guess I just never wanted another reason to lose faith in people."

I let her words wash over me, as the heat from the stove warms my skin. In truth I've never felt a particular allegiance to people. Too many of my own parts were cleaved away, excised like rotting flesh and replaced with titanium and circuitry, leaving me both more than human and less. I wonder if that's still how Inesa sees me. As a machine wearing the skin of a girl.

247

But I don't ask. I just watch as she sets to work dismembering the deer. It's a neat, efficient process, and she seems totally unperturbed by the gory aspects. Gutting the animal and draining it. Skinning the pelt. Carving the meat. She has a bucket to catch all the blood and innards, and her hands are soaked red up to the wrist.

I'm unable to take my eyes off her. For all Inesa's self-deprecation, she looks anything but weak now. She's focused, assured. Capable. And even though there's a gulf between killing people and cleaning the carcasses of dead animals, I understand now—we've both seen plenty of ugly things.

"We'll have to clean this up quickly, then salt and dry the meat," Inesa says. "So it doesn't attract the Wends."

I nod and sink down into one of the chairs, eyelids growing heavy. Half asleep, half awake, I find myself thinking about what it would be like to do this every day. Going out to hunt, coming home to a blazing fire and Inesa's earnest smile. My life in the City feels inconceivably distant. The long, sleek black shooting range, the enormous glass windows looking down on the ever-glittering lights, the dresses and the parties and the sapphire-blue liquid. The climate-controlled rooms and the showers with a dozen different settings.

All the things I thought I needed seem less important now. I've been surviving without them. Maybe more than just surviving.

I don't know when I stopped wondering how Outliers lived like this and started imagining myself among them.

"Mel? Can you pass me that other knife?"

The sound of my name jabs me like a syringe. Fire breaks across my vision. Crackling tongues of flame.

My name.

I go still in my seat, blood turning slowly to ice.

Inesa just watches me, brow furrowed. "What is it? What's wrong?"

I swallow hard around the stone that's formed in my throat. When I manage to speak, my voice is just a thin croak. "That's not my name."

"Oh," Inesa says. "I'm sorry. I wasn't thinking, really. It just slipped out."

The tip of my nose and my cheeks are starting to burn. I blink and blink, to put out the fire behind my eyes. It doesn't work. Through it all I see Inesa, watching me, her gaze glimmering with concern.

"No one has ever called me that," I whisper at last, "except for Keres."

A sudden, strong wind buffets the cabin—just a shack, really. Its walls are thin, rotted wood. They could collapse on us at any moment.

When the wind subsides, Inesa asks softly, "Who is Keres?"

My memory is as rotted as the wood. Filled with dark holes, spaces to fall into. But if I close my eyes, I can see her clearly: her shiny black braid and blue eyes, the way her teeth flashed when she smiled. I still remember her bones, when I helped zip up her hunting suit, the notches of her spine pressing against her pale skin. The delicate, swanlike column of her neck.

"She was another Angel," I say. "There are only three or four of us. I don't get along with the others. Just her."

"Keres," Inesa repeats. "What was she like?"

"Kind." It seems insufficient a word to describe her, but it's a start. I've never been good with words, anyway. "But in a natural way, as if she couldn't imagine being anything else. It's not natural at all for an Angel to be kind, but she was. Azrael must have programmed her that way. To fulfill a certain role." I've always known it to be true, but I've rarely wanted to admit it, even to myself. That maybe the things I loved about her were just the parts that Caerus made.

I clear my throat and go on. "Whenever either of us had a procedure, we would stay in the other's room, just in case we need anything . . ." I trail off because my chest is aching. I feel like my ribs could crack.

"A procedure?" Inesa frowns.

"Surgeries. Sometimes they're functional, like the eye. A lot of them are aesthetic. They did my lips and my nose. They made Keres do her breasts."

For some reason, this is the most shameful thing I've admitted to Inesa so far. The shame feels almost airborne, heavy and hot. Maybe it's because the surgeries are the epitome of pointless wealth, of excess, and that hearing about them will make Inesa start to hate me again. Or maybe it's because it's evidence of how little of me there is left. Not even my face is my own.

I wait for Inesa to curl her lip in disgust, to turn away. Instead, she just says, "That sounds painful, too."

"It is."

The wind howls again, rattling the door.

"What happened to her?" Inesa asks, voice low.

This is the clearest memory I have of Keres now. Her glazed, uncomprehending stare. The same eyes that had shone with laughter, drained of their glimmering light, turned dull and matte. The pain explodes inside me like shrapnel.

And there's the fire again, blooming in the theater behind my eyes.

"They made her forget."

"Forget what?"

"Everything." I can almost feel the syringe in my neck, the needle's cold, sharp bite. "They do it to all of us, at some point. It's called a Wipe. They can take away your memories of a specific event, or a specific person. Some of them. Or all of them."

Inesa draws a breath. "Why would Caerus want to do that?"

Azrael's explanation jumps readily to my lips. "The mind is the most complex organ in the human body. But it can break, too, like a bone. Certain things get stuck. They don't register in your brain like an ordinary memory. Instead, they feel immediate, like they're happening to you over and over again. It makes you scared and weak. The only way to get rid of them is to forget they ever happened at all."

"Surely that can't really work." Inesa has put the knife down, and her fingers are curling and uncurling around her bandaged palms. "Just going in, picking through someone's brain and taking out the bits you don't like . . ."

251

"It doesn't always work. That's the problem. Some memories are too stubborn to cut loose." My gaze burns into the floor. "I've gotten Wiped dozens of times now, and still . . ."

Silence washes over the cabin. There's only the wind, shrieking thinly, trying to beat down the walls around us.

"Still?" Inesa prompts quietly.

"There are things I can't forget. Stupid, small things." I feel a sudden flare of anger. "They've made me forget my real parents, my real name, my home, if I ever had one, but they can't manage to get that stupid girl out of my mind."

"The girl—you mean Keres?"

"No." My blood is electric now, making the tips of my fingers hum. The emotions are both new and familiar: grief, rage. I'm not supposed to feel them. But Caerus's chemicals have flushed out of my system and there's nothing to blunt them now.

I lift my gaze. Fire consumes me. "It was my last Gauntlet. My target was this little girl. She was twelve. Her father was a stinking drunk, and he used all his credits on booze. Her mother had died and it was just the two of them. And judging from the bruises I saw, I wasn't the first person to put my hands on her.

"It was raining. I remember that. The water was so heavy and cold that it soaked through my suit, and so loud that I could barely hear Azrael's voice in my ear. I kept sinking, sinking into the mud. The girl was wearing this white dress . . . she was so easy to find. I thought, if someone really cared about her, they would have told her to wear dark colors, so she would be harder to see."

Inesa's eyes have grown hard. She'll hate me for this, no

question about it. I don't know what purpose it serves, this pitiful confession. But the words just keep pouring out of me and I can't stop them.

"It's the type of Gauntlet no one really wants to do." Fire crackles in the stove behind me, and in the forefront of my vision. "Azrael would have sent Keres, but she was recovering from her surgery. She was usually best with the young Lambs. That was her archetype; she was supposed to be maternal. When she killed them, she could almost make it seem like a mercy.

"But he sent me. I was supposed to be—*am* supposed to be—the coldest one. The most merciless. It was a bad match from the beginning. I was never going to . . ." My voice breaks off. Inesa's gaze hasn't shifted. "I'd never done a Gauntlet like this before. I was cold and wet and confused. I was trying to remember what Keres did with the younger ones, how she got close to them and held them while she killed them, but Azrael was in my ear, telling me to just shoot. So I did. But it was a clumsy shot and it clipped her leg. She fell down in the mud. I ended up falling, too. I had to crawl after her, with the rain almost blinding me. She was bleeding and sobbing and begging me to stop. I couldn't stand to . . . I couldn't bear to listen to her. So I just put my hands around her throat until she was dead."

The deer's blood is in the air, but it has the same salt-tang as the girl's. When I inhale, I taste it.

"I don't remember very much about what happened afterward. But I remember the headlines. The streamers kept replaying the footage, reacting to it. A lot of them cried. They called me the most hated person in New Amsterdam. They hacked a holoboard in the City—then it caught on and everyone was saying it, going over my old Gauntlets, too. Azrael took my tablet away so I couldn't see it anymore."

Inesa lets out a slow breath. "Did he try to take the memory away, too?"

I nod. "Again and again. Wipe after Wipe. I must have lain on that table a dozen times. But it never worked. I couldn't even hold my rifle without thinking of her." My chest grows unbearably tight. "I couldn't do any Gauntlets. I could barely even leave my room. So Azrael tried a different tactic."

"A different tactic?"

"It's called an Echoing. Where they replay the memory over and over again. It's supposed to make you inured to it, kind of like working out the same muscle. Eventually you stop feeling the pain and you get stronger. But it only made it a thousand times worse."

By this point, I can barely do more than whisper. The deer's blood is dripping onto the floor.

"Those weeks were just a blur. I was in the shooting range. I couldn't even lift my gun. I was back on the table for another Wipe. I woke up in my room. A Mask forced food into my mouth. I went back to the range to try again. Another Wipe. Over and over . . . by the time I surfaced, by the time I was sort of lucid again, Keres was gone. Azrael had retired her and done a final Wipe. She didn't even remember my name."

Finally, the truth. At least, all the truth I know. I have no explanation for the fire. And I have no explanation for why, when

I close my eyes, I keep seeing Inesa's face; I keep remembering her touch. There's some glitch in my mechanics, all the carefully constructed systems sparking and then going dead silent. It's gotten dark enough in the cabin that my night vision keeps flickering on and off again, plunging the world into eerie green and then back into low, golden light.

"That's why you didn't kill me," Inesa says. "I didn't understand before. You were on top of me, and then it started raining."

I press my fingernails into my palm. "All those Wipes and Echoings for nothing. I'm still weak."

"I can't exactly say I'm sorry you didn't succeed." Inesa looks down. The blood on her hands has dried to a bleak, rusty color, more brown than red. A few moments pass, and then she looks up again. "You don't remember her name, do you? The girl's?"

I shake my head. At least Azrael managed to strip that away, for all the good it's done me.

"Sanne," Inesa says. "Her name was Sanne."

Something flickers inside me, like the flame in the chimney of an oil lamp. And then I remember what I thought, when I first touched down in Esopus Creek. *I've been here before.*

My breath catches in my throat. The walls of the cabin are still standing, but I feel like every wall inside me has collapsed, folded in on itself, and I'm left crushed in the wreckage.

"She was from your town," I whisper. "I . . . I remember now."

I had been in Esopus Creek. My stomach fills with bile. All the Wipes that didn't take, the Echoing that jammed the memory like a knife between my ribs—all of it, just for Azrael to send me back again. A single word crests out of the dark water of my mind. *Why? Why? Why?*

"Sanne Dekker." Inesa's voice is low, but resonant. Without hesitation or contrition. "Her father is Floris Dekker. He brought her body into my shop, a few days after the Gauntlet. I saw her spread out across the table."

Sanne. I remember now. Her name humming on the screen above her vital statistics, Azrael pointing and gesturing. I felt sick to my stomach then, the way I do now. And then—

"It was a test," I bite out. "That's why Azrael sent me. That's why he chose you for the Gauntlet. He wanted to see if he'd fixed me. If I could kill another girl from Esopus Creek."

There's no silence in the cabin, because the wind is howling and beating at the wood, spasming off the tin roof with a thunderous rumbling sound. Inesa stares at me without blinking, and there's a damp glaze in her eyes. Anger at the forefront, and grief burning low behind. Moments pass in the eddy of what I know is a coming storm.

"And I've failed," I say. "Again."

The knife glints on the table between us, the blade slicked with deer blood. Inesa could snatch it up and have it at my throat within seconds. I could reach for it, too, and I'd probably be faster. But the instinct just runs through me and then vanishes, like an electrical current reaching a wire's dead end.

"You know," Inesa says at last, "there's something my dad used to tell me."

I stare back at her, brow furrowing. *Surely*, I think, *this is all just a preamble to killing me.*

But instead of lunging for the knife, she just continues: "He said that Caerus has created the conditions that allow some organisms to thrive and others to die. That we're land animals in a drowning world and they're sea creatures. But if the lakes and the rivers dried up and the sea level fell, we would survive, and they would die." She pauses. "He said a lot of nutty things, especially when he was drunk. But I think he was right about that."

A clever breeze sneaks in under the door, and the flames inside the oil lamps snap. But just for a moment. Then they flare to life again.

"So what are land animals supposed to do," I ask, "when the sea levels rise?"

"Survive," Inesa says. "Just survive."

There's a strange pricking at the corner of my real eye. "In order for some creatures to live, there are always others that have to die."

"That's true." Inesa holds my gaze. Steadily. "You know, everyone in Esopus Creek hates the mutations. They think they're disgusting aberrations of nature. I should hate them, too, considering they're eventually going to put Luka and me out of business. But I can't make myself hate them. I never have. They're just surviving. Even the Wends are just surviving. Who knows what they would do, if they had another choice? If they knew they were safe? If they were free?"

———

257

By the time we eat and clean the mess the best we can, the oil lamps are burning low, more dark smoke than fire. Hung close to the billowing heat of the woodstove, Inesa's clothes have finally dried. She picks up the shirt, the pants, the socks. Drapes them over her arm. Waits.

"I'll turn around," I say. My voice sounds odd and strangled.

"Okay," she says.

I face the opposite wall, where the cabin's original owner hammered in pegs to hold his various tools. The hand axe, the bone saw, the rusted rifle I haven't gotten a chance to test yet. My eyes trace the shape of its barrel, trying to focus on anything but the knowledge that Inesa is changing behind me.

I hear the rustle of fabric, the gentle swishing as her hair falls down against her naked back. I bite my lip, gaze boring into the wall. But I can't see what's in front of me anymore. Even the fire is gone. All I see is Inesa. She grows like ivy on the insides of my eyelids. The roots of her are in my rib cage, winding up around my heart. I can't help imagining what her bare skin would feel like under my hands.

TWENTY-FIVE

INESA

It's my turn to keep watch. I add more kerosene to the lamps and carry one over to the side of the bed. Melinoë is lying down, but her body is stiff beneath the covers, and her eyes are open. I sink down on the floor next to her. Close enough that I can hear her breathing, even over the vicious howling of the wind.

A voice in the recesses of my brain keeps telling me I should hate her. It sounds like Luka, like Dad, even like Mom. It sounds like Jacob and everyone I've ever known in Esopus Creek. It sounds like the robotic drone of the commenters in my stream.

But it's not my voice.

She killed Sanne. I knew that already, of course, but it was too easy to forget, when her hands were wrapping my wounds so gently and her gaze was full of very urgent, very human grief. She's killed dozens of people whose names and faces I'll never learn, and she tried to kill me, too.

Yet the pressure of her grip around my throat is a memory so distant that even if I try to summon it, it just lingers at my mind's

259

periphery, like a ghost. The more immediate memory is her mouth grazing my finger.

I ball my hands into fists. The storm has come, cold and sudden and furious, beating at the walls of the cabin. I'm very aware of how thin the wood is, how it creaks and moans around us, how the chill slips in through the cracks. Even with the woodstove blazing, my skin rises with gooseflesh and my teeth are chattering. The worst is the chill at the tip of my nose.

Melinoë's eyes remain open. Watching me. Even at the best of times she's pale, and her skin has that slightly purple cast, but now it looks almost gray. Whatever modifications Caerus has made to her, she's obviously not immune to the cold.

Surgeries upon surgeries, syringes in her neck, like the one that injected my tracker. Digging into her brain, as if with a scalpel, prying loose all the unsavory memories, optimizing her into a machine: sleek, immaculate, ruthless. Incapable of mercy, incapable of regret. And despite all of it, I've seen the memories cresting through, surfacing from the deep, dark water. Those illicit, stolen moments that should be impossible, the smiles and laughs and even the grief that Caerus couldn't manage to steal.

It's too cold for me to relax into the silence. I have to speak, to distract myself from the chill that seems to be settling in my very marrow.

"I remember the last time it stormed like this," I say. "We lost power for a week. We kept having to borrow a generator from the Wesselses and haul it over on our rafts. Luka and I both fell overboard at least twice."

Melinoë bites a blue lip. "The Wesselses?"

"They're another family in Esopus. Upper Esopus." I give a small smile. "Where it doesn't flood quite so badly. The father is Dr. Wessels. He treats all our broken bones and cures our fevers. And his son is Jacob . . ."

Jacob. I can't think of him without thinking of the kiss. It feels slippery in my mind, like scum on stale water. Something I don't want to touch.

Melinoë watches me expectantly.

"He's a friend," I say at last. "The Wesselses are the ones who loaned us the car."

"He sounds like a good friend," Melinoë says, and I can't read the tone in her voice.

The memory sloshes around in my head unpleasantly. "I guess so. But not—not like Keres."

Suddenly Melinoë is tense. She props herself up on her elbows, eyes shifting.

"I just mean," I go on in a rush, "we would never sleep with each other. Sleep next to each other, I mean."

My mouth tastes a little sour as I say the words. I can't pretend I haven't pictured it: Melinoë in bed with this other girl. Maybe they curled around each other, like twin mollusks. Maybe they just joined hands, linked pinkies. Either way, it makes my stomach simmer with a strange emotion. Jealousy? I have no reason to be jealous of a girl I've never met, and one who is lost to Melinoë anyway.

"I see." Melinoë's tone is curt.

Silence falls across the cabin. Well, not really silence. The

261

wind is keening like a wounded animal. With each blast of air, a new wave of cold washes over me, and my teeth chatter even more furiously. I'm starting to regret washing up earlier. My hair is still slightly damp around the nape of my neck, and it's making me even chillier.

"It wasn't like that," Melinoë says suddenly.

I blink. "What?"

"With Keres." She looks down at the worn bedspread. I can't see very well, in the chiaroscuro of the room, but it almost looks like she's blushing. "It couldn't have been. We're not allowed . . . Azrael would never . . ."

She's definitely blushing—that odd violet color, which I'm starting to think is sort of beautiful. Like the underside of a lilac petal when it's shot through with sunlight.

"I see," I echo. I have to bite the inside of my cheek, because a smile is threatening to push across my face. Another gust of wind makes the whole cabin shudder. Frigid air slithers in under the beaten door. I shiver violently. I can hear Melinoë's teeth chattering now, too. After a beat, I add, "I'm sure it never gets this cold in the City."

"No."

"It might be easier to stay warm," I say, "if we were closer together."

As soon as the words are out, a fierce blush rises to my face. I stare down at the floor, because I can't bear to look at Melinoë, to see her scandalized expression. She doesn't reply, and a long stretch of silence passes between us. The wind keeps up its brutal howling.

When the silence has gone on for so long and my cheeks are so hot that I'm considering just walking out into the cold and freezing to death just to escape the utter humiliation, Melinoë says, very quietly, "Okay."

The next moments unfold without words. Haltingly, I get to my feet. Melinoë sits up and shifts backward, nearly to the edge of the bed, to make room for me. I bend down and unlace my boots. The whole time I can feel her gaze on me. It draws my blood up near the surface of my skin—almost like a knife, but without the pain.

Once my boots are off, I lie down on my back, tense. Melinoë drapes the covers over us both. She hesitates for a moment, then slides down onto the mattress beside me.

The bed is too small for us not to touch. We're pressed shoulder to shoulder, both staring up at the ceiling. In the cold, our breath drifts up above our heads, mingling in soft wisps of white.

"I'll stay up and watch the door," I say, but the effect of my words is diminished by a very ill-timed yawn.

"It's okay. I'm a light sleeper."

Exhaustion is weighing on my eyelids. "Okay."

It doesn't take long for the warmth of Melinoë's body to start seeping into mine. Under the covers, the tips of my fingers begin to regain sensation, chasing away my fear of frostbite. I flex them in relief, and when I do, my thumb brushes against Melinoë's palm.

I expect her to flinch away, but she doesn't. We just lie there in silence. I slow my breathing until it matches hers exactly, our chests rising and falling in an identical rhythm.

I don't know if I've ever lain beside someone like this before. Maybe Luka, once upon a time, but I was too young to remember. In fact, I can't remember the last time I was this close to someone who didn't hurt me. Even Jacob, whose kiss I never asked for, tasted so bitter in my mouth. And I can't remember ever wanting to be touched like this by someone. Held. Maybe more.

Melinoë falls asleep before I do, long, pale hair spread across the pillow, shimmery in the low light, and it's impossible to remind myself to be afraid of her. I'm only afraid of waking her, of spoiling this moment that seems held in timeless suspension—this moment where she looks so much like an angel to me, but not the kind that Caerus makes.

The lamps burn hazily, running the oil down to its last drops. My eyelids slide shut, and sleep claims me.

I wake slowly, in warmth and in silence. Morning light bleeds through the cracks in the walls, falling in bright bands on the floor. One stripes across my face. The woodstove has gone dark, but the chill has been banished from my bones. I no longer feel the cold at all. I can only feel the slight scratchiness of the bedsheets, and the gentle pressure of Melinoë's arm around my waist.

I'm curled on my side, and so is she, her face so close that her slow breath tickles my cheek. I go completely still, listening to her low exhales and inhales, hardly daring to breathe myself.

I wonder if it was a conscious choice, or if her body simply folded into mine, in the muddled throes of sleep. Pressed together like this, the world takes on a bleary, luminous glow, like the vestiges of a dream. I close my eyes again.

If I am dreaming, I want to stay asleep for just a little bit longer.

In the end, it's the faint simmering of anxiety that jogs me fully awake. It was my turn to keep watch, but obviously that was an utter failure, and who knows what could have been attracted to the cabin overnight. Even though I know it's unlikely due to the storm, I'm compelled to check, just to make sure.

But when I extricate myself from the bed—very, very slowly, so as not to disturb Melinoë—and nudge open the door, it's not the muggy, suffocating aftermath of a rainstorm that awaits me. It's snow.

A fine, crisp layer of frost lies over the ground. It lines every tree branch and makes a pale crown over each jutting stone. Where sunlight finds its way through the canopy, it makes the snow sparkle like broken glass. The albedo effect is so strong that I have to raise a hand to shade my eyes.

I let out a breath of amazement, which floats from my mouth in a white cloud. I wonder if, somehow, I could still be dreaming.

From behind me, inside the cabin, there's the sound of Melinoë stirring. I shut the door and turn around to see her sitting up, stretching her thin arms. I wonder if she remembers holding me in the night. I feel a faint thud of disappointment at the thought that she doesn't.

Her hair is mussed from sleep, falling loose around her shoulders. Her eyes look brighter than I've ever seen them, the hollows of her cheeks not so pronounced. The bruise on her temple has all but vanished. I can't seem to find her sharp edges anymore, the cold Angel qualities that once terrified me. Now she looks delicate, almost ethereal. My heart skips a beat.

I must have the most indecipherable look on my face, because Melinoë frowns. "What's wrong?"

"Nothing." I shake my head, as if I can banish the traitorous thoughts. "But you should come outside."

Warily, she rises from the bed. "Why?"

"Just trust me." I bite my lip on a smile as Melinoë crosses the room, heading to the door. "Wait. Hang on."

The oversize flannel shirt I wore yesterday is hanging on the back of the chair. Melinoë watches with no small amount of consternation as I pick it up and drape it over her shoulders, buttoning the top button so it looks like a cloak.

"There," I say. "That should help."

"You're very strange, you know," she says.

"I know." I zip my jacket up to my chin. "Come on."

I push open the door, and light pours into the cabin. Wind blows back Melinoë's hair. Standing there beside me in the threshold, shock—and something gentler, maybe wonder—works its way across her face.

"I've never seen it before," she says, softly.

"Me neither," I admit. "Except on TV."

"Everyone says the earth is too warm for it to snow. At least in New Amsterdam. It still snows sometimes in New England, I think. North."

She looks like a natural part of the environment for the first time: a creature of ice and snow at home in this frost-veiled world.

If she were dressed in white instead of black, she would blend in perfectly, like a fox shedding its russet coat for the camouflage of winter.

The snow that spreads out in front of us is unmarred, not yet pocked with fallen branches or the prints of animals. Everything is new.

"Do you ever wonder if they're wrong?" I ask. "The scientists, I mean. They keep telling us that the planet is getting warmer, less hospitable. That eventually it won't be able to host any life at all. But do you think they could be wrong? That maybe there's a chance things could get better?"

She looks at me with her dark, doe-like eyes. "I don't think I'm qualified to say."

"Just your best guess, then. A gut feeling."

Melinoë casts her gaze around the clearing, and for a long moment there's no sound except the snow slowly melting, dripping from the branches and onto the fresh sheet of frost. "I don't know," she replies at last. "I don't think it's up to nature. It's up to people. So I suppose it depends on whether you have faith in people."

"You don't have very much faith in people."

"No." She looks down at her gloved hands. "If humans were collectively capable of compassion, we never would have gotten here in the first place."

"I don't know about people as a whole. I haven't met enough of them. Until now I'd never left Esopus Creek." A small smile comes over my face. "But I think individuals are capable of compassion. Actually, I know they are. And maybe that's all it takes—at least at the beginning. Just a few people who care. And that caring matters, even if it can't cool the earth or lower sea levels or turn back time to before a nuclear blast."

Melinoë doesn't answer, but she does lift her gaze to mine. At her sides, her fists clench and unclench. We're standing close enough that I could reach out and take her hand. I remember the warmth of her body last night, her arm around my waist, and I flex my fingers. I could touch her. I could—

There's a rustling in the distance, faint, like leaves in the wind. At first I think nothing of it. But then it grows louder, closer. A Wend? I can't smell the familiar odor of rotting flesh. A mutation? Maybe. But it would be uncommon for one to venture so near the cabin, especially in the light of day.

The snowy brush around the clearing begins to part. The cans fixed in the trees rattle like tinny wind chimes.

Melinoë's head snaps up, as quick as a mountain cat scenting the air. All that violet color drains from her face.

And then, hoarsely, she whispers, "*Run*."

I'm too shocked and bewildered to obey. The thing that parts the bushes is nothing animal—at least, nothing of the natural world. It has a sleek metal hull, a lithe rectangular body mounted on four mechanical legs. Gears whir as it stalks closer, its steps too measured, too stilted. It's an aberration, but not like the mutations.

It's not a creature that has evolved for survival. It's a machine that was crafted to kill.

Before I can react, Melinoë grabs me by the back of my jacket and hauls me inside the cabin. She slams the door shut and forces one of the chairs under the handle, jamming it. I catch myself against the table before I fall, breathing hard.

"What *is* that?"

Melinoë has already shed the flannel shirt and has her rifle in hand. "A Dog. One of Caerus's mobile robots."

"But why—how—is it here?"

"I don't know," she says. "But it means Caerus found us."

There's a heavy scrabbling on the other side of the door. Blood roars in my ears. I kneel down and search under the bed, where I stowed Melinoë's knife, not that I'm convinced it will do me much good.

With enough force to knock the breath out of me, Melinoë shoves me to my belly, flat on the floor. "Get down," she hisses.

I hold my body completely still, though every nerve ending is fizzing with panic. Melinoë crouches beside me, peering through the scope of her rifle. There's a tiny crack in the wooden door, hardly wide enough to fit a finger through, and that's where she aims her gun.

She shoots.

Abruptly, the scrabbling stops. As the smoky smell of gunpowder fills the air, my muscles relax slightly, but Melinoë doesn't even twitch. She's staring down the barrel of her gun, the side of her face with the prosthetic eye turned toward me, so I can't begin to guess what she's thinking.

Thud. Thud. Thud.

The sound makes my heart leap into my throat. It's on the opposite wall this time, the pounding of forelegs against wood.

269

Melinoë whirls around. She fires another shot, right through the cabin wall, and the scrabbling ceases again. My body is starting to ache from being pressed against the floor, my muscles stretched and taut like copper wire. Melinoë's finger hovers over the trigger. Waiting.

Thud. Thud. Thud.

Thud. Thud. Thud.

It's coming from both sides now, from the door and the wall to my right. My blood curdles to ice.

"Two of them?" I whisper.

Melinoë gives a small, tight nod.

"How?" I manage, my voice breaking. "How did they find us?"

A swallow ticks in her throat. "I don't know. Maybe—maybe your tracker. Maybe it came back online."

I'm all too aware of it now, that second, alien pulse. When I focus on it, all other sounds turn distant and obscure. It becomes a timer again, ticking down the seconds to my death.

Melinoë shoots again, and my ears ring. This time there's no pause in the scrabbling, and after a moment, the wood splinters inward as the Dog's black foreleg punctures a hole in the door.

It's stuck there briefly, gears whirring, and Melinoë fires. The bullet glides right across its metal hull, leaving a silver scuff mark but nothing more.

My heart drops back into my stomach. *This is how I'm going to die,* I think, *not by my Angel's hands, but blasted apart by some Caerus machine.* Melinoë shoots again. Again.

The second Dog plunges through the wall, its body wedged

halfway into the cabin and halfway out. I can't help it—I scream. Melinoë whirls around and fires, but the bullets just ping off like pebbles. The next scream gets caught in my throat, strangled before it can come out.

"We have to get out of here." I manage to push up onto my knees, as the Dogs make more and more progress through the wood. "Come on."

Melinoë shakes her head, without taking her eye from the scope. "They're faster. We can't outrun them."

As her bullets continue to ping off, I almost want to laugh, in the blackest, most humorless way. Of course Caerus would make their Dogs bulletproof. And now, with them closing in, I understand that the Gauntlets really are a mercy, because at least the Outliers stand a sliver of a chance against the Angels. We have no chance against such monstrous machines.

TWENTY-SIX

MELINOË

Something is rising behind my eyes as I shoot, a red-tinged wave, blistering at the edges of my vision. This should be the easiest thing in the world. It's what I was made for. Caerus scientists labored over my body for hours and hours so that I could kill anything that's put in front of me, without fear and without remorse.

But I'm terrified now, and not just for myself. It's Inesa, kneeling by my side, who stays at the forefront of my mind. Her blanched face, her panicked stare. The gears of the Dogs whir like helicopter blades as they crush and crush their way inside the cabin.

I shoot, because there's nothing else to do. And because the whistling of the bullets is so familiar, almost comforting, like a song, a prelude for the end of my life.

Quickly, before I can stop her, Inesa gets to her feet and darts across the cabin. My finger slips from the trigger. "Don't!" I cry. "Stay down!"

But she's already skidded to her knees in front of the wood-stove and grasped the bottle of kerosene. She meets my eyes, gaze flickering between fear and determination. "What about this?"

What about this?

Somehow, these are words I've heard before. The fire blooms upward behind my eyes. I feel like everything is converging, except I don't know what *everything* is, only that the flame isn't a dream, isn't a glitch in my system; it's a memory. It layers over my vision and makes Inesa's face flicker like static in front of me.

"Maybe," I say, in a voice that seems too distant to be my own. "We have to try."

My limbs feel dull and heavy as I cross the room to Inesa. I take her hand and pull her to her feet. She swallows and squares her shoulders, as if to steel herself, and then, with a surprising show of strength, she hurls the chair away from the door. Almost dragging me after her, she bursts out of the cabin, into the cold, brisk air that seems to cut my eyes like broken glass.

The fire is so vivid that the real world is just its backdrop now. The Dogs, still caught in the cabin walls, start to reverse, their robotic legs pumping in a furious gyre.

We only have enough time to make it to the trees before they've extricated themselves. They back up with mechanical precision, eyeless metal hulls trained on us. Their sides are scuffed with bullet marks, and one of them is limping, the end of its front leg missing.

Inesa still has her fingers laced with mine, the bottle of kerosene grasped in her other hand. She raises her arm, the bottle arcing over her head. I lift my rifle, bracing it on my shoulder, and try to tunnel my vision into the scope, but suddenly everything is engulfed in flames.

And then the real world drops away. Memories flower up in its place. I can feel the heat of the remembered fire, taste the smoke in the air. And I can see Keres in front of me, black hair loose and wild around her shoulders, her eyes smoldering like embers. Their fury sears my skin.

She's holding a gun—a handgun, not a rifle, silver instead of black. It's Azrael's gun, I realize with a start, the one he always keeps tucked under his coat. She raises it until the barrel is pointed at her temple, her finger trembling over the trigger.

Azrael's voice comes, and it's too smooth, too casual.

"Put that down, Keres," he says, as slick as oil. "That's enough now."

"*No*," she bites out.

We're in her room. I've been here a hundred times before. There's the bed, the sheets tucked in neatly by the anonymous hands of a maid. There's her wardrobe door, flung open, dozens of identical black suits hanging like strung-up corpses. There's the window, spreading from floor to ceiling behind her, the City lights gleaming behind the glass. And to her left there's the fireplace, flames licking upward, the only disturbance in the still, heavy air.

I think I'm too stunned to speak. The rest of the memory returns in increments. Moments ago I had been lying in Keres's bed, our limbs entwined, our hair tangled on the sheets. And then there was Azrael, wrenching me from my half-dreaming state, pulling me up by my elbow and marching me to the door. And then there was Keres—up on her feet in the span of a breath, grabbing the gun strapped to his belt.

"You can't keep doing this to us," she says, her voice strangled with tears that will never fall. "I'm finished. I'm done."

"Don't be ridiculous," Azrael says. "You're making a fool of yourself."

"Shut up!" she cries. "Just shut up!"

Her finger brushes the trigger, but she can't bring herself to pull it. A hard lump is lodged in my throat and my mind is swimming. All the words I might say are lost to me, falling and falling endlessly through a thousand black spaces.

"Put it down," Azrael says, more sternly this time. "I mean it. Or I'll do the final Wipe and you'll be on Van Wyck's arm in a week."

I remember now. I'd been having nightmares about the girl. Sanne. I'd snuck into Keres's room, in the cold cover of night. She'd blamed herself, for not being able to do the Gauntlet, for Azrael making me do it in her place. She was still woozy from the painkillers, from the antirejection medication, some of her stitches still leaking, and she told me she'd hardly slept in weeks. She told me her body was betraying her. She told me it had never really been her own.

She was a fuse that had burned nearly to its end.

Azrael takes a step closer. Keres doesn't move. Her arm is trembling, the barrel of the gun pressed hard against her temple. Her blue eyes are like smoked glass.

"Come on, now," Azrael says. He's mere feet away from her. Close enough, almost, to reach out and grab the gun. "It's not worth this, Keres. I'll do a Wipe, and you won't even remember it by tomorrow."

Her gaze flashes, welling with impossible tears. Her lips pull back into a snarl, half anger, half pain, like a wounded animal, and she says, "No. You'll never do that to me again."

And then she shoots—but not at herself. In the space of a breath, she aims the gun at the base of the fireplace and pulls the trigger. The bullet flies.

"No!" I shout. I lunge for her.

But the fire divides us. Her bullet hits the gas tank, and the world explodes in red and gold. Heat billows outward. Smoke engulfs her. I inhale it and it chokes me and I drop to my knees, gasping. There's the acrid scent of burnt leather in the air. And then there's Azrael, his hand on the collar of my shirt, dragging me backward as if I'm a dog he's got by the scruff of its neck. Keres has vanished behind the flames.

The memory melts away and the real world resurrects itself before my eyes.

I'm in a universe of ice and snow. Keres is gone; Azrael is gone; there are only the Dogs pacing toward me, crunching the frost under their robot feet, and Inesa, still holding my hand. The warmth and pressure of her grip bring me back to myself. She's real; she's here; she's alive.

I can save her. I might have failed Keres, but I won't fail her.

In one brisk, rough motion, I yank the bottle of kerosene from her hand. She's too shocked to protest, to fight back. Her eyes grow wide with bewildered horror.

I give her a harsh shove and she tumbles backward, falling into the snow. I feel the reverberation of the impact in the soles of my

276

feet when she hits the ground. She scrambles upright, brushing her hair out of her face, but by the time she processes what I'm about to do, it's too late. I step between her and the whirring, man-made monsters.

"No!" she cries. "Don't—"

I hurl the kerosene at the Dogs. In the fraction of a second that it's still airborne, before it can bounce off them and land in the snow, I pull the trigger.

One perfect shot.

Heat. Engulfing me like a cloud of polluted air, heavy and black. Light sears through my eyelids, turning everything a sharp, burning white.

And pain. Pain like I've never felt before, crawling up my limbs, scorching every inch of my skin. Caerus has worked hard to prevent this, reaching into our brains and turning off pain receptors, toggling them like switches. Increasing the production of endorphins with injections and pills. But they can't go too far, because pain is protective, too. It lets you know when your life is in danger. It helps keep you alive.

I can't move or speak. Every nerve ending in my body is crackling like a fuse. This is the pain that says *Run. Hide.* But my muscles won't obey.

The next thing I feel is pressure under my arms. My legs skid across the ground and it feels like my skin is being scraped off, scraped down to the sinew and bone beneath. I manage to choke out a singular sound, but I can't tell if she hears me. Inesa. Dragging my body through the snow.

My vision returns to me in slow, agonizing increments, in brutal stops and starts, sharpening and then blurring again. I'm lying on my back, head tilted upward. I see the threshold of the cabin, dark wood against the white sky. I see smoke curling in the air. There's a foul, charred odor, and beneath it, something even more putrid. My own skin, burning like meat on a grill.

"Mel? Mel?" Inesa clutches my face in her hands. Her palms are cool and her touch is soft.

I blink, and her features clarify. Her pink-touched cheeks, freckles strewn like stars. Her earth-colored eyes, brimming with tears. Strands of dark hair falling wildly, caught on her lips and her thick lashes.

"Wait here," she says—as if I have any other choice. Her voice sounds distant, muffled; the pain is holding me at a distance, like I'm trapped underwater.

I blink again, and she's gone.

As long as I stay still, the pain keeps a sort of equilibrium. Embers and ashes, not blazing blue flame. More of my vision returns. There are the walls of the cabin, wood warped by water stains, and the gashes left by the Dogs that let the light bleed through. Distantly I can hear fire crackling. There's no room in me for panic, but I don't have to worry about whether Inesa will return. She will. She does.

Her face hovers above me, her brows knitted with fear. "I'm so sorry," she says. "It's going to hurt."

I can't really imagine how she could make it worse, but I don't say that. Instead, I part my cracked lips and whisper, "Did it work?"

She lets out a breath, almost a laugh, though without humor. "Yeah. It worked. The . . . the Dogs are dead. Blown to pieces. I don't think they're coming back, unless Caerus also dabbles in necromancy. But I guess they were never really alive."

"No," I say. The heaviness of exhaustion has settled over me, and I can't add anything else.

Inesa swallows. "It's mostly just your legs. It'll be easier if you can sit up . . ."

I give a faint nod of permission, and Inesa puts her hands under my arms again, propping me up against the wall. From this vantage, I can finally look down at my body.

I'm surprised to see that from the waist up, there's little damage. My gloves have burned off, but the flame-retardant material has kept my palms unmarred. Even my thighs aren't too bad, except the patches where my hunting suit has dissolved, leaving my skin raw and bright pink underneath.

But below the knee, my legs are a mangle of flesh and fabric. Long strips of the material have melted right into my skin. Around it, the flesh is raised and puckered, even blackened in some places. There's already a line of blisters, bubbling with yellow pus. Feeling the pain was one thing. But seeing the ruin is enough to make my throat fill with bile.

Inesa works fastidiously, as if she's done this a hundred times before. She's gathered a bucket of snow and very gently presses it in handfuls against the worst of my burns. Pain shoots from my legs and drills into my temple, making me gasp.

"Sorry!" She grimaces, eyes wavering with unshed tears. "I'll try to be quick."

The pain is coming in irregular jolts now, whenever the snow touches my skin. I'm not sure about the effectiveness of this particular method, but I don't question her. I'm not in the City now. There are no Caerus medics to anesthetize me and graft on new skin.

Inesa takes a knife from the table and slowly begins to work at the pieces of my suit the fire left behind. Even the slightest tug is agony. I inhale sharply.

"I'm sorry," she says again. "I just need to take the fabric off, or it will get infected . . ."

"Wait," I say hoarsely. "There are pills. On the table. Pain medication."

Inesa rises and sorts through the items on the table—the matches, the candles, the bandages, the meal replacement packets—and returns with a handful of tablets. Crouching down beside me again, she asks, "These?"

I nod. I try to reach out for the pills, but my limbs won't move the way I want them to. Inesa hesitates. And then, very gently, she puts a hand on the back of my neck. Tips my head back. I open my mouth and she places a tablet on my tongue. With immense difficulty, I swallow.

I close my eyes. Luckily the medication works quickly. If there's one thing Caerus is good at, it's making you numb. After a few heavy, shuddering breaths, I can hardly feel the pain at all.

"Better?" Inesa asks quietly.

"Much."

When I open my eyes, she's staring at me. Her face is close enough that I can see the tears daggered through her dark lashes. The smudges of ash on her cheek. Her throat ticks.

"I watched Dr. Wessels do this once," she whispers. "He cooled the burns with cold water. Then painkillers. But he said . . ." She pauses, swallows again. "He said it was important to remove tight clothing. Before the wounds swell."

Blunted by both the ebbing pain and the painkillers, my mind is slow to grasp what she means. All I can do is blink back at her. Then the word rises, almost unconsciously.

"Okay."

Inesa draws a breath. Then, with utmost gentleness, she takes me by the shoulders, tipping me forward at the waist. Just enough to reach the zipper on the back of my suit.

As she tugs it down, cool air brushes my bare skin, making goose bumps rise along my spine. I bend over farther, palms against the floor to steady myself. When the zipper reaches the small of my back, Inesa pauses. She repositions herself and then begins to pull the suit down from the front.

The fabric peels off my shoulders. My chest. It feels like my own skin is being cut away, like I'm parting with an essential piece of myself. But by the time my suit has been shed completely, when it's just a crumpled heap of black fabric on the floor, it feels like nothing at all, and I can't imagine how it ever seemed so vital.

Inesa brushes my hair back, baring my collarbones. Without even looking up at her face, I can feel her gaze running over me. From the scars on my wrists to the ones on my elbows, the crooks of my knees. My hips. They're garish and ugly, raised like maggots under my skin.

"They take us apart and put us back together." I stare down at the floor. "And then they have to cover up how hideous it looks."

"They're not hideous." Inesa's thumb touches the scar on my wrist. "They're just . . . adaptations. It means you've survived."

"Maybe." Slowly, I lift my gaze. "Maybe that's all, but . . ."

My voice tangles in my throat. Inesa just watches me. Her eyes are bright and deep at the same time, like light filtering through the leaves.

"I'm sick of just surviving," I whisper. "I want . . . more."

Fear floods me as I say the words. I'm curled naked on the floor and confession has made me even more vulnerable. Nothing dooms you quicker than desire.

Inesa raises her hands to cup my face. Her fingers are trembling.

"Me too," she whispers back.

She leans forward, closing the space between us. Our foreheads touch. And then our lips.

It all bleeds away. The pain. The smoke in the air. The cold prickling my skin. All I can feel is the warmth and pressure of her mouth, gentle but insistent. It sends heat through my body, through the marrow of my bones. I wrap my arms around her waist to pull her closer, and she folds into me, as if our bodies were made for this. As if it's the most natural thing in the world.

Maybe it is. Maybe I've survived this long so I could know how it feels to hold her. Maybe all my life has been one long gauntlet, running, fighting, searching for her.

TWENTY-SEVEN

INESA

I kiss her, and it feels like I've finally learned to breathe. I've been panting, struggling for air, and living by half measures. Everything I want just barely out of my grasp. Now I don't have to fight.

There's only a sliver of space between us, but it's still too much—her hand presses the small of my back, drawing me closer. My hands tangle in her long hair, the strange, beautiful color that looks almost silver in some light. It's even softer than I imagined it would be, sliding through my fingers like water.

Melinoë is the one to break the kiss. We're both breathing hard, our chests rising and falling, the rhythms perfectly synced.

Her heart is beating so close to mine that I can feel it. Like the pulse of a thousand tiny wings. "I've wanted to do that for a long time."

She bites down on her slightly swollen lip. "So have I."

"I was afraid to do it," I say quietly. "I was afraid you would hate me."

"I never hated you." She pauses, looking up from under her

pale lashes. "That was always the most terrifying thing. That I couldn't hate you even with my hands around your throat."

The memory of it—that horrible, clenching pressure—is as distant as a dream. All I know now is the softness of her touch. The warmth of her body, her lips.

"Oh," I say. "I was just afraid you would hate me for being a terrible kisser."

She laughs. I think it surprises us both, how easily the sound slips out. It's low and breathy, but it's real, and threaded with affection.

"No," she says. "But I'm easy to impress. I've never kissed anyone before."

I laugh, too. A dark-gold, molten feeling pools at the bottom of my belly.

"Well," I say, "you're the first person I've wanted to."

Jacob doesn't count. Neither does Adrian Pietersen, or the handful of other boys who awkwardly stuck their tongues down my throat while I stood there, still and cold as a fish. With Melinoë holding me, I feel as new and alive as shoots of green showing themselves in the earth.

I reach for her again. Cupping her face, my thumbs brush her cheekbones. Her dark eyes are like pools under the new moon, showing me my own reflection. I remember how I once cowered under her gaze, the prosthetic staring down at me, depthless and inhuman. With her so fragile now, stripped in every sense of the word, the eye becomes a lovely thing, as precious as a rare jewel.

"You're so beautiful," I whisper.

That faint purple flush comes over her. "It's just the surgeries. It's not real."

"You feel real to me."

Our lips meet again, with more insistence this time. She pushes herself up on her knees, and I can only imagine how much it hurts, with her legs as blistered as they are—but if she feels any pain, she doesn't let me know. She just holds me tighter, so that her bones are pressed against my bones, her bare skin against the fabric of my clothes, and I want to wrap her up, envelop her, keep her safe from the danger and the cold.

The air is still sooty with the remains of the fire, smoldering to ashes outside the door. There are holes in the wood where the light spills in, bright white as it reflects off the snow. It could be a dream: the outlying Counties of New Amsterdam, covered in a layer of impossible frost.

I know it will melt. Already water is dripping from the leaves and the branches, and the ice is draining into the dirt. But beneath the surface, there is a metamorphosis taking place, in the mud and the flower buds, just curling out of their seed hulls. The earth doesn't remember snow, either. To the soil and the seeds, all of this is new, too. How could anyone expect it to stay the same?

We lie facing each other in the bed, close enough for our noses to brush. Our hair streams over our bare shoulders, tangling like a nexus of tree roots. Light braiding with dark. Melinoë closes her eyes, breathing softly.

I remember the tug of jealousy I felt when she told me she had slept in the same bed as Keres. Now I have to bite my lip to keep from smiling, because I'm the one who gets to hold her, to touch her. To kiss her. I trace my thumb along her collarbone. Her lashes flutter.

"Can I tell you something?" I whisper.

She opens her eyes. Nods.

"I think you were wrong."

"About what?"

"About people." I tuck a strand of hair behind her ear. There's a scar just by her ear, too, a very faint one, half hidden beneath the soft fuzz on her temple. That's where they must have implanted her comms chip. "There's lots of reasons to have faith in them."

A small furrow appears between her brows. She's quiet, but after a moment, she replies, "Maybe just a single reason. Maybe just a single person."

I slow my breathing until it matches hers. "Sometimes all you need is one."

TWENTY-EIGHT

MELINOË

Sleep finds Inesa quickly, but it can't seem to get a hold on me.
The pain has receded into the background, just nipping at me
lightly when I move too quickly or too suddenly. It's more the opposite sensation that keeps me awake: the way my skin is still warm
and humming with the memory of her touch. The way my lips are
swollen, throbbing with the echoes of pleasure. I touch them and
feel the pulse of my own heartbeat, dragging and low.

When I do close my eyes, the world behind them explodes
with color. Bright white and deep green. Even with the more-than-
perfect vision my prosthetic grants me, it all feels new. Shades I've
never seen before. Hues I didn't believe were real. Extinct colors,
long-erased from the City, from the world Caerus built, but spring-
ing quietly back to life out here.

Inesa's bare shoulders rise and fall with her breathing. The
bruises I left on her neck have nearly faded, but there's a smaller
one blooming up in its place, violet and tender, in the shape of my
mouth. I want to kiss her again. I want to touch her. I want to fall

asleep next to her and know nothing will wake me.

But I remember it all now. Azrael jerking me out of Keres's bed. The icy fury in his eyes. I extricate myself from the blankets, taking care not to disturb Inesa. When I rise from the bed and put my weight gingerly on my feet, pain shoots up my legs and jolts my heart. I have to bite my lip to keep from making a sound.

I wait until the pain returns to its bearable equilibrium, and then I walk over to the table. My hunting suit still lies puddled on the floor, torn and charred. Streaks of my blood are drying on the wood. The jagged holes in the wall and the door where the Dogs clawed their way in are exposing planks of shivery light. The woodstove is cold.

There's no putting my suit back on. Instead, I take the oversize flannel shirt from where it's draped over the chair and button it to my throat. The pants are hopelessly large, so I just leave them. The shirt falls all the way to my knees, and I figure my legs and feet may benefit from exposure to the numbingly chill air.

I open the cabin door and step into the snow. Outside sunlight is glancing off the fast-melting layer of frost. Even though it's barely been an hour since I blew up the Dogs, it feels like an eternity has passed. The new world that hangs before my eyes is beautiful and strange. Maybe I did fall asleep and this is a dream. Maybe it will always be this bright and I'll never see the setting sun.

But I can't quite convince myself it's true. I take slow, halting steps through the snow, my whole body feeling clumsy with both the returning pain and the residual numbing effects of the pill. Eventually, I reach the smoldering pile of metal.

The Dogs are in pieces, legs snapped off their bodies, hulls crushed inward. I have to admit that I'm surprised how easy it was to destroy them. From all the stories I've heard, from all the demonstrations I've seen, I thought they'd be a lot more durable. It surprises me, too, that they never shot back at us, even though examining them now, I can see the charred remains of their mounted machine guns. If they had wanted us dead, they could've killed us instantly, in a spray of bullets.

I kneel down beside the nearest one and begin picking through the rubble. The metal is still hot enough to burn my hands, so I pull down the shirtsleeves to cover my palms. The pieces of the Dogs are all warped. I can't shake the feeling that this is wrong. Admittedly, my knowledge is limited, but how can kerosene burn hot enough to melt such tough, durable metal?

Something gleams from the mass of rubble, smooth and black as a piece of polished obsidian. I brush off the ash with my sleeve.

It's a large square object, unmarred by the explosion—not even scuffed. When I tap it with my index finger, there's a faint reverberation, suggesting it's hollow inside.

A literal black box. I run my hands around it until I find a small latch, just barely big enough to flip open with my thumbnail.

Inside there's a rolled-up length of fabric, also black. I recognize the insulated, heat-reflecting, Kevlar-lined material at once. I unfurl it onto the snow. A hunting suit.

My heart starts pounding. Underneath the suit, the box is full of other supplies: bullets, syringes, bandages, decon-tabs, meal replacement packets. My fingers tremble as I remove each item and set it down beside me. Total numbness overtakes me. I can't even feel the cold on my bare legs.

The last item is an even smaller box, made of the same sleek, polished metal. It looks like the sort of box that would hold a wedding ring, but when I flip it open, I find a tiny black object, curled like a mollusk. I struggle to even pinch it between my finger and thumb. I raise it up to the light.

It's an earpiece. My heart lurches.

Still trembling, I place it in my ear. There's the crackle of static, the high-pitched hum of a searching signal. And then a low, familiar voice.

"Hello, Melinoë."

Azrael.

"I'm sure you have plenty of questions. Don't worry. I'll answer them all in good time."

His voice is so smooth, so controlled, that at first I wonder if it's a recording. I stay silent, my heart hammering painfully against my sternum.

"Okay?"

Dry-mouthed, I reply, "Okay."

"I'm glad to see you survived your encounter with the Dogs."

Something twinges in my stomach. "You didn't mean for them to kill me. If you did, I would be dead."

"No," he agrees. "You're smart enough to figure that out. You're also smart enough to know that we've been watching you."

My vision tips. The ground seems to switch places with the sky. I stare and stare into the middle distance until my eyes burn, until I hear Azrael inhale, impatience evident in just that single sharp breath.

"How long?" I ask hoarsely. "How long have the cameras been on?"

"We did lose connection briefly. And after your encounter with Luka, your comms chip was indeed disabled. But the Lamb's tracker eventually came back online, and so did the cameras. Just in time to see you fall asleep next to her in that cave."

"But I didn't hear the cameras. Not once, since . . ." I trail off. My voice is smaller than a whisper.

Azrael laughs, a raspy, pitying sound that makes me feel like I'm eight years old again, my hand slipping out of my real father's grasp. I can almost remember that now, too. My real parents: Their faces are blurry, like reflections on the water, but if I focus, they sharpen and clarify. I'm starting to remember it all.

"You think we can't keep them below your detection?" Azrael clucks his tongue. "Making them audible was always a favor to you and the other Angels, so you would perform well. But as it turns out, your best performance has been when you believed the cameras were off."

"I'm not *performing*," I bite out. "I've been trying to stay alive. Because you *abandoned* me."

Azrael is silent, leaving only the faint hum of static in my ear, as anger surges like fire through my veins.

"You saw me get hit in the head," I go on, feeling almost breathless with fury. "You saw me almost get killed by the Wends. I could have starved or frozen, and you didn't help."

Azrael lets out a breath, full of indulgent contempt. "You must have forgotten how this works, Melinoë."

"No," I say, "I haven't forgotten. I remember everything now."

Silence. The static skips and hums irregularly, like the staggered beating of my own heart. I know the cameras are on now, hovering close to pick up every twitch of my mouth, every flash of emotion in my gaze, but I don't care. I want to claw out the hideous machine they've given me in place of my real eye. I want to scream until it tears my lungs.

"I remember everything," I say again, bitterly. "I remember what you did to Keres. What you did to me. What you've done, this whole time, to all of us . . ."

The buzzing static in my ear is wretched and almost painful. I hear Azrael inhale sharply.

"And what good has it done you, to remember?"

My righteous fury starts to wither. I feel myself slipping back into the body of the girl who was happy to forget. Who begged for the Wipes. Who had lain still as cold hands worked on her, as a black-clad body arched over her—I remember that, too. And the words I want to speak turn to ash in my mouth.

"I have been kind," Azrael says. "I have been merciful. Do you wish I had let Keres put a bullet in her brain? Do you wish I had left you mired in guilt and misery forever? I've given you the gift of oblivion. It's something many would kill for, or die for."

Something essential inside me cracks. Because he's right. It hurts to remember. As painful as it was to become this icy, unfeeling creature, it's even more painful to revert. The backward metamorphosis is like a thousand small deaths. Terror, grief, and shame all hammering into my titanium-grafted bones.

"You never gave me a choice," I say. "And now I'll never know what I might have chosen."

Azrael lets out a short, cold laugh. "All of New Amsterdam has witnessed your choices, Melinoë. They've seen what you've done when you thought you were alone. They've seen everything."

I lean over, bile rising in my throat.

The only thing that stops me from vomiting into the snow is the cameras. I was an idiot to think they haven't always been there, carefully keeping just out of earshot. Seventeen years of life, nine years of Angel programming, and I'm still so naive and stupid. I should have known.

"*Everything*," Azrael repeats in my ear. His tone is lofty, gloating.

They saw me save Inesa's life, over and over again. They saw her save mine. They heard me talk about the little girl on my last Gauntlet. Sanne. They heard me talk about Keres. They watched me strip off my hunting suit, baring my whole naked body to their unblinking eyes. They watched me say *I want to do more than just survive.*

They saw me kiss her. They saw me do far more than kiss her. Our bodies running under the blankets, her mouth grazing my shoulder, my hands running the length of her thighs.

I tip forward, catching myself before I land face-first in the melting snow. My breaths are coming in short, hot gasps. It's the very last thought that breaks me. The realization that they've seen Inesa, too. I've always been strung up, stretched out for the consumption of the audience. I've seen every comment, from the most laudatory to the most contemptuous and every intrusive, vile thing in between. I was shaped and trained for the cameras. But she wasn't.

Now the audience is dissecting Inesa, too. Zeroing in on all the places she has a right to keep hidden, the quiet words that passed between the two of us, the tender, secret, wounded places she thought she was showing to me and me alone.

"Please," I whisper. "Please—turn them off. Just . . ."

Azrael doesn't reply. He merely sighs, with the disdainful pity I know as well as I know my own heartbeat.

"What do you want from me?" I finally choke out.

"The only thing I've ever asked of you, Melinoë. To do what you've been made for."

I draw in a breath, try to prepare an answer, but my tongue feels numb in my mouth.

"Don't speak now," Azrael says. "Just listen. You have plenty of time, still, to make this right. But it can't be done just any which way. You know that. Especially not after everything the audience has witnessed between you two. This is the most-viewed Gauntlet in history. There's not a household in New Amsterdam that hasn't clicked on the live stream at least once. The CEO is very, very pleased."

Millions of people. My face plastered across their tablet screens. Inesa's bare body. I've protected her from Wends and Dogs, from freezing and starving, but I couldn't protect her from this.

"Obviously they are very invested in the narrative you've

created. The Angel who fell in love with the Lamb. They don't know, of course, that you aren't capable of such a sentiment. None of you are."

I swallow, tasting blood and bile. "Just turn the cameras off," I beg. "Please. Just for a little while—"

"It's too late for that now. All of New Amsterdam is watching."

They'll only be able to hear my end of the conversation, not Azrael's voice in my ear. And I don't want them to hear my pathetic wheedling anymore. I force myself to sit up, ignoring the agonizing pain in my legs and the urge to whimper.

"And what if I don't?"

Saying it aloud sends a thrill of fear through my chest. Defying him is terrifying. Even more so, now that I remember what he's done.

"Then you'll have failed," he says. "I'll have no choice but to decommission you. Do a final Wipe. And then I'll hand you over to Visser."

The memory of his hand on the small of my back is enough to make me want to retch again. Visions of the party swim through my mind. The glasses of sapphire-blue liquor, the shine of Keres's silk dress. Her empty, empty eye. All the damage the fire must have done, erased, her scars cloaked in new synthetic skin so she won't remember that once, at least, she had tried to be free. I can't choke out a reply.

"I don't want to see you fail," Azrael goes on. His tone is soft now, and I realize that I remember the softness, too. Just as much as I remember every blow. "I'll even make you a deal. Kill the Lamb,

296

and I won't Wipe you when I decommission you. I won't give you to Visser."

He's actually negotiating with me. My mind is in overdrive, trying to make sense of it. He must be truly desperate. The connection between Azrael and the CEO has always been shadowy and somewhat mysterious to me, probably by his design. But just like everyone else in New Amsterdam, Azrael is obligated to please him. If Azrael's Angels fail, Azrael himself will be a failure in the CEO's eyes, too.

Especially now, with this being the most publicized Gauntlet ever. It would be shameful. It would make Caerus look weak.

"You understand, of course," Azrael goes on, "that she cannot be allowed to live. Think of the precedent it would set. That a Lamb could seduce an Angel into sparing their life. You have already done untold damage to your reputation—to the reputation of every Angel in the program. It will take a lot to undo this. But you must kill her. There is no other option."

Light slants through the branches and onto the snow. It all seemed so immaculate just moments ago. Now the white is mottled with shadow. Where the snow is melting, damp brown patches of dirt emerge. The air starts to feel dense with humidity again, impossibly heavy.

When I still don't reply, Azrael says, "There's a new countdown timer fixed to the hunting suit. I would recommend looking at it. And look for the last box. You have everything you need now."

And then, with a crackle of static, he's gone.

I just stare ahead, unseeing. There's only carnage behind my eyes. Sanne's arms flailing as I pinned her down. Visser's hand sliding up the small of my back. Keres's blank, unknowing gaze. It all pours down on me like water. I feel drowned. Only a Wipe could save me from this, could pull me back onto dry land. That merciful oblivion. The worst part of it all is knowing that Azrael is right.

The memories are so blinding and the blood in my ears is pulsing so loudly that everything else fades into the background. I don't hear the crunch of snow behind me. And I don't see Inesa until she lays a gentle hand on my shoulder. I turn around.

"Mel?" Inesa's eyes are wide, her chin quivering. "What is it? What's wrong?"

At last, the truth. It comes flooding out of me, all at once, before I can even think to stop it. Maybe it would be smart to hide some things; maybe it would protect her. But I can't reason with myself through the woozy glaze of fear.

I take the earpiece out and show it to her, flat on my open palm. I gesture to the new hunting suit spread out on the snow. I show her the box, crammed full of syringes and bullets and other supplies. My whole body is shaking, but not from the cold. In fact, I can't feel anything but nausea, pooling slick in the bottom of my belly.

The whole time, Inesa doesn't speak. I only see her throat tick as she swallows.

"I was stupid," I whisper. "So stupid. I should have known they'd still be watching. I should have . . ."

Inesa just shakes her head. She reaches out to me, then stops, hand hovering in the air. Who knows how close the cameras are now? If they're zooming in on her face, or mine? And who knows what all the people behind the screens are thinking? Nothing we do is private anymore; none of our words and actions are our own. We're being laid out and dissected by millions of viewers. We're being chewed and swallowed.

I know there are going to be hundreds of clips of us, maybe thousands. Of our kiss and more. They'll be embedded in news articles, replayed on other people's streams, uploaded to unsavory websites. If I linger too long on this thought, I can't breathe. Even if we both survive, we'll never escape this. One way or another, we'll always be on this Gauntlet.

At last, Inesa speaks. Her voice is hoarse. "Did you check how much time we have left?"

"No." The word falls between us into the snow. "Not yet."

Inesa stares down at her open palms. The blisters are only partly healed, with pale, slightly raised streaks of pink with yellow bubbles of new skin beneath. Her lips quiver.

"Maybe," she says, "we should look in the other box."

TWENTY-NINE

INESA

I'm numb as Melinoë digs through the rubble. I'm numb as the snow soaks through to my skin. I'm numb as the whole clearing seems to ripple and shudder, as if, at any moment, I'm going to lurch awake from a hazy and obscure dream.

Melinoë unearths another shiny black box and sets it down before me. I feel my way around the edge until I find the tiny clasp.

Inside there are even more supplies: syringes of pain medication, bandages and gauze, decon-tabs, meal replacement packets, even matches and a tightly rolled Mylar blanket. It's all fitted in so neatly that if the circumstances were different, I might believe it was a care package, put together with consideration and sympathy. I remove each item methodically, even though my fingers are shaking.

Underneath the last package of gauze is a tablet. The screen is black, reflecting my face, my eyes gleaming with a hot flash of unshed tears. Melinoë's face hovers over my shoulder. Her skin is pale and mottled gray, like ashes on the snow.

Carefully, I lift the tablet up. As soon as I do, the screen flickers on.

It doesn't show the usual checkerboard of icons—the weather app and the web browser, photo library and system settings. There's only the bar at the top of the screen that indicates the time, and the battery life. No internet connection, of course. There's a single icon in the upper left corner, a blue folder. I double-tap to open it.

Inside is a video file. One unlabeled mp4.

I swallow hard and tap it with my thumb.

The video starts to play immediately, so it must have been pre-downloaded. It opens in full screen, showing me a large, neon-lit room. There's a wall covered nearly inch-to-inch in framed posters, crammed with shelves holding plushies and plastic collectible figurines, still in their plastic boxes. Strands of twinkling lights are draped everywhere, in a rainbow of colors.

Sitting in the center of the room, in an enormous high-backed leather desk chair, is a face I instantly recognize. Well—not really a face. A figure in a skull-shaped mask, with large and incongruous pink rabbit ears. He's wearing a bright green hoodie advertising some sports drink, and fingerless gloves that show off his black nail polish.

It's Zetamon, the most-watched creator on Caerus's streaming platform. No one knows his real name, and he's never shown his real face, but every day tens of thousands of people tune in to watch him play video games, or, more often, react to various videos. The reaction streams have always seemed ridiculous to me, because you can't even see his expressions. And he says everything in his famously deadpan voice.

301

Melinoë recognizes him, too—her eyebrows shoot up in surprise.

"Hey guys, welcome to the stream," Zetamon says, with his trademark dourness. "Today I have a special guest joining me. If you haven't heard of him, you've been living under a rock, or you've just gotten out of a fucking coma. Anyway, everyone say hi to New Amsterdam's latest internet boyfriend, and try to keep your thirst comments under control."

The door to the room opens, and Luka steps inside.

My heart stops. Just for a moment, and then it stutters to life again, beating painfully against my sternum. Luka sits down in a second oversize chair, next to Zetamon, his gaze on the ground.

He's alive. The relief that shudders through me is enough to make my vision blur and my bones turn to jelly. He doesn't even look any worse for wear. In fact, his face is smooth, radiating with a subtle glow. There's a healthy flush to his cheeks. When I look closer, I notice other subtle changes: his cheekbones are higher and more prominent, dusted with some faint gold powder. His lips are redder. Even his eyebrows have been plucked, though the scar through his left one remains.

Caerus has done some work on him. The rough-edged gauntness of a life in the outlying Counties is gone. Well, almost gone. He still has Dad's strong, square jaw. And Dad's hazel eyes. My eyes.

"So, Luka," Zetamon says, "aka the most famous guy in New Amsterdam right now. Tell us how it feels to be here today."

Luka's gaze shifts. He won't look at the camera straight on.

"Uh, relieved, I guess," he says. "Lucky that Caerus found me when they did."

"Yeah, it was pretty, like, cinematic, them pulling you into the helicopter to save you from those zombie cannibal things." Zetamon regards his nail polish. "Are those, like, common where you live?"

"The Wends? Yeah." Luka's fingers curl into a fist.

"Creepy," Zetamon intones. "Anyway, take us back to the beginning. How did it go down, finding out your sister was put up as a Lamb? How did you feel?"

"Afraid." This answer comes more quickly, though Luka still doesn't look up from his lap. "The last Gauntlet, it was another girl from our town. Sanne Dekker. She didn't survive."

It's obvious that Luka has been coached on his answers. And I'm sure Zetamon has been told explicitly which questions to ask. Caerus has arranged every aspect of this interview.

"But you had a plan," Zetamon prompts.

"I mean, we didn't have much time to figure it out, but we knew we had to get as far away from Esopus as possible," Luka says. "We borrowed a car, brought some supplies. We figured our best chance was just to run."

"That didn't work out for you, though."

"No." Luka's knuckles are white, bones pressing up against his skin. "She caught up to us."

"Yeah. So let's talk about her now, the Angel. Melinoë." Zetamon glances at his computer screen. "Chat really wants to know how you managed to fend her off—not once, but twice."

"The first time was mostly luck."

"Nah," Zetamon cuts in. "You're too humble, brother. The moment in the car was insane. Everyone thought you killed her. How'd you get to be so good with a gun?"

Luka talks, awkwardly and haltingly, about our taxidermy shop. He doesn't mention Dad. Obviously Caerus doesn't want people to know that anyone has managed to escape them, to live off their grid. He doesn't mention Mom, either. It would hurt the narrative, if he told the truth. Better to let the audience believe that Mom is an innocent victim, and that I was a willing sacrifice. Azrael must have cut the cameras when I told Mel the truth about Mom, the same way he did when Luka and I talked about Dad.

"Okay, so you've run into the woods," Zetamon says. "Those creepy fucks are chasing you. And then the Angel appears out of nowhere. What are you thinking?"

"It was hard to think." For the first time, Luka sounds sincere. Vulnerable. His voice is low, almost too quiet for the mic to pick up. "It was just instinct. In that situation, all you can do is try to survive."

"Mm-hmm," Zetamon says. "Chat is going crazy right now, by the way. They're spamming that clip of you knocking her out."

Zetamon switches the camera to screen-capture mode and replays the clip. Melinoë throws her knife, pinning Luka to the tree. He snarls at her—*bitch*—with such venom that it makes my skin prickle. And then she's wrestling me to the ground, hands around my throat, but the cameras linger on Luka, watching him tear himself free. Grabbing the rifle. Thrusting it against her temple.

The violence of it is sickening, and my stomach turns. This is the moment that made the audience fall in love with him? Melinoë was right—they hate her.

But as Zetamon replays the clip, I realize it's even simpler than that. They just want blood spilled. It doesn't matter whose. It's not like they were cheering just as hard for Luka when he helped me to my feet.

There's something about a man—because Luka looks like a man, even if he's only sixteen—beating a girl that's especially exciting to them. Something about watching her degradation. As Zetamon plays the clip for a third time, I have to squeeze my eyes shut.

They talk through the rest of Luka's time during the Gauntlet, until the moment that Caerus picked him up. I get to watch that clip, too. Blood running from a gash on Luka's forehead, him too dazed to protest as two Masks descend and shove him into a helicopter.

And then, at last, the conversation turns to me.

"It's obvious to everyone watching how much you and your sister care about each other," Zetamon says. "And you've been watching the rest of her Gauntlet, too, yeah?"

Luka nods.

"So if there was one thing you could say to your sister, what would it be?"

Finally, Luka lifts his head and stares directly into the camera. He swallows hard. Then, slowly, he reaches into his pocket.

He takes something out, closed tightly in his fist. When it's in view of the camera, he unfolds his fingers. Resting in the palm of his hand is the compass, Dad's compass, that fits the broken case I kept. That feels like an eternity ago.

Tears gather in my eyes. But the cameras are on me, too. I tell myself not to cry.

"I would tell her I want her to survive," Luka says, as he holds the compass out. "For both of us. That I don't want to lose her. That I don't . . ." He stops, and for the first time in years, I see tears gather in the corners of his eyes, too. Looking just like mine. "That I believe in her. That I know she's strong enough to make it. Please, Nesa."

"So, wow," Zetamon deadpans. "Powerful stuff."

The video cuts off abruptly. The screen goes completely black.

Without speaking, I set down the tablet and examine what remains in the box. There's only one item left: a rolled-up length of white fabric. I unfurl it.

It's a dress. Long-sleeved, slightly old-fashioned looking. I turn it over in my hands, examining every inch.

Inside the bodice, along one of the seams, are words stitched in black thread.

Wear this and he lives.

We carry everything into the cabin in silence. Every time a word rises in my throat, I remember that the cameras are on, and I swallow it down again.

Melinoë has the replacement hunting suit draped over her arm. When we get inside, closing the door behind us, she lifts up one of the sleeves. Attached to it is a new timer. Ticking down the seconds until the end of my Gauntlet. I cross the room with heavy steps so I can see how long I have left.

Two days. Seven hours. Fifty-two minutes.

Azrael has accelerated the timeline. He knows the audience is on the edge of their seats. I sit down in one of the chairs. My legs feel boneless, my knees weak. Melinoë stands, gripping the edge of the table so tightly her nails could splinter the wood.

There are a thousand things I want to say, but none I can risk with the cameras on. The knowledge that they've been on this whole time makes me sick—a full-body, hot-blooded sickness, an amalgam of anger and fear and hate. I hate Caerus for doing this. I hate them all for watching, for typing out their smug and casually cruel comments.

The force of my loathing surprises me. I never blamed the other Outliers for our circumstances, or even the City dwellers, with their decadent Damish accents, but now I understand: There would be no Gauntlet without an audience.

Maybe I've finally become a person Dad would be proud of. A person full of righteous, stomach-churning hate.

Dad.

I reach into the pocket of my coat, and my fingers close around the case of his compass. I'd forgotten about it, until Luka held his half up during the interview. As I touch the cold metal, I feel another sickening jolt of anger, remembering how Dad left us with nothing except this worthless piece of junk. Nothing except—

The tiny scroll of paper. With the cameras on, I'm too wary to remove it from my pocket, but I clamp my fist around it. It seems to somehow warm my skin.

Melinoë still hasn't spoken. Her eyes are trained in the middle distance, a muscle pulsing in her throat. No words can pass between us that won't be heard by a million people in New Amsterdam, by Azrael and all of Caerus. Hopelessness pools in my stomach.

"Azrael doesn't make idle threats," she says at last, in a voice that's hardly more than a whisper.

With my other hand, I finger the seam of the white dress. *Wear this and he lives.*

"I didn't think he was bluffing," I reply bleakly.

"It's always been like this." Finally, she meets my gaze. Her eyes are haunted. "He just takes and takes. I—we can't stop him."

A lump rises in my throat, because she's right. We have nothing to bargain with. What are two girls against Caerus? They could kill us in an instant, in a spray of bullets. They already proved that, with the Dogs. Every second I'm still breathing is a mercy they're granting us both. Another debt—one that I can repay only with my life.

"If I don't do what he wants, he'll turn me into an empty shell," she whispers. "Like Keres. And marry me off to someone in Caerus upper management. It's what he does to all of us, in the end."

And somehow, even though I've never set foot in the City, even though all I've seen are photos, I can envision it. It's clearer than a dream; it's almost as real as a memory. Melinoë, strapped down to the table, syringe in her throat. A blank, glassy look in her eyes, unknowing and unknowable. Some nameless, faceless man slipping his hand around her waist, between her legs, pressing her onto the bed.

Before I can even process it, I'm on my feet. I rise so suddenly that my chair topples over and clatters to the floor. And then, with a strength born only of adrenaline and sheer rage, I flip over the table, sending all the supplies, the hunting suit and the white dress, careening into the wall. Decon-tabs scatter everywhere.

"*Fuck!*" I scream. "Fuck him—fuck this—fuck everything—"

Melinoë just stands back and stares as I lurch through the cabin, smashing everything I can get my hands on. I kneel down and pick up a package of bandages, just so I can tear them apart. I hurl the rusted, ancient rifle against the wall, and the stock breaks off the barrel. It doesn't matter; it's useless against Caerus. All of this is useless. I stomp on the meal replacement packets until they burst. By this time, I'm breathing so hard I can't even speak, but I can still hear the pulse of the tracker, as ceaseless as my own heartbeat.

I pause, chest heaving, my gaze blurred with unshed tears. I look over at Melinoë. Somehow, impossibly, her eyes are damp, too. She told me that Caerus had removed her tear ducts. But maybe that was another one of Azrael's lies.

Suddenly, she drops to her knees. She fishes through the supplies until she finds the knife, her knife. She holds it up for just a moment, a furrow between her brows, lips quivering. And then she brings it down, slashing through the middle of a Mylar blanket.

Her movements are not swift, not graceful, not Angel-like. They're blundering and staggered, made clumsy by her anger. I kneel down on the floor and join her, tearing through the remains of the Mylar blanket, throwing whatever other supplies I can get my hands on, both of us breathing hard in tandem, the air growing thick and hot with our shared fury.

At last, the rage runs through and out of us. We're left kneeling, shaking, and struggling for breath. The tip of my nose prickles with oncoming tears, but the rest of me just feels heavy and numb.

Melinoë lets a strip of Mylar drift from her hands. Her hair is around her face and her cheeks are filled with that purple flush. Her lips are still swollen, with the memory of my kiss, and I want to grab her and kiss her again, again and again, as if the only touch she'll ever know is mine.

THIRTY

MELINOË

I'm sure the cameras loved it. Our unchecked, desperate fury.
Azrael would find it very cinematic. It's nothing anyone has ever
seen before: an Angel, finally cracking her cold facade. The clips
will be famous. But I'll never get to see them. I won't kill Inesa, and
he'll Wipe me the moment the helicopter touches down in the City.

I lift my gaze to Inesa's face. I see every detail of it, from the
constellation of freckles across her nose to the nameless green-
brown color of her eyes, and think, *I'll forget this, too.* I'll forget how
it feels to touch her, to be held by her.

The bile of rage rises in my throat. We both breathe heavily
into the silence.

And then, suddenly, Inesa bites out, "*No.*"

My brow creases with an unspoken question.

"*No,*" she repeats, her voice trembling. "This can't be it. This
isn't how it ends. I won't let it."

I feel my heart cracking with an emotion I'm not supposed to
feel. But it overrides my programming. It washes over me like a

dark wave, but it doesn't drown me. I'm just carried aloft in its great tide.

"There's nothing you can do," I whisper. "This *is* how it ends for me. How it ends for every Angel."

"No," she repeats stubbornly. Her hands are balled into fists.

"They'll kill him." My stomach feels acid with anger. "Luka."

At that, Inesa draws in a breath. She sits back on her knees, falling into silence. I look around at the mess we've made, all of Azrael's neatly packaged supplies, destroyed. It doesn't matter. They were useless against Caerus. He only sent them to serve his narrative. So the audience could be convinced that Inesa had a fighting chance. I have to swallow to keep from screaming.

Then, seemingly out of nowhere, Inesa cocks her head and asks, "Have you ever heard of the Drowned County?"

The unexpectedness of the question momentarily cleaves through the fog of despair. "No," I say. "What is that?"

Inesa hesitates a moment, as if she's listening for something. "They're not watching," she says. "Azrael has cut the cameras."

"What? How do you know?" I can't hear their faint buzzing, but only because Azrael is purposefully keeping them out of earshot now.

"He did it before," Inesa says. "When Luka and I talked about the Drowned County. Caerus doesn't want anyone to know it exists. It's a place north of here, near the border with New England. It's where Luka and I were headed. It's off the grid."

I believe her—about the cameras, at least. Especially now, with so many people tuned in, Azrael will be very, very careful about what he allows the audience to see and hear. But the rest?

"It can't be." I shake my head. "Nothing exists off the grid. Just bombed-out wastelands."

"That's what Caerus wants you to believe." Inesa reaches into her pocket. She pulls something out, clenches it in her fist. "They don't want anyone to know it's real. I thought it was just a myth, one of my Dad's stories, but . . ." She holds out her hand. On her open palm there's a tiny scrap of paper. "He left this for us. They're coordinates."

I stare down at the sequence of numbers. The ink is blurred, but legible. Degrees of latitude and longitude.

"I forgot about it until now," she admits. "Until Luka showed his half of the compass. Dad left the coordinates tucked inside it."

I just keep staring at it. A tiny scrap of paper with some hastily scrawled numbers. How can we stake three lives on it? Hers, mine, and Luka's. What she's talking about—this Drowned County— sounds like a fantasy. There's not supposed to be anything along the border with New England except for the irradiated aftermath of exploded nukes. If there were, Caerus would have destroyed it.

"No," I say, shaking my head again. "Caerus wouldn't allow something like that to exist."

"Maybe they don't know it's real." Inesa closes her fingers around the scrap of paper, hard enough to turn her knuckles white. "And they couldn't wipe it out—it's too close to the border. It would break the stalemate with New England."

I consider it. Inside the bubble of the City, all the talk of nuclear winter and radiation poisoning seemed hazy and unreal, like scenes from a movie. Horrible, yet too distant to fear. But I've already seen impossible things out here, things that shouldn't exist. Deer with webbed feet and scales. All sorts of creatures, adapting to a drowning world.

"Even if it is real," I say, "what about your brother?"

At that, all the color drains from Inesa's face. Her gaze flickers briefly, and then the light returns to her eyes, that blaze of determination, of defiance. I didn't see it in her photo, when Azrael first showed it to me on the holoscreen. But I saw it on Luka's face, and on her father's. Now the family resemblance is finally clear.

"He wants me to go," she says softly. "That's why he held up the compass. That's why he said he knew I could make it."

Luka's voice echoes: *I know she's strong enough to make it. Please, Nesa.*

Is it him making a sacrifice? Giving up his life for his sister's? I think back to the rest of the interview, to Zetamon's comments. *Everyone say hi to New Amsterdam's latest internet boyfriend. The most famous guy in New Amsterdam right now.* I can believe it. I know exactly how much the audience loathes me, and how desperate they are to see me—or any Angel—fail. Watching Luka—handsome, strong, and charismatic in his brooding silence—knock me out has probably become one of the most-watched clips of all time. And it's skyrocketed him to fame and adoration, instantly.

Which means Azrael can't afford to kill him. With how beloved Luka is, his death would provoke much worse than hacked holoboards. A Lamb dying on a Gauntlet is one thing—it's supposed to happen. Everyone has accepted this level of brutality.

Azrael has done a lot of things, but he's never coldly executed an unchosen civilian. It's beyond what even the callousness of the audience would allow. The ratings of the Gauntlet would plummet. The CEO would pull the plug on the Angel program. And Azrael would be the most hated person in New Amsterdam.

I meet Inesa's unflinching gaze, and I know she's come to the same conclusion. The unspoken message sparks between us, like a current through an electrical wire. That's what all of this is—every one of our gestures, down to our blinks or swallows—sparks that could kindle a blaze. The whole of New Amsterdam is watching. Which means that Azrael finally has something to lose.

Caerus wasn't always invincible. I have to remind myself of that, too. Their domination happened slowly.

Debts. It all began with debts. Student loans, medical bills, mortgages, credit cards—all of it weighing down New Amsterdam's government like an anchor attached to a bloated corpse. People died and passed their debts on to their children, on to their children's children. Shackled by the debt that followed them for generations, people stopped buying houses and cars. The birth rate plummeted. There was a shortage of doctors and skilled professionals because who was going to take on the extra debt of getting an advanced degree, on top of everything else?

In an act of apparent benevolence, Caerus bought all of New Amsterdam's debts. They began a staggered program of loan forgiveness to jump-start the economy. This was all while northern New Amsterdam was being ravaged by border skirmishes with New

England. And in order to entice people to buy houses and cars and to get their degrees, Caerus offered a massive line of credit to anyone purchasing their products: up to five hundred thousand credits.

The number was shocking. At first people couldn't believe it was real—five hundred thousand credits to spend on everything from groceries to home goods, anything that was sold on the Caerus website. The economy recovered in record time. The governor of New Amsterdam created a special cabinet post—economy czar—for Caerus's CEO, to help guide the state's recovery from its crippling depression.

To mitigate the effects of climate change that devastated the outlying Counties, Caerus was also given the grant for the Hudson River Valley Relief Project. They were supposed to build reservoirs, plant trees, mend power lines, and provide compensation to people whose homes were destroyed by flooding. And that's what they did, at first. But then they stretched the margins of the bill's purview. In order to account for who was receiving aid, where people were being relocated, and to track demographic trends, everyone in the outlying Counties was given a Caerus ID number. With the tablets they distributed freely to every New Amsterdam resident, Caerus could track your online activity, your movements, listen to your conversations. Everything.

At the time, the Outliers were all assured this was a temporary measure. Just until the recession ended. Just until the Counties were rebuilt, the flooding was managed, the border wars with New England settled with an armistice.

Looking back, anyone could've predicted what happened next.

The erosion of lines between corporation and government. People clamoring for Caerus's CEO to replace the governor. An election with questionable democratic integrity. Schools that used to be state-run dissolved and replaced with a new standard curriculum created by Caerus.

At the time, I'm sure it all seemed understandable, efficient. Caerus was running every other aspect of life in New Amsterdam—why not education, too? Why not military and defense? Why not housing and transportation? Why not health and human services?

But in spite of the Gauntlets, in spite of the economy that never really bounced back, the flooding that never really ceased, the border wars that continued to drag on to this day . . . approval ratings for Caerus's CEO are still above 90 percent. Because the truth is, things could always be worse. Sure, some people can't pay their debts and have to die for it, but those people are the stupid, the indulgent, the weak. As long as it's always somebody else, it's easy to blame them, easy, even, to cheer for their deaths.

I didn't fully understand it before. The Outliers love Caerus the same way I love Azrael. You can hate the person who imprisons you, but you can't hate the person who sets you free. So what do you do when they're one and the same?

The love is what Azrael—and Caerus—can't afford to lose. And maybe that makes love the most powerful force in the world, after all.

Inesa sets down the scrap of paper and the compass case, and the metal clinks against the wooden floor, jolting me from my thoughts.

Then she raises her arms and takes my face in her hands.

"Trust me," she whispers.

I just squeeze my eyes shut. It feels like too much to bear. All the systems so carefully constructed within me are short-circuiting, crumbling down.

Inesa pulls me closer. "Believe me."

Seconds drag past us. Outside, the snow melts into the earth. The dark soil rises again, fed by the cold, clear water from the sky. Finally, I open my eyes. I can't speak a word, but I give the slowest, faintest nod.

We can't risk saying much more. The cameras are greedily taking in every word, every expression. I've long lost my ability to keep my face a cold mask, revealing nothing. And everyone in New Amsterdam has now seen me stripped down to the bone, naked in ways deeper than my skin. Azrael is right. It will take a lot to undo what I've done, not just for my own reputation, but for the reputation of all the Angels.

It might be enough, on its own, to shutter the program completely. It might cost him everything. I should cheer at the thought. And yet a painful lump solidifies in the center of my chest.

He abandoned you, a voice reminds me. It's not the first time such a voice has spoken to me, but it's the first time it's felt like a voice of my own. *And then he exposed you to the whole world.*

Still, I can't exorcise the pain. Not entirely. My mind hurls memories at me: every time he embraced me, every time he pulled me into a helicopter and laid a Mylar blanket over me, stroking my hair as I shivered from withdrawal. I hate him for leaving me. I love him for saving me. All living creatures have a place they call home. And the instinct to return home is as essential as the drawing of breath.

Home. The cold metal of an operating table. The darkness of the shooting range, made sickly green in my prosthetic's night vision. The floor-to-ceiling window of my bedroom, showing me the glittering cityscape below, all the places I'll never reach.

Home. The low, smoky heat of the woodstove. The warm glow of the oil lamps, casting everything in pale gold. Inesa's hair spread out across the pillow, turned shiny in the moonlight that slips between the cracks in the wall. I could live like this, I realize. In just the spaces between walls.

Inesa is bending over the table, arranging the messy pile of supplies. We destroyed almost everything, but I can't make myself regret it. There's something freeing about being able to feel it, finally: All the rage that washed through me left a scorched wasteland behind. And yet even I know that flowers grow most brilliantly from ashes.

I join Inesa at the table. With fingers trembling faintly, I shove the intact supplies into a bag. There are some painkillers, a few bandages. A crumbling handful of decon-tabs. My gaze wanders to the white dress puddled on the floor. Part of me wishes I had torn it apart. Instead, I pick it up and let it unfurl.

It's a long dress, reaching nearly to my ankles. It has blousy peasant sleeves and looks strikingly chaste, like a nightgown. Or something a child would wear.

At that, I realize why Azrael sent it. He sent it for the same reason he chose Inesa for this Gauntlet. He wants to see if I can do it, if I can kill another girl from Esopus Creek. He wants this to be my redemption, and his redemption, too.

I have to swallow the bile that rises in my throat.

Inesa sees me holding the dress and says, "I can't imagine it will be very flattering. Not really my style."

Gallows humor. I wish I could force a smile onto my face for her. I can't deny that it would be cinematic: me in my black hunting suit, a stark contrast to my pale hair and face, descending on the innocent Lamb in her little white dress. Any concerns about my brutality or my fitness would be silenced. If nothing else, Azrael knows what makes a good show.

But there's no point in antagonizing him unnecessarily, of testing his limits further. Wordlessly, I hand the dress to Inesa and pick up the new hunting suit.

I don't have any modesty left to preserve; this Gauntlet has taken it all. The shame of being exposed is secondary to the physical pain of pulling the skintight suit over the blisters and burns on my legs. I bite down hard on my lower lip. Every tug of the fabric is pure agony.

Inesa helps me draw up the suit around my shoulders and then zip it in the back. With one final *snick* of the zipper, all my scars are hidden. With long, deliberate strokes, I comb through the tangles in my hair, and then pull it into a ponytail, sleek and high on my head. I could be fresh out of the helicopter, at the beginning of the Gauntlet. I can almost see the pleased gleam in Azrael's dark eyes.

When Inesa starts removing her boots, a sudden, fierce feeling of protectiveness overcomes me. I snatch the quilt from the bed and hold it out around her, like a curtain.

A smile lifts the corner of her mouth. "Thank you."

Behind the quilt, she slips off her shirt and pants. I stare down at the floor. Every thought in my mind is collapsing, like matter into a black hole. I go so long without blinking that my real eye starts to burn.

"I'm not used to saying that." Inesa's voice, sudden and unexpected, breaks the strange trance.

"Saying what?"

"'Thank you.'" She pulls on the sleeves of the dress, covering her bare shoulders. "It's kind of taboo, in Esopus . . . it sounds silly, but it's true. No one really likes the idea of being indebted to someone else. And you definitely never want to be the one who's needing."

I realize how much strength it must have taken for Luka to say *please* in front of the camera, in front of all of New Amsterdam. I swallow, not trusting myself to speak.

"It's funny, though," Inesa goes on, "because if we didn't need each other, we'd have nothing. Society wouldn't work. So it's a burden and a blessing at once. Even nature is the same. The plants drink the rainwater and the animals eat the plants and each other. Nothing is created without need. When we see flowers blooming or hear birds singing, we think it's beautiful. But when people need each other, it seems so ugly."

"Caerus has poisoned everything." The bitterness in my voice curdles my tongue.

321

Inesa bites her lip. Silence settles over us, like new-fallen snow. Then she says, "Will you help me with the buttons?"

I let the quilt slide from my hands and puddle to the floor. There's a line of tiny white buttons up the back of the dress, each one made to fit an equally tiny loop. Inesa reaches back and sweeps her hair out of the way. I'm careful not to catch any of the angling strands. Slowly, her bare skin vanishes, clad in impossibly clean white linen. The buttons go all the way up to her throat, the final one closing over the soft flesh at the nape of her neck.

When I'm finished, she lets go of her hair and it tumbles down around her shoulders. "Thanks," she says quietly.

My instinct is just to nod. But I force my mouth open and reply, "You're welcome." It feels strange to say the words, but not unpleasant.

"Well," Inesa says, tugging the sleeves down to her wrists and turning around, "how do I look?"

My eyes follow the line of her body, clothed in all white, from the bodice to the hem of the flared skirt, which falls to her ankles. My vision blurs. Reality starts to shiver away, and the memory rises up in its place, licking at me like flame.

"You look like her," I whisper. "Sanne."

The name I know and the face I'll never forget. She doesn't look anything like Inesa, not really, but my mind is caught on that memory like a fishhook, and it won't let go. Her limp body in the mud, rain pelting over us both, her skin growing colder and colder under my hands. And as the real world shudders in and out of my vision, the bald and ugly truth I've always known seeps into my skin: that I am a predator and she is the prey. That for me to survive, she has to die.

My fingers are shaking uncontrollably. Inesa reaches out and takes them, pressing my hands to her chest. Her heartbeat thrums through my skin.

"It's okay," she says. "It's okay."

She leans forward, and I lean forward to meet her. The tips of our noses brush. I think about how, just over a day ago, I wanted so badly to touch her but never thought I would get the chance. How do people love, I wonder, knowing that every moment is so precarious, that at any second, it could all melt like snow, or turn to ash?

"If, somehow," I start, in a strangled voice, "we knew each other before, without all of this, do you think . . ."

I can't finish, but Inesa knows what I mean to say. A small smile spreads across her face.

"If you were just another City dweller who came into my shop one day," she says, "I think I would be so flustered, I'd make a complete idiot of myself. And then I'd think: She hates me, she's never coming back."

"But I would come back," I whisper.

"Yeah," Inesa says. "But I'm clueless, so I'd probably think you were coming back because you have an extreme passion for stuffed deer."

I laugh, a low, breathy sound. "No, I'd just run myself broke buying them, so I'd have an excuse to see you again."

In this universe, there are no credits, no debts. No Gauntlets.

"And would you come live in Esopus with me?" Inesa's tone becomes hesitant.

"I suppose," I say. "I could hunt. You could cook. It would be very domestic."

This time, she laughs. "I'm a terrible cook. I'll microwave you pasta, but that's the best you're going to get."

"Deer meat and microwaved pasta." I chew my lip. "What a life it would be."

"Yeah," Inesa says. Her voice is soft. "A life."

THIRTY-ONE

INESA

Two days. Three hours. Twenty-six minutes.

Time seems to pass too quickly, clouds sweeping across the sky to blot out the sun. The snow has almost all melted by now, turning the dirt into sucking mud. I put my jacket on over the white dress. When I do, the case of the compass rattles in my pocket.

I think of the compass itself, lying on Luka's palm. I don't want to remember, but my mind throws up the images anyway: When Luka was eight and I was nine, Dad was on one of his obscure research kicks and he taught us about palmistry. We compared the sizes of our hands, the spans of our fingers. I was older and Luka was still a scrawny kid, so my hand was bigger. But we had the same pattern of creases in our palms. A very narrow, nearly invisible fate line, but a deep, fixed heart line.

Another memory. Hoisting ourselves up onto the roof of our house with a frayed rope, pretending to be mountain climbers, until Mom yelled at us to come down. I remember painting the sign for Soulis Taxidermy Shop. Luka was tall by then, and as he hung it, we both tried to smile proudly, even though our stomachs were roiling with an identical fear. *What if no one comes? What if we can't do this on our own?*

Something inside me cracks: a long, bleak fissure, like the earth itself coming apart and showing veins of slow-moving liquid fire beneath. I take the compass case out of my pocket and squeeze it in my hand, then raise my closed fist to my mouth. My lips brush against the scar on my index finger, the one that Luka gave me, the one that matches the healed white gash through his eyebrow.

"I love you," I whisper, voice muffled against the salt of my own skin.

We've never spoken the words aloud before. I think about all the walls we built around each other, and around ourselves, and all the time we wasted, being too afraid to say something so simple and so true. My lashes flutter as I blink back the tears that gather in my eyes.

For a moment, I wish Luka were the only one to see it, the only one to hear my words. Then, with a flash of anger, I realize that I want the audience to witness this. The only reason the Gauntlets continue is that the viewers can separate themselves from the Lambs, can imagine it would never happen to them. But the truth is, it can happen to anyone. We're not uniquely weak or uniquely indulgent or uniquely stupid, no matter what Caerus would have us believe. And all of a sudden, I'm furious again, furious with them for making us think that other people are less than human.

It's the first time in my life that I've let the anger fill me. That I've swallowed it down instead of choking on it. I was afraid to feel it, because I didn't want to be like Dad, drowning my righteous fury in a bottle, but now I think this anger might keep me alive. It doesn't obliterate everything else. It just rests beside my love for Luka, my love for all the small things like brilliant sunsets that make my life worth fighting for. It settles in my chest, as warm as hope.

I put the compass case back into my pocket. When I look up, Melinoë is standing before me.

She looks every inch an Angel again, zipped into her black suit, hair pulled back in a sleek ponytail. Without speaking, she unfolds her fingers.

Her knife rests in her palm. I lift my gaze to meet hers. My eyes are unflinching.

"Do it," I say.

The hum of my tracker is louder than it's ever been. It's like an enormous bird mutation, beating its wings in my throat.

This isn't the way the story is supposed to go. If I were a good little Lamb, I would run. If I were the girl my father always wanted me to be, I would take the knife, drive it into her heart. Instead, I tilt my head to the side and pull down the collar of my dress. I push my hair back and bare the side of my throat, where the tracker is embedded, a tiny lump pressing up from under my skin.

Melinoë's eyes, steady and gleaming dark, stare back at me without blinking. Then, slowly, she raises the knife to my throat.

I gritted my teeth, preparing for the pain, but it's more panic that shoots through me as I feel my blood leap up against the blade. Melinoë is delicate but quick, working the point of the knife under my skin, digging for the tracker. Her other hand comes to grip my throat, holding me in place. I squeeze my eyes shut.

It's over more quickly than I imagined it would be, and then Mel is pressing gauze to the wound. Blood sluices from my neck, soaking the bandage. Every swallow is painful now, breath squeezing out of me through a constricting siphon of fear. *What if she cut too deep, what if we can't stop the blood, what if—*

"Hold this," Melinoë says quietly.

I take over the task of pressing the bandage to my throat while she searches through the supplies on the table. There's not much left that we didn't destroy, but she finds a silver pill and raises it to my lips. I swallow, flinching.

The effects of the painkiller are immediate; I can almost feel the medication slipping coldly through my veins, numbing me to the tips of my fingers and toes. My breathing becomes almost even again. I look down and see the tracker on the table, gummy and red with my blood and bits of tissue. Nausea stirs in my belly.

"There are painkillers in the bandage, too." Melinoë brushes her thumb gently over the wound. "They should start to work in just a minute."

It's one of her fancy Caerus bandages, the kind that dissolve into your wound and form new flesh to knit it shut. The sensation of it soaking into me is strange, and it makes my skin prickle all over, a tiny needling through the numbness of the painkillers. My eyelids feel suddenly heavy. I remove my hand, the pads of my fingers sticky with blood. But the flow of it has stopped. Only the reddish stain on the collar of my dress remains as proof. That, and the still-blinking tracker on the table.

The absence of its pulse suddenly becomes the only thing I can focus on. I'd grown so accustomed to its second heartbeat that I feel oddly bereft without it. The tyranny of its ticking was a strange but familiar friend.

The timer on Melinoë's sleeve shows two days, two hours, and thirteen minutes. I take the knife from the table, its blade still slick with my blood. And the new anger that's found a home in my chest surges up, directing my hand, guiding it upward and then down again.

I crush the tracker under the hilt of the knife. It shatters, and its blinking light winks out like a dying star. For a moment we just stare at it, almost uncomprehending. The timer on Melinoë's sleeve freezes. It must have been linked to the tracker, just like the cameras. They might be able to follow us for a little while longer, but eventually the signal will die, when we reach the dead spot of the Drowned County. And Azrael will likely cut them before then, because he doesn't want the audience to see where we're going. There's nothing that threatens Caerus more than giving people the dream of freedom.

"It's over," I whisper, which is both true and not. The Gauntlet has ended, but we're still not free. Not yet.

Melinoë looks up and over at me. Her eyes are shining—even the prosthetic. It's stopped seeming depthless and impassive to me. Now I can see a thousand emotions reflected within it.

"I can't hear you anymore," she says, a bewildered note of grief in her voice. I'm glad she feels the same strange sense of loss that I do.

"Yeah," I say softly.

A furrow emerges between her brows—just briefly, and then it smooths again. Her face is so beautiful, it sort of hurts to look at.

"But I can feel you," she says.

We're not even touching. Yet my heartbeat brags so strongly as I reply, "Me too."

THIRTY-TWO

MELINOË

I pull out the cabin owner's ancient, yellowed map and Inesa unfolds the slip of paper with the coordinates. The owner was prescient enough to mark the cabin's location with a red X. Bending over the map, Inesa traces the lines of latitude and longitude with her finger. My eyes follow the arc she draws, and in my head, I'm adding up the miles. By the time I've finished my mental calculations, I'm shocked to realize we're little more than a day of brisk walking from the spot where the coordinates point.

"Did you ever imagine it?" I ask. "That we were so close?"

"I never really thought about it," Inesa admits. "I didn't believe I could survive. Much less . . ."

Much less escape. Much less be free. Fondness makes my chest swell, and along with it, a very foreign sensation: hope. It's perhaps the most dangerous emotion of all. The one that Azrael and all his countless procedures tried hardest to excise.

But the fire is mine now, all the mourning and all the fear and all the fondness that lick within me like tongues of flame. Azrael's voice echoes in my mind, marred by static and by my still imperfect memory: *You aren't capable of such a sentiment.*

And then an answer surges up within me, silent but fierce: *You're wrong.*

I reach out and take Inesa's hand. She links our fingers and squeezes.

"Come on," she says. "Let's go."

The sky is darkening but we can't afford to wait. I'm less afraid of the Wends than I am of Azrael. We've managed to fit a day's worth of food and water into our packs, and I have my rifle slung over my shoulder. Its weight is familiar and comforting. I managed to fend off the Wends once, even in my weakened state. I can do it again—especially now that I'm stronger.

As we step out of the cabin for the last time, hand in hand, I feel a tug of grief. I came to life within its four flimsy walls, like a corpse reanimated and lifted from its grave. I'll never be the creature I was when I first walked through the door. I'll never drift into that dreamless, annihilating slumber again.

But it wasn't the cabin that brought me to life. It was Inesa. I flowered up like ivy beneath her touch. And now, as we set off into the purple dusk, I can feel myself still growing, budding, blooming.

We walk for a while in silence, Inesa keeping her gaze fixed on the map while I guide us around tree roots and puddles. Birds flit in and out of the canopy of trees, their iridescent wings flecking the air. Squirrels and rabbits rustle in the brush. I stay alert for the scent of rotting flesh, for the sound of the Wends snarling and baying, but I smell and hear nothing. It's only the elements against us, for now.

The cold comes with the darkness, and I feel Inesa start to shiver. The night vision in my prosthetic clicks on, casting the world in an eerie green. I press Inesa close to me, maneuvering us around obstacles she can no longer see. But we've practically slowed to a crawl.

"Let's look for somewhere to take shelter," I suggest, my arm around her waist. "Until it's light out again."

"I'm going to leave that up to you," Inesa says through chattering teeth. "I'd probably lead us down a ravine."

It takes a good amount of circling before I find a rocky overhang. It's not quite a cave, but it reminds me of the place where we first sheltered together, after killing the Wends. If it starts to rain, at least we'll be dry. We decide to risk a small fire, just to keep warm, and dig into our rations of deer meat. We eat with our hands in the glow of the crackling flame.

"What do you think it will be like?" Inesa asks, when she's licked her fingers clean.

I lift a teasing eyebrow and reply, "Hopefully there will be forks and knives."

"Hey," she says in mock offense. "It's called being thorough." As if to make a point, she wipes at the grease around her mouth. Then her tone grows solemn. "But I like to think it will be different from anything I've ever known. People helping each other without expecting anything in return. Without worrying about owing each other. People living, not just surviving."

It's almost incomprehensible to me, really. So is thinking about the future at all. I never allowed myself to imagine a different fate for myself, other than what Azrael set out: a final Wipe, a marriage to a man I barely knew and could never care for. Total obliteration—of guilt, but also of love. The thought sends a thrill of fear through me, and I shift closer to Inesa.

"I hope they don't hate me," I say quietly. "For what I've done."

Inesa leans over and rests her head on my shoulder. "See, that's what I hope for most of all. That no one judges each other for how we've managed to survive. You're not an Angel anymore. Well—at least not a Caerus one. You still feel like some kind of angel to me."

THIRTY-THREE

INESA

I sleep fitfully, curled against Mel for warmth, and when I wake, I think of Luka. I wonder where he's waking up, and how. In a cell, jolted out of sleep with a gun pressed to his temple? I find it more likely that Caerus is keeping him in comfortable quarters, so as not to mar New Amsterdam's alluringly rugged hero. His interview with Zetamon was probably just one of many. I can easily imagine Caerus parading him around endlessly, proudly, as the ratings for my Gauntlet soared. They'll win themselves goodwill just by appearing to treat Luka kindly. At least in public.

Just because he's well-fed and sleeping in a warm bed doesn't mean he's not a prisoner. After all, that's how they kept Melinoë too. She could have anything she ever wanted—except her freedom.

It was never supposed to be this way. Luka was always meant to survive. It's hard to make myself believe I deserve it, to be the one who lives.

I have to push the thoughts from my mind. I glance over at Mel as she rouses herself. There was never any way for all three of us to make it. No matter what, someone has to lose the Gauntlet.

And in a way, Caerus is the only one who ever wins. I reach into my pocket and squeeze the scrap of paper with the coordinates, as if to imbue it with some of my skin's warmth. The cameras have definitely been cut by now. This is sedition, what we're doing. Maybe even open rebellion.

Even through the tree canopy, the sunrise is brilliant. Between the leaves are mottled bands of pink and gold, orange and purple, all radioactively bright. Melinoë stirs and blinks, raising a hand to shield her eyes. It's the most vivid the light has been since the start of my Gauntlet, and I feel my heart patter hopefully at the sight of it. A sunny day in New Amsterdam is as good an omen as there could be.

"Oh," Melinoë says. "That's beautiful."

"It's because of air pollution," I say. "Doesn't the sunrise look this way in the City, too?"

"No. The lights from the buildings and the holoboards are too bright. They dim everything else in the sky. But the window in my bedroom had different settings, so I could change my view. I could make a sunrise like this, but it wasn't real."

I bite my lip. With this image in my mind, I see Luka again, in a room just like Mel's, flipping through the settings on his window. I wonder what he would choose to look at. I wonder if he'd find comfort in seeing something beautiful—even if it was artificial.

Melinoë gets to her feet, then offers a hand to pull me up. The sunlight trickles through the branches and warms my cheeks, my fingers, the tip of my nose. I brush dirt off the white dress, which doesn't look quite so immaculate anymore, and then take out the map.

I bend my head over it, and Mel does the same. After a few moments, I lift my gaze to meet hers. My chest squeezes.

"We're close," I whisper.

She nods.

Only a few hours left, if we keep up a brisk pace. Energized by the thought, I draw in a breath, inhaling the cool, damp air. Melinoë slides her rifle onto her back, and then we're off.

As we walk, the forest around us begins to change. The bright green deciduous trees bleed into dark, spiny conifers. The ground is littered with dead needles that crunch beneath our feet. And then, slowly, the damp, soft earth hardens, bristling with the finest layer of frost. Mel and I exchange glances. Her gaze is half fear, half hope. A new world is hanging before us, almost within reach of our fingers.

The frost means we're nearing the border with New England. I soften my footsteps and slow my breathing, listening for signs of life. Human life, that is. But the longer I listen, the more I realize, with a jolt of panic, that I can't hear any animal life, either. There are no birds flitting from branch to branch, no scuffling in the underbrush. I sniff the air, searching for the rotting smell that always precedes the Wends, but I can't find it. Instead the air has a strange, tinny odor, almost like blood on my tongue.

I look at Melinoë, hoping that with her enhanced senses, she'll be able to pick up on something I can't. But her expression is as bereft as mine.

"Maybe we read the map wrong," I say. "Maybe it's a bit further. Let's keep going."

We walk on, and the metallic smell grows stronger, mixed with something denser and fouler. Smog or smoke. I strain my ears. I'm listening for the hum of an electric fence, the most basic and fundamental sign of civilization. Everyone needs a way to keep the Wends out.

The snow on the ground is getting thicker, but also grittier. Stained, as if with ash. I don't want to speak my fear aloud; I'm not even sure I could articulate it, if I tried. The fear is more somatic than anything, a twinging in my chest and a roiling in my gut. I reach out for Mel's hand.

The trees grow sparse and thin, and eventually, the path we're taking deposits us in a large clearing. There are only a few deep-green pines dotting the perimeter, stark against the whitening sky. The sun has all but vanished beneath a swaddling of gauzy clouds, and what little light leaks through is a blanched, sickish gray color. A wind picks up, snapping the hem of my dress and blowing my hair around my face. It lifts Mel's hair, too, and fans it out into the otherwise unnaturally still air.

We pause for a moment, facing each other, both of us working up the courage to speak. Melinoë swallows hard, a muscle feathering in her jaw.

"Something isn't right," I whisper at last. "We might have to double back. Maybe—"

My voice breaks off, my throat growing impossibly tight. I squeeze her hand tighter and I think I realize, then, why most people are too afraid to hope. The stronger your faith, the more brutal its shattering. The more vivid your dreams, the more agonizing the knife-twist of reality. It's a privilege, really, to desire, to imagine, to believe.

With my free hand, the one that isn't holding Mel's, I reach into my pocket, curling my fingers around the scrap of paper and the case of Dad's compass. Whatever warmth I managed to impart it with before is gone. The paper is flimsy and cold.

I thought it was cruel of him, to leave us only this. Now I understand that he left us with hope, too, and that's so much worse.

I'm going to tell Melinoë that there's still a chance. That I'm not ready to give up. But before I can open my mouth, there's a sound—at last. It descends on us, deafeningly, horrifyingly, like the flocking of a hundred huge bird mutations.

The bleak and frenzied beating of helicopter blades.

THIRTY-FOUR

MELINOË

🍃

All the color leaves Inesa's face.

We both stand rooted to the ground in shock. The whirring of the helicopter blades is so loud and so familiar that it turns my skin to ice. Familiar, but impossible. Impossible, but real.

I want to shout *run*. I want to tear back through the trees, into the forest, dragging Inesa behind me. Yet I'm frozen with horror, and it's too late. The belly of the helicopter lowers over us, parting the branches, snapping them against its metal hull. There's an even larger breach in the tree canopy now, baring the entirety of the gray-white sky.

Wind blows back my hair, nearly tearing it from my scalp. Leaves and dirt and hard, sharp bits of frost are kicked up from the earth. I raise my arm to shield Inesa, pulling her against me. Her body is stiff, her mouth hanging open and her eyes wide. She hardly even seems to register my actions.

The helicopter is sleek and jet-black, with Caerus's familiar logo painted on the door. The six-sided white gemstone. Or maybe it's a die. Wealth and fortune, or luck and chance? I've never known. No one has ever told me.

The helicopter doesn't land, just hovers about twenty feet in the air. The door slides open. Standing in the threshold, tall and leather-clad, is Azrael.

It's not surprise that floods me—how many times have I seen him in the same helicopter, coming to collect me after a Gauntlet? Instead, I'm filled with a fierce and burning rush of rage. Because ghosts are flowering up in front of my eyes. Keres, with his gun pressed to her temple. His huge body, arcing on top of mine.

"It's over!" I cry, though the deafening beat of the helicopter blades means it's unlikely he can hear me. "You're not getting your perfect ending! I'm finished!"

In spite of everything, he *does* hear. Anger whips across his cold, artificially youthful face.

"You promised, Melinoë," he shouts back. "You swore that she would die."

At the beginning of the Gauntlet, in the belly of this very same helicopter. *The Lamb has to die*, he'd mouthed to me, and I'd mouthed back, *She will.* It feels like a lifetime has passed since then. A lifetime in which I've become so much more than the creature he made me.

"I don't care!" The debris flying up into my face makes my eye sting, and water gathers along my lash line, trying to flush the foreign matter out. "I'm done! I'm not your Angel anymore!"

There's another flash of fury on Azrael's face. And then, rather than reply, he steps to the side. Two Masks appear in the open doorway. They're hefting a body between them, and the body is Luka's.

"*No!*" Inesa screams, tearing away from me. I reach out and catch her around the waist, before she can trip forward and fall.

But Luka stirs. He's not dead. Not yet. The Masks heft him onto his knees.

Azrael removes his gun from the holster at his hip. The same sleek, silver pistol that Keres once held. In one fluid motion, Azrael cocks the gun and presses the muzzle to the back of Luka's head.

"It's a pity," Azrael calls out, "that your brother's earnest entreaty wasn't enough to convince you to at least try to fight for your life. I thought the script I wrote for him was very moving."

"*Please!*" Tears streak down Inesa's cheeks. "Please just let him go. Please don't hurt him."

Luka's face is angled downward, half obscured in shadow. But I can see that his left eye is swollen and there's a gash across his forehead. I can see tears washing his cheeks, too—silent tears that turn his skin almost iridescent in the meager gray light. I remember Inesa telling me she hadn't seen him cry since they were children.

But he is a child, really. Younger than Inesa. Younger than me. And I'm sure the wounds are worse than just what shows on his face.

Over the brutal whirring of the helicopter blades, Azrael says, "I'll give you one more chance to make this right."

He never turned off the cameras. I know that now. While Inesa and I planned our escape, he was planning his own climax. This confrontation. What better way for Caerus to eradicate all hope than to let the audience watch us try and fail?

My rifle suddenly feels heavy on my back, its ridged edges pressing into my shoulder blades. It's not only Caerus's instrument now; it's mine. I can end this on my own terms.

Inesa just stares up at Luka, agony in her eyes. He lifts his head and stares back. Something unspoken passes between them, something I'll never be able to understand.

The rifle is slippery in my trembling hands, but I manage to get it aloft on my shoulder. Peering through the scope, I aim it right at Azrael's heart. Then I reassess. He's probably wearing Kevlar. I tilt the barrel upward, aiming it right between his eyes. Instant death, if I pull the trigger.

Azrael doesn't even flinch. And he doesn't speak, but his voice echoes in my mind anyway. *You are my perfect creation.*

Anger is what steadies my aim, what makes my finger brush the trigger. *Then you should never have put a weapon in my hand.* I'm furious at his arrogance, at his lack of fear. He could never believe that his own creature would turn her gun on him. As much as he wanted me to be strong, he's always known he was stronger.

Not anymore. I feel the warmth of Inesa's body, pulsing beside me, and I start to pull the trigger.

But in the millisecond before my bullet flies, Azrael shifts away. Closer to Luka and to the Masks, to make room for another figure to emerge in the doorway. A slim, petite, white-clad body, auburn hair laced in its customary crown of braids.

Lethe.

The shock of seeing her there unbalances me; the rifle slides

343

down my arm. Lethe leaps down from the helicopter in one clean, perfect arc. She lands in front of me, one hand on the ground to take the pressure off her knees. Then she stands. The top of her head barely reaches my chin—this was always her archetype, the tiny spitfire. Her hunting suit is identical to mine, only white. Azrael must have thought about the staging of it all. The cinematic qualities. The contrast of our height, our clothes, even our personas. I'm the ice to her fire.

Not anymore.

But I've never stared her down like this before. Like an enemy. It's one of Azrael's rules, that we never fight each other, not even to practice. I realize now that this is why. It's because he always wanted to have this trump card; he always wanted to be able to use us against each other.

Lethe's prosthetic gleams black; her real eye is a tiger-striped, synthetic amber.

"I knew you were weak," she says, lips stretched into a wide, crowing smile. "Azrael should have sent me instead."

My first shot is wasted. I'm still clumsy with shock, and the bullet sails over her shoulder.

She lunges forward, grabbing me around the middle. It knocks the breath from my lungs and I barely manage to stay standing. She lands one decisive blow to my forehead and my vision flickers with stars. Half-blind, I claw back at her, but Lethe grasps me by my hair and pain sears through my scalp.

As I'm bent over like that, she knees me hard in the stomach. Once. Twice. I cough, blood spurting from my mouth onto the frost. My body is as floppy as a rag doll's. With almost impossible dexterity, Lethe turns me over and pins me to the ground. Her expression is resplendent with pride.

I don't know why she doesn't just shoot me. One bullet to the temple and it will all be over. But the rifle is my weapon. Lethe prefers a more intimate form of violence.

And, besides, this is still a show. Azrael wants the most dramatic finale possible.

Pressing down on my throat with one hand, Lethe removes a knife from her belt. Its handle is sleek, white-gold, and well worn in the shape of her fingers. She has killed a dozen Lambs with this very blade.

She drives the knife downward but I catch her wrist, holding it back. The blade hovers a mere inch from my face, close enough that one slip would slice me between the eyes. Lethe's brow furrows, her gaze wild and glassy with rage.

Blood is still pooling in my mouth, almost choking me. I spit it into her face.

Howling furiously, she slackens her grip. With all the strength I can muster, I knee her in the stomach. Lethe falls over, clutching her middle.

"Fuck you," she snarls. Half of her unnaturally lovely face is caked in mud. "You always thought you were so much better than the rest of us."

I snatch my rifle from the ground and stand. Adrenaline is coursing through my veins, chasing away any pain, but my limbs are shaking as I raise the gun and point the barrel at her forehead.

"Yield," I say.

I do think I'm better than her, but not for the reason she imagines. Not for the reason I once believed, too. I'm better because I'm free now, alive with both hope and fear, guilt and fury, love and loathing. Kindness and mercy demand strength. Feeling nothing is true cowardice.

Once, Lethe was like me: a scared little girl dragged away from her parents and pinned down to a cold metal operating table. She's been jabbed with syringes, cut open with scalpels. She had knives thrust into her hands before she even learned how to tie her shoes. She only knows how to kill and how to hate. She's never been taught how to believe or how to dream. If she has ever been held without being hurt, she doesn't remember it now. Azrael has stolen away all her soft and fragile pieces.

Lethe's gaze is relentless and cold as she stares at me. The clouds overhead gather into a thick gray knot. Rain begins to patter through the branches. I keep my rifle trained on her forehead.

With a sudden, agile twist of her body, she sweeps my legs out from under me. I tip forward, and I have to let go of my rifle to catch myself on my hands and knees. Lethe charges me, pinning me down to the frost-encrusted earth once more.

"You don't have to do this," I tell her, gasping to get the words out. "I know you think you don't have a choice, but you do. Lethe—"

She strikes me across the face, so hard that my cheek bristles with pain.

"Shut up," she snarls. "Just shut up!"

The rain is falling more furiously now, the blades of the

helicopter spraying it in all directions. Cold rivulets stream down Lethe's face, dripping onto mine.

"Azrael can't win if you stop playing his game," I managed. As she reaches for her knife, I put an arm up to block her, and she screeches in frustration. "You're more than what he made you. You're not just a tool. You're a person. A human being."

She tries to drive her knife down, but I hold her back, and she howls again. Between the rain and the beating of the helicopter blades, her screams are almost silent now.

Even through the wet strands of Lethe's hair, through the broken black tree branches, I can glimpse Azrael's face. It's blurry, like a water-stained page, but the twist of his mouth is familiar enough that I could recognize it anywhere. All the times he watched me falter in the shooting range, paralyzed by memories that couldn't be erased, even after so many Wipes. I'm disappointing him now. Lethe is disappointing him. This isn't the climax he wants.

With another furious scream, Lethe drops the knife, and instead reaches for my throat. Rain beats down, making her skin slippery as I try to pry her arm away.

"You're just pathetic and weak," she sneers. "And now the whole world knows it. They've seen you bend to that Lamb. They're all cheering for me to kill you. But maybe I'll keep you alive just long enough to watch me gut your little lover."

Darkness is creeping into the corners of my vision. Beneath her crushing grip, only the faintest, wheezing breaths can slip in and out of my throat.

"Stop," I manage hoarsely. "Lethe, please—"

But there's nothing in her eyes except empty, vicious rage.

My vision narrows, winnowing away, until I see only black. Dying feels like going under. I can almost sense the prick of the needle against my throat.

And then, all of a sudden, the pressure stops. I gasp, sucking in air as if I've just been pulled from the water. As my vision returns in shuddery increments, I see Lethe topple over. I push myself up onto my elbows and watch as she gutters out a noise of shock, clutching her shoulder.

Inesa stands over her, frozen. The handle of my knife sticks out of Lethe's back.

Woozy, still trying desperately to catch my breath, I clamber to my feet. White-hot pinpricks of pain shoot through my temple and behind my eyes. Every breath scrapes and grinds my raw throat.

Lethe is doubled over, wheezing. When she looks up at me, she smiles, blood in the crevices between her shining white teeth.

"Too late," she whispers.

As quick as a strike of lightning, her fingers find her sleek, white-gold knife. And with her very last breath, she hurls it forward. Even on the brink of death, her aim is perfect. The rifle is my weapon, but the knife is hers. I have no time to react. I can only watch as she gives one last, ghostly grin and then slumps over, unmoving. I can only watch as Inesa runs toward me, hair streaming out behind her, the hem of her white dress damp with melted frost.

"No," she's saying, over and over again, "no, no, no—"

I look down. Lethe's knife is buried in my stomach. A stain spreads slowly over my hunting suit, turning the fabric an even darker black.

Shock keeps the pain at bay. I feel almost nothing at all as I touch my abdomen, even as my palms come away bloody. A deep-red color, drawn up from far, far below the surface. The blade must have punctured some internal organ.

I look back up at Inesa. Her eyes are bright with wild, frantic tears. She presses down on my wound, to stanch the blood, but it just soaks into her skin, too. All the way up the sleeves of her dress. The rainwater makes it run farther, down into the earth.

"I'm sorry," she says, her voice thick with agony. "Just keep your eyes open. Just keep breathing."

It's useless. This isn't a wound that time or pressure or bandages will mend. And she knows it.

I reach up—slowly, tremulously—and rest one arm on her shoulder. I hold her face in my blood-slicked hand.

"I love you," I say.

Inesa gives one short, stuttering sob. And then she leans forward, pressing her forehead to mine.

"I love you," she whispers. Her tears fall through the spaces between my fingers.

I try to focus only on that deep-green, hazel-flecked, earthy color of her eyes. Her skin feels warm, almost feverish, but I know it's just because mine is growing colder. I feel the pulsing of her heartbeat, but it no longer keeps time with my own. And I'm vaguely aware of the helicopter lowering itself into the clearing, branches snapping off under the weight of its belly. Lashing more rainwater through the air.

Inesa turns suddenly, arms slipping around my waist to hold me upright. The helicopter hovers only a few feet above the ground now.

The Masks heave Luka to his feet and push him out the door. He lands on his hands and knees in the mud, breathing hard. His bruises are a vivid purple in the light and the wound on his forehead is still dripping blood. I feel Inesa tense with the urge to run to him, but if she lets go of me, I'll fall.

Then the Masks step from the helicopter. One of them goes toward Lethe, to collect her body, and with unexpected urgency, Luka stirs. He stares at her, through the locks of damp hair falling over his forehead, and his gaze doesn't leave her until her body— even smaller in death, almost pitifully so—is bundled into the Mask's arms and lifted into the helicopter. His eyes are unreadable.

The second Mask starts toward me. Inesa's grip tightens, and she pulls me against her chest. My vision is darkening at the corners again. The world looks gray, washed clean of its color.

Azrael isn't far behind the Mask. He tucks the gun back into his belt, hiding it beneath his leather coat, and then reaches out for me with black-gloved hands.

Inesa doesn't let go. She opens her mouth and speaks, but I can't hear her words. I only see the defiant gleam in her gaze, and the current of grief running under it, making her eyes damp and shimmery.

The Mask is unperturbed. They don't even slow their pace. Inesa is still talking, protesting, in stammering, shuddery tones. I lift my hand again and, achingly, turn her face toward me.

"It's okay," I tell her. Over the sluggish pounding of my heart, I can barely hear my own voice. "It's over."

The rainwater falls in harrowing, heavy gouts.

The Mask lifts me into their arms with perfunctory gentleness. It's the fulfillment of duty, nothing more. I gasp, but my pain is incidental to them. Inesa keeps hold of my hand for as long as she can, until the Mask turns, and her fingers slip through mine.

They carry me into the waiting helicopter, hovering mere inches above the ground.

Even then, she runs after me, skidding in the mud and melting frost. It's only Luka, rising to his feet at last, who stops her. He grabs her around the shoulders and pins her to his chest. She cries and thrashes against him, but he doesn't let go.

Inside the helicopter, Azrael removes one of his gloves. He lays a bare hand across my forehead, and his skin is as cold as mine. To the Mask, he says, "Get to work on her at once."

I twist, straining in the Mask's arms, a sob breaking through my lips. I can just barely see Inesa, growing smaller and smaller as the helicopter takes off, blades beating the air violently. I watch her until she becomes just a streak against the frost, both dark and bright against the endless white. I watch her until she vanishes into nothing.

Azrael drives a syringe into the base of my throat. Instantly, my vision blurs and warps. The roof of the helicopter, with all its switches and blinking buttons, becomes an unknown constellation. But I can still see her. Inesa. Her memory is in my mind like the fire, keeping me awake, alive, even as the medication tries to numb me and pull me under.

I won't forget. I won't—

Even as I slip into my dreamless, anesthetized slumber, the world behind my eyelids explodes in color.

THIRTY-FIVE

INESA

If I'd paid more attention to past Gauntlets, I would have had a better idea of what happens when you win. But then again, none of the normal rules really apply to me. I won. Technically. But I lost more than what's accounted for on Caerus's stark, impersonal ledger.

There are plans for a series of interviews with Luka and me. They fly a reporter and a camera crew out to our house in Esopus Creek. The reporter complains unsubtly about the cold and the damp, the leaking roof, the dark, cluttered living room. Still, at least it isn't Zetamon. Luka and I sit on the lumpy couch as the crew fixes microphones to the fronts of our shirts. But just when everything is settled and the cameraman is counting down, the reporter's tablet pings and vibrates in her purse. The interview is off. She doesn't even try to disguise her relief.

When I turn on my own tablet, for the first time since the Gauntlet, I see why. My $ponsor app is flooded with donations, my inbox crowded with messages. For every earnest note of support, there's another that's snide and cruel and suggestive. Mostly, people send links to the clips of Melinoë and me. When we were both exposed. When we thought we were alone. They're trying to taunt me into an angry, defiant reply, so they can screenshot that and plaster it online, too. Or they're just pleased by the thought that they can humiliate and degrade me over and over again.

I delete my account, erasing everything.

Luka's accounts all get flooded with messages, too. His are equally suggestive—but none of them are cruel. It's hard to hate him, after watching the Gauntlet. He's the uncontested hero, really. Handsome and tall, stony and determined, a wicked shot with a rifle. It occurs to me, more than once, that he would have been the perfect Lamb. If Mom had chosen him, the Gauntlet would have been over in a matter of hours.

I want to ask him if he regrets it. Not killing her when he had the chance. But every time I try to speak her name, it withers like ash on my tongue.

Not all the attention is bad. As it turns out, Zetamon created a crowdfunding campaign to help us out. His subscribers donated tens of thousands of credits. It's more than enough to do all the repairs around the house—build a new set of stairs, replace the rotting floorboards—and even make the shop look shiny and new.

Someone reaches out and offers to pay to demolish our house and replace it with a sleek Caerus pod home. But I delete the message before Luka can see it. I don't think I could bear to live within their stark, white walls. Already it feels like everything is closing in on me from all angles, in all directions. I have to constantly remind myself to breathe.

I do take someone else up on their offer, though. He's a doctor at one of the big Caerus hospitals in the City, and he gives Mom her own personal, private suite in his wing. She can have as much testing done as she wants, all the food she could ask for, and nurses at her beck and call. She leaves a week after the end of my Gauntlet, in a Caerus helicopter, without looking back.

I wonder how long it will take them to realize that her sickness is an invention, a clever one, a shield against the grueling, daily miseries of the world. Everyone needs something, because most of the time, reality is too much to bear.

When I finally understood that, I thought I could teach myself not to hate her. But I can't make the anger fade and wash away. It lives inside me, like a second heartbeat, like the pulsing of the tracker, keeping me alive, but also killing me, slowly. Like water eating away at stone.

I do endless internet searches. I have a news alert set for her name. I think about reaching out to Zetamon, asking to be on his stream, so I can send a message that maybe, somehow, she might see. But I doubt Caerus would let me. They'd censor the stream for sure.

Instead, I focus on all the small, stupid things that build up the walls of my life in Esopus Creek. Stuffing and mounting deer. Piling sandbags outside the shop door when it rains. Patching our refurbished raft. We can always afford power now, and I never go hungry at night. Luka is even gifted a new rifle, sleek and state-of-the-art, and some proper hunting attire, a mottled camouflage of brown and green.

At night, I lie awake in my new bed with its plush mattress, the humid dark swimming around me. There's a proper wall between Luka's room and mine now. I can't see his silhouette through the curtain anymore. But we still don't have doors, so when I pass by his open threshold at night, I see his tablet shining in the otherwise unlit room. It's playing the Gauntlet. The last moments, when I drove the knife into Lethe's back.

When Luka realizes I'm watching, he immediately snaps the tablet off and turns around, drawing in a breath.

I see it all the time. My hand clenched around the cold hilt of the knife. The blood dripping between Lethe's teeth. Over and over again I see her slump to the ground, unmoving, her heart stuttering to its brusque and final halt.

Luka stands and meets me in the doorway. Light from the hallway pours in around him. I can't really place the expression on his face. It seems so stricken with grief, eyes shining hollowly.

"You didn't have a choice, Inesa," he says at last.

I don't reply.

"She would have killed you."

I didn't know it haunted Luka, too. Maybe it was just the fact that he watched it so closely, near enough to smell the tang of Lethe's blood in the air.

That's not why it haunts me, though. I've done ugly things to survive; so has he. What keeps me from sleeping at night is the knowledge that I gave everything I had, and it still wasn't enough to save her.

At last, after a month, it happens. A slant of light, slivering through the clouds. I'm stitching up a deer pelt when my tablet vibrates. I drop the needle, peel off my gloves, and tap hurriedly on the screen so it flickers to life.

The headline is short. Six swift, hard blows to the back of the head. *FORMER ANGEL TO WED CAERUS EXECUTIVE.*

It's accompanied by a video, just a minute and a half long. In it, Melinoë stands behind a podium inside a large glass theater. She looks painfully thin in sky-high stilettos, her long legs covered in beige stockings, not quite the right shade to match her pale skin. It must be to hide the burn scars, I realize. The stretches of still-healing skin, grafted over the old wounds.

Her dress is short, icy blue, with skintight sleeves down to the wrist and a high neck. Her hair has been cut bluntly to her chin, and it shimmers, smooth and white, beneath the production lights.

There's an eyepatch over her prosthetic. Or where her prosthetic once was. She told me that when Angels are decommissioned, their prosthetics are removed. Replaced with a glass eye that mimics their real one, aesthetic but nonfunctional. I guess not even Caerus technology has gone far enough to exactly re-create what has been lost.

Clutching her around the waist is a tall but slope-shouldered man. His face has the pillowy appearance of someone who has undergone too many cosmetic procedures, leaving him looking more bloated than young. His hair is too black to be natural, and it gleams like a slick of oil. He wears the charcoal-colored suit that's the uniform of Caerus upper management, and its sharp angles look unsettling against the puffy roundness of his cheeks.

Hendrik Visser, the article says. Caerus CTO.

He speaks in Damish, but the video is subtitled. His words sound slightly stilted in translation, just a little bit off. Too literal.

I'm pleased to reintroduce Melinoë to New Amsterdam as my wife. We are very happy together. The wonderful thing about love is that it makes irrelevant all that came before. A vow of marriage is stronger than blood, a promise to leave behind all previous appetites and indulgences. I look forward to our new life, and many happy years of matrimony.

They don't mention me. They don't talk about the Gauntlet. Caerus doesn't want anyone to think about the fact that I held her first, that I held her closest, before she was ever on this strange man's arm. And they certainly don't want Mel to remember anything.

The camera pans close to Visser as he speaks, but it never focuses on Melinoë. She stays in the background, partially blurred, and completely still. Her face is as smooth as a stone in the river. Her eye is glassy and empty.

The air is suddenly too oppressive and heavy. I could drown in it, I think, just like water. I slam out of the shop and step onto the porch, taking deep, shuddery breaths. But my lungs still clutch and seize, my throat too tight to allow them relief. I slide down against the shop's outer wall, putting my head between my knees. I might vomit, just from the lack of oxygen. But what I really want to do is scream.

I stare down at the wooden floor of the porch and watch the muddy water rush and churn through the gaps between the slats. How much has Azrael stolen from her, I wonder. Did he take enough that she hardly feels anything when Visser parts her thighs? Did he take enough that she forgot that she was made for anything else but this, that she was ever touched by someone who loved her?

I sit there for so long that my legs start to prickle with numbness. I wish it would spread through my whole body and into my heart. It's about this time that I start wishing for the relief of a syringe to the throat.

I go back inside, but I can't make myself return to work. Instead I just bend over the counter, replaying the video over and over again. What did Melinoë call it—an Echoing? Maybe, if I watch it enough times, I'll teach myself to feel nothing at all.

After six repetitions, the door to the shop swings open. I blink the tears out of my eyes so I can talk to the customer without choking, but it's just Jacob. I don't know if that's better or worse. Either way, my cheeks instantly fill with color.

"Hi," he says.

He doesn't cross the room toward me; he just waits in the threshold, hands in his pockets.

"Hi."

"I meant to come sooner," he says, gaze skimming the floor. "I just wasn't sure what to say. If you'd want me to."

I'm not sure I do, either. "Luka transferred the credits to your dad last week. For the car and all the gas. He got them, right?"

"Yeah, he got them." Rain begins to drum on the shop's tin roof. Jacob inhales, making his broad shoulders rise and then drop. Then, after a painful stretch of silence, he says, "I brought you something."

"You did?" After we wrecked his car, I can't imagine Dr. Wessels is feeling particularly generous toward us. Warily, I ask, "What is it?"

Jacob reaches into his pocket and fishes out a plastic package of chewable tablets, in a gleaming rainbow of colors. An instant fondness and nostalgia wells up in my chest. They're cheap cannabis pills, which Dr. Wessels gives to his patients with chronic pain. Jacob has been filching them from his dad since we were twelve. We'd hang out in his living room, giggling uncontrollably at things that only seemed funny in the haze of our mild high. I'm sure Dr. Wessels caught on to what we were doing, since we had all the subtlety one would expect from a pair of doped-up preteens, but he never reprimanded us for it. I remember wishing, sometimes, that Dr. Wessels were my dad, and it was my house, and I didn't have to go back to Mom.

We step out into the little grassy area behind the shop. The rain has lightened to a faint sprinkling that mists my skin like morning dew. It catches in Jacob's hair and gleams. I count out three of the raspberry-flavored red tablets. Jacob takes the lemon.

I only have to wait a few minutes for them to kick in. Then my flesh feels soft and soggy, like it could fall off the bone. My head feels like it's wrapped in warm cotton. I lean back against the wall of the shop and exhale, my breath white in the cold. Jacob stands next to me, close but not touching.

We don't speak. And nothing seems funny now. My mind is just drifting away from my body, like smoke escaping from the pipe of a woodstove. I can't think of much except what's in front of my eyes. Relief makes my vision fuzzy.

"Inesa."

Jacob's voice pierces through the haze. I turn toward him, his face a little cloudy. "Yeah?"

He stares at me intently, biting his lip. I'm afraid, suddenly, that he's going to try to kiss me again. My stomach curdles.

But he just says, "It's her, isn't it?"

"What?"

"*Her.*" The revulsion in his tone is obvious. "You can't let her go."

"I don't know what you're talking about." But the truth of the accusation thrums at me from the inside out, like a hollow drum. My mouth is dry.

"Yes, you do. And it wouldn't matter, anyway," he says, in a scratchy voice that makes me think his anger is just a guise for tears. "You would never really be just mine. I mean, all of New Amsterdam has seen you naked."

My own anger surges up, quick and burning. Heat blooms across my face. I've suspected it, of course, but now I know for sure: I don't belong in Esopus Creek anymore. The people who used to smile at me in the streets now turn their heads and avert their gazes. Mrs. Prinslew never makes small talk anymore, and when a customer comes into the shop, they say as few words to me as possible.

I'm ruined in their eyes. Tainted by the things I did on the Gauntlet. Not the murder or the violence. They wouldn't blame me for that. It's the fact that I held her and I loved her.

Blood sparking with outrage, I snatch the packet of pills right out of Jacob's hand.

"Then get away from me," I bite out. "Just leave me alone."

It will never stop. Not even now that the Gauntlet is over and the cameras are off. Jacob is right—anyone who wants to can search my name and find those clips, can fondle me in their mind. At first my life was Mom's to barter with. Now it's everyone's to consume.

I turn and flee back into the shop before Jacob can reply.

In bed that night, I take out the pills. Holding them up to the light, they shine translucently, like gemstones. I remove three, then four. Five. How many will it take, I wonder, for me to forget her? Forget her like she's forgotten me? They might give me an hour or two of reprieve, but I'll need something much, much stronger for the kind of true oblivion I'm seeking.

At this point, I'm starting to understand what Dad found so irresistible about the bottom of a beer bottle.

But I don't know if I want that. Not really. If I had a choice, would I excise her from my mind, as if she never existed? It would stop her from haunting my dreams. It would stop me from seeing her every time I close my eyes. But I would lose myself, too, I think.

I once told her it took strength to hurt, to grieve, that it was braver than feeling nothing at all.

I'm grieving for the living, though. It feels different than mourning the dead.

The door opens and closes with a *thud*. Luka is home. I stuff the package of pills under my pillow and try to look innocent as he strides past the threshold of my room.

Obviously I don't succeed. He pauses in the doorway, his hair dripping onto the floor. The rain has picked up again and I hear it pounding the roof. Under his wet mop of dark hair, I can still see it. The gash, which has healed into a thin, white scar.

He regards me for a long moment, silence stretching out between us in cords that I feel like I could touch.

At last, I say in a rush, "I'm sorry."

Luka just frowns. "For what?"

I glance from the scar on his forehead down to the ones circling his wrists, the not-quite-healed wounds that he hasn't explained to me. That I've been too afraid to ask about. When I look at him, I can see the compass held out so plaintively in his open palm. My throat starts to seize up, my breath growing hot in my chest.

"I'm sorry," I whisper, "that I didn't make it there."

Luka goes utterly still; he seems not even to breathe. In the half darkness of my bedroom, an unexpected metamorphosis takes place. He's a little boy again, appearing at my bedside, tears streaked down his face after a bad dream. It was so easy to hold him then, to comfort him. I don't know why it feels so impossible now.

And then, finally, he says, "There was nowhere to go, anyway. It was never real."

The truth that we've both been afraid to speak aloud, for weeks now. After the Caerus helicopter lifted off and vanished into the icy gray sky, we walked north for miles, following Dad's directions. But when we reached the marked place on the map, there was nothing. Just a vast, irradiated wasteland that reeked of smoke and oil, dead black trees forking out of the barren earth. If there was ever any life there, it had been wiped out in a brusque, decisive nuclear blast.

The Drowned County was just one of Dad's fairy tales. Maybe he even believed it himself. Maybe he left us those coordinates because he thought he could make it, too. Or maybe he never meant anything by it; maybe it was just some fumbling drunken scheme that he'd forgotten about by the next morning.

But it was Luka who believed, more strongly than I ever did. He wanted it to be real so badly that he mortgaged his life for it. He would have stayed Caerus's prisoner, if it meant that I could be free, if it meant that just one single time, Dad had told us something true.

Some ancient, half-buried instinct is resurrected within me, and it moves my body across the bedroom to where Luka stands. It wraps my arms around my brother and holds him tight and close.

He's stiff against me for a moment, tense with shock. And then he bends down to embrace me back.

———

The cabin isn't that far from Esopus Creek. On foot, it would take me only a few days to reach. I've mapped out the exact distance on my tablet. Of course, it would mean risking an encounter with the Wends, and I'm zero for two on fending them off successfully by myself.

But I can't leave Luka. And it's just a dream, in the end, that if I find my way to the cabin, I might also find some peace. The deepest, truest part of me knows that I would only find more to grieve.

Besides. I can't stop remembering what Melinoë said, about what it would be like for us if there were no Gauntlet. How she would walk into the shop, clear-eyed, pale hair damp from the ever-present rain. It's so easy to imagine it. The faint purple flush that would paint her cheeks. The way our fingers would brush over all the blood and guts—and it almost makes me smile; between the two of us, we've seen plenty of it.

So I wait. And every time the door swings open, my breath catches in my throat and I hope to see her face. A face that knows me. A face that remembers.

A week later, there's another ping on my tablet.

VISSER TO DEPART CTO POSITION

In a surprising move, Hendrik Visser is resigning from his position as chief technology officer at Caerus. A fellow executive, who has chosen to remain anonymous, states that Visser tendered his resignation this past Saturday.

"It was totally unexpected," says the source. "The CEO was blindsided."

Turnover among high-ranking executives at Caerus is exceedingly rare. As CTO, Visser not only oversaw all projects under the technological arm of the corporation, but a number of government initiatives on solar power, wind power, and hydropower; carbon computing; electric vehicles; and biotechnology.

Visser declined to comment directly on the reason for his departure; however, his office released an official statement.

"After many productive, fulfilling years at Caerus, including ten as chief technology officer, I will be voluntarily resigning from my post. This does not reflect at all on my relationship with other Caerus executives, dissatisfaction with the day-to-day workings of the company, or philosophical differences between myself and the company's direction. I maintain the utmost respect for my fellow executives and will look back fondly upon my tenure. And, of course, I am honored to have played a role in the development of technologies that have been used to promote the welfare of all citizens of New Amsterdam."

Visser also did not disclose whether he would be taking a new position elsewhere. The same anonymous source stated, "He is essentially retiring. He's going to Elan, of course."

Elan is the City's most exclusive luxury apartment

complex, which has long been home to retired Caerus executives. Elan's reputation as child-friendly and family-oriented lends credence to the theory that in light of his recent marriage, Visser is retiring to focus on domestic life.

The article includes a slideshow of photos from Elan's website. It's a mammoth cluster of buildings, all glass and smooth gray metal, surrounded by squares of immaculately landscaped grass where children play and dogs chase after Frisbees. There are swimming pools larger and longer than the main street of Esopus Creek, glistening with clear, artificially blue water. Naturally, all of it is housed within a climate-controlled dome, to keep the polluted air out.

And the rain. I wonder if, somehow, she'll be able to hear it. See it. Maybe the dome can't fully muffle the sound of rolling thunder. Maybe the droplets will still audibly patter on the glass. Maybe she'll wake in the dead of night, lightning streaking across the removed, distant black sky. And maybe, as the clouds gather overhead, paradoxically, the haze will clear from her eyes.

She told me that the brain is the most complex organ in the human body. When something breaks, it can't just be set in a splint and left to mend. Brain cells, when they die, can never regenerate. You can only hope that the mind develops new pathways to circumvent the hole. And memory is the trickiest element of all. Not even Caerus has mastered the science of it. There will always be gulfs in their understanding—long, black chasms large enough to fall through.

And there will always be those things that shoot up like river rocks in the dark water. The current pulls your raft downstream, and maybe you don't know there's anything in your path until the wood splinters under your feet. And you can strike and strike your flint, but you don't know how many strokes it will take until the tinder goes up in flame.

It was the rain that undid her. Or rather, undid all of Caerus's hard work. Wipe after Wipe, and there was always the sharp stone in the water. Always the spark that caught fire. I wonder how many times she's been strapped down to the table, syringe in her throat. I wonder if maybe it's impossible for Caerus to take everything, no matter how hard they try. I wonder, and the wonder turns to hope.

One of the splurges we made with Zetamon's crowdfunded money was a car. It's even older than the one we borrowed from Dr. Wessels, and it came to us with mud painted up and down the sides and three airless tires, but it runs okay for short trips. And the train station isn't far.

As we drive down the bumpy, unpaved roads, the car jostling us as it rolls through puddles and potholes, neither Luka nor I speak.

The train is waiting when we arrive, as sleek and silver as a bullet. Passengers are gathered at the doors. Luka puts the car in park and just stares, fingers tightening around the steering wheel until his knuckles turn white.

"Luka?" I ask softly.

He turns. A muscle feathers in his jaw. His eyes are my eyes, and when I look into them, I see them shining with unshed tears. "Yeah?"

"I'm coming back," I say. "I promise."

He just avoids my gaze, and the air in the car grows thick with silence. I don't blame him for his distress. All our lives, there's been nothing but leaving. I can't undo the pain of what came before, the months we spent waiting and hoping that Dad loved us enough to return, the hours we spent waiting hand and foot on Mom and wondering if she saw us as anything more than servants. But I can start shaping a new world, one that isn't marked by closing doors and hollow, silent, lonely grief.

I'm going to reiterate my promise—I'll say it over and over again until he believes me—but then, astonishingly, Luka leans over in his seat and wraps his arms around me. I'm so surprised it takes me a moment to hug him back. I press my face into his shoulder, the darkness behind my eyes fuzzy and incomplete, and my heart cracks and then mends itself, with a fiercer, stronger bragging than before.

"I'll see you soon," Luka says, when he lets go.

"I'll see you soon," I echo.

I'll step off the train. I'll follow the crowd anxiously through the station, stumbling and fumbling through unfamiliar corridors. I'll navigate the gridded, smog-choked streets. My hair is long and loose down my back, and I wear all white.

I'll take another train, if I have to, or a cab, or a bus. I'll find my way to those hulking glass buildings. I'll walk circles around the manicured lawns; I'll peer through the windows; I'll pass by the pools and the tennis courts and the little patios where the City folk drink candy-colored cocktails and stretch out under the rare and precious rays of sun.

Maybe she won't appear today. But I'll come back tomorrow, and the next day, and the day after that, if I have to. I'll push through the crowds. I'll watch and I'll wait. I'm seventeen, and I have a thousand brilliantly hued hazardous sunrises to spare.

And yet not a moment of it will feel like a waste. Because I know that when our eyes meet, through the glass, over the heads of strangers, in the bright, shining dawn or the soft, fading twilight, she'll remember.

ACKNOWLEDGMENTS

Thank you, first and always, to my incredible agent, Sarah Landis, who didn't let me give up on this book even when it felt impossible that it would ever reach shelves. Thank you to Sara Schonfeld, my wonderful editor, for championing it, and to my publishing teams on both sides of the pond, who didn't balk too much when I told them my next book was going to be a dystopian romance. Thank you to Stephanie Stein for that very first yes.

Mel and Inesa's story would not exist without the dystopian YA fiction of my youth. I found my passion on fanfiction websites and roleplay forums dedicated to the Hunger Games, so thank you to Suzanne Collins for writing books that made me want to write books.

Thank you to all my friends, especially Manning, who has known me since my fandom days and has seen many, many iterations of this story over the years; and to Sophie, who—as always—consoled me through the trials and tribulations of publishing; and to Courtney, who was one of *Fable's* earliest and most generous readers.

Thank you to all the writers and grown-up fandom kids and queer creators who came before me and alongside me. This book would not exist without you. Let's keep making each other love and hurt and hope and feel.